Not Having It All

A brazen comedy about the perils of midlife

By Jennie Ensor

First published in 2019 by Bloodhound Books

www.bloodhoundbooks.com

Print ISBN 978-1-912986-34-7

To Stuart, the king of my heart

Part one

Chapter 1

Portrait of a stranded scientist, weary wife and make-do mum

28 July

1am

Right now, I can confidently tick all of the above. All three strands of Bea Hudson seem to be plummeting to a nadir.

Where to begin? Too many thoughts to put down. But if I don't, they'll spend what's left of the night partying in my cerebral cortex and sleep will be even more impossible.

Before I forget, I'd better mention it's 3.03am sometime in late May — or is it June already? My brain has switched off. It's definitely still 2018.

Academically, I'm still floundering in a sea of two-star journals without hope of rescue any time soon. On the plus side, there's still some way to go before self-annihilation George Price style — or some other style, as I'm not good with gore. (He killed himself after being fleeced by homeless alcoholics — so my tutor at uni impressed upon us — while trying to perform random acts of kindness to disprove his theory of altruism as he didn't want to believe that everyone is essentially selfish.) Perhaps I need a more positive role model than an underappreciated, mentally questionable biologist.

Motherhood ranking is nearing an all-time low following another battle with Fran over her habit of putting Mr Gruffy on top of the wardrobe so he falls on anyone opening the door, hot on the heels of yesterday's announcement at dinner that from now on she will not be eating anything orange in addition to anything green (thus excluding runner beans, Katya's carrot and parsnip mash, and the mango I'd bought for dessert).

Marital satisfaction index in steep decline after this week's arguments with Kurt — who left the freezer door open and who should be responsible for vetting Fran's use of stray computing devices, come to mind (and other arguments I'm too weary to recall).

Then there's Kurt's cattier-than-ever comments about Maddie — our text messages to each other take up more bandwidth than a week's output from BBC iPlayer (!) and she's a bad influence on our daughter, not to mention me, for exposing us to foreign films about transvestites and Channel 4 documentaries about bodily hang-ups. (A huge exaggeration, apart from that Almodóvar film we watched one Friday afternoon while Fran was trampolining and a program about people with tattoos in unusual places, which I turned off at the first sniff of age-inappropriate content). Soon I won't even be able to ask Maddie over for a cup of tea without Kurt dissecting the teabags afterwards.

Things can only get better.

I wonder — what are the chances of Kurt finding this?

Probably shouldn't worry too much. If anyone manages to extract this clapped-out WH Smith exercise book from the bottom of my stack of Neuron journals, has the slightest inclination to open it, wade past the evidence of how much I've spent on cappuccinos at every conference I've attended since 2013 and then has the gumption to decipher this scribble, good luck to them.

That's what the man from the halfway house wished me yesterday when I was walking back from the park with Big Ears. 'Good luck' I mean. That's the only thing he seems to say, apart from 'With looks like that you shouldn't be allowed out.' (??) I certainly could do with some good luck. Maybe the reason my research never yields gobsmackingly brilliant results isn't because I'm not doing the right experiments or my team is too small or I'm too damn tired most of the time to do anything properly — I'm just unlucky.

Picked up another batch of hairs from the shower yesterday (long and brown so not Kurt's). At this rate, I'll soon be going bald as well as grey. Hope Kurt won't mind — better book an appointment at the hair salon. My hair is no longer as big as a squirrel's tail, as he used to tell me in wonder and admiration. At least I still have my big eyes, big hips and big bosom.

Better stop, Kurt's hissing about a pencil rustling.

Chapter 2

What to do about Madeleine?

WARNING TO INTRUDERS

This is Kurt Hudson's digital record of his attempts to penetrate the dark heart of whatever is going on between Beatrice and Madeleine. Anyone found to have accessed this document without the express permission of KH will be liable to the full weight of whatever draconian penalties he might care to devise.

3/6/18, Sunday, on plane to Istanbul

The discovery

I found it this morning while putting the spare BMW key back in Bea's underwear drawer – a midnight blue camisole, 100% silk from the 'Intimacy' range according to the label. Also, on top of the chest of drawers, I spied a birthday card showing a kitten sticking its nose out of a bucket. Inside, exaggerated swirls of handwriting in garish green ballpoint:

Happy birthday, Bea! Hope it fits. All my love, Maddie xxxxxx

Why would Madeleine buy my wife lingerie for a birthday present?

I have been pondering this question for hours but no satisfactory answers have been forthcoming. Bea's responses to my question have been variations of:

- It's not really lingerie darling, don't be so silly!
- How can you possibly think there's anything going on between Maddie and me?
  and
- I love you, you idiot!

I was almost convinced by this articulate and impassioned defence of her integrity. But something's not right.
Could Beatrice and Madeleine be having an affair?

How many times over the years have I stopped to ponder whether Bea might be tempted by another? There was that excessively vain and muscular so-called colleague she met at a conference in San Diego. Then there's the French prat who always winks at her whenever we go near his pretentious restaurant on the High Street, and Sweaty Mike from the university...

But an affair with a woman? There's no evidence for that. I'm jumping to conclusions.

Or am I? We've been married six years – it must be close to seven by now. Maybe she's getting restless. Maybe she's had enough of me. Maybe she never really loved me and I was just the guy who could give her the child she wanted – and the security she needed.

Has Bea stopped loving me? Maybe she feels stifled by our marriage. Maybe she's had enough of a bossy, opinionated husband who drinks more than he should. Maybe she's had enough of Fran, too. She'd rather come home and have her buttons twiddled by a brazen hussy than scold the au pair, clean up Fran's mess, cook dinner and listen to me expound on the frustrations of corporate life.

Of course, I may be barking up the wrong tree. Bea told me when we got married she wasn't the type of woman to go astray. She wanted one man for the rest of her life, and that man was me.

But what if there's room in her life for a woman, too?

How did I miss the signs? There have been so many, now I think about it. Madeleine's excessive texts. Her attempts to lure Beatrice into seedy salsa sessions whenever I'm away on business. The way I sometimes catch those two looking at each other... and that other blue thing.

On the eve of our wedding, Bea had a particularly restless night. After a murky groan accompanied by a vicious roll onto her side that nearly bounced me out of bed, I asked, half joking – no, completely joking – if she was having second thoughts. She didn't answer. I thought she must still be asleep. Then, as we were getting ready for the trip to the registry office, she sat on the bed in front of the mirror, her breasts delightfully filling the new set of La Perla lingerie I'd surprised her with the day before, her silky hair swaying slightly as she lifted a leg and nudged a foot into a stocking... She looked so sexy, I was tempted to delay us further (the alarm hadn't gone off, I remember – we only just arrived in time for the ceremony).

I love you, I whispered, kissing her bare shoulder.

She carried on with the stockings then tied a cobalt blue silk scarf around her thigh, above the garter.

Something borrowed, something blue, she said in a distracted tone. From Maddie.

A little smile paused on her face.

That was my first warning bell about Madeleine, Bea's 'artist' friend. When she first came over to the house I foolishly imagined her to be just another friend, squeezed in for infrequent cups of coffee whenever Bea's hectic schedule permitted. But 'Mad' has special status, I quickly learned. She comes to our home on Bea's only day off from university to dispense advice on our garden, dog, daughter and myself, and drink copious amounts of camomile tea, spearmint tea or Chablis while watching DVDs about French couples having affairs. She lures Bea away from looking after Fran to go to yoga and pilates classes, and delights in titillating anyone who will listen with stories of her shameless, oh-so-artistic past (the 3Ms – Men, Melodrama and Melancholia).

The central problem

Beatrice knows I am devoted to her. She is my sumptuous shapely wench, the natty, slightly nutty neuroscientist who bewitches me with tales of the brain's endless mysteries, the woman I hurry home to as soon as I'm loosed from the corporate cage. In short, the queen of my heart.

It would take a great deal to destroy my love. Infidelity would be one of those things, though – infidelity with another woman included.

Of course, I realise I'm married to a woman who probably has half her life behind her. Not that I mind her having experience of the world – and more than a sprinkling of male friends. I'm a broad-minded guy, I believe in equal rights for women. I've lived a bit myself, to be fair. But

I mind the thought of a friendship becoming something other than friendship. I mind that very much.

Yes, I'm sure Bea does find married life somewhat challenging – she has to put up with me for a start. Also, to be brutally frank, despite the many joys of our togetherness, Life Since Fran hasn't been wrinkle-free – more the texture of an elephant's trunk.

I admit I wanted a family as much as Bea did. More, if anything – it was the one thing we agreed on 100%. On reflection, though, family life is proving a tougher test than either of us imagined. Having finally dispensed with the near-constant crying, we now have to contend with Fran's battles for supremacy with everyone around her. Despite all my constructive suggestions to Bea, the wilful side of Fran shows no signs of abating. I only hope Bea will be able to cope while I'm away, with only that incompetent Polish ex-au pair to help. Bea's scattiness and absorption in her work, combined with Fran's need to be centre of attention at all times, could prove disastrous.

I suppose Bea has a point – I shouldn't have left her alone so often with a difficult baby and a string of next-to-useless au pairs who had never touched a nappy in their lives before they came to us. But I couldn't suddenly stop being CEO of ComputerCorp UK just because my wife was having a baby – the Yanks haven't even heard of paternity leave.

Of course, Fran wouldn't be an easy proposition for the most gifted mother. She can charm anyone from passing poodles to grey-haired men with walking sticks, just by fluttering her long lashes. She's delightful – everyone insists on telling us. But they have no idea what a terror Fran is when she decides to be – stubborn, bad tempered, opinionated, oversensitive… (Who could she have got those traits from?) The list is worryingly long.

Thinking about Fran, it hasn't escaped my notice that a certain type of woman is highly susceptible to her charms – resolutely independent females unencumbered by their own trying children. In particular, Madeleine. Which brings me back to the reason I've started this document.

Up until now, I've always had a grudging soft spot for Mad. The way she does her own thing, living entirely outside the bounds of convention, getting by on odd jobs, sales of her 'art' and visits from former boyfriends. (Not a bad-looking woman either – a shame she never spends any money on herself and doesn't have any normal clothes.) For all her faults, though, I've always thought of her as entirely straightforward and honest.

But what sort of woman gives her friend a silk camisole as a birthday present? Yes, it was on sale in an Oxfam shop (according to Bea), it was only £7, it's the fashion to wear underwear as outerwear and it didn't mean anything. Really?

I'm starting to have serious doubts about Madeleine. She had better keep her twitchy little nose out of Bea's bucket – and her claws well away from Fran, while she's at it. If she does anything to corrupt my wife while I'm away, she will regret it. That, dear Madeleine, I promise.

Chapter 3

From: Bea Hudson (bhudson9@blueyonder.co.uk)
Sent: 3 June 2018 9.35pm
To: Allie Loff (allie53@outlook.com)
Subject: **Hello again**

Hello Allie

How are things in deepest Queensland? Are you getting used to the exotic accents, creatures, and so on? It will take time to settle, I should think. You can't expect to be instantly smitten with the place. You'll probably need at least a year before you get the hang of things.

Sorry I've not been in touch for a while, have been more stressed out than usual with Kurt and Fran.

The spiders you found under the garden chair sound repugnant, am jolly glad there aren't any funnel webs over here! I've been exposed to rather too many of our eight-legged friends lately – close-ups of tarantulas that Ben has unearthed from the web. We're going to use them in our next set of experiments. Hayley (our migraine-prone PhD student) has been tracking down spider phobics from ads all over campus. Each volunteer will get a free therapy session with a phobia specialist in return for forty-five minutes of being scared witless in our scanner tube. She's even managed to lure three spider-phobic males. The control group seem to be mainly students who owe Hayley for her agreeing to become a victim of their experiments. By the way, did you know that around 5% of the female population is arachnophobic, four times the percentage of males?

Miss you, big sis. Wish I could beam you up to Godalming every now and then. Especially today – Kurt and I had another row. This time it wasn't about Fran's behaviour or the condition of the house or the amount of time I spend at uni. He found the present Maddie gave me, a snazzy silk strappy number she got from a charity shop (I'd put it away in my drawer), and said she's obviously got a 'thing' for me! I told him she's not Mata Hari, she's one of my oldest friends, of course there's nothing going on between us.

It might be amusing if it wasn't so effing ridiculous. He's quizzed me before about my male friends, guys at work, etc – but nothing like this. He must be getting insecure about us being apart for weeks while he's off on his business trip. Talking of which, Kurt left for Istanbul this afternoon. He'll be gone a couple of months, apart from weekend visits every so often. They need him to turn around the Turkish arm of ComputerCorp's empire, which isn't doing so well. Their comms cards have quality issues and the company isn't selling enough to the tablet market. His boss thinks only Kurt is tough enough to do what's needed, i.e. sack the ones who won't mend their ways and get the rest to work harder. Kurt didn't want to go, he says the Turkish company is full of lazy swindlers and if it was his decision he'd shut it down and be done with it. But he hasn't got a choice – his boss is head of the parent company, so what he says goes. (K says he's lucky to have lasted five years, the average lifespan of a CEO in the group is 2.8 years.)

I hope the break will do us good. I miss him already. The bed is huge and there's no one to give me a back rub or talk to about why bees shouldn't be able to fly, or the pros and cons of Hypothesis A over Hypothesis B (Kurt is better at science than half of the students I supervise) – and no one to fix dripping taps and broken loo seats, or get up in the middle of the night to check on tapping noises coming from under the stairs (a rat, I have a horrible suspicion).

At least Fran and I will be able to eat microwaved fishcakes in front of the TV without him telling me off for feeding our daughter junk food and being a bad mother.

Am I a bad mother? I sometimes wonder. I feel so uncertain of everything these days. Everyone seems to know how to bring up my daughter better than I do. Kurt, my colleagues at uni, the mothers at preschool. Put her on the naughty step, don't let her play computer games... Even Maddie said last week that I ought to be reading to Fran for half an hour every night before she goes to bed. Oh yes, and the books I've got for her are old-fashioned and haven't got enough pictures! Though Mad's probably right about a lot of things, to give her credit. She's never had kids but she seems to know instinctively what they're about, how to talk to them and what it's like, the strange world they live in – whereas I don't get it, half the time (90%?)

Thank goodness for Katya! Or Katie as we have to call her now. She's great with Fran, far more patient than I am, and Fran has really taken to her. She came the month after you left. (She's got tree-trunk legs and acne, so no worries about Kurt. Also, she has a boyfriend. She moved out of ours and in with him but they're nearby so she can come over as much as we need her.) Unfort, I often can't understand what she says, what with her Polish accent and her odd grammar (goodness knows how she ever got into a course on hotel management). Her cleaning isn't that great, either – she says she needs new glasses and can't afford them yet. (That's just a ploy to get a pay increase, Kurt reckons.) But you can't have it all, can you? It was such a hassle finding her after Anya left.

Must go, a thousand things to do by the end of today.

Write soon. Say hi to Ray – and the dog, goats, chickens, horses, sheep and emus. Have I missed anyone out?

All my love, Bea.

From: Allie Loff (allie53@outlook.com)
Sent: 3 June 2018 9.58pm GMT
To: Bea Hudson (bhudson9@blueyonder.co.uk)
Re: **Hello again**

Have been missing your emails, thought you'd fallen through crack in pavement. Will call in 10 mins.

A xx
From: Bea Hudson (bhudson9@blueyonder.co.uk)
Sent: 4 June 2018 8.08am
To: Allie Loff (allie53@outlook.com)
Subject: **Your call**

Sorry not to make much sense last night. Went to bed early (knackered after a long trampoline session with Fran) and was asleep when you called. Weekends are the best time to talk but please don't call after 10pm (my time) Sunday evenings.

PS

I know you're a long way from the bright lights, Allie, but when are they going to get around to hooking up your place to broadband? Then we could Skype each other.

PPS

Forgot to tell you the latest Psychopathology Lab news. After weeks of hassles, we've finally got the Ethics Committee approval for our experiment – as long as we put a warning in the volunteer paperwork to say that the experiment could induce high levels of anxiety, which could potentially aggravate any pre-existing conditions such as phobias. So we start scanning soon, hooray!

PPPS

Why did you have to get hitched to an Australian? Nothing against Ray, he's a good bloke even if he is losing his figure...

(What do you expect? Send him to Weight Watchers!) Remember, you're allowed to change your minds and come back if things get too difficult. Failing that, I'll be over there to lend a hand.

Much love, Bea

From: Allie Loff (allie53@outlook.com)
Sent: 4 June 2018 8.45pm GMT
To: Bea Hudson (bhudson9@blueyonder.co.uk)
Re: **Your call**

No chance of broadband. Telstra told us that we live in a small rural backwater and we should be grateful to have a phone. Email better for me anyhow. Usually when I most want to talk it's 5am in the UK.

Re your experiment – why are you scanning spider phobics now? Do you think this will be your big breakthrough?

A xx

From: Bea Hudson (bhudson9@blueyonder.co.uk)
Sent: 4 June 2018 9.57pm
To: Allie Loff (allie53@outlook.com)
Subject: **Science stuff**

Ok sis, I'll try to keep this short. Forgive me if I don't.

A recap of the big picture first, in case you've forgotten my last lecture on the subject.

Neuroscientists are trying to uncover the so-called 'neural fear pathways' (includes the amygdala, hippocampus and other brain parts, some quite tiny and buried deep down, so tricky to explore). We think that some of them work too well in people with anxiety disorders such as phobias – the fight/flight response gets activated even when it's a false alarm.

We know that many phobics respond to exposure therapies (gradual exposure to the feared object). But therapy doesn't work well in all cases. Also some people's fears come back if they see a spider or whatever in a different context, instead of being safely imagined in the therapy room (say a big black blob hops onto the duvet in the middle of the night).

My team is looking at the brain parts activated when phobics are reacting to their feared object. We're aiming to find a part of the brain that could be targeted by drugs instead of/as well as exposure therapy. We already know that the amygdala and hippocampus are part of the 'normal' fear response. From our earlier experiments, we think that extra sites get triggered in the phobic fear response, especially animal phobias. I'm clinging to the hope that we'll be the first to identify these conclusively.

We started off by looking at snake phobics – remember I told you about our weird data earlier this year? Their fMRI brain scans had hotspots popping up in really unexpected places. The data was perplexing, to put a positive slant on it – in other words, not fit to be printed in the lowliest journal. This time, we're going to focus on spider phobics. If we get a strong response from any of the same brain parts that lit up for the snake phobics, we may be onto something – and yes, it could be the Big Breakthrough. If not, I will be in total despair.

But that's the fun of science, you never know what you're going to find next. It's no good getting fixated on one thing happening, because it almost certainly won't.

I think that's enough science for now. Watch out for tarantulas, funnel webs and black widows…

xx

Chapter 4

Portrait of a stranded scientist, weary wife and make-do mum

Early June

3am-ish

Can't sleep.

Keep thinking about Kurt. How when we were first married, he used to be my number one fan. He framed my PhD certificate and hung it in the hall beside the grainy old photo of his dad catching a monster trout. He encouraged me to apply for Senior Lecturer and when I got it he said I had the best neuropsychology brain in the country, leagues ahead of that 'wrung-out old Prof Hopkins' and he would support me in my career, no matter what.

Back then, we only disagreed about things like what colour to paint Fran's room and whether men are naturally better at science. Now we seem to argue about everything. How we ought to bring up Fran, why can't we get a better au pair and the latest, why can't I work two days a week instead of four?

These days, he hardly seems to care about my career. When I ask why he can't occasionally work less than twelve hours a day, five days a week himself so he could be around to cook dinner and kiss our daughter goodnight, he just looks at me as if I'm talking nonsense.

Has he changed — or is it me?

Not so sure if this journal is a good idea. Do I have time for lengthy, angst-ridden deliberations and inconclusive examinations of self, family and career?

Chapter 5

From: Allie Loff (allie53@outlook.com)
Sent: 5 June 2018 6.01pm GMT
To: Bea Hudson (bhudson9@blueyonder.co.uk)
Subject: **Farm girl blues**

Think I may need some animal phobia therapy myself soon. This morning went into the pen to feed the emus and they all marched towards me at once with their beaks wide open, hissing loudly! I dropped the container and fled.

Ray has no sympathy. He says I just have to confront my fears and get on with it. He can't afford to pay someone to help us on the farm – he expects me to support him in this new life, not whinge about how difficult it is.

Another thing, I forgot tell you. One of the cows nudged me the other week when I was trying to check its number. They are enormous – they could trample someone to death very easily – and those horns! I go cold and clammy just picturing them.

Things not going so well here. I love the space, the big skies and the sunshine. The people are very friendly when I go to town for supplies or auctions or whatever. But I miss going out in the evenings. There's nothing much unless you count the farmers' meetings Ray takes me to sometimes. I always have to go to bed around 9.30pm to be up at 5.30am. Hands looking worn and wrinkled, nails cut short, feel like a farmer's wife. Wearing jeans all the time, months since put on a dress.

I would kill Ray's dad for leaving us this place, if he wasn't dead already. Wish Ray's brother could come and take it over. But he's got more sense.

A

From: Bea Hudson (bhudson9@blueyonder.co.uk)
Sent: 5 June 2018 11.05pm
To: Allie Loff (allie53@outlook.com)
Re: **Farm girl blues**

Hiya Farm Girl

Just a quick note, worn out after long day.

Ray is lucky you don't mind getting your hands mucky and that you like animals – apart from your fear of emus and cows, that is. Hope you can pluck up the courage to confront the emus again. Try doing it gradually, e.g. just opening the door to the pen at first, then next time taking a few steps towards them. That's meant to be the best method for overcoming phobias.

Tell Ray from me that he can't expect you to adapt instantly to farm life. You'll have plenty of time to learn how to shear sheep, hoove horses, brand cows, feed emus and whatever else you have to do. You can't expect to become a country bumpkin overnight (JOKE).

Just an idea – why don't you check out the local pub scene? They might have folk nights or something. And why don't you ask Ray to take you to a cocktail bar once in a while or a dinner dance (do they have such things over there?) so you'll have an excuse to put on some of those languishing dresses!

Got a card from Mum – she and Janice have arrived in St Petersburg, along with Anna Karenina, Mum's thermal underwear and fur hat (she thinks there might not be heating on the night trains). I hope she will survive the summer travelling across Russia and central Europe with only Janice and thirty words of Russian. She says Dad would have wanted her to go, which I'm sure is true. But why couldn't she have started with two weeks in Wales?

Bea xx

From: Bea Hudson (bhudson9@blueyonder.co.uk)
Sent: 6 June 2018 10.03pm
To: Allie Loff (allie53@outlook.com)
Subject: **Crisis at home**

Latest news – Fran refused to get dressed this morning. I tried to cajole her into putting on her top but she just sat on the edge of her bed in her knickers and vest saying she didn't want to get up. After about ten minutes I was losing what patience I had – I tried bribing her with the promise of a giant toy rabbit she'd seen on the internet. In the end, I am ashamed to admit, I got so angry I yanked her clothes on while she shrieked loudly enough to wake the neighbours and the deaf woman at the end of the road.

I spent another ten minutes persuading her to eat her yoghurt.

Then, as I was unlocking the car (by then it was too late to walk to preschool), Fran announced that she wasn't going anywhere – she wanted to go back inside and play with her doll. I completely lost it. I opened the car door, took her by the arm and dragged her onto the seat while my little girl yelled, 'Mummy, you're hurting me!'

Behind the wheel, trying to breathe normally and feeling like a child abductor, I noticed Jackie next door standing by her gate and staring at me as if I'd just committed a criminal assault. (Could making one's own child get into one's own car be criminal assault?) I'm praying she won't call the police, or I might be interviewed soon by the SS (social services).

Fortunately, when we got to preschool Fran came in with me without any fuss. I told Mrs Drain in charge that Fran had been difficult this morning, and if there were any problems with her to call me, I'd be straight back.

For the rest of the day, I was useless. Ben asked me if he could get me a sandwich three times before I heard, then I somehow managed to mangle a male spider-phobic's scan data.

What's going on with Fran? Whenever I ask, she won't say. This evening she was well-behaved and went off to bed without a grumble. And Katie told me that when she collected Fran at lunchtime, she was as sweet as could be – apparently she'd had a wonderful morning making monsters out of egg boxes.

I'm totally confused. Was this morning a test to see who's the stronger, her or me? Or was it her way of saying that she doesn't want me to abandon her as well? She's been quite subdued since Kurt left last week – a week could be a year to a child her age, I suppose.

You know how stubborn Fran can be, but I've never seen her like this before. If she's going to be like this till Kurt gets back, I'm going to go mental. I'll either have to clone myself or stop work altogether. I'd go part-time properly, but that would be the death knell of my research career. Four days a week at uni is the absolute minimum you can do to be taken seriously. And I need all the help I can get at the moment. The project is hanging by a thread – the Prof's been on our collective case for months, moaning about the need to demonstrate the Cognitive Science Department's research prowess and the shortage of funds for projects that don't bear fruit. On top of that, we've all got to submit info for the REF (research excellence framework – another time-wasting exercise all universities have to take part in). They're counting how many papers each of us gets into top/middle/low ranking publications – in my case, precisely four in the past two and a half years, all distinctly low to middlebrow. If my team doesn't get some decent results soon, our funding won't be renewed and I'll end up like Moira and all those other dull-eyed academics, thrust out into endless teaching and committee sitting.

Kurt called earlier. His project's going well but he's not too keen on the hotel. They're still looking for an apartment for him - in the meantime he's got to put up with The Best Hotel In Town (it's tough for some). I haven't told him yet what happened this morning with Fran. There's no point worrying him, there's nothing he can do from over there. Anyway, he'd only nag me again about how I'm neglecting her by working all hours.

Better get to bed, eyes won't stay open.

I just needed to share this with you, Allie. No words of wisdom expected.

Bea

From: Allie Loff (allie53@outlook.com)
Sent: 6 June 2018 10.15pm GMT
To: Bea Hudson (bhudson9@blueyonder.co.uk)
Re: **Crisis at home**

Hang on in there, girl – and give Fran a slap from me. I know you don't believe in slapping children but one can't hurt once in a while, can it?

I'm not surprised you lost your cool, anyone would when their daughter suddenly turns into a stroppy little shit. Stop trying to be a model mum and cut yourself some slack! (I don't mean Fran is a stroppy little shit, just bloody trying when she wants.)

Fran's reasons – is she acting up to test you now Kurt's away?

Telling Kurt – not sure that's a good idea. If things don't improve, why not go to a counsellor?? You could talk about strategies for dealing with Fran – and your marriage. Yes, I know you'll hate the idea.

Ending up like Moira – of course you won't! You love your work, just keep plugging away and one day everything will fall into place.

Painting the town red – there's nowhere to go in the evenings except the RSL club in town and a pub belching poker machine noises and

Tammy Wynette – not my idea of fun, B. No hotels with dinner dances and cocktail bars, not even a lousy wine bar.

Hugs, A

From: Bea Hudson (bhudson9@blueyonder.co.uk)
Sent: 6 June 2018 10.32pm
To: Allie Loff (allie53@outlook.com)
Re: **Crisis at home**

Thanks for the comforting words.

No, I don't need to see a counsellor, things aren't as bad as all that! I'm just overstretched, overtired and frazzled to a crisp at the moment.

I suppose I could ask Mrs Know-It-All's advice (one of the designer-dressed, hair-always-brushed with part-time-job-and-perfect-home Super Mums at preschool who only talk to me when it is unavoidable). I heard she started a blog recently, 'How to Deal with Difficult Children'. And Maddie will be able to suggest something, I'm sure. Will call her soon, but she's got enough to cope with at the moment – her shower's packed up and she's got no money to fix it.

Big hug xx

PS

Sorry the nightlife is so dire there.

PPS

How many hours ahead are you now?

PPPS

Violence of any kind is against my principles – have vowed never again to use force with Fran (not even a brisk slap, tempting though it may be). I'm going to get the hang of this mothering thing if it kills me.

Chapter 6

Katie's journal

6 June

I dont know how to write all the things in my head. Here is for practise with English. I must try to look up all tricky words. Words dont come easy, they are like slippery plates in my hand.

Today when I pick up Fran from preschool she has thing in her bag like lots of egg boxes stuck together, the head with black teeth and big green horns popping out of the sides. I laugh, is so funny. She say it means to be scary, is called Diner Saw.

On way home she says her big toe rubs into shoe, so we stop at bench.

Why are you naughty to Mummy this morning, I say. Mummy says you do not want to go with her.

Fran sucks sweet very loud, swings legs very fast.

What, I do not hear you.

Sucking and swinging stop.

Mummy says I am bad girl. Do you think I am bad girl, Katie?

You can be very good girl if you like to be. Also very bad girl.

Is Daddy coming back, Katie?

Fran looks at me with pretty little nose like Mrs H's and big brown eyes like Big Ears when he wants pig's ear.

Yes darling, he comes back very soon.

She looks at me like it is Big Lie.

It is true, I say. Come on Little Miss, we go home now, Big Ears is missing you.

Fran takes my hand and skips and sings her new song again.

Katie kiss me, kiss me Katie!

7 June

Today when I pick up Fran she has face like sunk cake Mrs H makes once (after this Katie makes all cakes in Hudson Household).

What is matter, I say.

Nothing, she says.

What do you do this morning?

Nothing.

Nothing all morning?

She says one of girls on her table says that Fran's Daddy does not come back ever, like her Daddy who leaves her Mummy for Mummy 2. Also Fran's Mummy does not care about her because she is at work every day.

It is not true, I say, it is only what nasty little girl says. You must forget, is heap of crap.

Heap of crap, heap of crap, heap of crap!

After lunch I say we must take dog for walk, I do not have time this morning, too much washing ironing folding shopping.

I am tired Katie, can I stay here?

You cant stay here on your own.

Yes I can!

Dont be silly Fran, you are not big girl yet, please dont be naughty girl!

Fran runs up to room and slams door. Big Ears runs into kitchen, lead in mouth and drops at my feet. He is moving tail so fast I think it will come off and big spitty blob coming out of mouth.

I go to Fran's room. Please, I say, come with me.

She is on floor with beach box, lid open, talking to stones.

Leave that, you come back to box later.

She keeps talking to stones.

Come on Fran, dont be naughty girl, Big Ears wants to go for walk.

I want to play with my beach box.

OK, we take beach box with us.

Very big mistake. We are walking on doggie path for ten minutes and she throws stone at dog coming other way.

What are you doing?

I dont want all these stones, there are too many in box now.

You must not throw stones at dogs, is very bad.

I do not see next thing, she is behind me and Big Ears is long way in front, gone to scruffy dog like him and is sniffing his arse. No, it is a she, I see, he is getting it on with she dog. No owner I can see. Then I hear someone goes Aaaaaarr! I turn back, see man on path flat on arse and bicycle on top.

Fran comes out from a bush with hand on mouth. I run over.

Did you throw stone at the man? Tell me you do not throw stone at him.

Then man is up on feet shaking fist at Fran, shouting Look what she did, this horrid little girl, I cant walk now she hit me in knee, the little git!

He goes on like crazy man. I say I am sorry, she is very bad girl, take Fran's hand and go see what happens to Big Ears.

Thank god he is not shagging she dog now, owner is there with angry voice, tugging his dog away from panting Big Ears. I put lead on Big Ears all way back, tell him No More Hankypanky.

At home I take beach box away from Fran for punishment, tell Fran she must stay in room and no peanut butter samwitch, and this evening I must tell her Mummy what she does. Then I go sit in TV room with Mr H's special drink he hides in bottom of kitchen cubbud with black shoe polish and put on DVD from Mrs H's stash of naughty French movies. Little perk for Katie, I deserve. Today I have enough of Little Miss and Big Ears.

Chapter 7

From: Bea Hudson (bhudson9@blueyonder.co.uk)
Sent: 8 June 2018 9.55pm
To: Allie Loff (allie53@outlook.com)
Subject: **Crisis at home 2**

Further developments re Fran. Just as it's time for us to leave the house this morning, she bats her lashes and looks at me with her sweetest I-love-Mummy expression.

F: Can we go to the beach today?

Me: No, darling.

F: Why not? It's a Friday. You don't work on Fridays.

Me: I have to go in to work today for a meeting, I told you yesterday, and you have to go to Little Lanes this morning. Katie will look after you till I get home. We'll go to the beach at the weekend.

She sits at the table considering this while I clear away the remains of breakfast, gather up my books and half-marked essays then search for my handbag, which I find ten minutes later hidden under a pile of clothes on the laundry room floor.

Me: What's my bag doing here? Did you put it there, Fran?

F: (wide-eyed) No, Mummy.

Me: I don't think it was me, Fran. Why on earth would I have put my bag with all your dirty pants and socks? That only leaves you.

F: Maybe it was Big Ears.

Me: No, I don't think it was Big Ears. He never picks up anything in his mouth–

F: I saw him with a rat in his mouth yesterday.

Me: Don't tell lies, darling. I haven't got time for this, we have to get going.

F: I don't like Katie, Mummy.

This is new.

Fran has always been fond of Katie. Right from the start, she's been the bee's knees in Fran's eyes. I've always liked her too – plus she's the only au pair/childminder so far who hasn't been exhausted by Fran's demands for attention and need to turn everywhere she goes into a state of chaos. On the minus side, as I've said, I sometimes struggle to understand her and she has an irritating habit of forgetting what I tell her. But she always means well, and hasn't yet done anything badly enough for me to sack her (though forgetting to plug Kurt's alarm clock back in the day before an important 9am meeting made him demand temporarily that we (me) find someone else to look after Fran.) Most importantly though, Katie's always cheerful and engaged in what she's doing, and unlike me never complains or snaps or says she's worn out. In fact, thinking about it, I realise I can't possibly do without her. Katie may have her faults, but she's the perfect childminder for Fran.

Me: What do you mean, you don't like Katie? You liked her yesterday and last week and the week before that.

F: –

Me: (checking watch, wondering if the Prof will understand if I'm late again for a Psycho Lab meeting) Fran, let's get a move on. We can talk about this on the way to Little Lanes.

I walk towards the front door. Fran doesn't follow.

Me: Come on, Francesca! Please, I'm not in the mood for your silly games!

I must have said this a hundred times. Each time I tell myself I mustn't say it again.

F: (with no sign of movement) She took my box away.

Me: Your beach box?

For months she's been putting shells, bits of seaweed and chalky, holed, pock-marked pebbles collected on our weekend beach visits (the south coast, usually Worthing or West Wittering) into the shoe box that once held Kurt's hiking boots. The contents come out from time to time and get picked up, stroked, prodded and arranged in patterns on the floor.

F: (vigorous nodding)

Me: Why did she take it?

F: –

Me: I'm sure she had her reasons, darling. I'll talk to her later on.

She takes my hand without arguing, which is a relief, and we set off to preschool.

Me: Didn't you have a nice time with Katie yesterday?

F: –

Me: Did she take you to the park?

(It has a lake where Fran likes to throw crusts at the ducks, which Big Ears likes to chase.)

F: –

Later that morning, while rushing down a strong coffee, I phone Katie and ask if, and why, she took my daughter's beach box.

K: She was throwing the stones, Mrs Hudson. I was going to tell you yesterday but I forget.

Me: Throwing the stones? What, like a game?

K: Not a game. She threw them at man going by on bicycle. He is hit in leg and falls off bicycle. I go see he is ok. He is angry, that is all. I say so sorry, I will sort out girl.

Me: Why didn't you tell me this yesterday?

K: I wait but you come late. Then I have bad news from home, I forget to say. My mother has false teeth accident.

It's bizarre. Nothing like this has happened before. Why would my daughter throw stones at a man on a bicycle? That is quite out of character. She may be the worst behaved little girl in Godalming, but she's not a thug.

On reflection though, she's been acting rather strangely lately. Last weekend, I came into the kitchen and found her pulling Big Ears' tail until he started barking at her. She loves that dog, I've never seen her doing anything to hurt him before. This must a bid for attention – she sees (truthfully sometimes, I admit) that Mum can't wait to get back to her playground chockful of wonderful machines which she can play with all day long – and now Dad has abandoned her too.

What can I do – take her to work with me? I tried that once on a preschool-free day when Katie had flu (Kurt can never leave his office for non-work-related reasons, of course, unless he's at death's door, being CEO of AVBIC, aka A Very Big Important Company). Fran spent the day alternately interrupting me and charming Ben (who forgot to buzz in one of the volunteers, who followed someone into the lift and got lost inside the maze of the Psychological Sciences Building). Finally, I got so frazzled I snapped at Ben who threw a tantrum, walked out of the Psycho Lab and didn't come back till next day.

Giving up my job is tempting at times like this. Except that it's my life, my passion. I've worked so long and so hard for the chance to do this research. Dropping out for a year when Fran was born was nearly the death knell of my career. Another break now would be disaster – I'd never get back in. How can I give it all up now, just when I might finally be starting to get somewhere?

I've got a confession to make, Allie – please don't say anything to Ray. I love Fran with all my heart, but sometimes I wonder if I did the right thing having her.

Yours,

Mother at end of tether

From: Allie Loff (allie53@outlook.com)
Sent: 9 June 2018 5.53am GMT
To: Bea Hudson (bhudson9@blueyonder.co.uk)
Re: **Crisis at home 2**

Sorry no time for proper reply. Ray is shouting at me again for leaving the emus' gate open. I did what you said, approached them slowly, just a few steps, but one snarled and stabbed its beak at me and I ran away. When Ray got there three had escaped, now just four left. At this rate I'll be sleeping in the kennel tonight.

Re questions:

why would my daughter want to throw stones at a man passing on a bicycle? – that is bizarre

bid for attention? – odd way to get attention! maybe she would prefer to be throwing stones at you – or Kurt

take her to work with me? DEFINITELY NOT

give it all up now? DEFINITELY NOT

sometimes wonder if I did the right thing, having her – don't be a silly noodle

Chapter 8

Miss Madeleine Geen

7 June, Session 1, 4pm

Background

Miss Geen rang in the first week of May, insisting she have an appointment the next week. Jane explained to Miss Geen that my schedule was full and I could not take on any further patients. Then last week Mr Milroy had a heart attack while shooting grouse in Scotland. As this freed up the late Thursday afternoon slot before bridge evening and reduced the patient list to seven, I informed Jane that I have revised my position on not seeing middle-aged women.

Facts known about Miss Geen

1. She refused to disclose her age to Jane.
2. She lives in Wellfield Road, Streatham.
3. I was recommended to Miss Geen by her near-neighbour Mr Lode, who consulted me in 1998.

(I skimmed through Mr Lode's notes to reacquaint myself with the case a strange fellow with a fear of social interactions and insects, and a compulsion to talk endlessly about deeply unpleasant dreams involving squashed eyeballs. He left therapy after thirty-one sessions, able to hold brief conversations with neighbours and colleagues, and to enter his garden shed.)

Note on Miss Geen's physical appearance

Tall and slim, dressed in a black T-shirt and flared orange jeans. A large green stone on right index finger. Dangling silver earrings. Little make-up. Long hair the colour of straw, roots showing grey. A handsome woman. Fierce blue eyes, strong jaw.

Session notes (filed with tape in top drawer of small cabinet)

MG: Hello, I'm Madeleine Geen.

Voice strong, well-modulated. A regional accent loiters behind the clearly enunciated vowels. An actress? Cabaret singer?

NR: Good afternoon, Miss Geen. I'm Mr Rowley.

MG: Please, call me Madeleine. Or Ms Geen, if you prefer. I hate being called Miss Geen, it makes me think I've turned into a primary school teacher.

NR: I'm sorry, *Ms* Geen. I'll try to remember.

Invite patient to sit. Explain that I like to get the money part over with first.

Miss Geen looks at me and the empty armchair suspiciously then perches herself on it, placing a voluminous bag on the coffee table - more of a shopping bag than a handbag, though these days it's hard to tell the difference. After a long grope, a small fringed purse is extracted.

MG: It always gets stuck down at the bottom. (Smiles unapologetically.) Your secretary said I could pay you £30 as I'm not working at the moment.

Inform her that this is quite all right. (Note: Remind Jane to be stricter with middle-aged women. In future we should charge them all £50 minimum, whatever their circumstances.)

Miss G hands me three wrinkled notes. Nails short, unvarnished. Flecks of green (paint?) on her hands. Long fingers.

Obtain permission to record the session.

MG: I'd better be careful what I say then, hadn't I?

Explain my role and methods as Jungian therapist, and how the therapy requires the patient to talk freely.

Miss G nodded dubiously.

Explain re questions on personal circumstances, how the information is to help me assess how I can best help the patient.

Miss G nods dubiously.

NR: Age?

MG: Why do you need to know that?

Explain that it is a standard question.

MG: I'm forty-four.

NR: Single, never married?

MG: That's right.

NR: Living arrangements?

MG: Excuse me?

I elaborate.

MG: I live in a one-bed garden flat with two cats, Giblet and Mungo.

NR: Any current significant relationships?

MG: Apart from with my cats, you mean? Hmm. I don't know if you'd call them significant, but I'm still friendly with one or two of my ex's - does that count?

NR: Occupation?

MG: I'm an artist, I make sculptures from found objects. And I paint - paintings are easier to sell.

NR: Is this a regular source of income?

MG: Not exactly. I sell something maybe three or four times a year. I do casual work from time to time - bar work, gardening... I've been an extra in six films.

NR: Do you have any family?

MG: My mother died ten years ago. My Dad lives in Nottingham - I go over when I can and help him with his place, his health isn't too good. My sister and I had a blazing row one Christmas, I haven't seen her in three years.

NR: How would you describe your childhood?

MG: Not so good. My parents hated each other. My father was violent and my mother was addicted to everything in the bathroom cabinet.

NR: I see. And how is your health, in general?

MG: I look after myself as best I can. Yoga, acupuncture, healthy food. (Smile.) I try to avoid doctors.

NR: Have you ever been diagnosed with any psychiatric condition or mental health issue?

MG: No, I'm pretty sure I haven't.

NR: Have you ever had any counselling or therapeutic help of any kind?

MG: I was sent to a child psychologist because I pinned up my painting of the headteacher in the corridor. She confiscated the painting too—

NR: Have you ever had any therapy as an adult?

MG: My GP suggested I see someone once, but I didn't want to. (Smile.) I don't have much faith in therapists, I'm afraid.

NR: What did you come to see me about?

MG: I thought I ought to talk to someone. Something's been on my mind lately.

The patient's gaze wanders from the owl painting to my desk, now behind me as Jane advised, though I'm not sure it makes me seem any less formidable to patients. I suspect that this one would have given anything not to have been sitting in that chair with only a coffee table between us. My smile only seems to increase her alarm. My teeth aren't in the best condition, I want to tell her, but I'm no ogre.

Her hands clasp each other as she appraises the newly polished chandelier, substantial collection of framed accreditations and carefully arranged bookshelves.

MG: You read a lot, do you?

NR: I have every significant work on psychoanalytic theory on those shelves, Miss Geen. They help to enhance one's aura of wisdom and mystique, I find.

I smile brightly to signal my attempt at humour, which I hope might relax the patient. She looks at me stonily for ten seconds before speaking.

MG: My friend has a daughter, Fran – I'm her godmother. I have these thoughts about taking her away and bringing her up as my own daughter.

Obsessive jealousy? Delusional? Can I possibly do anything to help?

NR: I see. And what happens to your friend?

MG: She gets put in prison or has to go to hospital, something like that. Or she gets lost in South America, or is taken away by a sect…

I suppress my urge to laugh, not so much at the sentiment itself but at the matter-of-factness with which she expresses herself, as if it were some commonplace thing she might say to her butcher (or greengrocer – types like her never seem to eat meat).

NR: Is that all?

MG: Isn't that enough?

NR: Do you ever think about harming your friend?

MG: Absolutely not! I could never hurt her. But sometimes I cringe at what she does with Fran.

NR: What does she do?

MG: I know it's difficult for Bea. Her husband works long hours and she has a full-on job at uni. But once she left Fran with a car park attendant for two hours because she couldn't get childcare

and she had to give a talk about her research…
And sometimes she forgets to pick up Fran from
preschool. Then there was the time she had an idea
for an experiment on the train and didn't realise
where she was till she was nearly in Portsmouth.
Kurt was in America and the au pair was on the way
to Gatwick for her flight to Poland so Fran was left
on her own at home. (Laughs.) I sound like a right
old biddy, don't I? Who am I to judge, I haven't
even got kids.

NR: Have you shared your opinions with your friend,
may I ask?

MG: Of course not! Well, just a few things, once
in a while. I told Bea how lucky she was to have a
daughter and I couldn't understand why she didn't
want to spend more time with her. She said I sounded
just like her husband.

NR: So, you would like to rescue Fran from your
friend?

MG: I wouldn't put it quite like that. Bea means
well… She isn't that bad a mother, she's just so
all over the place. I'm not sure that I'd be any
better at it. I'd probably get so wrapped up in my
sculpture I'd forget about everything else, too.

NR: Have you ever thought about having children
yourself?

MG: I did, once. But it's not going to happen now –
it would take a miracle, at my age.

NR: Did you always want to have children?

MG: I always wanted to, yes. But the men I loved
either left me or made me leave them. It wouldn't
have been fair on a child.

NR: And now you regret your lack of children and you want to take another woman's child?

MG: You have a way with words, don't you?

Ten second silence.

MG: I know it's not right, imagining all these things. But I get these thoughts more than ever, lately. Ever since Fran made me a card for my birthday, a few weeks ago. She drew a picture of me in a green mini and purple platforms with yellow hair down to my waist – God knows when she saw me dressed like that. Underneath she wrote, 'My number 1 Auntie'. It sounds soppy but it really got to me. (Long sigh.) Sometimes when I visit, I feel so torn up with longing. It's driving me mad. Bea's such a good friend, I don't want to lose her. But if she knew half of what went through my head, she'd never to speak to me again – are you listening?

NR: Of course, Miss Geen. Why do you ask?

MG: It looks like you're doodling.

NR: I make notes on all of my patients. Does it bother you?

MG: Is your memory bad, Mr Rowley?

NR: I don't believe so. Why do you ask?

MG: Because I asked you not to call me *Miss* Geen! Ms is fine, or Madeleine.

NR: I humbly beg your pardon – Miz – Muz – Madeleine. Have you ever suffered from delusions or paranoia, may I ask?

MG: Not unless you count occasionally feeling paranoid about a man with a balaclava over his face looking over my shoulder while I'm using a cash machine. And sometimes when I'm talking to elderly men in dark blue blazers with neat grey beards, I get the strong impression I'm trying to communicate with an alien who's never seen a human being before.

Inform the patient that, unfortunately, we have run out of time. I would be extremely pleased to take her on to work with her to address her concerns; however, I can guarantee nothing, etc.

Miss G hoists her bag onto her lap and fiddles with its strap for an excessive length of time.

MG: OK, why not? What have I got to lose? (Radiant smile.) Except my mind, of course.

NR: The standard minimum is ten sessions.

MG: Can't we just see how it goes? I'm not sure if my budget can stretch that far. Giblet is already on a no-biscuits diet.

NR: I'm afraid not, Miss – Madeleine. The rules are important, though they might seem pedantic to some.

MG: Put me down for ten sessions then. I guess in for a penny, in for a pound.

Initial assessment

An intelligent and self-aware though rude, argumentative and somewhat neurotic woman, clearly frustrated by childlessness. Anger management issues. Obsessive and manic depressive tendencies suspected. No signs of delusion or paranoia, as yet. An unstable personality, possibly? My intuition tells me to be careful.

Note to self: Can I cope with this woman? Is she worth the risk of elevated blood pressure and premature ageing? But the patient list is looking meagre with the demise of Mr Milroy and last week's defection of Mrs Allsop to Mr Peabody in Balham.

Outlook

Some easing of the patient's symptoms can be hoped for, though I see little prospect of any substantial change. Over a long enough period, improvement is possible but appears unlikely, given Miss G's dismissive attitude to therapy.

Plan

Concentrate on Miss G's primary concern, i.e. attempt to reduce her thoughts and imaginings re her friend's unfortunate daughter. At any signs of Miss G acting out her fantasies, inform appropriate authorities.

Chapter 9

What to do about Madeleine?

Report on suspicious signs

Below I have noted my observations of Bea's suspicious behaviour on various dates (to the best of my recollection), as follows:

26/5/18

Continual texts between Bea and Mad (who was walking in the Lake District with ex number three) accompanied by sniffs, snorts, sighs, etc. When I asked what was going on, Bea replied, 'Oh, just girl stuff'.

27/5/18

Asked casually if Bea would ever consider having an affair. (I was in the final stages of preparing boeuf bourguignon followed by crème brûlée to mark the imminent departure of Bea's mother to central Europe and Russia, where she will spend several months train-hopping, vodka-sipping and trying out her stumbling Russian on unwary locals.)

No, of course not!

Not even an incy wincy one?

Not even an incy wincy one. I love you, Kurt, how many times do I have to tell you! I'm not interested in anyone else.

What about if something should happen to me, what would you do then? Say if I died in a freak accident.

What?

Say I got electrocuted while installing some lights in the kitchen.

Oh, in that case I might be tempted. There's that hunk round the corner who drives the Aston Martin, and…

She tossed in several other examples of prime manhood then gave me an impish smile before carrying on.

But I think if I had another relationship, darling, it would probably be with another woman. They're much less demanding than men, they don't yawn when you're in the middle of saying something, they don't leave the house in a mess the moment it's been cleaned, they don't nag about unmatched socks and they don't snore like hyenas.

And they don't give you what you like on a Sunday morning!

She laughed and so did I. Then we kissed and cuddled until interrupted by Bea's mother's arrival.

2/6/18, night before leaving for Istanbul

Over dinner, when I asked Bea what she would do while I was away, she replied, 'Oh, have lots of fun.' Then she listed the tasks to be performed, along the lines of:

Get quotes for a new damp course and decoration of hall; get a plumber in to fix the dripping toilets/taps; get a roofer in to fix the gutters; look after/cook for/punish/entertain Fran when Katie's not around and while I'm at it, try to keep my research job by making a few major discoveries in neuropsychology.

I ignored this poor attempt at sarcasm.

Later, while I was packing, Bea applied white goo to her face and clipped/painted her toenails. She seemed to be going to a great deal of trouble.

Going somewhere nice?

Oh, you never know, Maddie and I might head off to a hot nightspot in town tomorrow night, get pissed and see who we can pick up.

Assumed she wasn't serious. Now wondering if I may have missed something.

When we made love (after I reminded her how long I might be away), she closed her eyes and moaned (no scratches or obscenities since Christmas Eve). Afterwards, she didn't put her head on my chest as usual.

When I told her she was the queen of my heart and I would love her up until my last breath, she looked thoughtful and a little sad. I said I would miss her very much and I would not be happy again until I returned to her arms. She said she knew I would be OK without her, I just had to keep busy and promise not to drink too much. We would talk on the phone every day and before I knew it, we would be together again.

6/6/18, afternoon

Calls to Bea's mobile redirected to voicemail for two and a half hours.

When I called the home number that evening, she explained that she had been 'talking to the Prof about the ref'. Did not understand but too tired to ask.

She seemed relieved that I did not ask any further about what she had been doing, and changed the subject to the rogue rat in our cellar that she had not witnessed but was certain was down there from various signs such as tappings and droppings. I suggested a trap, then poison, then ear plugs.

7/6/18, evening

Bea did not answer the phone until my fifth attempt. Said she was 'in the loo' then 'looking for rats in the cellar'.

12/6/18, evening

1. Mad answered phone not Bea.
2. Bea would not talk to me.
3. Overwrought hysterical laughter overheard from Bea (feeling guilty about something?)

Actions to take ASAP

Find out whether or not Madeleine is having sexual relations/improper closeness with my wife. Use whatever means necessary to conclusively ascertain. (Photos of kissing? Video of illicit behaviour?)

If the result is:

No – Apologise profusely for meddling. Ask forgiveness, try to make amends and work on being a better husband with immediate effect.

Yes – Take Appropriate Action depending on the degree of Unreasonable Behaviour:

i) Moderate (errant behaviour including but not limited to excessive time together, communication breaching the normal bounds of friendship) – try to forgive but advise her of the unfortunate consequences that will result if she continues such behaviour.

ii) Bad (transgressions of a sexual nature happening once/a very small number of times, without attendant feelings of love/infatuation) – forgive, if possible, otherwise seek immediate divorce and damages.

iii) Severe (unforgiveable transgressions, e.g. repeated wanton acts of a sexual nature) – seek immediate retribution.

Immediate retribution? Like what? And how can I possibly check if anything's going on from here?

Jesus, the air in here is as stuffy as a gorilla's armpit. I wish I could rip this miserable hotel room apart. The thought of someone else's hands on Bea's private places, or her hands on someone else's private places... It would be the end of everything. It would be even worse if the someone else was a woman, not a man. I can't imagine I'd get a milligram of pleasure from watching two women getting it on; it would only represent failure on a grander scale.

But why am I sitting here tormenting myself over what my nearest and dearest may or may not be up to? I'm losing my sense of perspective. She's probably up to nothing more sinister than an overlong phone call or two. Instead of these masochistic machinations I could be enjoying the pleasures of modern corporate life. If the Chief Executive of ComputerCrap, Inc. didn't insist I stay put in this doomed outpost of decrepit technology, I'd be out of this place in a nanosecond and back to Godalming. A video conference from home to start with, maybe, then a top-down cruise in the BMW through lush Surrey lanes to the office, popping in to see a client in the Thames Valley on the way, or lunch in Datchet overlooking the river with a good bottle of red…

Today was just impossible, trying to get these pesky Turks to pull their thumbs out of their backsides and get down to work. They prefer to stand around gossiping and sniffing rose petals, or nipping out for fixes of that foul soup they call coffee. No wonder the Turkish operation is going down the gurgler. They seem to think they've got the upper hand, that I'm some soft-bellied squidgy-livered corporate imposter who's powerless to change their cosy set-up. But they'll be reeling by the time I've finished with them. No one is going to mistake me for a doormat – at work or at home.

Remember that, Beatrice darling. Your long-suffering husband isn't about to sit around like a prize pumpkin while his woman is making out with another woman. If Goldilocks lays the tiniest finger on your beautiful body, I will not be held responsible for the consequences.

Chapter 10

From: Bea Hudson (bhudson9@blueyonder.co.uk)
Sent: 12 June 2018 10.40pm
To: Allie Loff (allie53@outlook.com)
Subject: **Crisis at home 3**

Hope Ray calmer by now?

Sorry to hear that my suggestion re gradual exposure didn't work. Those emus sound nasty, it might be better to stay well away from now on.

Today's crisis as follows:

I was trying to make Fran eat more than three spoonfuls of Rice Crispies and at the same time trying to find my laptop with the slides for the presentation I've cobbled together about the Phobia Group's latest non-findings before rushing to catch a fast train to Birmingham.

Me: What are you playing at, Francesca? I'm in a hurry. I can't wait here forever while you finish that. If you don't hurry up, you'll have to go to Little Lanes without your breakfast.

F: (banging her spoon on table) No!

Me: What do you mean, no?

F: I don't like Little Lanes. I want to stay here!

Me: You can't, I have to be at a conference in three hours.

F: No!

She picks up her beaker of orange juice and chucks it at me. I'm standing next to the table, three feet away, an easy target. The beaker bounces off my collarbone and rattles to the floor. A gush of cold liquid drenches my shirt.

I'm so shocked I can't utter a word, let alone a shriek. Fran leaps up from her chair and runs out of the kitchen faster than I've ever seen her move. The juice seeps under my bra, down my stomach into a puddle at my feet. My white linen shirt is covered in several large, bright orange splodges. I pull off shirt and skirt and fling them in the sink, then have an urge to run upstairs after Fran and slap her.

How dare she do such a thing? Whatever happened to the smiling, affectionate little girl who used to jump onto my lap and hug me as we watched Mr Bean, or grab my hand and kiss it at the Waitrose checkout?

I lean on the sink, head in hands, not giving a toss that I'm in the kitchen with the blinds open wearing only a bra and knickers in full view of the neighbours. When I finally go upstairs, Fran is sitting on the floor playing with a headless Barbie.

Me: Why did you do that?

F: –

Me: Come on, tell me. I want to know.

F: I don't know, Mummy.

Me: (yelling) How can you not know!

F: (looks at me in horror)

I take a deep breath, imagining a tropical beach and a gentle breeze cooling my bare skin.

Me: You must not throw things at people on bicycles – and you must not throw orange juice at Mummy. Especially you must not throw orange juice at Mummy! She loves you very much and tries to do what is best for you and Daddy. Sometimes what she does won't make sense to you, but you must know that she is doing the best she can. Do you understand?

Fran: (looks at me as if I had thrown juice at <u>her</u>)

Me: I love you very much, Frannie. I'm not going to hurt you. But I'm not going to let you behave like that in my house. (That last bit is what Kurt says when he's angry with her.) Don't you dare do that again, or there'll be no more trips to the beach.

I got out Fran's picture book, made a cup of tea and took a shower. I couldn't think straight, didn't know what to do – I couldn't face trying to get Fran in the car again after what happened last time. I was about to call Katie and ask her to come over early, then remembered her 10.30am hospital appointment (NHS, so no telling how long she'd be).

So I called Maddie.

Maddie drove over (took less than an hour, so must have been at 90mph), told me I must go to the conference. She would stay and look after Fran, so I could call Katie and tell her she wasn't needed this afternoon.

Thank heavens for Maddie! When I got back to Godalming this evening, Fran was a sweet little girl again, eating out of Mad's hand – in both senses! They were sitting side by side on the sofa sharing a plate of bread with peanut butter. I'm not sure who was enjoying it most. Mad likes her food, that's for sure. Actually, I was a bit taken aback to see them sitting so companionably together. Not jealous, exactly. Well, just a little.

Fran jumped up and wrapped her arms round me and said she was sorry she had been so horrible. I was touched, though I think Maddie put her up to saying it.

The three of us spent the evening together. Maddie cooked dinner and Fran showed me drawings she'd done. Mad had got her drawing deep sea fish from photos on the web, scary-looking creatures with enormous serrated snouts. I told her they were fabulous and she looked so pleased. She was a totally different child to the one I was with this morning – it's so confusing.

Maybe she feels bad about throwing the juice. Or maybe it's because Maddie is great with children. She has so many child-friendly skills that I lack. She talks to Fran differently to me, as if she's a child herself. Yet she can be firm enough to get Fran to do what she wants, even helping to dry the dishes!

I sat in a daze, letting Mad take over, enjoying the peace – no fighting about how much ice cream Fran can have, how much TV she can watch or when she has to go to bed. And M's such a wiz at practical things – on top of looking after Fran, she fixed the wonky gas ring, wound up the kitchen clock, put the damp remover thingies in the cupboards and swept away the bits of cobweb hanging from the hall ceiling that I keep forgetting to tell Katie about.

After we'd said goodnight to Fran, Maddie joked that I should be married to her instead of Kurt. I said yes, a wife would be much handier – Kurt does nothing around the house except watch TV, make a mess and demand food, back rubs and sexual favours (gross exaggeration, of course). We couldn't stop laughing. It was almost as funny as years ago when the chemistry teacher at St Mary's stopped in the corridor, blew her nose and farted (even louder than Dad used to after a helping of Mum's stew).

Just at that moment, Kurt rang. I couldn't speak so Mad answered, still chortling. She said I was busy, could he wait a minute? He said, 'Please, I'd like to talk to my wife, is that too much to ask?' and hung up.

He still hasn't called back, which is just as well. He can stew in his own sour juice, imagining whatever he likes. By now he's probably cooking up visions of Mad and I in bed together, getting up to no good.

Anyway, Maddie has offered to come over and look after Fran whenever I need her to. She loves the space and light here, she can paint out on the terrace and do her yoga in the living room. I might take her up on her offer next month, when preschool ends. Then (thank God) there's only the summer to get through before Fran starts school full-time in September.

xx

From: Allie Loff (allie53@outlook.com)
Sent: 12 June 2018 10.58pm GMT
To: Bea Hudson (bhudson9@blueyonder.co.uk)
Re: **Crisis at home 3**

Poor thing. You did well to avoid immediate retaliation. I would have smacked the little brat and banished her to her room for the rest of the week, and no more OJ for a year.

It's a good thing your friend was OK to come over. She sounds like an ideal part-time mum. I'd be dead jealous.

Re sleeping in kennel – Ray and I made up, he's forgiven me for being such a useless farmer's wife.

A

From: Bea Hudson (bhudson9@blueyonder.co.uk)
Sent: 16 June 2018 10.09pm
To: Allie Loff (allie53@outlook.com)
Subject: **Crisis at home 4**

Positives first.

This morning I took Fran to play with her friend Skye up the road then got through two hours of essay marking. Then we trampolined until my legs were ready to drop off (calf muscles more defined now). This evening we stuffed ourselves with pizza and coke while watching 'Babe' for the fifth time. Fran seems happy again. She's been well behaved all day and hasn't pulled Big Ears' tail once – I even came across her stroking his head.

A scarcely legible postcard from Mum came this morning. I think she is in Vladivostok and has been having a fabulous time except for a row with her friend over the dinner bill, and being afraid to open the window of their compartment at night because her friend has a cough. No need yet for any fur hats.

The incident was this morning. I'd put Kurt's top-of-the-range Garmin satnav (which I gave him for Christmas and he said was one of the best presents I've ever given him) in my dressing gown pocket to take downstairs to go back in the car. But I forgot to take it out of my pocket, possibly due to early dementia – memory has been bad lately – or a delayed effect of yesterday's stress. Was chopping strawberries for muesli when Big Ears jumped onto the pedal bin and tried to snaffle Fran's toast. I saved the toast but spilled coffee all over my dressing gown sleeve, so took gown off and put in the wash.

Unfort, as I found out when I went to get the washing, the satnav has not come out as pristine as when it went in. The thing doesn't come on when I press the on button and the screen has a crack in it.

Am ridden with angst and remorse. I don't dare tell Kurt, especially as he spent hours customising its voice to that of a husky-toned female who's just cooked dinner and is about to present her stockinged leg.

Re Maddie helping with Fran – I'm lucky to have a friend like that around. If she wasn't, I'd be in deep shit.

Bea

From: Allie Loff (allie53@outlook.com)
Sent: 16 June 2018 10.52pm GMT

To: Bea Hudson (bhudson9@blueyonder.co.uk)
Subject: **Second thoughts**

Thanks for the satnav story B, I've not laughed so much in ages

Maddie is probably fine to look after Fran – but what will Kurt say?

I'm doing my best to keep my spirits up. Ray's not been talking much lately, he prefers to watch TV.

I know I've disappointed him. I wish I could be more like a farmer's wife but can't kid myself anymore, I'm not cut out for this outback life. Oz is great – by the sea or in the mountains, where the flies aren't constantly in your eyes or up your nose. Wish I could be honest and tell him this myself, but can't bring myself to. He loves it here, he is so happy looking after the farm. He just needs someone else to help him with it.

A

From: Bea Hudson (bhudson9@blueyonder.co.uk)
Sent: 16 June 2018 11.23pm
To: Allie Loff (allie53@outlook.com)
Re: **Second thoughts**

Sorry life is so tough right now, Allie. I hope things get better v soon. Haven't got any incredibly useful advice.

Just a thought - does it have to be you who helps Ray with the farm? And what about getting some fly spray/bug traps/ electric zapper things?

Over here, have just finished packing up the satnav so that it will withstand DHL taking it to a factory in the Czeck Republic - however that's spelled - where the technicians will mend it (for £150 - ouch!)

All my love, Bea

Chapter 11

Miss Madeleine Geen

21 June, Session 2, 4.10pm

NR: Good afternoon, Miss Geen.

MG: Sorry I'm so late, nothing's going right today! And sorry about missing last week. I had dreadful PMS… Well, you won't want to know the details. (Breathing heavily, she drops her voluminous bag onto the coffee table.) I couldn't get a parking place anywhere. Then I went to the wrong house – I was knocking on the door of number thirty-one for ages before I realised you're number thirteen. (Grimace.)

NR: Perhaps unconsciously you didn't want to see me.

MG: I don't think it's anything like that! I gave myself an hour to get here but one thing after another went wrong… I won't bore you with the details.

Inform Miss G of my policy of not extending sessions to latecomers and of charging the full amount if a patient misses a session without twenty-four hours' notice.

MG: I'll try not to be late again, then! Gosh, it's like I'm talking to my old maths teacher. He was always giving me detentions for coming in late.

(Miss G studies me.) He had a moustache, too - no beard though. We all thought he must gay. Not that I'm saying you're gay…

NR: Is there any chance that you could pay me before we begin, Miss Geen? I may have forgotten to explain, but I like to get the money matters out of the way, first thing-

MG: No, you did tell me, I forgot in all this rush. (A rummage in the bag delivers two ten pound notes followed eventually by a heap of coins.) I'm sorry for all the change. I meant to go to the bank this morning but it slipped my mind.

NR: Perhaps you'd rather not have to pay me at all?

MG: Excuse me? (Grips the arm of the chair) I've come all this way to see you, hoping you can help me, and all you do is malign my intentions and try to draw me into an argument!

NR: I must apologise, Miss Geen-

MG: And will you stop calling me Miss Geen!

NR: I'm so sorry, I meant to say… (Clear my throat.) So, Madeleine. How was your week? Are you still having fantasies about kidnapping your friend's daughter?

MG: (Deep sigh.) Not at the moment. I've mostly been thinking about how I can get to spend more time with her, then I feel guilty for deceiving Bea - not deceiving her exactly, just not telling her the whole truth. I was with my goddaughter just the other day, as Bea was having trouble with her… I fell in love with her all over again. I know it's a weird thing to say - you probably won't understand. But she's the loveliest, most affectionate little girl. When she saw me in the hall she ran up to me and hugged me as if I'd been trapped in the Arctic for the past year. (Wistful smile.) Shall I go on? Or am I boring you?

NR: Not at all, I was just taking a few notes. Carry on, please.

MG: She took my hand and took me to her room. I helped her put a tattoo of a starfish on her arm – a temporary one – and she put a rose on mine. (Taps the top of her arm.) I'm not going to wash there, for a while. (Lowers her voice.) There's something I want to ask you – I'm sorry if you're offended, but I'd like to know. Is there any chance you might repeat anything I say to anyone?

NR: I wouldn't worry about that, Ms Geen. Whatever you say to me will remain strictly confidential. Apart from certain extreme circumstances, that is, which I very much doubt will arise–

MG: Extreme circumstances?

Explain the procedure if a patient becomes a danger to themselves or others, stressing that it would be most unlikely that this would ever apply in her own situation.

NR: Many people have fantasies of committing acts that they would never be prepared to carry out in reality. The best thing is for you to tell me everything that comes into your head, omitting nothing. In this kind of therapy, I need you to be as open as possible. I hope you will gradually be able to trust me enough to tell me everything, even your deepest secrets.

I smile reassuringly.

MG: I'll do my best. (Smile.) Now, where was I?

NR: The tattoo?

MG: Oh yes, the tattoo. Fran said I reminded her of a rose – I laughed and said it must be a thorny one. It was so sweet… I've always got on well with her but we've never been quite as close as this. After what Bea said about Fran being so naughty, I was wary about going over. But she wasn't at all difficult. Anyway, as time went on I started to work out how long we had left until Bea came home. Then I started thinking how nice it would be if she *didn't* come home, if it could just be me and Fran all the time. I even let myself imagine *I* was Mrs Hudson, but that was too awful. (Miss G smiles, displaying her extremely white teeth.)

NR: How often do you see Fran?

MG: Every three or four weeks – it all depends. Lately I've been going over to Bea's on a Friday, her day off. Fran's home in the afternoons, so I get to play with her a bit. And I've been over to babysit six or seven times. She's a lively little girl, to put it mildly.

NR: And now you're captivated by her, and believe you could become her surrogate mother?

MG: You think I'm crazy, don't you?

NR: It's a fantasy, Ms Geen. You know it couldn't really happen – don't you?

MG: I suppose it couldn't, unless something really did happen to Bea. She could get a long-term illness and be confined to bed, maybe. Or she could get even more sucked into her work… Bea's asked me to look after Fran again. I said yes, of course, but part of me doesn't feel good about it. I know it's all in my head — this fantasy as you call it — but I feel I'm deceiving my friend. I can imagine Bea's reaction if she ever found out.

NR: How do you think she would react?

MG: I'm certainly not going to tell her — I hope you're not suggesting I do?

NR: It sounds as if you've been keeping quite a lot from your friend, if I may say. Sometimes honesty can be the best policy, in my experience. Then again, one must be pragmatic. From what you say, I have the impression that your godchild brings you a great deal of satisfaction.

MG: Fran is the greatest source of happiness in my life, I can honestly say.

NR: Is being a surrogate mother easier than being a real mother, do you think?

The patient glares at me.

MG: I'm not stupid, Mr Rowley — can I call you Nigel? Mr Rowley is so formal. Of course, spending a few hours with my goddaughter here and there isn't the same as being a real mother, coping with a difficult child day in, day out. I'd be hopeless at it, probably. As bad as I am at relationships.

NR: Would you like to tell me about your relationships?

MG: (Scowl.) They just don't work for me. I've tried loads of times, but I always end up feeling I want to go into a dark tunnel and scream my head off. The frustrations, the compromises… Though it would be nice to live in a big house in the country, like Bea's. Maybe I should find a rich man who can keep me and my cats. (Smile.) Bea's always telling me I should learn to compromise, that there aren't too many fit, frisky guys with a decent income and a thing for penniless forty-four-year-old women with two cats.

NR: That may well be true, I'm afraid.

MG: Don't get me wrong, I'm not anti-men. I've had plenty of men in my life – some have meant a lot to me. Sam was the first, then Vic. He moved in with me briefly and broke my heart. Then there was Toby–

NR: Did you ever think of having a child with any of these men?

MG: Sam wasn't the fatherly type. Vic wanted me to have his baby. I was going to – I came off the pill. Then I found out he'd been unfaithful… I got a termination. (Looks sadly into her lap.) I didn't think a single mum raising a child in poverty would be the best thing to do. And Toby… He was always out gambling–

NR: Would it not be possible for you to get pregnant now?

MG: Not without IVF – or a miracle. And who would I have a child with?

NR: It's clearly very painful for you that you've remained childless, Madeleine. But isn't it some compensation to have a good relationship with your friend's child?

MG: I don't know. Being with Fran reminds me how much I'm missing. She's four – little girls that age have always got to me.

Miss Geen moves her bag to her lap, rummages inside and brings out a tissue.

NR: I'm afraid we're going to run out of time soon.

MG: You told me to open up.

NR: I did, and thank you for doing so. You can tell me the rest next week.

MG: I'll have forgotten what I was going to say by then.

NR: I'm sure we will find other things to talk about, if that's the case… (Smile.) So, I take it you're willing to put up with me for a little while longer?

MG: I'll do my best.

NR: I'll see you next week then, Miss - pardon me, Ms Geen.

MG: See you next Tuesday, Mr Rowley. Pardon me, I meant Thursday.

Chapter 12

Colin Settle
18 Tudor Drive
Woking, Surrey GU21 3NZ
England
(email cmsettle@blueyonder.co.uk, mobile +44 7939 551012)
Gary Settle
14010 RANCHO SOLANA TRL
San Diego, CA 92130
21 June 2018

Dear Gary,

I don't know how to start this, so I'll launch straight in. Please forgive this sudden intrusion into your life – I very much hope you will not view my letter in a negative light, more as an overdue attempt at restoring brotherly bonds.

Firstly, I trust you are well and still enjoying the delights of San Diego. Do you still swim every morning? It must be the dog's bollocks at this time of year, before the onslaught of tourists. I often think about my visit. I can still smell the pines on the breeze and the perfume of beautiful women flitting between those pricey La Jolla boutiques.

Clare and I have parted since we last saw each other, though you probably already know that. You were right about her being easily distracted.

On the work front, for the time being I'm still at the insurance firm. (I'm writing this from my usual spot by the canteen window, watching the flotsam of Canary Wharf as I stuff a sandwich into my gob.) The place is filling up with youngsters in pinstripes tapping into their iPhones. Some glance disdainfully at my scratched laptop and very unsmart phone. I'm sure none of them have chronic back pain, clapped-out knees and sleepless nights worrying that they haven't got long to go before they get the chop.

It looks like the shears have started cutting back the old growth. Dave was out last week – a bloke everyone loved, never too busy for a 'How's it going, Col?' But evidently Messrs Clifford and Spelt noticed his greying hair and more frequent visits to the doctor, or perhaps his frequent phone calls about credit card repayments. They don't want the sick and needy working for them, nor do they want the desperate committing criminal acts on their tempting asset base, heaven forbid. Safest to cull the questionable ones, i.e. anyone who doesn't pass the Clifford-Spelt Test.

Rumour is, Messrs Clifford and Spelt have drawn up a profile of the ideal employee of Clifford & Spelt Insurance. According to the Compliance Manager, who saw it on Mr Clifford's PA's computer screen, the ideal employee is mentally and physically alert, is healthy in mind, body and financial circumstances, takes no more than four days average sick leave per year and doesn't have a hearing aid, artificial body part, diabetes or a depressive condition. (That excludes two-thirds of us, I should think.) Apparently they're going to start applying the test more rigorously over the next three months to streamline the operation. Old geezers like me stand no chance. (Eight sick days so far this year, three dental implants and mild to moderate depression.)

I'm not going to just take this on the chin, Gary, whatever redundancy payout they might try to lure me with. For twelve years I've toiled in this company, fleecing people who've been sucked into buying third-rate insurance policies that they're too lazy or stupid to understand, and now the bosses expect me to graciously stand aside. Not just me, either – all those hardworking cogs in the machine that are no longer needed. It's time I showed Messrs Clifford and Spelt what Colin Settle is made of.

On the train back to Woking

Sorry for the rant earlier, Gary – you must think that I've finally lost it, if you didn't already. I know we haven't been close lately, especially since the incident with Clare. But I hope you will carry on reading this letter, if it ever reaches you that is. I cross my fingers that the address I have is your latest, as your 'friend' with the sultry drawl seemed to think. (Your friend also said she would appreciate a phone call, and you left your flowering cactus behind – she intends to throw it away if you don't pick it up soon.)

No, I'm not planning to create mass carnage with a shooter or set fire to this great tower dedicated to The Gods of Finance. What I'm thinking of is much better. With a suitably executed parting gesture, I reckon I could, in one fell swoop, pay back Clifford and Spelt for making me do their dirty work, and make amends to the customers who've been shafted by our next-to-useless insurance policies. A Robin Hood-style scheme, if you will.

To a man of my calibre, it presents very little challenge. I'll just have to shift the numbers around a little, make one figure higher over here, another lower over there, by an amount X, say £100. No one will notice until next year's audit, and by then I'll be long gone.

You're shocked, aren't you, dear bro? You thought I was a nice, well brought up boy, the sort of bloke who gives coins to bucket-rattlers, offers his train seat to pregnant women and reports suspicious strangers to Neighbourhood Watch. Well, I am. I'm still the kind-hearted, considerate, put-himself-down, have-a-laugh-at-himself Colin that you know and (dare I hope?) love. But now I have another side too. I'm no longer going to be Colin Settle, Colin Settle-for-anything as long as it's tiresome, pointless and completely demeaning.

I know you won't have much sympathy for me, Gary. You'll probably think I've gone bonkers or I'm suffering from the male menopause, and you could be right. Right, bloody right! Will continue later – Woking coming up.

Train stopped at junction

Maybe I'll have to shelve my plan – or make it less risky. I don't want to end up in prison.

I *am* under stress, to answer your anticipated question. Things haven't been very rosy lately in any department. I still miss Clare – this week it's a year since she left. I've heard from Facebook that she and her intrepid BA pilot are about to tie the knot. Sometimes I go and sit on her chair under 'her' eucalyptus, close my eyes and imagine she's coming home. (She would sit in its shade with a Sophie Hannah novel and caress its bark – she loved that tree more than anything else, I reckon.)

It's sad, I know. Since Clare's departure, no woman has planted a foot inside my humble abode, with the sole exception of my cleaning lady.

But Clare was right, I realise. I've turned into a bitter, boring middle-aged man, resentful of everyone who has done better than me and I'm scared of making any changes that might upset the status quo. No wonder she left me.

If it hadn't been for you nudging things along a bit, as it were, it might well have been someone else. Did I really expect her to keep on loving a man who's conditioned himself to have everything in his life just so, who's set on following the narrow tracks laid out in front of him for as long as he's got left?

Clare and I went to the Isle of Wight every June to see Dad, God bless him, and to Scotland every Christmas and Easter to see Mum. Then, if we had a week to ourselves, we went to Rhodes – I always insisted on the same beach, the same two restaurants, and never wanted to explore the mountains because we might have got sunstroke or been attacked by bandits. I can't seem to do anything without considering the downside. It's definitely time for a change, methinks.

So, Gary, what about you? I hope you are still enjoying life, the ladies, etc?

Much brotherly love,

Colin

PS

Please forgive me for what I said the last time we met, especially the bit about never wanting to speak to you again. The stress I was under was considerable, you can imagine.

Chapter 13

What to do about Madeleine?

16/6/11, ways to check on Bea

I'm getting ahead of myself – how do I conclusively ascertain that Bea and Mad are having an affair when I'm stuck in this goddamned country full of bells that ring fifty times a day, and cold meat and cheese for breakfast? (There are other items on offer, such as congealed pigeon's egg, but I've not had the guts to try them yet. Complained to the manager yesterday that this is supposed to be a five-star hotel not a one-star hostel, and got the evil eye – he probably thinks I'm some xenophobic cretin who can't hack foreign cuisine.)

a) Ask Adrian next door to look in on Beatrice occasionally. The guy is friendly enough and, more importantly, as inquisitive as a woman. He's at home most of the time with his exterior design consultancy or whatever he's calling that gardening business now – always pottering about outside his front gate with his hedge clippings, where he can check that no undesirables are about to move into the street, eye up the ladies and peep on the men (I wouldn't be surprised if he's on the bi side, the way he looks at me sometimes). He'd enjoy the mystery and intrigue, I bet.

b) Ask Dad to take a rest from living it up in Florida Keys/lining up wife number three, and hot-tail it over for a childminding/house-tending/wife-watching break in Glorious Godalming. No point asking Mother – she will be recovering from her latest face job/lip suction/eyelid stretching, or else far too anxious about being blown up over the Atlantic to consider a visit to her neglected daughter-in-law.

c) Get a pro on the job. Hire a private eye who knows what he's (she's?) doing.

d) Spy on Bea myself. The latest gizmos are amazing, I read in the *Financial Times*.

17/6/11, web search results

Amazing what you can find on the internet. Half the world seems to be in a state of paranoia about their loved ones.

This one sounds good: 'The world's smallest DVR and motion-detect spy camera – the ultimate 007-style surveillance kit, perfect for discreetly checking on kids and *promiscuous partners,* comes with three false buttons for hiding the camera in one's jacket and matching real buttons for camouflage...'

Wow, they've thought of everything! There's more... 'A sound-activated miniature pinhole camera disguised as a car cigarette lighter!'

And this: 'A tissue box made of one-way-view plastic that hides a camera and digital video recorder, suitable for low light levels with a wide-angle 2.5mm lens that can take in the entire room!'

I'll catch them in the act with all this kit, no problemo!

20/6/11, the eagle has landed!

8.15am

Picked up a hefty package from reception, delivered express by DHL. The brunette who a few days ago upgraded my room to an Executive Suite gave me a look of puzzled concern tinged with pity. Worried over breakfast she may think I'm a closet weirdo who has ordered bondage equipment that will horrify the cleaning staff – which reminds me, have to get on with finding a more suitable residence. This place has no privacy whatsoever. Maids constantly come in without knocking despite the Do Not Disturb sign. And lately there is a tanned, very muscular, mid-thirties guy who stares at me from the apartment block opposite. Whenever I go to my balcony to inhale the hot dusty air, he is out on his, drinking coffee or towelling down his triceps.

9.15pm

Everything seems to be in order. Opened the package and spread out all the kit on the bed – a fully-functioning alarm clock, which just happens to conceal a tiny wide-angle camera, ditto for the crafty tissue box, and the fully-functioning wireless smoke alarm (doubly useful as the ones we have already have never detected a whiff of smoke) plus dozens of plastic bags containing all the extras – batteries, cables, SD cards, software CDs and copious instructions.

I put all the stuff back into the boxes and secured them with heavy duty tape. Will inspect properly tomorrow eve after office social, if not had too many drinks by then.

Must lie down now and cool off. Air con still not working properly. Complained but they say the system is designed not to make the air too cold.

10.02pm

On the bed with curtains shut, stripped to underpants. Would sit out on balcony but for muscle man across the way.

All this heat and spicy food – I feel something stirring. If only I could be at home with Bea right now. Instead, as usual, I must make do as best I can without her. I could work out in the gym downstairs until exhausted then take a cold shower, or I could investigate the massage parlour a few doors down, where they will supposedly pull you off for cost of three Manhattans. I saw two of our engineers go in there yesterday afternoon, giggling like girls on a shopping expedition. No wonder the repair centre has such a backlog.

No, I couldn't go with another woman, not even for a ten-minute hand job. I love Bea too much. Maybe I'll bring my trip home forward a week. My system is going into overdrive.

This nonsense I've got in my head about her and Mad getting it on together – where did it come from? It can't be true. She's told me several times that she still loves me, even when we're at each other's throats, and she's never looked at anyone else since that fateful evening when I inadvertantly jostled her with my trolley in Waitrose. And I'm about to go home and plant a spy camera in our bedroom in case she's getting up to no good with her best friend.

How much of a dick can a man be? I should just tell her I've been an idiot, I don't deserve her, and send this lot back.

Chapter 14
Katie's journal

21 June

I need holiday. Mrs H is gone mad, so is daughter. Fran said to me this morning, Katie you should wash, you stink. I said little girls should keep their little mouths shut. But I was hurt inside. She would never say anything like that to me before beach box went. Now she says anything she likes.

Katie is Ninny Nanny, Smelly Fanny! Katie bad, Katie likes to wee wee, Katie drinks cat pee!

Hear Little Fiend singing this when I am cleaning her room. I hear Mrs H tell Mr H about one of mothers at preschool with this name, like it is curse. She spells for me. Fran I will call Little Fiend now. Little Fiend deserves. I never knew children could be so horrible, sweet as a ripe mango one day and you're sure she loves you even though you are only ex O Pair, and next day she turns you away like broken biskit.

I break another plate yesterday and didn't tell Mrs H, or she might say I am out with the trash. Yesterday she says I have my brain scrambled, I do not remember what I am doing, I unplug electric doorbell on top floor for hoovering so we do not hear FedEx man with secret box for Mrs H.

Another thing that is My Fault. Mrs H is always telling me I must be more careful with dusting and washing up, or Mr H will say I must go. Now she does not listen to my stories of Warsaw or help me write words like before. Cardigun, biskit, cubbud. Fran hates me, Mrs H will hate me soon. Now I am Katya to

Mrs H when she is in bad mood, not Katie like before or 'the girl' in case of Mr H. For months he wants to get rid of me, he is always leaving notes.

Tell the girl to iron my shirts again!

Why didn't the girl empty the bins today?

Please tell the girl not to smoke in house/on terrace/ in garden, it is bad example for Fran!!!

I think Mr H needs his arse grabbed more often. I see why Mrs H gets tired of him when he is growling and snapping like the little dogs next door when you come near. It is just as well he is at work most of the time.

Mr H is gone now and Mrs H's Mad friend is over again tomorrow afternoon. Mrs H asks can I work longer hours like before, now preschool is closed for summer. Mad friend is nice to Mrs H also very nice to Little Fiend. I see her when she comes here for tea. Always biggest slice of cake she takes. She is trying to take Fran away from me, I am sure. Mrs H says I must make house VERY NICE before Mad friend visits and dust every corner, No More Cobwebs! She said she wants to ask friend to stay for night in guest room but Mr H would not like. I wonder if Mad friend will be moving in here soon, like cuckoo in other birds nest. Then I will be out on my ears, I must find new family.

Why this makes me sad? I do not like it so much here, do I?

Chapter 15

Letter to Gary continued

4 July

6.30pm, on train to Woking

Hello Gary, it's me again. Didn't get round to sending my letter after all, so I may as well carry on from where I left off.

On Saturday I went to the tennis club's summer party – live band, lots of booze, you know the score. My social life these days is based around the tennis club and the local over-fifties footie team. They're a good bunch, I can't complain, and there's always plenty of women around. But no one to get excited about. I don't go in for the diamond-braceleted, Mercedes-driving types that inhabit much of Surrey.

Work today was enlivened by an incident in the lift, which I shall relate for your amusement.

At the second floor (home to a motley collection of employment agencies, cosmetic procedure salons and developers of gambling software), a tall blonde gets in and starts jabbing at all the buttons at once.

'Where do you want to go?' I ask.

She says she has an interview with a Judy Smith Associates. 'They're supposed to be on the second floor but I can't find them anywhere. Someone said to try higher up.'

Her cheeks are pink and she breathes heavily as she stares impatiently at the indicator panel. The lift doors close.

'They could be on the seventh floor,' I say helpfully.

She stares at her watch. Her hair is a rich creamy blonde, and ripples past her shoulders as though she's just stepped out of bed. I press the seventh floor button.

'I'm already too late. It's nearly twenty to eleven, I can't go in forty minutes late. I've blown it.'

'A job?'

'Yes, part time, it would have been ideal. It's the first interview I've had in months.' She takes out a small rectangular folded tissue from her handbag. For a moment she looks as if she's going to cry. I try to look concerned and capable, as if I'm used to gorgeous women unburdening themselves in my presence. I make a mental note to start working out again.

'I understand,' I say as she wipes her forehead. 'Being late for a job interview can be very stressful.'

At the seventh floor, the woman makes no attempt to move. I keep my finger on Door Open. 'Aren't you getting out?'

'I can't go in now, it would be ridiculous. What would I say? It wasn't my fault I'm late, it was just a series of coincidences. Giblet left me a half-dead rat on the kitchen floor, which Mungo finished off, then I burnt my toast and set off the smoke alarm, which I couldn't get to stop for ten minutes. Then I forgot to take the map I'd printed with the address of the place for my interview!'

I take my finger off Door Open. The lift resumes its journey towards the fourteenth floor, and my office. 'Perhaps you weren't meant to get that job after all.'

She has a lovely smile. She also has perfect skin, apparently unmarked by blemishes or wrinkles, surely as soft as the skin on her generous breasts – as far as I can tell from my limited view of them, encased opaquely behind her blouse (36C?). Clare, you may remember, was an unexceptional 34B, shapely but not much to get a grip on.

'I think I'll just go and get a coffee somewhere. Thanks for your help...' She pauses.

'Colin. And you're?'

'Madeleine.'

The doors open, revealing the familiar plaque on the wall. This is the moment of truth. Terror threatens to overwhelm me as I reach out to clasp her hand. 'Madeleine, pleased to meet you. If you don't mind, I'd like to show you where you can get a really good cup of coffee... You look like you could do with one.'

She looks startled but agrees. I am startled too. Before either of us can change our minds, I lead her up to the fifteenth floor and my usual table in the staff canteen with its view of grand phallic edifices.

Things went downhill from there. We chatted for maybe twenty minutes about our favourite places for coffee, the disadvantages of working in an alienating environment such as an office and her relief that she wouldn't be working in Canary Wharf after all (she'd much rather be at home working on her art, though it doesn't bring in quite enough money to live on). But then she said she'd better be getting home to her latest sculpture, inspired by an object she'd seen while hitchhiking in Mexico.

I'm not sure if it was something I said that made her hurry off. I tried to convey as subtly as possible that I had a high-paying, responsible job in senior management and that I was a normal, sociable guy who wasn't currently attached. Or maybe she picked up that I was attracted to her and didn't reciprocate (I did my best to avoid glancing at her cleavage). Or maybe she was just playing very hard to get. Women can be infuriating, don't you find?

I do have one ray of hope, though. She gave me her email address. She wrote it, rather huffily, on a sheet of paper torn from the notepad that she carries everywhere in case she gets artistic ideas. I've folded it and put it inside my box of cufflinks. I haven't sent anything yet as I don't want to appear too keen – and in any case, I'll need time to conjure the appropriate words.

The hopeless loser in me is already regretting this hasty action.

Women are traps to be avoided at all costs, he reminds me. You've learned that lesson, haven't you? Now it's time to let go of your foolish hopes of finding another mate and accept reality. Walk on, Colin. Don't kid yourself that this will come to anything. We both know it won't.

The rest of the day was tediously normal. My pleasure at walking into the office halfway through the morning was offset by the sight of my nemesis, Mark Hollis (aka Mr Smarmy Pants), who looked up from his desk with a dazzling smile.

'Morning, Colin.'

'Morning,' I mutter.

'Everything OK at the doctor's? Did he do anything to relieve your permanent state of irritableness and misery?' Snigger snigger, smirk smirk.

'Bugger off, you charmless cretin.'

'Ooh, sensitive, are we?'

The youngster's gob was within punching distance. I'm normally restrained to the point of cowardice, but today my fingers itch to transform my junior colleague's face into 2D. But I sat down at my desk (as usual groaning with reports to be read, tasks to action and things to be put on one side) not nearly far enough away from Mr Hollis, whose permanently cheerful, freshly-minted mug all too often strays into view.

Mark Hollis is tall and slim, has no grey hairs and a face that could have been sculpted by Michelangelo. He goes about his work enthusiastically, to say the least – he's as unstoppable as a dog on heat. All day long he dispatches policyholders' queries and complaints with unquenchable aplomb, quashing the difficult or rude without a qualm in his studiously courteous manner, as one might destroy an irksome fly with a well-aimed swat.

'Can I please find out why my claim was refused? I don't understand, there was absolutely no reason…'

'I have to say, the way I'm being treated beggars belief…'

'Why the f– has it taken you thirteen months to turn down my claim? This is totally unacceptable!'

His reply is nearly always along the lines of: 'I'm sorry sir/madam, I can appreciate your concern/frustration/distress but I'm afraid the claim is still being assessed/a final decision has been made on the claim/perhaps I could draw your attention to the policy wording…'

There are surprisingly few permutations. The most troublesome customers are given an email address where they can send their complaint (only a minority do), after which they receive some permutation of our standard set of excuses for our lack of haste in dealing with their claim, appalling customer service, or whatever.

It's the same every day in this place. As soon as I turn on my computer, I'm sucked into the whirring machinery of dodgy policies and false claims, lives gone wrong, senseless accidents and premature deaths… And underneath it all, our futile cravings to outwit our cruel impermanence, to lull ourselves into a blissful ease while we head remorselessly towards death.

Gloomy, aren't I? Well, this job would steal the cheer from anyone's heart. We spend our days exploiting massed human frailty, taking advantage of people's fears and insecurities. Clifford & Spelt Insurance will provide whatever the customer requires and the market provides, as long as it looks like a winner to us. We ferret out the most profitable types of risk, and the most profitable customers. Devoted pet owners worried in case their beloved animal succumbs to diabetes or kidney disease, hypochondriacs awaiting numerous life-threatening conditions, holidaymakers planning to indulge in camel riding or alligator wrestling, newlyweds concerned that one day they might be at each other's throats… The list gets longer each year. And when all the hopeful claims come in, rest assured they'll be dispatched with the maximum of ruthlessness and the minimum of compassion – I make sure of that. By now, I am adept at casting aside what remains of my integrity.

In case I haven't mentioned it before, Gary, I authorise all payments, partial payments and non-payments on behalf of Clifford & Spelt Insurance. (Not the ideal arrangement, according to the Financial Conduct Authority and the consultant's review we had a few years ago, but no one can be bothered to change the process – Mr Clifford least of all.) I ensure that our customers are treated badly but not badly enough that they feel fleeced and lodge such vast numbers of complaints that the company's reputation suffers or (rather less likely) the financial watchdog takes action. Of course, even the best companies get complaints – it's all in the numbers. Our ethos has mutated from what it was back when I joined, i.e. to provide a service second to none while making a modest profit for our trouble. Now we aim to fleece those with modest incomes while making a profit second to none.

Suckers, where are you? Enough cash to fritter some away on a policy that will never pay up? (We'll make sure of it, don't worry.) That should be printed at the top of every new policy form. We stay inside the letter of the law and avoid too brazenly breaching the codes of conduct. We're not scared of toothless regulatory bodies, we know they have too much to do in too little time.

Sorry about that interlude – where was I?

You may not understand this, Gary, itinerant drifter that you are, addicted to the pleasures of life and suspicious of anything resembling graft. But to someone like me, without any overwhelming talents or excess of courage, tenacity or insight (a rather timid, plodding soul, it has to be said), the allure of being respected, if not exactly held in esteem by one's colleagues, and the sense that I was an important (though clearly not crucial) part of a substantial organisation, was seductive.

I hope you noted my use of the past tense in that last sentence. As I write this, the prospect of losing my job is no longer as grim as it was. I shall wave goodbye smiling, on my own terms. I shall start to execute my cunning plan ASAP, to make amends for the wrongs I've inflicted. If only I have the guts to carry it through.

Fondest wishes,

Colin

Part two

Chapter 16

From: Allie Loff (allie53@outlook.com)
Sent: 15 July 2018 9.50pm GMT
To: Bea Hudson (bhudson9@blueyonder.co.uk)
Subject: **Accident with goat**

Shoulder nearly wrenched from socket, arm extremely tender and knee swollen like football after I was kicked and chewed by Dimpla. I was trying to stop her baby goat from eating Ray's merino jumper – his favourite!

Ultra Mega Pissed Off.

A

From: Bea Hudson (bhudson9@blueyonder.co.uk)
Sent: 15 July 2018 10.05pm
To: Allie Loff (allie53@outlook.com)
Re: **Accident with goat**

Sorry to hear about the incident with Dimpla – it must have been scary. Your injuries sound very painful. Hope you get better quickly (and you can buy Ray another jumper). Trust you will be allowed to take time off your farm duties for a proper rest? I don't want to hear about any more distressing incidents involving goats, emus or anything else.

No emails recently as have had a run of late nights, too exhausted to turn on laptop after tucking in Fran. Weekend passed in blur of obsessing over research data, trampolining and playing with Fran's dolls.

Bea x

PS How did the goat get to eat Ray's jumper? Wasn't Ray in it?

From: Allie Loff (allie53@outlook.com)
Sent: 15 July 2018 10.12pm GMT
To: Bea Hudson (bhudson9@blueyonder.co.uk)
Re: **Accident with goat**

no, he dropped it while he was milking the goats – winter over here. another jumper? don't think so.

got to go, Ray taking me to the doctor, can't drive yet.

xx

Chapter 17

Letter to Gary continued

16 July

8.12am, on train to Waterloo

Still not managed to post this, Gary, so will keep on until a convenient time arises. It may well be different in California, but it's hard to face going to the post office over here these days, knowing that an hour-long queue awaits before one's letter can be anointed with the correct postage.

To summarise the latest developments in my nascent romantic life, dear bro – after nearly two weeks of cajoling emails to the object of my desire, I met Maddie yesterday at her local café. It was a long way from Woking, in the scruffy fringes of south London and not the best run establishment. But it's her favourite place for a cup of tea, she told me, so I was more than willing to overlook its deficiencies.

I get there first. I sit out on the terrace in the sun with my sunglasses and Ted Baker shirt, bought especially. It's quiet for a Sunday afternoon and you can see for miles across blue-tinged hills.

Maddie arrives fifteen minutes late, carting a pole with a ceramic moon fixed to one end and a bag of bone meal.

She's gorgeous. She's wearing a floppy sunhat, sleeveless cotton dress and flat sandals. Her long pale arms match her long pale legs. Her long blonde hair has a faint strawberry hue and almost reaches the middle of her back. Blue eyes, as near as damn it, a soft misty morning blue.

'The sale's on at the garden centre up the road,' she says.

'It's good to see you again, Maddie. Really good.'

'Did you think I wouldn't come?'

I watch her languid limbs settle and make a mental note not to fall in love with her. She won't be perfect, oh no. She'll have smelly feet and wobbly thighs. She'll like folk music, Abba songs and Wagner operas. She won't like lovingly restored old Jaguars and she'll hate going down to The Green Man on a Friday night for a beer or three and a chicken tikka masala. She'll have faults far worse than Clare, most likely.

'I'm glad you did,' I say. 'My day would have been ruined if you hadn't.' Stir her interest, laughter and sympathy, but under no circumstances aim for pity.

'I knew you'd come.' She looks straight at me. Her face is natural and her nails are dirty. She certainly isn't trying to get me interested; she doesn't seem to care if I fancy her or not.

'You don't normally go out on dates,' I venture. 'Do you?'

'I'm not desperate to meet someone. I haven't got money to waste going on dating sites – or time. I'd rather meet someone naturally.'

'Like we did?'

'That's right. At least this way you have some idea about who the guy is, and they're less likely to tell you a load of horseshit. I've heard that on some sites all the guys lie about their jobs. I don't want to meet any arrogant financial wheeler-dealers or crooked businessmen.'

'Well, I'm not one of those–'

'Which one?'

'One of either, I'm neither of those. I'm a decent, normal chap – you've got to believe me.'

A smile comes to her eyes and she starts to laugh. I relax a little. The conversation gets into gear. She likes old cars and driving fast and hates Abba and folk music. I tell her that I too love gardening (well, looking at gardens) and sculpture, especially Rodin and Moore (they're the only sculptors I can think of). I tell her about my six unhappy relationships and the disastrous marriage and she tells me about hers (she's single but has had far more break-ups than me). She's gone off men since her last bloke, who was unfaithful (ditto, with genders reversed). Like me, she enjoys spaghetti westerns and disaster movies. We're a match made in heaven.

'Any more job interviews?'

She finishes her tea and takes a large bite of scone. 'There's no jobs out there, not for someone like me.'

'Never mind–'

'I don't. I'm busy working on my sculpture. This is the concept.' She shows me a drawing of what looks like a demented bull (outsized horns, protruding black tongue) squatting on top of a pile of pound notes.

(A comment on the state of modern capitalism? Best not to ask.) 'It's fabulous.' I gather up my courage. 'So, Maddie, when can I see you again?'

'I don't know, I'm pretty busy at the moment. When I'm not working on my sculpture, I'm working on the garden – I'm replanting the lawn and putting down a patio. I do a lot of stuff myself – none of the men I know can bend or lift anything heavy because they have bad backs, or they're at work all day–'

'I could help.'

She looks doubtful. I change tack. 'We could go to a film, if you like. Or a play. There's one on at the National–'

'I don't know, Colin. I really enjoyed meeting you this afternoon, but to be honest…' She shrugs.

Keep it light, I tell myself. 'I'm not your type?'

'To put it bluntly – no.'

'What type am I?'

'You're a lovely man, Colin. But I'm more into sporty, muscular guys–'

'I'm sporty! I play tennis twice a week and I play golf quite often – and crochet. Croquet, I mean.'

'I'm not saying we can't meet up, now and then, for a cup of tea.'

'I could help you with your garden. I can bend and lift things. Heavy things! I'm stronger than I look.' Tell myself to smile. Remember, humour not pathos.

'Er – maybe. Sorry, time's getting on, I have to get back to get the chicken on. My friend Vic's coming over this evening for a bite. Shall we get the bill?'

Chapter 18

From: Bea Hudson (bhudson9@blueyonder.co.uk)
Sent: 18 July 2018 10.05pm
To: Allie Loff (allie53@outlook.com)
Subject: **Latest on research**

It's all go here. We've been working flat out to finish analysing data from our spider-phobic experiments (especially since I asked Ben and Hayley to take fewer coffee/Instagram/game playing/phone checking breaks) so we can get a move on with the project. We don't want anyone else getting results ahead of us, that would seriously affect our chances of getting a paper into a decent journal. There's a group in California working in the same area. I don't think they're quite there yet, fingers crossed, but you never know. In American universities everyone seems to be glued to their computers and lab coats 24/7.

Lunch today was a bag of roasted peanuts – fortunately there's a machine down the corridor dispensing diet cokes and Mars bars. I didn't leave the Psycho Lab until 8.15pm this evening!

Something is definitely going on. The data suggests that the snake phobic findings we got before weren't a fluke. The results still aren't conclusive, though (the hotspots in the phobic brain scans still vary too much from one subject to the next, and generally aren't all that 'hot'). Unless we can get something more definite, we probably won't get our results into the Journal of Neuroscience, let alone the hallowed pages of Nature. One particularly odd hotspot has showed up again, from within the 'smell centre' area of the brain. It doesn't look like an error in the analysis, as we assumed before – it could be that the phobics were responding to a smell in the room that wasn't present when we scanned the controls. (Ben farting nearby?)

I won't freak you out with any more science, I know you're allergic to anything involving numbers and I'm in no fit state to explain. Suffice to say, we will have to do some follow-up experiments soon, with a twist. I have a hunch we need to rev up the brain response. Maybe we could use film clips instead of static pictures for extra impact. There's so much to chew on and not enough hours in the day. Talking of things to chew on, are you recovering from the goat mauling?

xx

From: Allie Loff (allie53@outlook.com)
Sent: 18 July 2018 10.30pm GMT
To: Bea Hudson (bhudson9@blueyonder.co.uk)
Subject: **Après goat**

better than was it was, thanks

taking a few days rest

can't do much, shoulder still sore

Ray to feed all the animals from now on

A

Chapter 19

Miss Madeleine Geen

19 July, Session 6, 4pm

Miss G's hair is blonder than last time, if I'm not mistaken. After her usual grope inside her voluminous bag, she extracts a purse and hands me a battered ten pound note and a motley collection of coins.

MG: I'm sorry, Nigel, I'm fifty pence short – I was buying Mungo some biscuits and ended up getting some art supplies as well… Would you mind very much if I paid you the rest next week?

I briefly contemplate outright refusal – if I tell her to come back next week with the correct money, I'll be able to get to bridge club on time and enjoy a brandy with Harry instead of having to listen to the progressively more disturbed Miss Geen. But I'm developing a fondness for the woman, despite her infuriating habits, and her case is interesting…

NR: I think I can survive without the fifty pence until next week, though please don't get into the habit of bringing the incorrect fee – this is an important part of our therapeutic alliance, you see. (Authoritative smile.) So, *Ms* Geen, how was your week?

In summary: Miss G recently met a businessman in a lift on the way to her job interview, which she did not attend as she was forty minutes late. He bought her a cup of coffee and asked to see her again. Though reluctant to meet him, she met him briefly at her local café on the weekend.

MG: He offered to pay for my two slices of chocolate cake, as well as my tea – I accepted, I don't believe in too much equality between the sexes. (Smiles as she circles her bare right foot, slender and lightly tanned with fluorescent orange toenails.) Anyway, we had a nice chat before I had to tell him he's not really my type–

NR: What type is that?

MG: Oh, firm and muscular… This guy's got a bit of flab around the belly – I can't believe he plays tennis twice a week! He's not bad looking, just a bit… ordinary, I suppose. But he's easy to talk to and we had a few laughs. And he didn't try to interrogate me, like this guy I met a few years ago – he spent the whole evening asking where I went to school, what I'd achieved so far… Dating these days is like going for a job interview!

NR: That would be most unpleasant, I imagine.

MG: You're married, aren't you, Mr Rowley? I bet you've not been on a date for years. No, I know, you're not supposed to tell me anything about yourself, this is all about me transferring my stuff onto you. You don't have to tell me all that again.

NR: How did you feel when you were talking to… (Frown.)

MG: Colin, his name's Colin. You're not good with names, are you? (Left leg slowly crosses right.) It was fun, I suppose. Though I felt a bit awkward, like I wasn't really in control of things – a bit like how I am with you, actually. He called me 'Maddie' in a voice like warm oil being rubbed over my body. I wanted to take his hand, I had to stop myself. And he told me about his ex-wife who'd dumped him after eight years. He sounded really cut up about it.

NR: Did you find him attractive?

MG: Yes and no. I liked him to chat to but I don't know if I could go any further than that.

NR: You couldn't sleep with him? Or you couldn't have a relationship with him?

MG: Neither, really. It would only complicate things.

NR: Why?

MG: With his history and mine! The odds are stacked against us. I'm sorry, Mr Rowley, I don't mean to be rude, but sometimes you seem to have no idea about what happens in the real world.

NR: Perhaps you're putting obstacles in the way of potential happiness because you're scared to let anyone hurt you again.

MG: Isn't that a sensible thing to do?

NR: You didn't have a very happy childhood, Madeleine, did you?

MG: I suppose a lot of things come down to our childhoods, don't they?

NR: Would you like to tell me about yours?

MG: I'd rather not. My parents were on the harsh side. My father used to hit me with his belt when he got angry. My mother didn't have much time for me, she was always telling me I was a bad girl. At school I was always getting into trouble.

NR: Do you think you're a bad girl now?

MG: Sometimes, yes. Sometimes I still feel like a naughty little girl.

NR: A naughty little girl who's jealous of what her friends have?

MG: I care about Bea – very much. But yes, I do feel jealous of her sometimes. Not her husband – we'd be at each other's throats within hours. Or her job – competing with a bunch of guys out to prove themselves better than she is, who secretly think all women belong by the kitchen sink. But her house – they live in a big old house with a huge south-facing garden looking onto miles of countryside! And when she complains about how difficult her daughter is, I feel like saying, 'Don't you know how lucky you are?' I'd give anything to have her daughter – a daughter like hers, I mean.

NR: Jealousy is a very natural emotion. Most people have envious feelings at one time or another, but they're not socially acceptable so we suppress them–

MG: (Twirling a lock of hair.) Sometimes I think about Bea and I living together. If things don't work out with her and Kurt, I could move in with her, Then I could be with Fran all the time–

I don't quite manage to suppress my groan.

MG: I'm not serious! It's just my imagination going wild, that's all.

NR: Perhaps we could explore this fantasy. How would you go about moving in with your friend?

MG: Goodness, it's five past five! Have I just had five minutes for free? You'd better dock me five minutes next time.

NR: Thank you, Ms Geen.

MG: Don't mention it, Mr Rowley.

Chapter 20

From: Bea Hudson (bhudson9@blueyonder.co.uk)
Sent: 25 July 2018 10.02pm
To: Allie Loff (allie53@outlook.com)
Subject: **Domestic stuff**

Sorry, got to let off steam for a few mins.

When I came home this evening, Katie handed me a long note about Fran listing every detail of this week's bad behaviour, starting with Fran getting into a fight with a boy in the local playground because he wouldn't get off 'her' swing.

I placed this beside my list of the things I must do before Fran starts school in September, such as fill in forms, buy uniform, sports kit and appropriate shoes and the list of what needs to be done in the house – I must arrange for someone to fix the overflowing gutter and the damp kitchen wall, which I promised Kurt I'd sort out over the summer. I also have to order carpets for upstairs and blinds for Fran's room and take Big Ears to the vet (Katie refuses as he tries to jump out of the car whenever he's within sniffing distance of the place).

I haven't been sleeping well – at 3am all the tasks I haven't done rise up into a vast cloud of dark matter and torment me, and I lie there fretting about how I'm neglecting my home and daughter. These past two weeks I've hardly seen Fran except for an hour in the morning, an hour or two in the evening, and weekends. Now preschool's ended, Fran's got all day to give Katie a hard time and Katie never stops complaining. (Mrs

Know-It-All says I should get Fran referred to an educational psychologist or she will turn into a 'delinquent child'!)

I wonder if Fran is trying to get Katie to leave us, so I have to stay at home every day to look after her? The poor girl has been looking after Fran all day until eight or so in the evening, except for the Bright Faces playgroup mornings (only three days a week this year due to lack of parental support) and a couple of times when Maddie came over. Katie wasn't pleased when I told her I wouldn't be home until nine this evening – she was meant to be welcoming Konrad back from Warsaw.

Re homecomings – Kurt's back this weekend for three days. It's his first trip home since he left. Fran's looking forward to it – it's all she talks about lately. She's been planning what we're all going to do. Madame Tussauds, the dinosaurs at the Natural History Museum, a rollercoaster ride at Brighton Pier, face painting at the local summer fair – and that's just Sunday!

I miss him far more than I thought I would. Our wacky conversations, his jokes and funny voices. His big hairy chest... I crave his hands on me (the whole works, to be blunt). My super, shiny, new multi-gizmo high-tech vibrator is certainly effective, I've discovered. 'Better than fingers or tongues,' it says on the box. I wouldn't go that far, but it's been in use quite a lot lately, though on top speed the thing buzzes so loudly it's like having a hornet's nest in the bed. I just hope Fran can't hear it, or Adrian and Jackie next door (they would probably notice someone farting a mile away). Talking of the neighbours – Adrian has been much chattier than usual, asking how I'm managing without my husband and if he can do anything to help (always when Jackie's at work). I was very tempted to say, 'Why don't you come in, Adrian? You can get dinner ready, fix the vacuum cleaner and trim the hedge.'

I've been dipping into my old journal from when Kurt and I first met – a few pages in I found, 'Made love all afternoon then had long foamy bath together.' Can't remember when we last made love all afternoon, let alone had a bath together. I want the Kurt back who flirts with me in the supermarket and shamelessly squeezes my bottom at his company dinner dance, and the Bea who never says no to sex because of being tired the next day, or Fran overhearing.

So, when Kurt gets home, I'm going to surprise him. I've bought some Elle Macpherson underwear – a skimpy G-string and a black lacy corset thing that makes my breasts stick out a mile. They look great with my black patent leather stilettos!

Anyway, how are you doing?

Lots of love, Bea

From: Allie Loff (allie53@outlook.com)
Sent: 25 July 2018 10.30pm GMT
To: Bea Hudson (bhudson9@blueyonder.co.uk)
Re: **Domestic stuff**

Much better now, thanks. Doing tasks well away from any animals.

Postcard from Budapest. Mum and Janice were being hassled by an inspector about not having a valid tram ticket and a man came up and saved them from a massive fine. They've spent the day sightseeing with him. He's a retired doctor.

Know what you mean about passion needing rekindling. Ray is getting bigger – in the wrong places. I'm finding it harder to get interested in sex, especially with the lights on.

The outfit sounds wild. Let me know how it goes down with Kurt. Reading between the lines, it sounds like you need a long holiday – or a long bout of passion. Dr Loff prescribes three a day for the next three days.

A xx

From: Bea Hudson (bhudson9@blueyonder.co.uk)
Sent: 27 July 2018 1.13pm
To: Allie Loff (allie53@outlook.com)

Subject: **Brainstorming meeting**

Glad mum is having an eventful trip.

Looking fwd to long bouts of passion.

Thought you might like this insight into the weird and wonderful world of a university researcher. Haven't time to explain, have just copied my notes from the meeting this am.

Chapter 21

Intro

[Bea] This is a group brainstorm to get ideas for effective, cheap, simple fear and anxiety-inducing stimuli. I want to create higher anxiety levels in the volunteers (within reason) than we're getting using pictures of spiders. Hopefully this will create both more consistent data and stronger hotspots, so we will be able to identify with a degree of certainty each brain site involved in phobic fear.

Noted: Most volunteers have indicated they will be available for a further scanner session in mid-August. Hayley to finalise arrangements with volunteers and book the scanner for a week.

Initial suggestions

'Warm-up tasks' for the volunteers to do before the scanner session:

1. Find a parking place outside the Psych Sci Building at 9am on a Monday morning. [Bea]
2. Navigate through the Psych Sci Building to the Small Lecture Theatre using just a GPS and their initiative. [Ben]
3. Ask them to do the typical useless puzzle you get in a Christmas cracker, e.g. unlinking linked metal tubes or getting two balls lined up on a plastic thingy. [Bea]
4. Ask them to match a set of keys to a set of locks within ten minutes, not telling them that none of the keys actually fit. [Ben]

5. We build a maze for humans to go into instead of rats
    – in the empty storage room with movable partitions
    and 'a dead end or two' – then blindfold the volunteers
    and put them inside. [Hayley]

Hayley suggested that if we can't get all of our volunteers back
this time, we could use her 'claustrophobic, navigationally
challenged, mechanically inept' mother for all of above tasks.
['You don't take after her do you, Hayley?' – Ben]

Stimuli to use during the scan:

1. Put a spider in the scanner tube with a preferably
    female spider phobic and 'leave it to crawl around'.
    [Ben]
2. Show them part of a medical documentary on a guy
    getting 'something unpleasant done to his pecker'??
    [Hayley]

Bea reminded the group that:

1. The subject is not allowed to move in the scanner. ['We
    could strap them down.' (Joke?) – Ben]
2. We can't ask volunteers to do anything that we ourselves
    wouldn't do.
3. We need to concentrate on suggestions that have a
    chance of being passed by the Ethics Committee.

Shortlisted stimuli to use during the scan

1. Non-phobia fear/disgust stimuli:
    * edited YouTube clips of people in high-anxiety
      situations, e.g. a climber dangling from a rope [Ben]
    * brief clips from films, e.g. the 'razor eye bit' in 'Un
      Chien Andalou' and teens being preyed on by a
      masked man in 'Scream' [plus many more examples,

all from Ben]. Ben to compile a list of ten suitably scary/horrible/disgust-inducing film clips
* a VERY BRIEF excerpt from a documentary showing 'some kind of medical eye procedure', e.g. retrieving a stray piece of contact lens or an injection into the eyeball [Bea]
2. Phobia-relevant stimuli that we could put in the scanner tube with the subject:
   * a realistic model of a spider [Hayley]
   * a realistic animated model of a spider [Ben]
   * a dead spider [Hayley]
   * a live spider enclosed within a transparent box so it can't escape, suspended a suitable distance from the subject [Bea]

Discussion

* Will the volunteers want to stay in the experiment if we subject them to all this? [Bea]
* We should remind them that they can press the speaker button at any time to ask to stop the experiment. [Hayley]
* We should also remind them that if they do it will look bad, as none of their fellow volunteers have bottled so far. [Ben]

From: Bea Hudson (bhudson9@blueyonder.co.uk)
Sent: 27 July 2018 11.58pm
To: Allie Loff (allie53@outlook.com)
Subject: **Maddie**

Just had the weirdest evening. I want to tell you all about it but I don't think I can. Condensed version: Maddie came over and gave me a massage, which felt a lot better than it usually does.

Bea

Chapter 22

Portrait of a stranded scientist, make-do mother and weary wife

28 July

1am

Can't sleep. Can't stop thinking about this evening. Need to write it all down. If I don't, I probably won't get a wisp of sleep — and in eight hours Kurt will be here.

Maddie turned up ten minutes after I got back from uni (Katie scarpered the second I came through the door). She made dinner for the three of us — her, me and Fran — haddock and chips then raspberries and ice cream with chocolate sauce. I couldn't bring myself to say that I'm trying to lose weight.

Needless to say, Fran was delighted to see Maddie. M brought a dress for Fran's doll that she made herself. She's pretty nifty with her sewing machine — I can't even sew on Kurt's buttons properly, let alone make something from scratch.

After I put Fran to bed, M and I sat chatting in the living room. She's been seeing this therapist who supposedly trained with a leading analyst and has years of experience, though most of what he says seems to rub her up the wrong way. I asked why she's going, as she's always said that she'd never go to a therapist, they're a lot of money-grabbing charlatans. She said she's not sure where her life is going, and she doesn't want to spend the rest of it with just two cats (plus she's met this guy in insurance who's keen on her, but she isn't sure about him). It's strange, Mad has never said anything before about being lonely. Her life always seems so full.

We were discussing the dilemmas in our lives (her lack of money to buy art materials/fix up her flat, and my lack of time to go to work/look after my daughter and husband), when she asked why I don't find someone who doesn't have a full-on career and wouldn't mind staying at home and looking after Fran.

Me: A house husband, you mean? I don't know any men who want to be house husbands!

Mad: There's all those scientists at your university. What about hooking up with one of them?

Me: But I love Kurt.

Mad: You said you didn't think you could put up with him for another seven years.

Me: Did I? It's just that things are particularly difficult right now.

Mad: You're always saying that. Maybe you should accept that things aren't going to get better.

That made me want to go to bed, bury my head in the pillow and sob.

Me: I think I need an early night.

Mad: I'm sorry, Bea, I have the tact of an elephant. I didn't mean to upset you. How about I give you a massage? You look like you could do with one.

As I felt beyond weary and my neck and shoulders felt stiffer than usual, I said yes.

So there I was, lying on my stomach on the sofa, a towel covering my lower half, lights dimmed, Bach on the stereo, a glass of wine within reach and my friend's hands on my body, musing on what Kurt would say if he came in.

Maddie was kneeling down on a cushion beside the sofa. I could smell her jasmine scent and every so often her long hair swished against my back. She made her way slowly down my spine. It felt wonderful.

When she got to the base of my spine, the most amazing shivery tingly sensation went through my body — every part of it.

I opened my eyes.

Mad: Enjoying it?

Me: Yes — don't stop.

Mad: You're sure you want me to go on?

Me: Yes — no — well, maybe you should stop.

She said she'd go wash her hands and make us some peppermint tea. I put my dressing gown on.

Later, we were drinking tea, side by side on the sofa. Maddie looked up from her Cats mug.

Mad: Have you ever kissed a woman?

Me: No, never. What about you?

Mad: No, but I've always wondered...

Me: Me too.

I almost kissed her then. On the lips, softly.

Just in time, I came to my senses. I finished my tea and got up, saying I needed to get to bed, it was getting late.

That was two hours ago. I've been puzzling over what it all means.

Am I turning into a lesbian? Is Mad turning into a lesbian?

Or did I just respond perfectly naturally to a moment of intimacy between friends who care about each other? Maybe this is a sign that I need to go in an entirely different direction, so I can discover my true sexuality.

Sexuality isn't a black and white thing, they say. People can change.

I feel guilty for enjoying that massage so much. Which is ridiculous, isn't it?

Chapter 23

From: Allie Loff (allie53@outlook.com)
Sent: 28 July 2018 1.45am GMT
To: Bea Hudson (bhudson9@blueyonder.co.uk)
Re: **Maddie**

just back from communing with the goats
    little sis, pls explain
    what did you and Mad get up to?

From: Bea Hudson (bhudson9@blueyonder.co.uk)
Sent: 28 July 2018 1.47am
To: Allie Loff (allie53@outlook.com)
Re: **Maddie**

Nothing happened, thank goodness. It could have but it didn't.

From: Allie Loff (allie53@outlook.com)
Sent: 28 July 2018 1.48am GMT
To: Bea Hudson (bhudson9@blueyonder.co.uk)
Re: **Maddie**

Bea, what are you playing at? What will Kurt say?

From: Bea Hudson (bhudson9@blueyonder.co.uk)
Sent: 28 July 2018 1.49am
To: Allie Loff (allie53@outlook.com)

Re: **Maddie**

Nothing – he isn't going to find out. Nothing happened, anyway. For goodness sake, Allie! Since when were you such an angel?

From: Allie Loff (allie53@outlook.com)
Sent: 28 July 2018 1.50am GMT
To: Bea Hudson (bhudson9@blueyonder.co.uk)
Re: **Maddie**

Be careful, B. You don't want anything not to happen again. Or do you?

Chapter 24

What to do about Madeleine?

Phase 1, Operation GROM (Get Rid Of Madeleine)

28/7/18, Day 1

Due to easyJet's uncharacteristically prompt arrival at Gatwick, immediate repatriation with baggage and reckless minicab driver, I get home at 8.10am, forty-five minutes earlier than expected. Let myself in quietly and put on coffee machine.

No sign of life from upstairs – Beatrice and Fran must be sleeping in. Saturday, after all. Decide to grab the opportunity for initial reconnaissance prior to planting spyware.

Where to put the gizmos

Smoke detector:

First, I checked out the living room. Given the AP's sporadic and ineffective house cleaning and Bea's lack of domesticity, was expecting to find crumbs on the carpet, dented sofa cushions and the coffee table stacked with unwashed mugs. But everything is neat and smells of cleaning fluid.

The smoke detector, I decided, after careful scrutiny, will go on the ceiling next to the hall door to give an unobstructed view of the entire living room – also when the door is open, a good part of the hallway. Bea will not notice anything amiss. Her brain is usually preoccupied with far more cerebral affairs than logging the contents of the house. She probably hasn't even realised that we already have two smoke detectors downstairs.

Alarm clock:

This will have to go in the bedroom or Bea will be suspicious. But that's OK because if anything happens, it is quite likely to happen in the vicinity of the bed, *n'est pas*? I put the clock on my bedside table, close enough to the ideal position in the corner of the room. Must remember to tell the AP not to dust/pick up/disturb the new clock – an ultrasensitive piece of hi-tech German engineering.

Tissue container:

This will go next to the toaster in the kitchen, where the unadorned box of Kleenex is now. Or should it go in the bathroom? If I put it in the bathroom Bea or the AP might move it back into the bedroom, then there'll be two cameras in one room and none in the other. Also, what if Bea should examine the tissue container when she's changing the tissues? If you peer in for long enough and have a good imagination, you can make out a coin-sized disc lurking behind the dark glass. But she's far too busy to spend her time peering into tissue containers.

Decide to wait to install everything until I'm alone in the house. Two to three hours should be enough.

After I've finished recon of downstairs and second cup of coffee, I'm standing on a stool in the hall doorway trying to yank off the old smoke alarm and ascertain the best installation method for the new device (may need a hammer drill to get through this plasterboard) when Bea comes through the door in underwear (black, lacy and very sexy) and three-inch high heels.

Hello darling, I say, wobbling. You look nice.

Kurt, I didn't hear you come in. How long have you been here?

Oh, not long. I didn't want to wake you up – thought I'd get started on a few jobs round the house. I've bought a new smoke detector for the living room, this one's clapped out. What's with the gear?

Why don't you leave that and come upstairs?

I smell the Jasmin Noir perfume I gave her for Christmas and jump off the stool. Bea leads the way to the bedroom, sits on the bed and unzips my flies. Fortunately Katie isn't working on the weekends anymore and Fran doesn't stir.

We have the best sex we've had in two years, maybe three. She is wildly passionate, as if she's just been released after ten years in a convent and I'm the captain whose leave will expire in twenty-four hours.

Afterwards, in each other's arms, I tell her that I want our marriage to last. And that I love her as I've never loved anyone, as I'll never love anyone ever again.

I love you too, she says. With all my heart.

She sounds genuine. But afterwards I can't help wondering how nun-like has Beatrice been these last few weeks. Could this unexpected welcome be intended to put me off the scent? Is it to cover up something she's done that she shouldn't have?

The rest of the day passes very pleasantly, with further home comforts – lying on the sofa watching cricket and Formula 1 for most of the afternoon, interrupted by occasional beers on the terrace, trampolining/frisbee throwing/drawing with Fran, and garden shed pottering/ dripping kitchen tap fixing/hinges oiling. Bea cooks scallops and king prawns for dinner.

Bliss.

11.15pm

Complete the transfer of this Operation GROM document to a three-level-deep, innocuously-named, password-protected folder within the iPad, which seems the safest option given my presence on home turf.

Feeling increasingly bad about the surveillance thing, about this entire Get Rid Of Madeleine thing. Consider throwing out the devices, or returning them and getting a refund. Do I really need to go to such extreme lengths to assess Bea's fidelity (or otherwise)? Am I really such a suspicious, mean-spirited, hard-hearted etc bastard that I don't trust my own wife?

29/7/18, Day 2

8am

After sleeping on the matter, the way ahead is clear. If, after thorough investigation, I find evidence of Bea's disloyalty, that will sufficiently exonerate me from my growing sense of guilt at being a sneaky-creepy-over-the-top compulsive weirdo. If, on the other hand, my wife is blameless, I resolve here and now to fully admit to her the depths I have sunk to in order to ascertain this fact.

While Bea is downstairs making me a coffee, I meet Fran in her PJs on the landing beating her ragdoll's head against the wall. She stops when she sees me.

Morning, Daddy. Selima is getting her punishment for being naughty.

I see. What has the poor girl done?

She spat at a little boy. And she said a very bad thing to him.

What was that?

She smiles.

I don't want to pry, sweetie-pie. You don't need to tell me.

She said his face was one big zit and he smelled like a toilet. Her smile broadens so I can see the gaps between her teeth.

That wasn't very nice. Are you enjoying the summer holidays so far?

She shrugs.

What have you been doing over the holidays?

Playing with my friends… Drawing in my new book… Making a crane with my Lego set… Taking Big Ears for walks. Swimming, going to the park. Lots of things with *Katie*.

She makes a gargoyle face.

You don't like doing things with Katie?

Katie isn't nice, Daddy. She's always cross with me. I wish we didn't have her.

Why isn't she nice – because you're being naughty?

Much headshaking.

I'm not naughty, Daddy.

Run that one by me again?

Only a little bit!

What have you and Mummy been up to while I've been away?

She scratches her head.

I don't see Mummy very much. Only on Saturdays and Sundays.

Does she take you out anywhere on Saturdays and Sundays?

We went to McDonald's once – and Thorpe Park. But she wouldn't let me go on the rollercoaster though I really, really wanted to.

9.30am

Over coffee and brioches, I tackle my wife.

Fran tells me that she's being badly treated by Katie. And that you only see her on the weekends.

She's exaggerating. Katie gets frustrated with Fran sometimes, but so do I. So would you, if you had to look after her. Fran's been extremely difficult since you left. It's been one thing after another. She refused to leave the house one morning, then she hid my handbag, then she threw stones at a man on a bike...

Bea hides her head in her hands and continues to speak, faster and faster, running her words into each other so I can't make them out. Something about being a hopeless mother. She is very upset. I comfort her, suppressing my urge to pull off her dressing gown. (She got up this morning before I was fully awake, and before I had a chance to coax her into my arms.)

Is it my fault for being away?

No darling, I'm not saying that. It's just that Fran misses you – and now with both of us being away from home so much...

Is it true, you hardly ever see her except on weekends?

We're very busy at work at the moment, she says defensively. So I get home later than usual sometimes.

What – six o'clock? Eight o'clock? You always seem to be out whenever I phone the house.

She gestures as if brushing away a fly.

Around then, yes.

When? Six or eight?

Around eight, this week – a bit later, sometimes. It depends. Katie has stayed on most evenings, it's been quite all right.

Are you still cooking dinner? Or is Katie doing that too now?

Hesitation. I have hit the maternal guilt button.

Look, Kurt. I cook when I can, or we have a takeaway. Fran's been helping out too–

You're getting our four-year-old daughter to cook?

Of course not. She opens packets and sets the table and puts things in the fridge and the microwave, that's all–

Beatrice, I really don't think Fran should be messing around with the microwave, not at her age.

She isn't messing about with the microwave!

This isn't going to become a fight. I hold my words inside. No more confrontations. No more voice-shaking, fist-thumping, purple-faced exchanges. We are man and wife, joined in holy matrimony. I put on my most empathetic voice.

Things aren't easy for you just now, darling.

Bea looks at me in amazement.

What about a slap-up breakfast, sweetheart? I haven't had a full English for months.

10.07am

Task 1 Get house to self

Finally managed to get Bea and Fran out of the house for a trip to the warehouse-sized, eight-miles-away Waitrose to get mushroom, tomatoes and bacon for brunch as well as a long list of other delicacies, essential after a month of cold sliced meat and insipid cheese that passes for the hotel's breakfast.

Calculate that by the time Bea has waited in Sunday morning traffic, found a place to park, rounded up the food, given in to Fran's demands for liquorice allsorts, coloured pencils, furry animal pencil cases, flower power tights, strawberry cheesecake Häagen-Dazs and returned home, it will be 11.30am or even 11.45am – plenty of time to get the gizmos in place.

Task 2 Configure and install spy devices

I tried to stay calm and methodical throughout.

Fortunately, I had already read the installation instructions three times, studied each device carefully, noting key points, warnings, tips for optimum positioning, etc.

Unfortunately, now in urgent need of them, I discovered that my only pair of glasses in the house no longer contain the right lenses, rendering the print in the manual unreadable, so was forced to hunt for the relevant installation manuals on the spyware company's website. (Did not forget to clear the browsing history.)

For some reason, I had imagined that installing three spy cameras was bound to be a good deal simpler than assembling Fran's Ikea wardrobe. However, setting up each spycam and its accompanying miniature DVR involved adjusting the numerous settings and options – picture resolution, mike sensitivity, focus, auto recording parameters (flexible scheduling, motion detect, zoning feature for blocking out unwanted parts of the field of view, you name it). By the time I'd worked all this out (each device works slightly differently, of course, but the variants helped to keep boredom at bay) it was:

ETA-22 mins

I started to install the smoke alarm cam on the living room ceiling (spot marked on Day 1), which went nicely until I dropped the screw, which rolled under the sofa. I finally retrieved it along with a hairgrip (of the kind that

Bea never wears) entwined in a long blonde hair, which looked suspiciously like Madeleine's. Curious.

The sleek black plastic tissue container fitted snugly beside the kitchen radio. I popped a brand new box of Kleenex inside and ran to the bedroom.

The crafty alarm clock was more of a challenge. Positioned on my side table so as to capture action from anywhere in the room with its little 72° viewing angle lens, the damn thing stubbornly refused to tell the time until I had reinserted the battery four times, shaken the device and threatened to send it back from where it came.

ETA-3 mins

Collected stray instructions, spare batteries, memory cards and cables and shoved the lot inside the Tesco plastic bag serving as our bedroom bin's liner (along with a few sweet wrappers and a crumbled Mars bar which I didn't have time to remove). Then shoved the bag into my sock drawer.

Doorbell rings.

Daddy, we're back!

Had minor heart attack, then wiped my sweaty palms on my jeans and embraced Miss and Mrs H. Then a testicle-shrinking moment when Mrs H spied my trusty laptop displaying a document entitled, 'Instructions for Setting Up your Hidden Camera System'.

At work already, darling? Isn't this meant to be a holiday?

I flipped down the lid and bundled the laptop under my arm, praying that the font was small enough for her not to have read anything. Explain that it's just research for some new product lines we're considering.

Now I'm wondering if this covert surveillance plan was such a good idea after all. Will my constitution survive the next phase of Operation GROM – spycam testing? That has to be done before I leave, so I can reconfigure the devices if necessary, or there might be no video of unsanctioned goings-on stored on 64G SD cards, or, in the case of the smoke alarm cam, beamed real-time to a remote internet connection via the wonders of modern technology.

30/7/18, Day 3, trip to Brighton

7.43am

Bea snoring softly. Doll-playing noises from Fran's bedroom.

One more day left before departure to the hubbub of the corporate world, interspersed with calls to prayer and soggy breakfasts. Why do I do it? Would be so much pleasanter to stay on here in this Surrey idyll and tell the Chief Executive of Bullshit Inc. and his Houston cronies and all those pesky Turks trying to muscle in on the action to shove this lousy job up their backsides.

But, of course, the corporate life has its compensations, not just the financial ones. Free travel to exotic locales with high-class hotels to broaden the mind, reduce the boredom of domesticity, pep up one's sex drive, increase one's appreciation of one's wife…

Must get to work. Thirteen hours left to tie up all loose ends.

Tasks to complete by 9pm:

1. Take family to the beach.
2. Go next door and make proposal re Phase three of Operation GROM.
3. Reassure Bea of our future/my feelings/her competence, etc.

4. Warn Fran that bad behaviour will not be tolerated.
5. a) Test devices. b) Take any necessary remedial action.
6. Pack mouthwash, ibuprofen, iPad, laptop and REMOVE ALL REMAINING SURVEILLANCE ACCESSORIES FROM MY SOCK DRAWER.

9.30am

Where's my bucket and spade, Mummy?

Daughter appears at foot of stairs in new pink flip-flops, five-sizes-too-large sunglasses, shorts and Marilyn Monroe T-shirt. Mummy nowhere in sight.

Daddy hovering at front door in shorts that accentuate paleness of legs and floppy hat that makes him look like prize dork, hoping to seize opportunity to accomplish task 2.

Tasks 3 and 4 ticked off, and inadvertently 5a when managed to lure woozy wife to horny hubby. Words cannot describe ensuing ecstasy until a belated realisation that my thrusting backside is in full view of alarm clock cam, no doubt providing a surfeit of motion with which to trigger the motion-detection software. Felt like a past-it porn star. Had absolutely no wish to watch my naked buttocks in their full, close-up glory. Bea's buttocks, though, are another thing. Tried to shift her on top of me to no avail.

Bea appears at top of stairs in sundress, wide-brimmed hat and ten-sizes-too-large sunglasses, clutching sun cream, Selima and an inflatable plastic ring.

Where did you put your costume, Francesca?

Judging our departure to be another ten to fifteen minutes off, I slip out of the house unobserved.

Adrian answers the door after three rings. He looks like he just got out of bed, hair standing up like a porcupine's and shirt buttons misaligned with buttonholes.

Hi Kurt.

Hi Adrian, glad I've caught you at home. I haven't got you at a bad time, have I?

No mate, I was just doing a bit of DIY.

How's the garden redesign going? I see you replaced the shrubs while I was away.

He gives me a look of surprise/annoyance/suspicion.

The dogs didn't like the greenery, mate. So we decided to go with tiles instead – and much easier to keep clean.

Dogs?

Yeah, two bulldogs, we got 'em a month ago. Bea came over and said hello, you'd just gone off to Turkey... How's it going out there?

I have to leave for Istanbul tomorrow morning, unfortunately.

You're not keen on the place?

It's not that bad, as they go. Just lacking in home comforts.

I get your drift, mate.

He smiles broadly. Adrian has never called me anything except 'mate' in the five years we've been neighbours, though we've not talked of much apart from what one normally discusses with a neighbour – our houses and cars, the eccentricities of other neighbours, notable incidents in the street. I check my watch. Five minutes to go before Bea starts wondering where I am.

Actually, mate, I was going to ask you a favour.

His eyes glaze over and his mouth flattens into a thin line.

Oh, nothing too onerous, I say brightly. It's to do with Bea, actually. I've been rather worried about her lately. She's been behaving a bit oddly... I wonder if she might be – well, I'm sure I don't need to spell it out. I wasn't all that worried at first, but now, what with me having to be away so much... You know how it is. I wouldn't want to think of her making a fool of herself or getting into any trouble. But if someone nearby were to keep their eyes and ears open…

He stares at me. Finally, I see the delight of comprehension on his face.

You think she's having an affair!

I glance behind, aghast at the loudness of his voice.

No need to tell the whole street, Adrian. And I'm not saying she is – necessarily. It's only a possibility.

He winks and pats the top of my arm.

Don't worry mate, I know exactly what you mean. I'll keep an eye on her.

Thanks, mate, that would be very good of you. Nothing too obvious, of course. Maybe drop round every so often and check out anything that looks–

A bit dodgy, yeah of course, I can do that, no worries. I'll have a nosey at your place from time to time and suss out anyone who's in there who shouldn't be. Blokes, especially.

Actually, in this case, it might not be a bloke.

His face clouds. I check my watch. Bea will definitely be wondering where I am. How long will it take for this thicko to catch on?

Women of a certain age, you know. They can yearn for a toy boy, or…

I grit my teeth. She has a friend, a tall blonde. She's been over quite a lot lately.

Oh, I get it! Sorry mate, I'm a bit slow this morning – late night 'n all. No worries, I'll keep my eyes peeled for any tall blonde birds.

Thanks, Adrian… I'm sure I don't need to say, but you'll keep this to yourself, won't you?

Mum's the word. I won't even tell the wife.

Cheers, mate, I owe you. Let me know if you need any dog walking. Maybe our childminder could do something.

10.00am

Our first disagreement is over whether we ought to take the satnav. I want to take it in case of traffic but Bea insists that it is safely put away and we know very well where Brighton is.

Roads thankfully clear of Monday commuters. Nice to drive the BMW again, after those taxi drivers in Istanbul who can sniff out a foreigner from the other side of the city.

Bea and Fran play I Spy while I curse the blind/ignorant/incompetent drivers who try to take our lives.

Disagreement over where to park resolved by me taking executive decision.

Disagreement over whether we should go to pier or beach first, resolved by Fran announcing she will sulk/throw tantrums for rest of day if not allowed to immediately experience a) rollercoaster and b) swinging cars.

Disagreement over whether to bring heavy beach bag to the pier resolved by Bea marching off with said bag, which later (50% heavier) is of course returned to me.

Sunshine becomes intermittent after Bea stops at a refreshment kiosk to cover Fran in vast quantities of factor 90.

The 'amusements' of Brighton Pier prove a drain on our finances, patience and nervous systems. After taking her fill of the bouncy castle, the trampoline, the helter-skelter and the giant slide, our daughter insists one of us accompanies her on the wild river ride. Two goes later, Bea takes hold of my hand and says she is feeling dizzy and is going to be sick. I tell her she should not have eaten the sandwich from the kiosk and volunteer to accompany Fran instead on one last ride.

Big mistake. Premonitions of death as we hurtle downwards, dispelled by the shock of being drenched with cold water. Can't tell whether my scream or Fran's is the louder.

3.00pm

Bea and I stretch out on our towels, grateful for the absence of motion and water, and the solidity of the ground. I try to appreciate the sunshine and ignore the small rocks pressing into my spine and the constant crying/yelling/wheedling/cackling from numerous small children in the vicinity. Fran busies herself transferring large quantities of pebbles from the beach into her small plastic bucket. Then the game changes direction.

What are you going to do with those stones, little lady?

Fran stops halfway between us and two small children sitting contentedly on a rug beside a large hamper, ten metres away.

Nothing, Daddy.

There's a glint of mischief in her eye. She sets down the bucket, sits down and examines its contents, stone by stone.

Bea groans and lifts her head a few inches to ascertain that no one is in immediate danger.

I ask if Fran has thrown any more stones at passing cyclists lately.

Not as far as I know, Bea replies. Only at inanimate objects. Gnomes in front gardens, that sort of thing. She's been a lot better behaved this last week. It's because she knew you were coming back soon.

So I'm the big bad wolf, am I? Can't you discipline her too? Why does it always have to be me?

Fran picks up her bucket and moves to a spot a few metres further away.

Bea roots about in the beach bag for the factor 90. She applies more white goo to her nose, cheeks, neck, arms and décolletage, then cleans her hands with a wet wipe, shaking her head sadly.

She doesn't listen to me when she's in a strop! I either have to yell as loudly as she is or threaten violence. Immediate disembowelling usually does the trick. Decapitation works quite well too.

For a second or so, I am lost for words.

Darling, it doesn't sound like you're managing Fran very well. That isn't the way to talk to our daughter.

Bea fumbles in the beach bag then crunches into a Granny Smith, spattering juice.

Well, what do you suggest I say? When she's determined to be disobedient, nothing I tell her makes any difference. Last weekend, she insisted on taking a chocolate bar from the cupboard before we went out and refused to put her toys back in the box. I can plead, shout and stamp my foot and it won't make any difference, she's as obstinate as a bloody donkey! It's like she's become a teenager nine years early.

Her tone suggests imminent tears. I avoid pointing out that Fran is never like that with me.

What's she like with the au pair?

Katie has to put up with it too now. She never stops complaining about Fran.

Don't you know anyone who can help, or give you some advice? Your friend at preschool – what's her name?

I haven't got any friends at preschool! When I picked up Fran on Fridays I always said hello but the other mums ignored me.

What about Mrs Know-It-All? Aren't you talking to her still?

Another loud crunch.

She wasn't much help. She thought I should take Fran to an educational psychologist.

Well, we might have to if you can't manage. Or you'll have to go part-time again.

I am working part-time.

I mean properly part-time.

Maddie is very good with Fran. She's been over a couple of times to help out.

Really? I was going to ask you if she's been in the house. I found something of hers on the sofa.

Bea starts to choke. She sits up and leans over the towel, face red, eyes streaming. I thump her back until a yellow globule shoots out of her mouth.

When did Madeleine last come over, I ask when she's recovered.

She waves a hand.

Oh, Friday evening, I think it was. She helped cook dinner. I was done in.

The evening before I arrived?

That's right.

She avoids my eyes as I consider this information. There's something going on that I should know about. Bea sounds awkward. She's hiding something. But I sense that a direct interrogation won't yield any results.

I hope she hasn't bought you any more underwear while I've been away?

Of course she hasn't, don't be silly! She's my friend, that's all.

It was a joke, Bea.

A bloodcurdling shriek interrupts us.

We stand simultaneously. Fran is throwing stones at the children on the rug. The boy is pointing wildly at Fran, the girl is trying to shield herself behind the hamper and their flabby-thighed mother has flung down her *Vogue* and is staring open-mouthed at our daughter.

Neither child appears to be hurt. Fortunately, Fran's enthusiasm for stone throwing is not matched by her target-locating prowess. Gratefully, I seize the opportunity to escape the conversation.

I feel distinctly poorly, as if I've just eaten too many servings of chocolate cookie/strawberry cheesecake Häagen-Dazs. My symptoms are getting worse each week. Now I need only think of Madeleine, or even hear her name mentioned, to have increased heartbeat, hyperventilation and an overpowering need to squeeze the life out of the nearest object to hand, which today happens to be the paper bag containing Fran's half-eaten banana. Familiarity makes it no easier to bear – the opposite, in fact. If Goldilocks were to appear this very moment, I would be sorely tempted to wring her neck.

Chapter 25

Katie's journal

31 July

This morning Mr H went back to his job in Ottoman Outpost as he calls it. Now Mr H is going mad as well as Mrs H and Little Fiend. If I stay here, I am going mad too.

I come over at 8.30 in morning as usual on Tuesdays. Mr H comes to door in dressing gown, does not speak, just runs into kitchen and shuts door. I knock on door, say Can I come in? He calls out, I am busy on important thing, I will be ten minutes, please will you clean other rooms first. I say, Please I want to make cup of tea first also the cleaning box is in kitchen. Will you sit on sofa, he says in voice like teacher with naughty child, I will call you when I'm ready.

Katie, he says in nice voice when I am nearly asleep, You can come in now. I am so surprised I drop my glasses onto floor, he never calls me Katie before.

He asks if he can make me cup of tea, which bag I like? No Mr H, I say, that is my job. He says he is sorry he snapped at me, he does not mean. He trusts me, he thinks I am good O Pair, very good with his daughter and wife and dog, he would like me to stay with all of them for very long time. I say yes, I would like too.

I give him Lapsang Something tea and Hobbs biskit. Ask if Mrs H wants tea too but he says she is sleeping still, she is very tired last night.

I have something to ask you Katie, he says. It is about my wife.

Then Mrs H comes in kitchen in silk nightdress to show her breasts for Mr H and he forgets to say rest. She has very nice underwear, I see in her drawer when I am bored and have peep (also there is sex toy). She says she forgot I am coming today, she is not at work today because it is Mr H's last morning, so I can leave early and see Konrad.

Later when I am dusting cobwebs in guest room, I overhear Mrs H talking to Little Fiend next door (the door is open, it is easy to hear). Little Fiend is crying and Mrs H sounds like teacher with bad student.

I love you very much Fran, but you are very naughty girl. That little girl could have been hurt yesterday if the stone had hit her. Did you mean to hurt her?

No answer I hear. I move closer to the bedroom door.

You're going to go to the big girls school soon and if you try to hurt other children there you're going to get into very big trouble. It will be serious, do you understand? Daddy and I will be very unhappy. Very very unhappy.

I put chair on landing outside door so I can reach the ceiling with duster. Mrs H is always complaining about cobwebs. I tell her I can't reach, she says no excuse to be short you can always stand on chair.

Darling please listen to me. I am not cross with you, I just want to understand whats going on. Why are you doing these things? I don't understand. Don't you know how much we both love you?

LF carries on crying. Then she runs out of room and into my chair. I fall to floor. Big noise from LF like cat is scratching her. She runs down stairs. Mrs H runs out of room.

What the hells going on Katie?

I am dusting, I say, from the floor.

Have you hurt yourself? You are silly girl to put chair there. Now, I was going to ask you Katie, please don't take this the wrong way but I want to ask you for favour, I hope you don't mind. If Mr H asks how many times my friend Madeleine comes over, can you say it is one time only, no more? It is very important Katie. Do you understand me?

She must think I am age four too because my English not so good. But I am not cabbage head. I smile and say, Yes Mrs H, of course I will do.

Next when I am hoovering Mr H can't find his I pad. He is running around house looking into cupboards, under cushions, like mice after cheese. He is going to give himself hurn ear, Mrs H says. She puts on her yoga DVD in living room, she says is very good for relaxation. I go to kitchen to stay out of way.

Little Fiend is back in her room, does not come out. She has new box for beach stuff - shells, dead starfish, stinky seaweed, a piece of coconut and a long pointed thing like shark tooth. No stones now, Mrs H takes away after Incident On Beach. She says to me after Incident On Beach, Katie will you please make sure that Francesca does not carry any stones and she is not near any stones she can pick up. I wish to say, How it is you expect me to do this, I do not carry around stone detector.

When Mr H is on toilet I go in Mr and Mrs bedroom to put clean clothes away. He comes in room when I open drawer to put in a big pile of underpants he will need when away.

NO DON'T GO IN THERE!

He runs at me like lion onto kitten, pushes drawer shut with big bang so my right ear pops.

Please leave it, he says, I will put away. Sorry I am stressed out, I still do not find I pad.

When I am out of room, I hear big shout.

THANK CHRIST IT'S IN HERE!

After this I go downstairs as Mrs H says she will be busy with Mr H for a while, I must listen to LF read story.

They have good fuck, I hear, the floor goes Thump Thump. I turn on TV loud to hide. Fran is happy, she is bored with reading. She is not good reader, I am not good listener, we both prefer to see Arnold S shoot the bad guys.

She is not such Little Fiend now, I think. She is lovely little girl who is my friend.

Where is Miss Naughty gone today?

I am Miss Nice today, she says.

Why can't Miss Nice stay always? We all like her much more than Miss Naughty.

She laughs like I say funniest joke in world.

You are very funny Katie, I like you.

I am pleased, I say.

She comes up to where I sit and kisses my cheek then goes to sit on carpet again. I am surprised and yes it pleases me, though I know tomorrow Fran will be Little Fiend again.

Did Mummy and Daddy give you big telling off yesterday?

They want her to be good girl always she says or they will not let her into the big girls school, she will have to go to School for Bad Girls instead.

I wonder if that will be such bad thing.

After fucking, Mrs H glows in face and Mr H makes big chest like Arnold S. He pats her arse and she gives him tickle. They are puppies playing in the sun.

You can go home now Katie, Mrs H says, we're all going to the airport to see Kurt off. Thank you very much for your help this morning. I see you tomorrow morning.

It is pleasure. Bye Mrs Husdon! Bye Mr Husdon! Bye Fran!

Chapter 26

Miss Madeleine Geen

26 July, Session 7, 4pm

Miss G had the correct money this time, though she arrived seven minutes late, out of breath and quite bedraggled in dirty trainers and a sweatshirt with a large hole in the sleeve.

I began by pointing out that lateness in a therapeutic relationship is highly significant, that it may indicate the patient's lack of commitment to the process. As I expected, this produced an immediate negative reaction.

MG: Oh, for goodness sake! Will you stop piling so much into every tiny thing I do or say? I'm late because I had to fix the radiator hose on the way here because my car is a wreck and breaks down at every opportunity it can. I can't afford a decent one because all my spare cash goes on coming to see you! (In a gentler tone.) I'm sorry, I didn't mean to shout. But it does get my goat.

NR: I see, Madeleine. (PMT? Told myself to tread carefully.) So, how have you been?

MG: I had a terrible dream the other night – are you interested in dreams? I suppose you think dreams have a deep significance, don't you?

Tell Miss G that I would be honoured to hear her dream; explained that this therapy is about accessing the secrets of patient's unconscious by means such as slips of tongue, freely expressed thoughts and, especially, dreams recounted to the therapist.

MG: OK, here it is. The doorbell rang and I went to the door to get my delivery from Waitrose. But instead thére was a plastic carrier bag on my mat with a baby inside. It was very small and I wasn't sure if it was alive, so I put it under the tap to see if that would wake it. The baby smiled and reached out to touch my face. I found some baby boots I'd knitted and put them on her. For some reason I thought I would keep the baby, that she must have been left for me on purpose… But then it began to cry, so loudly my eardrums felt they were going to burst. That wailing, I couldn't stand it. So I… (She screws up her face.) The next bit is horrible. I don't know if I can tell you.

NR: Please try.

MG: I flushed it down the toilet!

Nod soothingly, hoping to disguise my grimace. Tell the patient that she has done well to unburden herself to me and that this dream must be highly significant to cause such mental distress.

MG: I told you it was horrible. It stayed with me for hours, what I did to that poor baby. What do you think it means?

NR: What came into your mind when you were telling me your dream?

MG: That I was a wicked woman for doing such a thing. And that I wouldn't be any good at raising a child, even if I had the chance.

Miss G stares down into the cavernous bag at her feet, bulging with packets of bird seed and paint brushes. My mind wanders to the cruel flushing from Elizabeth's womb of what would have been our first child, then swiftly on to Harry's drunken exploits at last week's Bridge Club, ending memorably with the flushing of his Johnnie Walker bottle into the vicar's kitchen sink.

MG: Hello, anyone at home?

Apologise for being so deep in thought. Tell her my interpretation – the baby is a symbol of her yearning for a child. The fact that she kills the baby in her dream means that she is killing her hopes of ever having a child.

MG: I never thought of that. (Stares at me.) So, the dream isn't saying I'd be a bad mother?

Nod sagely.

MG: I was wondering, Nigel – well, if this dream could be telling me something about my scientist friend. That I should stop having thoughts about taking her daughter away from her.

NR: Perhaps your dream means that, as well.

MG: Can a dream have more than one meaning? That doesn't seem right.

Explain that the unconscious has its own rules, which often don't make sense to our conscious minds.

MG: You see, last week with Bea…

Ten-second silence.

NR: Do you want to tell me about it?

MG: I don't know.

Explain that the patient will have to trust her own instincts but I will promise to listen with compassion, without judgement, etc.

MG: I suppose I should tell you – this is costing me thirty quid a week. (Crosses one long leg over the other, smiles and leans towards me.) I was giving my friend a massage – she has problems with her neck sometimes. After a while, the massage went a bit astray. I could tell she was getting into it too, from her smile.

Nod sagely.

MG: I knew I had to stop, or we'd be in trouble. Then later, when we were sitting together, I nearly kissed her. But she got up then, so I didn't.

I spend several seconds visualising the scene.

NR: Do you regret that?

MG: No, it's just as well. Bea wouldn't be able to cope with the idea that she's not straight. She loves her husband too much.

NR: You told me last time about another fantasy involving your friend – you were wondering whether you could lure her away from her husband then move in with her and her daughter.

MG: That was just a crazy thing that came to me, I wasn't serious. (She smiles sweetly.) It wasn't an actual plan.

NR: Perhaps your unconscious mind softened the ground, as it were. Then you went ahead and sowed the seeds…

MG: Hmm. I don't know about that. (Jiggles foot.) I felt bad, afterwards. I think I've confused her. She enjoyed my massage more than she expected, and now she feels bad because she's a married woman. She doesn't want to see herself as a bit on the bi side, or a closet lesbian.

NR: Perhaps you're confused about your own sexuality?

MG: Oh no, I like sex too much – with men. (Hand flies to mouth.) God, I sound like a nymphomaniac! I suppose what I'm saying is, I'm pragmatic. I know that men do it for me, but if there's an opportunity to try something new, why not take it? I like new experiences – so long as they don't have a down side.

NR: And sex with your friend would have a down side.

MG: (Expression of distaste.) If I was going to get off with a woman, I'd be better off finding one who isn't my best friend, don't you think?

NR: I'm not here to dispense advice, Madeleine.

MG: What *are* you here to do, then?

NR: I'm here to help you understand yourself better. Through mechanisms which may not at first glance seem particularly transparent.

MG: Oh, please, not the unconscious again. (Sits upright on the edge of the chair, clutching the handles of her bag.) It's about time I was going, isn't it?

Reassure the patient that we have five minutes left, in case she has saved something up for the end of the session. (Could there be anything to top what's gone before?)

MG: I've had enough of the unconscious for one week. Can't we finish early today?

Remind the patient that the patient needs to continue in the therapist's presence for the full hour, that the most productive parts of session may come from periods of discomfort, etc.

MG: In that case… Colin's coming over to my place on Sunday – the insurance guy, remember? He's getting quite keen. I'll probably have some things to say about that next week. My unconscious desire to make him fall in love with me so I can steal all his money – only kidding.

She laughs, picks up her bag and settles it on her lap.

MG: You know, Nigel, there isn't anyone else I can talk to like this. I don't have that many close girlfriends, and I couldn't tell any of this to a bloke – not even my exes.

NR: Because they might think badly of you?

MG: No, I wouldn't worry about that. It's just you know what it is with men, how they have a thing about girls getting it on with each other.

NR: Our time is up, I'm afraid. Thank you, Ms Geen.

MG: Thank you, Mr Rowley.

Chapter 27

Letter to Gary continued

26 July

7.50am, on the way to Waterloo

Well, bro, I have found indisputable evidence to support my hunch that my neck is soon to be placed on the chopping block.

Yesterday evening I was 'working' late on Contentious Claims for Review in another attempt to execute my cunning plan that will give Messrs Clifford and Spelt something to think about other than the size of Clifford & Spelt Insurance's annual pre-tax profit. (I've put it off twice due to a heavily pounding, highly irregular heartbeat just as I'm about to do the deed, only too aware that I'm about to commit a criminal act of gross deception against my employers, who have provided my bread and butter for innumerable years, not to mention a generous pension, four weeks paid leave per year, and during office hours, a supply of warmth, light, shelter and reliable, if not always congenial, companionship.)

No one was around except the cleaners. Noticing that the door of Mr Clifford's office was open rather than locked as it usually is, and wondering what interesting morsels I might find within, I casually loitered inside. (His PA has been off sick and her temp replacement is enthusiastic but gormless.) After a good root around various folders inside a filing cabinet, I found a folder labelled 'Reorganisation Plans'. Inside was a printed email from Mr Clifford to the Head of HR which referred to the 'current economic climate', 'uncertainty over Brexit', 'increased customer fraud' and 'staff members whose antiquated attitudes do not fit with the tough and enterprising demeanour that modern times have forced upon us'.

There followed a list of six names under the heading 'Deadwood'. Colin Settle was the fifth name, I can reveal. The first four were in Claims Processing (not Mr Smarmy Pants of course, one of the stars of the show). Last was the deaf chap in Finance who keeps forgetting to wear his hearing aid.

Stunned, I had an urgent need to use the lav, along with an urge to tear the document into small pieces over the framed photos of Mr Clifford's photogenic wife and children, then stamp on them a large number of times (the photos, I mean). But I summoned my reserves of cool, put everything back and made a hasty exit to the gents, mercifully unoccupied.

This discovery has crystallised my resolve. Today is Do Or Die Day. By this evening I shall either be as elated as a giant panda after a shag, or as mortified as a newly-snipped tom.

Stopped at signals near Vauxhall

The first case in my unofficial list 'Cases for Reconsideration (by undisclosed persons)' is Mrs Hurt Puss, eighty-two (not her real name). It was rejected for various reasons, as are a large number of claims we receive, especially where the policyholder is likely to be less than fully mentally alert or else lacking the gumption, stamina or bloody-mindedness to stand up for her rights. I say 'her' for good reason. It's seventy plus women (our favourite customers) who generally cave in the quickest. They're also the most easily pressured into buying a policy that can't possibly meet their needs.

Mrs Hurt Puss has been particularly badly treated by us, I fear. Last March she put in a hefty claim for her cat's medical treatment. It contracted diabetes in 2006 and ever since then has suffered palpitations following the stress of being inexpertly injected by the cat sitter (who literally stabbed it in the back). The poor woman called us repeatedly in tears, according to the case notes. The cat, Derrida, is everything to her, she would sooner die than see it suffer. But she can't afford to keep up the cat's various treatments (insulin injections, pills for hyper-anxiety etc), despite not putting on the central heating and only eating twice a day (Derrida eats three times a day and gets all the meat).

The claim was initially refused by Tim 'Tough Titties' on the grounds of a delay in lodgement, which she disputed, then secondly by yours truly on the grounds of the likelihood that the diabetes was as a result of poor diet (too many sugary treats and tins of condensed milk, which she admitted after some detective work by the enterprising claims assessor) and as such was a preventable condition as detailed in the policy document that she had signed seventeen years before.

To date, I have selected thirteen cases by two admittedly subjective criteria – 'degree of ripped-off-ness' and 'degree of deserving-ness'. (I may cull one from the list in the interests of superstition, but can't decide which.)

You may well be asking how I intend to settle these claims without drawing undue attention to myself, especially since the provisional grand total concerned comes to £749,953. That's right, close to three quarters of a million smackers, enough to trigger a spot of the collywobbles in our esteemed partners Gideon Clifford and Rory Spelt. (The Finance Director won't be too pleased, either.) Don't worry, I've got it covered. As Head of Claims Settlement, I have authorisation to approve payments of up to 100K from several accounts without additional signatories. I will disguise each undisclosed settlement by making transfers between various accounts that I have ferreted out, e.g. 'Collection for Frugal Fred's Retirement', opened in 2007 and not used since. Touch wood, my activities will remain undetected at least until the accountants start work on the next set of company accounts, by which time I should be long gone from the Nation's Number One Pussy Insurer.

So, rest easy bro, I haven't taken complete leave of my senses. Mrs Hurt Puss will soon be able to live in the comfort that she deserves, along with her cat – and I will feel a lot better too. Becoming a Robin Hood is so much more satisfying than the prospect of defrauding my employers for mere personal gain. Not that I couldn't do with a spot of personal gain to redress the savage removal of my final fifteen premium-earning years. But if all goes according to plan and no one links me to the dodgy transactions, I should be in a reasonable financial situation after I'm shown the door. Redundancy payments tend to be quite generous for senior managers in their early fifties. So no, I won't be carrying out this unauthorised activity for any personal gain – all financial benefits will be squarely targeted at the Deserving Thirteen.

What if I should be caught with my pants down? I have a Plan B, which I trust will mitigate against the downside scenario (ranging from interrogation under duress to forcible withdrawal from premises, public shaming and prosecution for fraud and other heinous corporate crimes).

Waterloo approaching

I suppose I'd better print this letter soon and send it to you, Gary, or the thing won't fit in the envelope! Though the printer at home only prints in cyan at the moment – I'd print it at work but the Corporate Ethics Committee has been on the warpath again, warning against the misuse of company resources and so forth.

6.40pm, on the way to Woking

Leaping cane toads, I can breathe again! I feel as if I've just shot an elk!

At 10am, I found out from Mr Smarmy Pants that for the next ninety minutes he would be away from his desk. Instead of delivering his spiel to woo Grannies with Imminently Ill Moggies and Houses Full of Untold Costly Potential Repairs into the clutches of The Insurer You Can Trust, he would be in a training session, 'Risk Management for Insurance Managers: How to Spot the Perpetrator of Insider Fraud'. I decided to take advantage of this to conduct my activities unobserved in company time.

By the way, I went to one of these sessions last week. Apparently, there's been a horrific rise in internal fraud in the finance industry since 2008. Now, not only are we being duped by the sort of person who would run over their cat on purpose for financial gain, we have to deal with two-faced insiders who aren't content with spending their lives flogging over-complicated, often worthless policies while refusing to consider the claims of the genuinely distressed. The Senior Audit Manager, Mr Guy Relish, has put up posters with exhortations to call the employee hotline should anyone notice any 'suspicious behaviour', such as someone who routinely prefers to stay at their computer rather than joining in a few rounds of after-work drinks. (To Mr Relish's chagrin, most of the calls to the employee hotline are to rat on colleagues who sneak in to make excessive personal use of the photocopier.)

Anyway, on with my story. It took barely fifteen minutes to get into the system, change the Mrs Hurt Puss case status from Rejected to Settled and authorise the transfer of £29,800 into the No. 2 Settlement Account for next-day payment to Mrs Hurt Puss (which, being under 50K, will go through without requiring a director's authorisation). I had sweating palms and a racing heart for nearly an hour afterwards (also three trips to the lav). Hopefully, next time will be less stressful.

So, Gary, I hope these thirty-odd pages will give you a flavour of my life as it's become since we last spoke. Now, what I've been working up to saying.

I wish I could say that I forgive you entirely for the havoc you created in my life by drunkenly propositioning my ex-wife at the first sign of our marital discord.

However, I now see that you are not wholly to blame for what subsequently happened. When my wife knocked on your door two months later saying how deeply unhappy she was, her offer must have been tempting. I blame Clare far more than I blame you, Gary, rest assured. Also, you had the decency to tell me exactly what you and her had been up to, hard though it was for me to deal with at the time. I thank you for that.

Please understand that I did not really mean what I said to you when we parted. I'm sorry.

I'd like very much to hear from you. I would like to have you back in my life, bro, what else can I say?

Colin

PS

I'll be visiting the lovely Madeleine on Sunday afternoon. Fingers crossed, she won't be too unhappy when she finds out I am not the DIY and gardening expert that I may have implied during our early conversations.

30 July

8.15am, on the way to Waterloo

Before I send this off, I may as well describe my latest (last?) adventures with M, which took place yesterday:

I wake bang on 10am with a severe twinge in my lower back (from my match the day before – too many fast serves), cramp in my left calf and a hangover from the tennis club's summer party. I do back exercises, agonise over whether or not to wear my new shirt (on the bright side) and arrive fifteen minutes late at Maddie's newly painted, letterbox-red door in the middle of a row of down-at-heel south London terraces.

'Hiya, Col! You're out of breath.'

'Oh, it's nothing, I've been hurrying, that's all. Left the house a bit later than I meant to–'

'You shouldn't have worried, honestly, I never notice the time. Come in, let me take that bag. It's heavy – what's inside?'

'I thought I could cook us something later, maybe. All the ingredients I need are in there.' I squeeze her arm in what I hope is a suitably friendly, not-too-forward gesture.

She gives me a quick smile. She looks ready for some serious manual labour – jeans, sweatshirt, hair tied back.

'It's good of you to offer to help with the garden, I do appreciate it. Come through, I've got everything set up for us outside. Do you want a glass of water? I thought we could get going on the path and stop for a cuppa later. I've got some hummus and whatnot ready that we can snack on if we get peckish... The flat's a mess – you don't mind if I don't show you round, do you?'

She ushers me through a narrow hall into a cluttered room, its walls crammed with paintings, the surfaces a jumble of artistic bits and bobs, and two armchairs, each occupied by a curled-up cat. On into a narrow kitchen with a table bearing a plate of chopped raw carrot and some unappetising beige dollops. Then she wrenches on a pair of earth-daubed wellingtons and opens the door onto the garden.

A strong urge to change my mind strikes me when I see the roller parked on the patio, which wouldn't have looked out of place pressing down tarmac on a motorway.

We work for two and a half hours

- heaving the roller over a richly varied assortment of stones pilfered from gardens and municipal parks
- hauling a collection of enormous pots across the garden to M's patio
- hacking off the roots of the ivy that has enmeshed itself with her fence
- hammering the broken fence back in place

with only one snatched bathroom break when her attention is distracted by the phone ringing. I gratefully rest my weary haunches on the lav, dab the sweat from my arms and chest (using a flannel folded over the bath that I rinse thoroughly afterwards) and recover my breath.

To be fair, Madeleine does her fair share of hard yakka – almost as much as me – and I'm sure she would have done more, if I'd let her. But it feels unmanly to let her do more physical labour than myself, so I gird my loins, grit my teeth and ponder the gourmet meal I plan to prepare this evening à la Heston Bloomin' Tool – vegetable tagine followed by poached pears (if that doesn't woo her, nothing will). The lovely M doesn't cook much, she has admitted.

By the time we stop for a break, the stones are flat enough to look like a path, my muscles ache as if I've run a marathon, my back won't move more than ten degrees off vertical and I could eat an entire farmyard. I'm frothing at the mouth at the thought of a cold beer.

'Sorry,' she says, inspecting the fridge. 'There's no cans left. I must have finished them last night. I'll nip down the shop when we've finished and get some more… More carrot and hummus? Hey, are you all right? You look knackered.'

'No, no, I'm fine. My back's troubling me a bit, that's all…' I stop grimacing and rubbing and try to smile. 'Too many aces lately, it's not good for the back.'

'Let's stop then, Colin. I can do this by myself. No need to do yourself in on my account.'

'No, I'll be ok, really. Let's finish the job.'

What am I saying? I don't want to end up a cripple. But even more, I don't want to look like a wimp.

The final hour is no easier. We hoe the killer-dry soil at the far end of the lawn and flatten the vaguely chair-shaped mound (she made it for a laugh once, it used to be very comfortable) before planting grass seed. Then she asks if I'd mind fixing the bird feeder (which fell off when Mungo jumped up and killed a wood pigeon a few weeks ago) halfway up a worryingly tall lime tree.

'It's rock solid, I'm holding on down here, don't worry!' she yells as I gingerly climb up to the top of a rickety stepladder, cursing my eagerness, my foolish desire to appear invincibly male and my ridiculous, leg-wobbling, stomach-dissolving fear of heights. While stretched out diagonally, hammering the bird feeder into place, the ladder jerks. I nearly wet myself.

'Let's call it a day, shall we? Sit down, I'll get you that beer.'

My face has betrayed me. I stagger towards the garden seat Maddie is waving at. My legs have lost whatever firmness they once had, my hands are trembling, I am ready to sit down and pass out. For a moment a black wall comes down and the world recedes. Fortunately, this is interrupted by the arrival of an ice-cold metallic cylinder in my right hand, otherwise known as a can of Carlsberg, generally not my favourite, but who's fussy at a time like this?

I gulp it down before the can has a chance to warm.

Maddie sits down beside me with a glass of water. The seat is only just big enough for two – her ear nuzzles mine, our aromas of exertion mingle. All thoughts of cooking vanish.

She thanks me again for helping her. I put my hand just above her knee.

'I'm just glad I could be of service to such a lovely lady–' A twinge of pain shoots down my back.

'Are you all right?'

'Gardening isn't the best thing for my back, I'm afraid.'

Swig on beer, grit teeth. Come on, Col. Show some moral fibre, assert your manliness. Are you a wimp, or what?

'Do you want an aspirin or an ibuprofen – or some Voltarol? I've got half a pharmacy in my bathroom.'

While she's gone, in between periods of nausea, I notice how pretty the garden is. Wispy sunlight catches on a fishpond. A cloud of pale pink flowers ripples suggestively in a nearby flower bed.

Maddie hands me a glass of water and a half-dispensed sachet of ibuprofen tablets.

'That should do the trick. Giblet, come and say hello to Colin.' A fat black shape bounds up, nudges my legs and springs into my lap. 'He likes you.'

The cat is head butting my chin. I whisper sweet nothings, twiddle its ears and carefully stroke its back, bracing myself for those claws to sink into my exhausted muscles. They all do that, these fickle creatures, sooner or later.

'Don't you like cats?'

'I like well-behaved cats... This one looks a little fierce.' The cat's glaring at me, front paws on my chest, tail whipping from side to side.

My hostess laughs. 'He's a sweetie, he wouldn't hurt a flea. It's Mungo you have to worry about – he's a biter. The dominant male, you see. He gets very possessive whenever someone sits down near me. And you're in his seat.'

I scan the garden nervously. No sign of Mungo. With any luck, the other feline is still inside the house, profoundly inert upon the armchair. 'How many cats do you have?'

'Just two at the moment... Bagpuss got cat aids last year. He was always out chasing pussy, he was such an alley cat! I had to take him to a place where they could look after him.'

She sounds sad. I would have put my hand on her arm to comfort her, only the fat black lump of fur is now settled on my lap and I don't want to startle him. God, I hate cats.

'Oh dear,' I say. 'That's a shame. Well, at least you've got two left.'

'Yes, we're one big happy family.'

'Well, it helps to have company when you live alone. When my wife left, my place felt like a morgue. I'm surprised you haven't been snapped up by some charming chap though, Madeleine.'

'Please, call me Maddie. I get nervous when people call me Madeleine. Sorry, I've forgotten your question.'

'I don't mean to pry.' (Of course, I do.)

'I haven't been lucky with relationships.' She sighs. 'The men I've loved the most have all been total shits. I'm friends with some of my exes now, though–'

'Friends? What sort of friends?'

'Oh, we don't get up to anything much. Vic would love to get into my knickers again but he has four women already and I'm not interested in being number five. Toby's found a serious girlfriend – we give each other a massage now and then, that's all.'

This does not totally put my mind at ease. But oh, what wouldn't I do for a massage right now from those lovely capable hands. I feel a stirring inside my jeans, just below the cat's paw. I want to rescue this damsel immediately from the unhappy chaos of her life and take her away on my galloping steed.

Suddenly the cat leaps off my lap and hurtles towards the kitchen.

'It'll be supper time soon,' Maddie says.

'I can get the tagine going, if you like.'

'No, I mean the cats' supper!' She rumbles with mirth. 'You were married once, Colin, didn't you say?'

'The divorce was finalised seven months ago.'

'What happened?'

'I – She – It was all pretty horrible...' I can't decide what to tell her. Certainly not the truth, that you propositioned then slept with my wife, which prompted a sexual rampage ultimately leading to her eloping with a devastatingly handsome bastard who flies passenger jets for British Airways and owns a palace overlooking the Thames, not to mention a beachside retreat in the Seychelles.

'Never mind, Col. I understand. It was obviously a difficult thing for you to go through. I don't think I could stand being married.'

'Why not? Marriage can be great, if you find the right person–'

'Exactly. What are the chances of that?'

I'm about to tell her the latest divorce statistics, which I know because the UK's Number One Pussy Insurer now offers divorce insurance alongside its other top money-spinners – pet insurance and funeral insurance.

'Of course,' I say, 'things don't always work out. Clare and I loved each other. Then one day she said I was... I'm sorry, I'm being a party pooper. You don't want to listen to me going on about my failed marriage.'

Maddie smiles. 'No, I love hearing about other people's relationships. Especially ones that end in disaster. It's comforting, somehow.'

'You're a strange one – strange in a good way, I mean.' Triple damn, have I offended her?

'I'll make a start on some dinner,' she says brightly, getting up. 'For us, as well as the cats.'

'But I said I'd cook.'

She stands in front of me, hands on knees, and speaks sternly. 'You're not in any state to cook, Colin. I'm grateful for you for offering, but I can easily knock up something. You've helped me enough today, let me do something for you. You just sit there, I'll bring you another beer. The shop is just across the road.'

Dinner is parsnip soup liberally dosed with black pepper and parmesan – jolly tasty. I sit on the uncomfortable chair and try not to stare at her cleavage when she takes off the sweater to reveal a low-cut T-shirt. Her eyes are warm but watchful, as if she thinks I might suddenly grab her and carry her up to bed. (That's not my style, Gary.) Her lips are plump, ever so kissable... And her smile – it comes from nowhere, making me long to carry her up to bed. Oh, what would I do to her!

These lustful sensations distract me from my aches and pains, if nothing else. She shows no signs of reciprocation. She asks how my work is going.

'Not bad, still jogging along.' Like a man wheezing up a hill just before he's struck by a coronary... For a moment, I'm tempted to tell her about my Robin Hood scheme. 'How's the job hunting going?'

She groans. 'I've given up, to be honest. I'm too old to get anything except jobs in call centres and school canteens. Anyway, I need time to do my sculpture.'

'You're not old, for heaven's sake. You're years younger than me, I bet.'

'How old are you, Col?'

I tell her I'm fifty-one (two years less than my actual age).

She smiles mysteriously. 'I'm a fair bit younger than you, then...'

She's in her early forties, at a guess.

'So, Maddie. How do you manage without a steady income?'

'My mother's estate helps. She was into collecting antiques and old rugs, stuff like that. It won't last forever, though. I either have to sell some more art, or find a wealthy man who's about to kick the bucket... Only kidding. I would never do anything like that.'

It crosses my mind that she could be lying, she might be on the lookout for a loaded bloke to keep herself afloat so she can carry on producing her artworks. But no, I don't believe she's capable of being that manipulative. She explains that she's sold three sculptures in the last year – the last one three months ago, when it was shown at a Whitechapel gallery.

'I'm impressed.' To make any money whatsoever out of art seems worthy of celebration, regardless of the cost-ineffectiveness of the activity and the high probability of ending up broke. 'Doesn't it worry you, Maddie, all the financial uncertainty?'

She shrugs. 'Not really, I'm used to it. I don't understand how people can do a job for years that bores them witless and makes them feel insane, until they finally keel over with a stroke, then wonder why they didn't spend their lives doing something they actually enjoyed. To me, that's plain daft.'

'You're far braver than me. I'm not sure why I got into insurance – I think it was because my uncle was in the industry. He always had beautiful women on his arm. I remember him telling me how insurance was a maligned but essential part of our society. And it offers one a decent income and a stable career.'

'That's what you wanted?' She looks as if I've admitted to sniffing glue every weekend.

'Not anymore. I've gone off insurance.' Gratefully, I accept another ice-cold beer.

'So, what are you going to do instead, Col?'

'I haven't thought much about it. Maybe buy a yacht and retire to the Seychelles.' I smile at the thought of the near infinite number of unlikely possibilities, and wonder how long it might take to decide on one. Do I want to decide on one? Perhaps, for the first time, I could let the next big step in my life happen without a preparatory phase of agonised mulling over options. I could just jump off and hope that the water's warm, with no sharks waiting.

After dinner, Maddie shows me her 'spare room', which contains various works in progress constructed from an ensemble of junk materials – packaging, bottles and other stuff that most people would dump in the recycle bin. Perched on a toilet flush handle, a parrot sprouting a perky plume of sprayed shredded-plastic-bag feathers. Looming from a huge cardboard box, a giant snail trailed by sparkly, glue covered polystyrene blobs.

'It's more fun than painting. But people aren't always into sculptures of found objects, so I may have to go back to painting again.'

I stand in the doorway and gawp, as there's not enough space to stand among the rubble of materials and partly constructed creatures. Then I recognise a rabbit emerging from a hole and a monstrous rat gnawing through a three-inch thick length of cable, and burst out laughing. 'I'd have that rat in my porch, I'm not kidding! Just to see people's reactions as they go past.'

'Do you think I'm odd? Tell me, I don't mind.'

'No, I don't think you're odd. You just have an unusual mind. A gloriously fresh, inventive mind.'

'I'm glad you think so. Lots of people look at my work and wonder if I'm a crazy lady.'

A moment later, she's embracing me. I'm momentarily incapacitated.

'Sorry, I didn't mean to startle you.'

'No, I like being startled–'

'How's your neck, Col? You keep rubbing it.'

'It's a bit sore, actually.'

'Do you want me to give you a neck and shoulder massage? You've worked so hard this afternoon... Why don't you come into my room and lie down, I'll get you another beer.'

I nod and follow her to a bright room decorated with wind chimes, framed photos of eagles and bear cubs, further artistic creations etc, and arrange myself on the lemon and indigo-striped duvet. Maddie lopes away and returns with another can of Carlsberg, a bottle of oil and a towel. My heart rate kicks up a gear. For a moment I am back in the bedroom of my first love (the daughter of a Thames Ditton property developer) with the door blockaded by her desk in case her parents came home. I was obsessed with her all through the year of my O-levels, remember? Until you told me to forget her, she would go to bed with anyone who asked (you had, of course).

Back to the woman at hand. She instructs me to remove my shirt and begins masterfully kneading my muscles, to which I respond with occasional moans, unfortunately more of pain than appreciation.

'This will do you good,' she says several times. 'I feel the muscles relaxing. Just go with it.'

Of course, the massage does not result in any carnal satisfaction – it ends abruptly with a series of brisk slaps on my back. Afterwards, my neck and shoulders feel fantastic and my desire has multiplied tenfold. Yes, Gary, I know what you are about to say. I must curb my tendency to become infatuated with inappropriate and/or unavailable women who are bound to make me unhappy.

I try to thank Maddie with a kiss, which she dodges. I tell her she must come over to mine soon, where I will cook the meal I promised her – and my withering garden could do with a woman's touch (any touch, to be fair).

Her reply is less than promising, in retrospect. She wants to come over – would love to come over – but there are so many things she has to do. She must phone her Dad who's been rude to the meals on wheels lady and has forgotten where he put the front door key, cut Mungo's claws before tomorrow's vet appointment, finish a piece of sculpture... She gives me a hug goodbye and swings the front door open.

C'est la vie.

Chapter 28

From: Allie Loff (allie53@outlook.com)
Sent: 31 July 2018 3.59am GMT
To: Bea Hudson (bhudson9@blueyonder.co.uk)
Subject: **Life on the farm**

Over here, we're having a major bug invasion
    Flies all day, of all kinds – house, horse, you name it
    Horsefly bites now itching like hell
    Roaches the size of rats infesting our kitchen
    Nearly garrotted Nellie the sheep when electric shearer slipped (tired after no sleep looking out for roaches in the bedroom), had to call the vet
    Another postcard from Mum. She and Janice went their separate ways after a fight about whether to keep the hotel room window open or closed overnight and who's turn it was to pay for dinner. She's now carrying on alone
    A x

From: Bea Hudson (bhudson9@blueyonder.co.uk)
Sent: 31 July 2018 9.02pm
To: Allie Loff (allie53@outlook.com)
Re: **Life on the farm**

Sorry to hear you're finding farm life so tough at the mo, Allie. It must be hell to have flies buzzing around all day and cockroaches the size of rats. (How big are the rats over there??) You could get used to it after a while though, don't you think?

I hope Nellie recovers quickly from her injury. Maybe you need to do a course on sheep shearing.

Reading between the lines, it sounds like you need some support from your nearest and dearest. Why don't you confide in Ray? Tell him you're finding things extra difficult at the moment and you're not sure if you're cut out for farm life. He would be disappointed, yes. But the farm is his passion, not yours. In my experience, it's often better to tell one's hubby everything that is going on. (Yes, I should practise what I preach.)

Re mum – I hope she will be OK travelling herself. At least there will be more time for her to finish Anna Karenina.

Re the sexy underwear I bought for Kurt – it seems to have worked! Our passion was rekindled over the weekend. I didn't think once about either Maddie's massage or the possibility that I am turning into a lesbian.

xx

Chapter 29

Katie's journal

1 August

Fran is Little Fiend again. After Mrs H leaves house, I get big smile and What are you doing, Ninny Nanny Smelly Fanny?

I say None of your lip young lady, like Mrs H does, and Please wash your hands and get dressed, we must have lunch then get bus to the store to buy your uniform for big school. LF says I don't want to go, I want to stay here. I say Please be good girl, your mother tells me to take you.

It is like this for hour. She will not get dressed. She is not hungry. In the end I am so angry I shout at her, grab arm and force legs into skirt. She cries like baby, says I hurt her, she will tell Mummy I am Bad Katie.

In the evening I wait for Mrs H to give me telling off, but no word. She comes in while Criminal Minds is on, talking talking about her experiment and scanning hippopotomos and amigos. Is all nonsense to me.

Must get away from this family! Child crazy, parents crazy, now I am crazy. All my effort to be good ex O Pair are gone with the wind. I cant take this any longer.

2 August

Today I go to playgroup to collect Fran and one of play ladies shouts in my face, Your child is biting Molly! She is gone to doctor with broken finger! Fran is not welcome here, please leave at once!! No I dont care if you not mother I will phone mother!!! Please take this child away RIGHT NOW, she is frightening the other children.

I want to swallow myself, feel like witch who must burn. Fran is in toilet, she wont come out so I have to stand there looking back at the play ladies. They give me Death Stare. Never again I will go back to this place, I swear.

What has she done, I say, I dont understand. Then Head Play Lady comes to me. She is big and heavy, feet in slippers, has look on face like old kipper is stuck under nose. She holds arm of Fran like she holds escaped prisoner. Fran has big brown eyes in small white face.

You are the O Pair I understand, Miss Cow-Less-Car? I am afraid very serious incident is taken place today, this child has attacked Molly...

I take Fran's hand and we run out of playgroup. I do not speak on way back. I am shamed by this woman, she speaks to me like it is my fault. But I am not Mother. Mother is away at work, she leaves me to shovel the shit, I am just O Pair, the girl, the One Who Must Do All. Mrs H will have big shock soon.

We get to the front gate. Fran wails like end of world is come. She says it is not her fault, Molly pinched her very hard on arm so she hurts her back.

Inside house I say, Roll up sleeve, show me.

I see red patch, nothing much. Not reason to bite like animal. I tell her to go to room, I am fed up with her, she is Little Fiend.

Chapter 30

Portrait of a stranded scientist, make-do mother and weary wife

2 August

Trying to gather enough calm to write this. Hand trembling, can't hold pen properly. Feel like screaming and tearing my hair out then running out of the house to a Refuge for Scientist Mothers – failing that, a high security asylum.

Relax shoulders, take deep breath. Will try to describe it all coherently, despite this blotchy chewed-end pen (Fran?) Don't think I'll be able to read this afterwards – nor will anyone else, thank goodness.

OK. At 2pm I get a call from Mrs Watson, head of Fran's playgroup. My daughter has been sent home after she 'viciously attacked' another little girl, who has been taken to hospital with a bite wound and suspected broken finger. It was a deliberate, unprovoked attack, Mrs Watson says, according to 'the victim' and the three other children who were sitting at the same table.

I drive home straight away as fast as I can, straying into a bus lane and nearly knocking over a cyclist. Arrive home in state of desperation to be accosted in the hall by the au pair, who threatens to leave immediately and not come back. Her hands wave about like demented starlings as she shouts at me in mixture of Polish and English.

Me: Calm down, Katie, I can't understand what you're saying!

K: I am going mad, little fiend is sending me mad, you are all mad! I need holiday...

Me: Yes, it does sound as if you need a holiday. Why don't you take a few days off? We'll talk about it later... Where's Fran? What happened at playgroup?

K: She is bad girl, she is too much for me. I can't work here anymore. I am going to Poland to see my mother, I will not be back!

Me: Please Katie, calm down, we'll talk about this later. First, I must talk to my daughter and find out what happened.

K: She says it is not her fault. Don't you listen to her, Mrs Hudson!

I run upstairs and find Fran lying on her bed staring at the ceiling. She doesn't look at me. Her hand rests on her stomach, the fingers smudged with blue and yellow paint.

Me: Fran, sit up.

F: —

Me: Tell me what happened at playgroup. What did you do to that little girl?

She hugs her knees and lowers her head.

Me: Fran, I'm speaking to you! Please answer me.

F: I don't want to go back there, Mummy.

Me: Answer my question. What did you do to Molly?

She presses her lips together.

Me: Well?

F: I bit on her finger.

A chill goes through me. For the past hour, I haven't been able to believe my daughter could have deliberately harmed another child badly enough for her to be taken to hospital.

Me: You bit her finger?! You know she had to go to hospital because of you? Her finger might be broken. She might have blood poisoning.

F: She hurt me first.

Me: Hurt you? How?

F: She pinched me. Then she makes paint go all over my painting. She says my painting is stupid and I am stupid too. And she says no one likes me and no one wants to sit at my table.

Me: Are you telling the truth, Fran?

She nods, face solemn.

Me: Mrs Watson says you hurt Molly for no reason. So do the other three children at your table.

F: (as if I'm the stupidest mother who ever lived) They're Molly's friends.

Me: It's all right, darling. I believe you had a good reason to be upset. But it's very wrong to bite people. Now go and wash your hands, then come downstairs. I'll get you a Ribena.

My phone rings as I'm pouring our drinks (a dash of Triple Sec on ice for me). Mrs Watson from the playgroup tells me in a stiff-as-a-corpse voice that Molly has been released from hospital after having had her finger examined, which is not broken after all.

Me: Oh, thank Christ for that.

I'd imagined a permanently scarred finger, lawsuits and demonisation of Fran and myself on the Bright Faces playgroup Facebook page.

Silence, except for the howl of Katie's vacuuming upstairs and a loud clank followed by an unintelligible curse. Fran peers up at me from her seat on the kitchen step.

Mrs Watson: Mrs Hudson, I'm very sorry, but given the nature of this incident, I'm afraid we won't be able to welcome back your child to our group. Her behaviour contravenes our Conduct and Discipline Policy...

She doesn't sound very sorry. She goes on. Since my daughter joined Bright Faces playgroup last week, Fran has also contravened the Hand Washing Policy and I have fallen foul of the Parental Involvement Policy (not appearing in person at the playgroup least once in a given week), and Katie has dissed the Child Collection Policy (picking up child more than fifteen minutes after the end of session, on at least two consecutive occasions in a given week).

I want to kick her pudgy arse.

Me: That's just as well, Mrs Watson, because after the disgraceful way she's been treated by the other children, my daughter has no wish to come anywhere near your sodding playgroup ever again!

Fran is looking at me, her mouth open. I toss my phone onto a pile of folded towels.

Me: That told her, the fat old bitch.

F: (delighted smile)

I want to pick my daughter up and hug her. Instead I give her the glass of Ribena then make her sit down at the kitchen table. I tell her sternly that this doesn't mean I've forgiven her for what she's done — and that no matter what hurtful things someone may say to you, you mustn't use violence to hurt them back. And you certainly can't go around biting the people who upset you.

F: Why not?

Me: Just imagine if Katie or I bit <u>you</u> every time we were cross with something you did, how would you like that?

Katie: (appearing in the doorway) Maybe we should try.

She hauls the silent vacuum cleaner across the kitchen into the laundry room. I glare at Katie and send Fran back to her room.

Me: She's my daughter, I won't have you speaking about her like that!

K: I am sorry Mrs Hudson, I am fed up with back teeth. At first I like Fran very much, now she is worst behaved child I ever know. She is rude to me all the time, she never does what I say, she makes mess in house on purpose so I must clean again...

The catalogue of complaints goes on. I am sympathetic, until we get to the issue of Fran finding Katie's mobile, left out on the kitchen worktop, and accidentally dialling one of the numbers stored on it.

Me: Thank you, Katie, you've made your point. But no child is a saint. I wish you'd told me about some of this before, we could have talked about it—

K: Please, madam, I have not yet made my point. I must leave this house. I cannot look after your child any longer.

Tempted as I am to say, 'Sod off then, you obviously aren't suited to this job,' I remember how caring and enthusiastic Katie was with Fran for so long. And what on earth I am going to do without her, without a friendly playgroup around the corner?

How will I manage to get a replacement childminder at short notice, just after the start of the summer holidays?

How will I find someone willing to work four days a week from 8am or 8.30am until 6pm, 7pm or 8pm?

Not least, how will I find someone able to cope with Fran? It's my daughter I need to change, not my childminder.

Me: Katie, don't be silly. Why don't you have a think about this? I'm sure we can sort something out that will suit us both. It's been very stressful for you lately, coping with Fran all by yourself, I didn't realise how much... How about you take a week off? Or two weeks?

K: No, Mrs Hudson, I am sorry. I have made my mind.

Me: Please, Katie. You've been so good with Fran, so patient — better than anyone else has ever been!

Stony silence.

Me: Kurt won't be back till September. I need you, Katie. How will I cope without you?

K: You will find way, I am sure. I have friend who is childminder, she lives in Guildford — I tell you her name if you like.

This is delivered with casual coolness as she turns away, checking her watch.

K: I must go now, it is five already.

What else can I do — bribe her? I'm willing to try anything.

Me: I'll give you a pay rise. A big pay rise.

She stops moving towards the door.

K: All right, I will think about. Tomorrow I let you know, OK?

Now I'll have to wait to find out her decision. I would phone Kurt and tell him what's happened, but he's bound to be in the middle of firing someone or in his room having a nap — or in the bar, sipping on a G&T.

Rather tempted to have a G&T myself.

Chapter 31

From: Bea Hudson (bhudson9@blueyonder.co.uk)
Sent: 2 August 2018 9.04pm
To: Allie Loff (allie53@outlook.com)
Subject: **What to do about Fran?**

Fran got expelled from the playgroup today. Also, Katie tried to resign, saying she can't cope with Fran.

What else? Oh yes, I found out today that my latest funding proposal has been knocked back, despite the 'excellent science'. They mentioned 'fitful progress to date' and 'numerous other highly deserving candidates'.

How are things there? Did you talk to Ray?

Bea

From: Allie Loff (allie53@outlook.com)
Sent: 2 August 2018 10.01pm GMT
To: Bea Hudson (bhudson9@blueyonder.co.uk)
Re: **What to do about Fran?**

What has Fran done this time???

ThInk you need Katie, give her a pay rise FFS

Feeling a bit blue lately

No, haven't yet talked to Ray

Don't know what to say or how to say it

Wish I could go away somewhere

Will go for a long drive maybe

A

From: Bea Hudson (bhudson9@blueyonder.co.uk)
Sent: 3 August 2018 10.09pm
To: Allie Loff (allie53@outlook.com)
Re: **What to do about Fran?**

You don't sound yourself, Allie. Where did you drive to?

Re Fran – she got very upset after one of the girls in the playgroup was nasty to her. Fortunately, things not quite as bad as they might have been.

Other news – Kurt and I had a fight on the phone this evening. He says I should 'just go in to work one day a week' until he gets back from Turkey (I can just 'shunt my work onto the rest of the team') so I can be around for Fran. Told him I will take some extra days off in the next couple of weeks, though I'm really not sure if I can – I can't leave the team at this crucial stage with only Ben to keep the project going. The other night I woke up in a sweat dreaming I'd been locked out of my office and I was mopping the corridor, which was littered with the debris of fruit flies, dead spiders and dehydrated volunteers who had lost their way in the building.

Also, the Powers That Be in the School of Psychological Sciences would be certain to notice were I to have the gall to take off any more than one day a week (no one 'serious' ever does, because they know that if they did they would immediately be shunted to 'Mummy Track'.) Three years ago, Moira (who used to be a full-time researcher in the Trauma Group) told one of our brown-corduroy-suited old fogeys that she was going to take maternity leave and was hoping to return to her job at 60% FTE (full time equivalent) afterwards. He said, 'Oh dear, just when you were doing so well! We all thought that you were going to have a serious career.' That's the mentality here – either you're a full-time researcher, or you're a dilettante.

Kurt and I also fought about my idea of taking Fran to a counsellor. He says it would 'stigmatise her for life' – we (I) must deal with her and make her understand that what she's done is wrong. (At this rate, I will be asking Mad for her therapist's name for myself.) He's come up with a 'suitable punishment' for Fran. For one week she will be left alone in the conservatory for two hours every day with only the trampoline and her drawing books to amuse herself with, no dolls or other toys allowed. (That may not sound particularly harsh but to Fran, being without attention/TV/computer/my mobile/visits from friends is hell itself.) I said yes, that's a good idea, because by then I had a headache coming on.

Got to go and take another ibuprofen.

Bea x

Chapter 32

Portrait of a stranded scientist, make-do mother and weary wife

3 August

Kurt's other idea was for me to make Fran apologise to Molly, the child she hurt at playgroup. Molly's mother lives just five minutes' walk from us as I found out after a brief phone call to her (her number was grudgingly given to me by one of the playgroup mothers). So this afternoon I swallowed my pride and set off with Fran, determined to be a sensible and responsible role model for once.

Molly's mother (in trainers, T-shirt and tracksuit bottoms, red cheeks, breathing heavily) opens the door. She nods and gestures for us to come in, goes to turn off the booming Abba song in the next room and yells for Molly to come down. We wait in the hall. Halfway down the stairs Molly sees Fran and stops with an audible gasp.

MM: Come here, darling, she wants to say something to you.

Molly approaches us.

MM: Show her your finger, darling.

Molly's hand is lifted with trepidation. The finger is hidden under a chunk of bandage. I nudge Fran in the back.

F: I'm very sorry, Molly.

M: (glares at Fran)

MM: (icily, lifting plucked-away eyebrows) Sorry for what?

F: (looking at MM) I'm sorry for biting your finger.

MM: It wasn't my finger.

F: (in hoarse whisper) I'm sorry for biting your finger, Molly.

M: –

Molly's mother regards Fran with a hostile flick of her eyelashes and a contemptuously lifted chin. I feel an unreasonable jolt of hatred towards Molly's mother and contemplate the surprise she would feel if I stepped forward and took a bite out of her finger.

MM: Thank you, Fran. I sincerely hope that you don't make a habit of this.

Before my daughter can answer, I tug her arm and propel her away from the awful scene.

Chapter 33

Miss Katie Kowalski
Flat 2B
18 Douglas Walk
Godalming
4 August 2018

Dear Mrs Hudson,

Miss Kowalski will continue work for rest of this week as she does not wish to cause big problem to her employers.

Unfortunately Miss Kowalski will be in Poland for two and a half weeks from Sunday, 5 August, to Wednesday, 22 August.

She will be available to continue her work as au pair from Thursday, 23 August, subject to ALL of following:

1. Hours 9.30am to 5pm (strict) 4 days per week (strict).
2. Pay to increase from £12 to £18 per hour.
3. No cleaning inside cubbuds.
4. No cleaning of cobwebs in cellar.
5. No cleaning of Miss Hudson's bedroom unless it is not looking like garbage bin.
6. No picking up from floor of Miss Hudson's dolls, dirty nickers, squashed marsbars etc.
7. Punishment for bad behaviour to be given from Miss Kowalski as follows:

Smack on arm for ordinary bad things.

Hard smack on back of knee for very bad things.

Sending to her room for the whole day for the most bad things.

I look forward to start of our new relationship.

Your Faithful Servant,

Miss Katie Kowalski

Chapter 34

From: Bea Hudson (bhudson9@blueyonder.co.uk)
Sent: 4 August 2018 6.03pm
To: Allie Loff (allie53@outlook.com)
Subject: **Fucking au pair**

Just read a letter from the Katie – she must have come over and put it through the letterbox.

Faithful Servant, my arse!

My first impulse was to scrunch up Katie's coffee-stained list of outrageous demands, go over to her flat and shove it up her sodding T-shirt. After second thoughts I messaged her, agreeing to her ultimatum.

When Kurt calls, I'll tell him Katie will be staying on with us – after a short break. (She has to go back to Poland for a two and a half-week holiday.)

I suppose I'll have to work from home as much as I can while she's away. The research will have to carry on without me – I'll just have to gee up the team over the phone. They can call me if they need anything.

Bed calls.

From: Bea Hudson (bhudson9@blueyonder.co.uk)
Sent: 6 August 2018 8.44pm
To: Allie Loff (allie53@outlook.com)

Subject: **Ben's accident**

Bad news this end – yesterday my postdoc Ben had a crash on his motorbike. He's in hospital with a leg broken in three places, a dislocated shoulder, a fractured wrist and a cut face. As awful as he looks, the doctor says he'll mend soon enough with no permanent injuries or scars, thank goodness. It'll be two weeks or more before he can return to work, though.

This morning I went in with Fran and his books, papers and laptop, as he insisted (he can't type or write and is still too groggy to read, but it seems to comfort him to have them nearby).

I'll have to manage without him, Lord knows how – our next experiments are due to start in eight days. The scanner is booked for the whole week, two hours morning and afternoon (phobics in the mornings, controls in the afternoons). Our radiographer looks after the technical side and preps the volunteers, but someone has to be in the control room to run the experiments. And before that, we still need to finalise the experiment design.

Hayley can't really cover for Ben. She's having enough trouble coping with her own work, and she's always off with a migraine just when I need her to be getting on with things. Plus she doesn't have the project knowledge that Ben has – and Ben would go nuts if I let her do the scans on her own. She doesn't have much practical nous, either. Last week she got locked inside a toilet cubicle in the Psychological Sciences Building and had to be rescued by the caretaker.

I suppose I could delay the experiments. But time is running out. The project will be done for, unless we get some decent results soon. Besides, if we delay, we'd have to wait for another six weeks for the scanner to be free, by which time many of the volunteers wouldn't be available. There's no way around it – if Ben's still off sick on the 15th, I'll have to go in myself to look after the experiments. Kurt won't be pleased, nor will Fran. (I've promised to take her to the beach next week and the week after.) Goodness knows who's going to look after her. Maybe I can find a flexible childminder/playgroup that's open all day and close to home, which doesn't have a mile-long waiting list and doesn't close over August?? The uni childcare is only open two days a week during August, and anyway I promised Fran I'd never take her there again after three hellish days last summer. I suppose I could take her into the Psycho Lab again if I have to – she loves pressing buttons. But what if she went near the scanner tube, or the Prof turned up? There's a No Children rule due to health and safety. Plus she'd distract everyone from the experiment with her constant chatter.

Ben's accident feels like an omen spelling out the end of my research career.

Must go and prise Fran away from 'Postman Pat'.

Let me know the latest on the farm. How are you and Ray getting on?

Bea x

From: Allie Loff (allie53@outlook.com)
Sent: 7 August 2018 10.07pm GMT
To: Bea Hudson (bhudson9@blueyonder.co.uk)
Subject: **More farm news**

Ben's accident – bad timing, yes

end of your career? don't be so negative

how are Ray and I getting on? whenever I try to talk to him he says he's too tired. and he doesn't want to talk about anything except the farm. want to tell him what's in my heart, but too scared. don't want to let him down

back feeding the animals – feel I ought to do my bit, despite my fear of being kicked or pecked to death. Ray's got a guy from town to do fence mending, etc popped into the town pub yesterday eve on way back from buying supplies, cos needed to use the toilet (it was gross)

band on, very good (the hunky-to-the-max singer-guitarist kept smiling at me)

didn't stay long, felt guilty about leaving Ray working on the farm, also I was the only woman on her own

From: Bea Hudson (bhudson9@blueyonder.co.uk)
Sent: 8 August 2018 9.30pm
To: Allie Loff (allie53@outlook.com)
Re: **More farm news**

I know it's tough for you out there Allie – but what's all this about going to the pub on your own and smiling at strange men? That's asking trouble, in my opinion.

This morning I left Fran in Maddie's capable hands and went into the Psycho Lab. Mad came over yesterday morning and stayed the night. She's agreed to look after Fran every day till Katie gets back from Poland, and to take her to the beach instead of me. (She'll stay in the guest room, I can't expect her to travel back and forth to Streatham every day.) So, all should be hunky-dory. Fran loves being with Mad and Mad loves being with Fran, and I shall save my project from oblivion. What could possibly go wrong?

Interesting day at work. Persuaded migraine-struck Hayley to go home, in case she vomits over the keyboard again. Got stuck into sorting out the latest problem with the volunteers (one threatening to drop out as she thinks she may be recovering from her spider phobia) and forgot about my 3pm appointment with the admin bitch who's been scrutinising last year's conference receipts and says I've claimed £11.50 too much in Geneva. Remembered appointment fifteen minutes late then nearly twisted my ankle while galloping downstairs. Arrived sweating, flustered and unprepared to defend my extravagance at ordering two glasses of white wine with my evening meal.

Highlight of the day was definitely meeting Elaine, a Costa Rican zebra tarantula delivered to the lab by Pedro, Ben's mate in Zoology. She was in a glass box full of sand, rocks and bits of cacti, and was about twelve centimetres across with a big fat middle covered in grey hairs and the most horrendously long, thick and hairy black-and-white striped legs – I can't believe some people keep them as pets.

'They're not dangerous to humans,' Pedro said, 'but very good at freaking people out.' He gave me a leaflet: 'Introduction to Elaine, our Costa Rican zebra tarantula'. She's eleven years old and enjoys a varied diet including live cockroaches and fruit flies (sorry if you're eating while reading this), which of course are plentiful round here. They were trying to get her pregnant but gave up when she ate her last carefully acquired mate after having sex with him. Pedro asked if I wanted him to lift the lid so I could have a better look at Elaine – but not to touch her as it might unsettle her! I said thanks, but I'd prefer Elaine to stay safely enclosed inside her box.

Left for home at 6.30pm, exhausted. No time for a walk to the canteen, a tea break or chats to colleagues. But feeling chirpier now the next phase of our research is about to get underway.

When I got home, a chicken was browning in the oven, the table was laid and Classic FM was exuding relaxed vibes. Both Mad and Fran seemed perfectly content. Not sure what I was expecting – mayhem? Fran insisted she'd spent her two hours punishment in the garden helping Mad weed and prune. Mad swore that Fran had not turned on the computer or TV all day. Not the least sign of trouble.

During dinner Kurt rang to say he hates his hotel, his boss and his work. The Americans are pressuring him to fire the head of the New Products Division but the guy has five kids and has shown Kurt the highlights of Istanbul in his RX5 and like Kurt is a David Byrne fan. Also, K is desperate to be with me and can't face another Turkish breakfast. He's off to a bar to drown his sorrows, he says. I said be careful not to overdo it, I love him and I'll see him soon.

I didn't get around to telling him that I went into uni today, and that Maddie's staying with me and Fran for the next ten days. He'd only have a fit about her being here all that time and berate me for not being a proper mother. I'll wait until he's in a good mood to tell him.

Just got a text from sodding Katie. She's having a nice time swimming and sunbathing – and by the way, Big Ears has a vet appointment tomorrow. She wrote it down on the calendar but forgot to tell me. Got to go – Fran's trying to get my attention and Mad's yelling about clean sheets, don't I have any?

Bea x

Chapter 35

What to do about Madeleine?

8/8/18

9.57pm, report from Havana Joe's

Can't cope with this godforsaken town much longer. Hot and muggy as a belly dancer's armpit in my hotel room, the aircon still refuses to go below twenty-five degrees despite repeated complaints to management. The closest place to go for relief is a noisy, pretentious bar (recommended by Yalom, along with a clutch of brothels, gambling dens and 'nightclubs' that I have carefully avoided). It's full of potted palms, ceiling fans, kissing Frenchmen, hugging Italians and cigar-toting cocktail-swilling Yanks. Most of the clientele seem to be expats living in Istanbul. The Turks wisely steer clear of the place.

I'm sitting in my regular spot at a side table away from the bar-side scrum where I can watch the show and blend in with all the other lonely people.

Everything goes on here, sooner or later – currency trading, drug trading, men picking up girls, girls picking up men...

Missing Beatrice. Wish I could find the words to tell her how I feel. They get trapped somewhere and when I want to find them I can't. Not just how I yearn for her day and night – especially nights. How I love her, so very much, far more than my mediocre words could ever convey. So much, in fact, that I can't help speculating what she might be up to. Breathing harder as a slim feminine hand creeps up her thigh, perhaps, and a lipsticked mouth smudges her belly button?

I'm losing it. I'm becoming an obsessed lunatic, set to destroy the love of my life for a tawdry half-cocked fairy story that a child of five would laugh at. Live and let live. Who cares if a rampant corrupter of morals is woman-handling my woman? Human beings aren't possessions. That sort of patriarchal nonsense went out two centuries ago, as Bea might say. Except over here, of course, where half of the women sneak around shrouded in black.

Missing my darling daughter too – hoping desperately I shall be back home in time for her fifth birthday. It's at the end of September. The 29th – or is it the 30th? She was meant to arrive on the 29th, that was it. But she actually came out on the 30th.

God, I'm wasted. I can hardly type into this sucker of a keyboard. Why does the collective genius at Apple think that a grown man has fingertips the size of a matchstick head? The fourth martini was probably a mistake, on top of that Manhattan. The lights are starting to swirl and my stool seems to be getting higher. It's a long way to fall from up here.

Tried to get some sense out of the damned spyware company this afternoon but the guy I spoke to had a thick Glaswegian accent and was unconcerned about a matter so trivial as customer satisfaction. Yes, sir, the wireless smoke alarm device should be able to transmit its signal through up to two walls into your router. Yes, sir, in theory you should be able to observe the spycam output remotely and in real time. But in practice, any number of things could be the problem. Are you sure your internet service provider allows you to receive high bandwidth data? Are you sure that the router is switched on? Maybe it has been disconnected from your broadband connection? Could the battery have run out? You may need to go back and check your equipment, sir.

I hung up when he offered to check my equipment. God knows where these helpline staff are trained. What's the point of explaining that I can't just go back to check on all of my spying paraphernalia, because I'm not going to get out of here for another month? The staff are doing their best to fuck this fledgling operation with their bureaucratic fumblings and admirably well-honed excuses for avoiding work. Running off to pray every few hours or to smoke a bit of hash. No quick nip out for a sandwich – every lunch has to be a three-hour job enhanced by generous quantities of gut-stripper and flesh-wobblers (more flesh than wobble, in many cases). The ex-pats are even worse. The Yanks especially, trawling the brothels and getting pissed in bars and fuck knows what else.

I know, I know, people in glasshouses... Jesus, I sound like a racist twat. I'm being a xenophobic asshole. I love the Yanks. They invented Manhattans and movies and rock n roll. The Turks aren't so bad, either. They have some amazing dancers. Even the men. That Whirling Dervish is damned impressive... And my best friend here is Turkish. My only friend, sadly. I'm getting pressure to axe him too but I can't bring myself to do it. He's invited me to dinner at his place again. Looking forward to that. His eldest son wants to show me the film he made. His wife makes a cracking dolma and her Kuru fasulye is to fucking die for. Who knew white beans and meat stuffed into vine leaves could taste so heavenly? Will have to get the recipe for Bea to cook when I'm back home again. If they ever let me out of here.

I guess I'm just feeling sorry for myself. I want to be back home with my family, not stuck in a hotel for months on end. I haven't even got the weekends to look forward to anymore. Every day it's up at 6am, work till 7.30pm or 8pm then back to the hotel for dinner, a wave from the friendly bodybuilder across the way, a cold shower and (if I have the stamina) a stroll through the neighbourhood for a drink/or two/or three before I collapse under a sweat-soaked sheet and the weary cycle repeats itself.

I need to get a grip. I'm losing it, I'm getting paranoid. So what if none of the spycams I've installed are working? I shouldn't be spying on my wife. And what if she ever finds out what I've done? She'll hate me. I won't have any shred of moral authority left. What if she's found them already? Is that why they're not working, she's deliberately taken out the batteries?

No, don't go there. Anyway, it's only the smoke alarm cam that's not working. The other two aren't connected to the internet, they'll be working fine. They could be beavering away this very moment. Some new movement may have triggered another twenty-second burst of secret recording…

Finish my drink in one. Wipe sweating brow with napkin. New thought, please.

All this angst about Beatrice is more than likely a product of my rampant imagination. Anyway, what could Bea be up to while I'm away? Impassioned debates about Earth's dying ecosystems with Sweaty Mike at the water dispenser? Occasional sparkly-eyed chats with Adrian next door and the bagpipe-playing Scot from number thirty-three? Though

I recall she was giving Scottie the glad eye last Burns Night while his wife was blessing the haggis or whatever it is they do with that collection of sheep innards.

She's not doing anything untoward with Madeleine, surely. Do I seriously believe she could desire another woman? She ogles Daniel Craig and that snooty oh-so-English twat on *Downton Abbey*, and the entire Welsh rugby team. And she smiles at random passing men, especially that Froggie bandicoot who runs Le Bon Gout.

That weekend we were together was no show, either. That was the woman I know and love, who can still make me as stiff as a rhino's horn and send my heart into a flutter strong enough to set off a tsunami. What am I thinking?

I have to ignore the fact that Madeleine sent my wife a schmaltzy birthday card and a wispy silk garment that you can't honestly call underwear because it isn't substantial enough to cover a third of her bosom. Just because the two girlies have been like long-lost buddies ever since the freethinking, visionary 'artist' returned from her inspirational (i.e. pot-smoking, man-baiting, freeloading) trip to southern climes, texting each other every other minute and whispering and laughing about God knows what whenever they are alone together. And that time when I called and Goldilocks was staying for dinner and I could hardly get a coherent word out of Bea… Come to think of it, when I called Bea earlier, she sounded a bit uptight, as if she was trying not to let on about something.

Something's going on, I know it.

Two strapping chaps have arrived at the bar with packs on their backs the size of houses, and legs with the hairiness and girth of an Amazon jungle plant growing out of their khaki cut-offs. Vile Australians. I listen with mild amusement turning to horror as they conduct a crass conversation about what they would like to do once they have finished their drinks.

Hey, mate, what are you looking at?

Tie me kangaroo down, one is getting up from his stool. The other's busy trying to cram another note into his wallet.

I avert my gaze and tap furiously into my iPad. Pretend to be deaf mute.

A hand thuds onto my shoulder. Overhead lights swirl in ever-decreasing circles. Ffffffffffffffffffffffffffffffffffffffffffff uuuuuuuuuuuuuuuuuuuuuuuuuuuuuuuccccccccccckkkkkkkk kkkkk

Chapter 36

From: adriansmith@luciouslawnsltd.co.uk
Sent: 8 August 2018 10.49pm
To: khudson@computercorp.com
Subject: **Report 1**

Hi Kurt,

A quick word to keep you up to date with the situation at home.

I've been keeping my eyes open for anything out of the ordinary next door as you asked. Last week (Friday I think it was) the Polish woman left your house and hasn't been back since.

Since then a tall blonde (I assume it's the same bird as you mentioned before, lean with boob-length hair) has been in and out of there a good deal. I haven't seen her leave the house in the evenings, so either she slips out very late or stays the night.

This morning (Wednesday) when I was casually looking out of the back bedroom window, I caught sight of her in the garden pegging up large quantities of tights, undies and other female kit.

At 10.30am I wandered over for a sniff around just as she was coming out of the front door with Fran. I introduced myself and looked at her enquiringly.

She smiled and said, 'I'm Maddie, hi,' and she was sorry but she was in a hurry to get to the beach before the roads clogged up. No sign of or mention of your wife.

I said, 'Good to meet you,' and she gave me a friendly wave. I noted her revealing top and very short shorts. I also noted that her and Fran drove away in your BMW. A few minutes later I rang on the doorbell and no answer, so I presume that Bea was out at work as usual. She must have taken the train.

The blonde returned with Fran around 6pm. I've kept an eye out but there's no sign of her leaving as of this minute (10.45pm).

I hope this is of interest.

Adrian

Chapter 37

What to do about Madeleine?

9/8/18, Thursday

11am

Survived to tell the grisly tale, I'm pleased to report. Now I feel hot and prickly all over, like the inside of a camel's mouth, and my head feels like it's been kicked by a camel's hoof.

Regret rages in me over last night. Fortunately my unconsciousness was temporary, no broken bones, just a bruised ankle and great embarrassment. I was helped to my feet by a po-faced gold-Rolexed yacht-owning tycoon who told me I should be more careful in future as the drinks are stronger here than they are 'back home'. Thanked the man for his thoughtful advice and said I had better be going.

Will stay in safety of my hotel room for the rest of today, content with room service deliveries of juice, coffee and toast. I solemnly vow to stay clear of that bar – and any other similar bars I come across – until I leave Turkey. No more cocktails, either. Certainly not Manhattans.

3.30pm

Found an email from Adrian, sent yesterday, re Bea and Goldilocks. Very bad news indeed.

7.20pm

Bea's mobile has just called me. I said hello but no one answered. Everything sounded muffled as if she were having a conversation with someone inside her bag. I couldn't make out who she was talking to until a gale of laughter erupted in my ear, which was most definitely Madeleine's. Naturally, I carried on listening.

A few minutes passed, containing occasional clinking sounds and more overwrought laughter. Then I distinctly heard the words, 'Have you told Kurt?' to which my wife replied in an alarmed voice, 'I'd rather he didn't know.' Madeleine then said, 'You should tell him, Bea. He'll be back soon. He's bound to find out.'

7.55pm

Have been unable to think of anything except for this inauspicious conversation, and Adrian's email. Operation GROM is officially resumed.

Chapter 38

From: khudson@computercorp.com
Sent: 9 August 4.45pm GMT
To: adriansmith@luciouslawnsltd.co.uk
Re: **Report 1**

Adrian,

Sorry for late reply, did not see your mail until just now as have been out of action last night and for much of today (work-related issues).

Yes, this is exactly the sort of thing I am interested in. Yes, this long-legged blonde certainly is the one that I am concerned about. No, I had no idea that she was staying in my house or spending time alone with my daughter or driving my car. This development is very worrying. Please do your best to check exactly what is going on. Use your discretion and please do not worry about propriety. Can you have a wander over one evening soon? And make sure to listen out for anything of interest when you're outdoors. I hear it's getting warm over there. Bea likes to go out in the garden on summer evenings.

Perhaps we should think about some incentive for your efforts? I will discuss this with you on my return.

Best, Kurt

From: adriansmith@luciouslawnsltd.co.uk
Sent: 9 August 10.22pm
To: khudson@computercorp.com

Subject: **Report 2**

Kurt, good on you mate. I am only too pleased to be your eyes and ears while you're away, though of course any token of your appreciation would not be declined.

Further incidents next door to report.

This evening while I was parking my van at about 7.30pm after a late hedge job I noted Bea parking the BMW (not very well by the way, I called out for her to mind the motorbike behind). She didn't hear me, she had just returned from work I assumed as she was weighed down with plassie bags and hurried into the house. A few minutes later I went out onto our back deck to have a can, given the pleasant sunshine and bearing in mind your comment about her fondness for the garden.

Saw Fran in the garden splashing about in the inflatable paddling pool. I moved to a spot behind the wisteria on the railing between our terraces so as not to be observed. A few minutes later the blonde came out in shorts and a top, lit the barbie and joined your daughter in the pool. It was like (I hope it is not out of place to say so) two sisters playing together. They were both laughing and splashing about so much I grew concerned that the blonde might accidentally hurt the little girl. I was just wondering where your wife had got to when she came out changed into shorts and put some kebabs on the barbie.

I nipped in for another can, say hello to the wife and feed the dogs. When I came out again all three were eating dinner at the patio table. I could hear bits of conversation, nothing of note but they all seemed to be greatly enjoying themselves. Fran called the blonde 'Auntie Maddie' I noted and I did not hear your wife shouting at Fran as she sometimes does in the evenings since you've been away. (I hope this comment is not out of place.) The impression I got was of one happy family.

After my own meal I ventured out to the deck again (as you requested, I have not told Jackie about the situation and was trying to behave naturally so as not to alert her). It was nearly dark by then and I thought that they might not come out again.

At 9.15pm, though, the two women came out and lay on the reclining chairs. Your wife said 'Isn't it lovely out here?'

'It's so hot still,' the blonde replied and something about a hose.

Bea said she had a report to read for tomorrow, she didn't have time. The blonde said she should forget about her work for once. Bea said she would go upstairs and look for her bikini. The other one must have said, 'No don't bother,' I presume, because next thing they were both stripping down to their panties.

I made sure they couldn't see me watching, arranging my seat so my line of sight coincided with a gap in the wisteria. Also, I was worried Jackie might come out and think I was perving. (You know what women are like.)

They were out there for nine and a half minutes spraying each other with the garden hose. I couldn't hear most of what they said. I don't think there was much talking though. There was a lot of laughing, which reminded me of teenage girls doing something they shouldn't. I had a strange feeling I tell you, watching two nearly naked women hose each other down. The light from your kitchen was on so I could see them quite clearly. It was a bit like a scene in a film. Not the sort I normally watch, but you know what I mean. The blonde started messing around with the hose and Bea was laughing and screaming. She did not seem distressed, more excited if you get my drift.

Then all went quiet for five minutes. They turned away from me and I couldn't see what they were doing. Suddenly Bea ran inside the house and the blonde followed.

That's it, Kurt. I'll let you know if there are any further developments. Hope you manage a decent kip.

Adrian

From: khudson@computercorp.com
Sent: 9 August 11.10pm GMT
To: adriansmith@luciouslawnsltd.co.uk
Re: **Report 2**

Thank you for your astute observations, Adrian. You have given me much to dwell on.

I am considering an impromptu visit to Godalming. In the meantime, please continue the good work. Please don't hold back on any aspect of your reporting. I am interested in anything that could possibly be relevant re my wife's inappropriate liaisons. The smallest detail may be significant.

Will try my best to get some sleep.

Kurt

Chapter 39

Colin Settle
18 Tudor Drive
Woking, Surrey GU21 3NZ
England
(email cmsettle@blueyonder.co.uk, mobile +44 7939 551012)
Gary Settle
14010 RANCHO SOLANA TRL
San Diego, CA 92130

Dear Gary,

9 August, 12.30pm, from the staff canteen

I was heartened to hear from you this Sunday, despite my initial grogginess – it was 3am, I'm not sure if you realised, and I'd had a fair bit to drink earlier at the tennis club social. You weren't sober either, I don't think. I don't know where it was you called from – a swimming pool, by the sound of it. I can't remember much of what we talked about or what in particular led me to deliver that long stream of invective. It wasn't what I meant to say to you at all.

Anyhow, I'm sorry. My overlong letter was a clumsy attempt to build a bridge between us, but it seems that in one fell swoop I have demolished whatever flimsy structure I may have managed to create. After stumbling back to bed, I swore at myself for being such a moron and resolved to try anew to rekindle the blaze of brotherly love. I was intending to call you back ASAP to apologise but as your number was withheld I had no way to do this – foolishly, I didn't think to ask for your number before you cut me off.

As you haven't called back, I'm guessing you are still upset. So for now I will continue with this slow and old-fashioned but perhaps more reliable method of communication. When you get this letter, Gary, I'd much appreciate another phone call or an email letting me know your current phone and email address.

In the meantime, I will continue with more news from this end.

My cunning plan is going well. I've made the payments to all except the final three deserving recipients on my list, including a man whose Labrador developed a heart condition which cost £1000 in emergency treatment and then £350 a month thereafter in vet bills. His lifelong pet insurance policy was promptly terminated by us after we coughed up £200 (after the generous excess was deducted) and informed him that he was now uninsured, and uninsurable.

Tomorrow is Friday – while everyone is in The Butcher's Hook getting blotto, I will be at my desk making transactions eleven to thirteen of the Deserving Thirteen.

Unfortunately, I have an idea that my most disliked junior colleague, Mark Hollis, is getting an inkling of my activities. (He must have been taking notes at the 'How to spot insider fraud' session.) Recently he's taken to following me around the office even when I am only helping myself to a cup of water, staring at me with an unusual intensity whenever I speak to him and hovering behind my desk to peek at whatever secret business I might be up to on my computer. (Generally, it's as harmless as placing a bet on the 2.30pm at Kempton Park, or looking up the weather forecast.) Yesterday, when I felt his hot gaze on me, I came up with a sharp riposte, 'Shouldn't you be busy doing something useful, Mark, like preening yourself in the lav?' He gave me another long stare and sauntered off.

I shall have to be careful.

Onto other things. Madeleine has finally ventured onto my territory.

She arrived yesterday evening, thirty minutes late, with a bottle of Prosecco, a bag of horse manure for the flowerbeds and two pots of fiery red camellias, while I was rushing around the house removing all dust, dirt and other potentially incriminating signs (my geeky anorak on hat stand, a dismantled seventies hi-fi occupying a corner of the living room floor and the photo of Clare's face with dart holes decorating the nose, stuck on the kitchen noticeboard).

Opened the door to find Madeleine in a gorgeously thin blouse, a skirt and sandals with heels! It was the first time since our lift encounter that I'd seen her in anything but jeans. She greeted me enthusiastically then launched into a story about her encounter with a 'shamanic healer' at the local arts and craft fair, who expressed an interest in looking at her sacred animal sculptures to enhance his studio. Supposedly he is from Lapland and in his thirties.

'Do you think he was really interested in your sculptures?' I do my best not to sound jealous.

She smiles broadly. 'Do you think he was after my body?'

'Well, maybe your body as well. Men can be pretty one-track-minded you know. You need to watch out for wolves.'

'Do you class yourself as a wolf, Col?'

'Me? No, I'm far too good-natured. I'm more like a loyal, licky Labrador.'

My imaginings of being a loyal licky Labrador are cut short by laughter. Her eyes shine, her creamy cheeks blush and my heart zooms into the stratosphere.

After pouring us both a glass of my pre-chilled, carefully selected New Zealand Sauvignon Blanc, I take her on a tour of the house, past the closed doors of rooms that I fear are too untidy or tasteless.

'Yuck!' She stops to examine one of the few decorative items on the walls, on casual glance a painting of a large, featureless greenish field resting above another large, featureless brownish field, which Clare sensibly decided not to take when she emptied my house of all that belonged to her (and much else besides). 'This place needs a woman's touch,' M announces when we're back in the kitchen. 'All this grey – doesn't it depress you? I could paint some murals, if you like.'

I swiftly accept her offer. She's right, the minimalist squalor of this place would depress someone who'd just won Lotto. I've let things slide.

We go outside into my somewhat bare plot of land with the garden items (I've promised to pay her back) and select an appropriate location for planting the camellias, away from the favoured toilet spots of my neighbour's black cat. I explain some of the methods I've used to deter it. Maddie replies with obvious shock that it is cruel to kick a cat, one ought to aim a water pistol at feline intruders. I keep my thoughts to myself.

What would it be like living with a woman and two inhospitable cats? The thought comes while M helps me extract slices of smoked salmon for our starter. I pour the Prosecco, lost in visions of becoming entangled with feline limbs, dangling forests of skimpy lacy panties and bountiful bras…

She's looking at me intently.

'Sorry, Maddie. Did you ask me if I liked salsa? I've never tried it – or did you mean dipping salsa?'

'No, dancing salsa. You should try it, sometime.'

My tagine is not 100% successful, owing to the lack of preserved lemon and a shortage of garlic. But my guest is unfazed and too polite to mention any disappointment. We discuss alternative realities and discover a mutual interest in sci-fi films. I invite her to come over and watch my *The Day of the Triffids* DVD this Saturday night. She says she'd love to – another time. She's planned to go to a salsa class that evening with her scientist friend Beatrice.

'How about Sunday afternoon, then?'

'Yes, I should be free then. I'll call to confirm.'

'Fabulous', I say, all set to wrap her in my arms and kiss her. Thank you, universe.

'What's happening in the insurance world?'

We're onto dessert, mercifully not homemade – a cheesecake from M&S. I explain about my employer's proposed employee headcount reduction, and my discovery that I'm number five on a list of 'deadwood'.

She looks so concerned I hasten to explain that I'm not quaking in my boots – I've come up with a plan.

Eyes huge, lashes aflutter with curiosity, Maddie leans towards me and whispers dramatically, 'A plan?'

'It's nothing much, just an idle thing I've been hatching for my amusement.' A diversion from the painful reality of becoming redundant in my prime, not to mention a way of relieving the guilt I've carried for having had to be such a bastard in my job.

'You're not going to tell me what it is? I thought we were friends.'

She's seen through my deceptively casual tone. I pick up her hand, which is resting on the table, temptingly close. 'Of course we're friends. Very good friends.'

'Well then, tell me about this plan. You're not going to steal money from your company, are you?'

'No, of course not!' I shake my head vehemently. 'Nothing like that, I wouldn't do anything like that.'

She's seen through me... almost. But I'm not stealing am I, if the money I take doesn't end up in my account at the end of the day? It's simply a redistribution of assets from the Haves to the Have-Nots. I'm not a rogue trader. Though sometimes, I must admit, I've felt a tiny temptation to transfer some cash into my own account while I'm at it. A few thou maybe. (I won't do it, bro – I have my principles.)

Fortunately, M's next question is stalled by her mobile phone ringing.

'That was my scientist friend,' she explains after a few brief, reassuring-sounding words. 'She's panicking about her husband again.'

'Really? Why's that?'

'He's been asking awkward questions – he's like a terrier onto a scent. Why hasn't she answered the home phone lately, is she really at work, who's the strange woman looking after his daughter? She tried to bluff it out.'

'So what's really going on?'

'I'm staying over at Bea's place for a while, looking after her daughter while the childminder's away. Bea's meant to be at home but she's really at the lab doing her research.'

'And her husband's getting suspicious?'

'You could say. My friend's getting worried, he's not the most tolerant of guys – or the most even tempered. He has this ridiculous idea that – well, I don't want to bore you.'

'You're not boring me. What's the ridiculous idea?'

'Oh, it's totally crazy. He thinks I'm trying to take his wife away from him.'

She's playing with my pepper shaker. A small trail is accumulating on the table.

'You're not, I take it?'

'Of course I'm not! I like her, yes. But I wouldn't take a man's wife from him, even if I could.'

'You're not interested in women, then?'

She moves her head to the side and gives me a quarter smile. 'No, not really. That's one thing I haven't tried yet.'

'You're quite adventurous, aren't you, Maddie?'

Her eyes sparkle. 'I'll try anything once – not absolutely anything, I'd never go potholing for example, I hate small dark spaces. But you know what I mean.'

'I've always been the opposite of you, I'm sorry to say. So cautious about everything, I could enjoy nothing.'

'Do you have lots of insurance policies, then?'

'I used to, quite a few. Until I realised what a racket it is.' My thoughts are wandering. Maddie's eyes are on mine and mine have strayed to her cleavage. I take her hand again and pull it towards me. 'I like you, Maddie. Very much.'

Our lips touch. My tongue finds its way into her mouth. Her tongue finds mine…

Then it's over. She pulls away from my grasping hands and studies her watch intently. 'It's getting late, Colin. I'm sorry, I don't want to disappoint you, but I'm not ready to… to go any further. Not yet.'

'Don't worry, I understand.'

The evening has come to an abrupt end, again. I stop panting and try to ignore the bulge in my jeans. It's my fault, I tell myself, outside the firmly closed front door. I was rash, leaping at her so suddenly like that. She'll think I'm a sex-starved, soon-to-be-jobless senior manager with a severe case of midlife crisis. It wouldn't be so far from the truth.

10 August, Friday, 8pm,

sipping a remedial glass of South West Trains' Chablis

My final illicit transactions were going well until interrupted by the untimely arrival of Mr Smarmy Pants during the penultimate customer payment, to the recently diagnosed MS sufferer Mrs Paterson. (In May, I deemed Mrs Paterson's Critical Illness Cover that she'd contributed to for seventeen years to be invalid, since she hadn't disclosed a recurring headache, toothache and various other ailments prior to taking out the policy – a decision that has nagged at me ever since.)

There I was, furtively huddled in front of my computer screen, debiting £84,311.50 from the No. 2 Settlement Account. I was about to transfer the same amount into Mrs Paterson's account when the telltale scent of my junior colleague's Brut assailed me. Assuming a nonchalant expression, I quickly restored the BBC's weekend weather forecast.

'Still hard at it, old chap?' In his habitual less-than-friendly tone, compounded by a lopsided sneer.

I sigh emphatically. 'Oh, you know how it is. Too much work, too little time. I've got a couple of outstanding cases to look at, they won't take much longer. What are you doing here? I thought you'd be on your third or fourth pint by now.'

'Just came back to pick up my overnight bag.' He unlocks the lower drawer of his desk. 'Didn't want to take it to the pub with me in case it got nicked.'

'Enjoy your weekend, Mark.' I will him a speedy exit into a waiting lift.

Instead, Mr Smarmy Pants positions his slim torso and David Beckham stubble beside me and scrutinises my screen. 'Sunny intervals, highs of twenty-five. Not a great weekend for repairing hi-fis, Col.'

I give him my most derisive look. Why won't the little shit get a move on?

He beams me his smarmiest smile. 'Hey, don't let me interrupt your important work. See you Monday, have a good one!'

'Have a shit one,' I mouth at his back.

Churlish of me, yes. But my colleague would go crawling to our bosses quicker than he'd accept another pint of London Pride at The Butcher's Hook.

After several wild flutterings in the region of my heart that I put down to delayed shock, I decide to complete the last payment of my Robin Hood scheme (to the thirteenth customer on my list) after a suitable length of time has elapsed. Two or three weeks should be enough to put Mr Smarmy Pants off the scent. Four, even, in the interests of my heart. I print out the evening's transactions, delete the confirmation file and perform the obfuscating transactions. Then I switch off my machine and rush to the lav, only to be confronted by Mr Guy Relish, mid-flow. I back out before he spots me.

Woking coming up, and a weekend of Sky Sports, renovating the hi-fi and (please, God) another meeting with the gorgeous Madeleine.

To be continued in my next instalment, all going well.

Fondest wishes,

Colin

Chapter 40

Portrait of a stranded scientist, make-do mother and weary wife

10 August, Friday

Maddie appeared in my dream this morning. She was reclining on top of a mound of rose petals, brushing her hair, naked except for a pair of high heels. We were inside an enormous room with a gold-tapped bath, one of those old-fashioned ones with claw feet. Nothing actually happened, but I woke up feeling so turned on I had to get out my latest vibrator (a super-quiet one).

Thought about the dream all day. Wouldn't dare tell Allie or Maddie, let alone Kurt.

I don't think I have any desire for Mad in real life — apart from that time when she was giving me that massage, of course. And, to be honest, when we were fooling around with the sprinkler last night (it was really hot and muggy) I did notice how shapely her breasts are. But there's no doubt in my mind — I don't want there to be anything sexual between us. She's my friend, and that's quite enough.

Still, I can't help thinking that this dream might be a sign. Could it mean that I have a latent lesbian streak which needs to come out? Or is it just a sign that I should use the vibrator more often? A long weekend with a sex-starved husband interspersed with weeks of abstinence is asking for trouble.

Chapter 41

From: Allie Loff (allie53@outlook.com)
Sent: 10 August 2018 9.01pm GMT
To: Bea Hudson (bhudson9@blueyonder.co.uk)
Subject: **Lost sheep etc**

Bad news first – Nellie has disappeared (our darling black sheep – except for a white patch over her left eye)

We've looked all over, no sign of her – think she must have wandered off when the fence mender left the gate open the other day

The other thing – went to the pub again after getting supplies in town – band was on, got chatted up by the singer I mentioned before (everyone calls him Mellow Marty)

He's about thirty at a guess, amazing looking, nearly seven feet tall, plays the guitar like Jimi Hendrix and sings like Van Morrison

Before I knew it, I was drunk – he kept buying me drinks – then he asked me to go outside with him

We smoked a joint in the pub garden, then (prepare yourself, B) we had sex behind a strangler fig!!

It was WONDERFUL

A x

From: Bea Hudson (bhudson9@blueyonder.co.uk)
Sent: 10 August 2018 9.59pm
To: Allie Loff (allie53@outlook.com)

Re: **Lost sheep etc**

Very sorry to hear about the loss of Nellie. Where do you think she went? Is there a ram around?

Re Mellow Marty – I really don't think it's a good solution to your issues with Ray to get drunk and stoned then pick up the first bloke you see in a bar, even if he is nearly seven feet, ten years younger than you and sounds like Van Morrison, Jimi Hendrix, BB King, Stevie Ray Vaughan and Stevie Wonder all rolled into one. I may sound like an old fogey, but **be careful,** you know what men are like.

From: Bea Hudson (bhudson9@blueyonder.co.uk)
Sent: 10 August 2018 10.15pm
To: Allie Loff (allie53@outlook.com)
Subject: **Spider ethics**

The experiments are still due to go ahead next week, tho we'll have to delay a couple of days as we've had problems with the uni Ethics Committee. Mrs J, the midwife, didn't like the idea of a spider at first. Must admit, the thought is starting to alarm me too. She wants us to add a clause to the volunteer paperwork stressing that they can leave the experiment at any time. Also, Hayley has now developed an ethical objection to experiments involving spiders. She's persuaded me to consider the possibility of putting an artificial spider in the scanner instead.

Mike, my colleague in the Memory and Learning Group, happened to mention a professor of AI he knows who's keen to test his group's newly developed robot spider (I'm not kidding). His name's Grommet. He makes a peculiar little rattle as he scuttles over the floor and he's covered in gingery hairs. I've never seen a spider like him, but hey, beggars can't be choosers.

We let him loose in the room that houses defunct scanners, which I thought would be the ideal test site. He was pretty nifty.

The AI prof had told me that Grommet (who he always referred to as 'he' not 'it') was designed to make 'moderate scurrying movements confined to a forty-centimetre square'. Hayley thought we might be able to place him on some kind of pedestal in the scanner tube above the prone volunteer. But it took three of us (me, Hayley and the scanner technician) nearly ten minutes to catch him. He kept changing direction just as someone was going to grab him and darted under a chair or up someone's leg. (He can climb up to just below knee height before he falls off – then he rolls over and picks himself up like an earwig.) There's supposed to be a setting in the software to control the speed and climbing ability but the AI prof couldn't make it work.

Re Mellow Marty – Are you going to see MM again? Has he offered you any more joints – or anything else? Does Ray suspect anything?

Bea

From: Bea Hudson (bhudson9@blueyonder.co.uk)
Sent: 12 August 2018 7.45pm
To: Allie Loff (allie53@outlook.com)
Subject: **Beach with Fran**

Maddie went back to south London this morning, so today it was just Fran and me for a change. (M's due back later this evening. I think she's seeing her insurance chap – she went to have her legs waxed and eyebrows threaded yesterday, both for the first time.)

I took Fran to the beach – we both swam three times, though the water was nearly ice. Fran had a great time collecting shells and pebbles and didn't throw a single one. (Kurt has banned her from throwing stones.) She didn't snap at me or sulk and did everything I asked first time – I couldn't believe it!

I think Maddie must be a good influence on her. She's only been with us one week but Fran seems even more fond of her.

She keeps telling me about things she's been doing with Auntie Maddie (face painting, toenail painting, frisbee throwing, goldfish chasing and helping M to colour her hair, to name a few).

I've told Fran not to say anything to Daddy about Maddie coming to stay with us, he wouldn't understand. It's probably not ideal, encouraging her to be deceitful, but Kurt would go mental if he found out I'm still at work and Maddie's here looking after Fran.

From: Bea Hudson (bhudson9@blueyonder.co.uk)
Sent: 13 August 2018 10.02pm
To: Allie Loff (allie53@outlook.com)
Subject: **More fun at uni**

This morning Grommet bounced along the corridor like a rubber ball while the AI prof was trying to reprogram him. Hayley and I gave chase. Hayley managed to rescue the creature just as it reached knee level on our Prof, who unfortunately happened to be outside the Small Lecture Theatre, absentmindedly staring through the window at the incinerator chimneys.

Prof: (white-faced, hand on crotch) What the hell is that?

Hayley: (picking up spider mid-rattle and transferring him back into his hutch) His name's Grommet, he's a synthetic spider. We're testing him to see if he's suitable to let loose on the volunteers.

Prof: Have you had permission for this from the Ethics Committee?

Me: Not yet – I was waiting to see if we'll be able to use him.

Prof: (crossly) I think perhaps you should review the rules covering the use of artificial intelligence in research.

Me: Right, will do.

Rush back to find a sedated Grommet. He now scurries at a more modest speed of five kilometres per hour but he still won't stay within the forty-centimetre square. I tell AI prof that we will have to ditch the artificial spider concept. We would be better off getting a toy one from a Halloween shop or a dead spider from Biosciences. He begged for one more chance to sort out Grommet, but I told him no. The road to research glory is ridden with potholes, much like the roads in Godalming.

In the afternoon, Hayley's mother came in to help us test the experimental setup with Elaine, the very-much-alive Costa Rican zebra tarantula, this time in a smaller glass box minus any obscuring rocks etc, which made her seem even bigger than before.

After Hayley and I had worked out how to insert the glass box containing the spider in the scanner tube with the aid of tape and string, Hayley's mother peered at Elaine and said she didn't want to go into the tube after all. (Hayley had reassured me that though her mother isn't keen on spiders, she doesn't have a phobia of them.) With Hayley's persuasion she changed her mind, only to faint as soon as we moved the creature from foot level to twenty centimetres above her knees. (Granted, Elaine was rearing up on her hind legs, and thrashing the rest alarmingly.)

On reflection, have decided it will be best to go back to Plan B and use video clips instead of 3D creatures, real or otherwise.

I've asked Ben (resting at home, in theory) to email me his 'phobic clips', which include a huge bulbous black spider scuttling towards the camera and a monstrously hairy one climbing over someone's bare back while they're sleeping. We've set up the projector to show a clip every ten seconds on a random part of the screen. I'll edit each clip down to half a second, which will hopefully be short enough not to trigger any fainting, panic or heart attacks among the volunteers, then insert them into the sequence of 'neutral' clips (people yawning, picking their noses, etc).

Hayley has already prepared the 'non-phobic' clip sequence from Ben's homage to Friday Fright Night, a splendid selection of B-list shockers and YouTube home movie nasties – at my request, without any razored eyeballs or distressed penises.

I thanked Hayley and Ben (via conference call) for doing such a great job of raising the anxiety stakes, and went home. Roll on Wednesday (experiment day one)!

From: Bea Hudson (bhudson9@blueyonder.co.uk)
Sent: 13 August 2018 10.07pm
To: Allie Loff (allie53@outlook.com)
Subject: **Mellow Marty**

You've been very quiet lately, Allie.

Sorry if I upset you with my comments re Mellow Marty – did I?

All my love, Bea

From: Allie Loff (allie53@outlook.com)
Sent: 13 August 2018 10.11pm GMT
To: Bea Hudson (bhudson9@blueyonder.co.uk)
Re: **Mellow Marty**

Yes, you did. But I'll get over it.

Re your experiments – feel sorry for poor Grommet.

Re Elaine – ditto. Can't imagine why anyone would agree to having a massive hairy spider come within a mile of them. Certainly not me.

Have seen MM again, you won't be pleased to hear, while Ray was out at meeting with the local rednecks (farmers, I mean). Went to his place this time. He serenaded me on his guitar. I think I am in love.

A

From: Bea Hudson (bhudson9@blueyonder.co.uk)
Sent: 14 August 2018 9.08pm
To: Allie Loff (allie53@outlook.com)
Re: **Mellow Marty**

You daft sausage! How can you be in love with this guy even if he is a seven foot, thirty-year-old musician who plays the guitar like Van Morrison?! You've only seen him a few times (and most of those were in the sack, or the great outdoors).

How's it going with him anyway?

From: Allie Loff (allie53@outlook.com)
Sent: 14 August 2018 9.15pm GMT
To: Bea Hudson (bhudson9@blueyonder.co.uk)
Re: **Mellow Marty**

Marty has told me he has to go on tour with the band for two or three months. Devastated at thought of not seeing him all that time. But it's probably just as well, Ray wouldn't have understood. A

From: Bea Hudson (bhudson9@blueyonder.co.uk)
Sent: 15 August 2018 9.30pm
To: Allie Loff (allie53@outlook.com)
Subject: **Experiment begins**

Sorry you're feeling sad, forlorn, lovesick etc – but to be honest, can't say I'm unhappy to hear Mellow Marty will be going away for a while. You're right, Ray definitely wouldn't understand.

Maddie was due to come over this morning to spend the day with Fran but she accidentally trod on her cat's paw and had to wait at the vet's half the day. The cat will be ok, but it won't go near her.

I did my best to persuade Fran to try uni childcare again but she refused to go inside so I took her up to my office and left her sitting at the table with Ben's pile of old Beano comics. (Hayley found them under his desk with his secret stash of porn photos, now safely locked in Ben's drawer.) She said she'd pop in every so often to make sure Fran was OK.

For lunch I took Fran for a veggie burger at the Psych Sci café. Some of Hayley's PhD pals came with us – they all made a big fuss of F, who purred with pleasure. In the afternoon, Fran pestered me to show her what we were doing, so I let her into the control room. She had a long chat to a volunteer who'd come to look at her brain scan, then (with Hayley's help) she lay in the scanner tube (not turned on) and watched our spider movie through the prism binoculars. After the scanning session, I settled her down with crayons and paper at the table in my office while I talked to Hayley about how she might contribute to the progress of our experiments (e.g. by cancelling her Wednesday afternoon sessions at the acupuncturist).

Re progress of day one – the first day has passed smoothly, thank goodness. The fMRI readings were a lot higher than last time, which is great news. None of our four subjects passed out or refused to go ahead with their scans, though one of the controls looked a bit pale afterwards, and Hayley had to offer her an aspirin and a glass of water.

Bea x

From: Bea Hudson (bhudson9@blueyonder.co.uk)
Sent: 16 August 2018 9.03pm
To: Allie Loff (allie53@outlook.com)
Subject: **Chaos reigns**

Just as I was about to bundle Fran into the car for another day at the Psycho Lab, Maddie turned up in her battered Beetle with her two cats in boxes. (M didn't want to leave her poorly cat alone. Her neighbour, who was going to pop in twice a day this week, had to cancel.)

Problems at uni today.

First, Hayley got a sudden migraine attack which reduced her mental capabilities even further than usual – she showed a spider phobic Ben's Fright Night montage instead of the spider sequence. I was not at all pleased, though she was so apologetic I bit back my sharp retort. Luckily I came into the control room before the sequence was halfway through, or we would have been in trouble – the scanner had been booked at 5pm by another group. I sent Hayley home and restarted the scan after much earnest pleading with the volunteer (who looked a bit shaky after what she'd seen so far and wanted to leave immediately to cook a meal for her husband) about her sense of duty, community spirit and her chance to contribute to the excellence of the UK's scientific research. Desperation can make one behave strangely.

Second, on the way out of the Psych Sciences Building, I had to walk past the Prof (nearly turned back but he'd already seen me). He was outside Room 12, waving goodbye to an important looking chap he's probably trying to poach from another uni.

Prof: (Smile turning to frown.) Hello Bea. I heard you brought your daughter into the scanner room recently. I'm sure she enjoyed the experience. But I wouldn't want her to be a distraction to the students – or to anyone else. And it's against health and safety rules, I understand.

Me: I know, I'm sorry. There was a last-minute problem with the childminder.

Prof: (hostile stare) I see.

He doesn't care one hundredth of a euro about the reason, he just wants me to know that his Psychopathology Lab is not the child-friendly environment that such centres of excellence might be in other universities. (His wife is the primary caregiver in his family, of course.)

Prof: I hope this isn't going to happen again?

Me: Of course not! It was just a one-off.

I hurried away to the safety of the car park.

Home at 6.50pm to the smell of burnt sugar, and Fran on the living room sofa.

She tells me she had fun with the cats today. Mungo likes her stroking him and hasn't bitten her yet, and Giblet has demonstrated an assortment of tricks, from peeing into Kurt's beer tankard to locating the most comfortable spot in the house (my brand new Dunlopillo pillow) and accidentally turning on the Blu-ray player.

A shriek brings me running into the kitchen. Red-cheeked, flour-flecked Maddie looks at a baking dish bubbling brownish goo in disgust, and slams the oven door shut. She pulls off the apron and tosses it to the floor.

Mad: Fuck this caramel pudding! I've just wasted three hours making this shitty pudding!

Me: It was a nice idea.

Mad: I'm going to get some fucking Ben & Jerry's!

The front door slams. In the back garden, Big Ears is on the patio barking at the cats, who look on calmly from their respective spots atop the shed roof and gas barbeque. I rescue Big Ears from the patio. Then the phone rings.

Me: Hello, Hudson residence.

It's Kurt. He sounds happy – and sozzled. He's had an upgrade to a superior executive suite on the other side of the building, away from the noisy mosque and the 'biceps-brandishing workout freak' in the apartment across the street. Work is going better than it was – so far this week he's not had to fire anyone (though the neck of the head of New Products Division is still on the chopping block). He's also found a Turkish guy who wants to manage the business over there and bribed some official to smooth the way for something or other, and if all goes well he'll be able to come back to the UK mid-September.

Me: That's not so long. Have you been drinking?

K: I'm missing you like crazy, sweetheart. I think of you constantly.

Me: I miss you too, darling.

K: How have you and Fran been getting on?

Me: Oh, fine. We've been making caramel pudding, it just came out of the oven.

K: Not missing your group at all?

Me: My group? No, no, not at all.

K: Are they managing OK without you?

Me: Yes, fine! Everything's fine.

K: Why don't you fly out here for a week? You could jump on a flight tomorrow.

Me: Tomorrow? What about Fran? Who will look after her? (And the experiments? And Hayley? And the volunteers?)

K: You could bring her with you. She would love it out here, staring at all the men with their long beards and the women in their black sheets. Then there's the whirling dervishes and the belly dancers. We could go for a boat ride on the Bosphorus. Make it a mini summer holiday.

Me: That sounds fabulous – but Fran's got the dentist tomorrow afternoon.

K: Can't you change the appointment?

Me: No, I can't – she needs to have some work done. She's got a wobbly tooth.

K: Aren't they meant to be wobbly at her age? What about Saturday then?

Me: A man is coming over to look at the damp patch in the kitchen. He's really booked up, this was the only day we could get. And Big Ears has an appointment with the vet in the afternoon-

Maddie: (yelling at the top of her voice as she comes down the hall) Got some ice cream!

K: Who's that?

Me: Just the TV. Fran's got it turned up really loud.

K: It sounded just like Madeleine.

Me: A lot of people sound like her, she's got one of those voices

Giblet jumps up on the counter with a piercing miaow. Fran runs in with a scream of excitement, clapping her hands and tries to prise off the lid of the ice cream container. Big Ears starts barking.

K: What the devil's going on there? Was that a cat?

Me: It's only Fran making silly noises. I'm sorry sweetheart, I'm going to have to sort things out here – I'm in the middle of getting dinner. I'll talk to you tomorrow.

Kurt growls and Mungo starts snarling at Big Ears.

I put down the phone and go to lock myself in the bathroom.

Chapter 42

Miss Madeleine Geen

16 August, Session 9, 4pm

Miss Geen arrived with flushed cheeks and messy hair, her shirt missing a button.

Before I could speak, we were interrupted by barking and a child's laughter from the reception area.

MG: Nigel, I'm so sorry about this. I hope you don't mind if Fran and the dog wait for me in the waiting room. I had to bring them - Bea's at work and I'm meant to be looking after Fran. I asked Jane, she said it would be OK so long as they're quiet.

I tell her they are welcome to wait outside, for this week only.

MG: I won't need to do this again, the childminder's due back next week. I'm sorry I couldn't make it last week, I was so busy looking after Fran and walking the dog and everything. I rang on Monday afternoon to explain and Jane said as it was a special situation there wouldn't be a charge-

NR: That's quite all right. You're here now, at least - your new family included.

Miss G smiles. Her skin is tanned. There are freckles on her nose and her teeth seem even whiter than

before. A faint scent of perfume, or hair product…
My thoughts are briskly interrupted by two barks.

Child: Stop it, Big Ears! What did I tell you?

Miss Geen bites her lip and frowns at the door.

MG: I'll go and tell them to be quiet, shall I?

NR: No, stay where you are, please. I'll deal with
it.

I open the door to reception and ask Jane to take
out the rubber bone, tennis ball and packet of
cheese pretzels from the bottom-right drawer of my
desk.

MG: Prepared for everything, aren't you? I'm sorry
I had to bring them, but Bea was desperate. It's so
weird, Nigel, being transplanted into a family. And
it's knackering having to look after Fran and Big
Ears all day, as well as my cats. (Smile.) I almost
brought them too, but thought better of it.

NR: Family life isn't quite the blissful scenario
you imagined?

MG: It's been eye-opening. I've had to yell at Fran
and threaten to lock her in the conservatory – Bea
says I have to make sure she goes in there for two
hours every day. It's a punishment from Kurt. I
understand now what it's like for Bea. Fran is such
a handful! So wilful! And so cunning! She tries
everything she can to get me to sit in with her
when she's supposed to be alone, or else Big Ears
or the cats – she feels ill or she has to go to the
toilet or there's something she has to tell me that
can't wait. Of course, I'm not her mum, I'm Auntie
Maddie – if I went away she would probably miss me
for a day and then forget about me. (Winds a strand

of hair around her finger.) But I love her so much. I love being with her, even when I have to tell her off – I love it all. I don't want this to end.

NR: You know that it must end, don't you?

MG: I suppose. Katie's back next week, Bea won't need me so much then. Things will go back to normal. I'll be back at home with my sculptures and cats for company.

NR: How are you going to manage without this little girl?

MG: I don't know. (A heavy sigh.)

NR: Have you had any more thoughts about setting up home with Bea and her daughter? Or could this be the first stage of your planned takeover?

MG: Do you think I'm a fruit cake, Mr Rowley?

NR: We all have dark undercurrents–

MG: She's far too attached to her husband for me to even think about anything like that – and she's convinced she'll become an instant lesbian if she as much as holds hands with another woman. Anyway, I've got a new lover. He wouldn't be too happy if I got up to anything with Bea.

NR: A new lover?

MG: The insurance manager. His name's Colin. I told you about him, remember?

NR: Of course, Madeleine. I thought you weren't interested in him because he's not athletic enough, or trim enough, or good enough looking.

MG: He's not that bad, after all. When we went to bed recently, I got quite a shock. His belly has melted away, he's actually got muscles – he says he's been working out. His thighs were rock hard and so was… Well, I won't bore you with the details.

NR: So, you had sex with him?

MG: Yes, it was amazing. A bit slow to start with – the DVD player went on the blink halfway through *The Day of the Triffids*, then he knocked his wine onto the floor while he was kissing me. We went up to the bedroom and he had trouble taking off my boots, then his alarm went off just as he'd got me undressed. It was so funny… Are you sure you want to hear all this?

NR: Please tell me whatever you are comfortable telling me.

MG: You're enjoying this, aren't you?

NR: I assure you I'm here to listen, not to get gratuitous pleasure. But sex is a very important part of the psyche, you know. To Freud it was–

MG: Why are you staring at my chest? Oops, my button's not done up. (Adjusts her blouse to remove the gap.) Why didn't you tell me my shirt was bulging open?

NR: It's not up to me to tell my patients how to dress, Madeleine. I apologise if I've caused you any concern.

Ten seconds silence.

MG: It's funny, now I've slept with Colin, things aren't the same. I want to see him again. Soon.

NR: Why is that, do you think?

MG: I suppose it's the same old story. Man gives woman a good time in bed, she falls in love with him and they live happily ever after - except that won't happen with us.

NR: Because?

MG: Because I've lost my faith in men, I think they're all out to hurt me. Isn't it obvious?

NR: But you want to trust them. You could make a start here, perhaps. With me?

MG: I could, I suppose. Then again… Some men are more trustworthy than others, don't you think? (Puts her head back and stretches out as if she's at home in front of a cosy fire.) Excuse me, I need a good kip. (Sandalled foot twirls. Strappy sandals, showing off sparkling blue toenails.)

NR: On the matter of our future therapeutic relationship, Madeleine - I note that our tenth session is coming up next week. If you would like to continue-

MG: Are you married, Nigel?

NR: Yes, I've been married for nearly thirty years - we have two grown-up children. Why do you ask?

MG: Just wondering. You seem like a respectable guy. Conventional, and so on.

NR: In some respects, perhaps.

MG: You wouldn't take a leak in the street, or run off to Bermuda with one of your patients?

NR: Do you think I'm too conventional to be able to help you?

MG: I'm not saying that. Why are you always twisting my words? I want to find out a bit about you, that's all. I tell you all my stuff, and you sit there doodling! And don't tell me it's a Freud thing!

NR: I'm sorry if I gave you that impression. I think we need to take a good hard look at whether our sessions should continue.

MG: You don't think they should?

NR: I wonder if you ought to consider another therapist. To be frank, Madeleine, you seem to find it hard to trust me. I know you had a difficult relationship with your parents-

MG: I'm sorry, I don't want to talk about my childhood yet again.

NR: You have only talked about it once, very briefly, in my recollection-

MG: That's quite enough. I am who I am. Dragging up the past won't change it.

NR: It's up to you what we talk about, and where we go from here.

MG: (Quietly) Colin could be a good father, I think. He's kind and responsible. He hasn't had any kids, yet.

NR: Does he want children?

MG: I don't know. He wanted them with his ex but she wasn't keen. She wanted to wait for her career to blossom - then his brother took her to bed and their marriage was history.

NR: Would you like to have a child with him?

MG: Yes, I would.

This seemed to surprise her.

NR: Thank you Madeleine, we'll have to leave it there, I'm afraid. Perhaps before our next session you could think about whether you would like us to continue for another ten sessions.

MG: Right you are, Nigel. See you next week.

She gathered up her bag and its disparate contents (which had spread across the floor during the session), smiled disarmingly and strode out of my office, leaving behind an elusive scent of jasmine.

From the waiting room:

Woof woof!

Auntie Maddie!

Hey, guys!

Chapter 43

From: adriansmith@luciouslawnsltd.co.uk
Sent: 17 August 2018 10.32pm
To: khudson@computercorp.com
Subject: **Report 3**

Hi Kurt,

Did what you suggested and had a wander over to the ladies this evening. As I could not think of a suitable pretext, I decided to offer my services should they need anything done around the place while the master of the house is away.

Your wife opened the door looking like she'd been asleep – her eye pencil was smudged and there were long, light coloured (dog?) hairs all over her blouse. She didn't twig who I was straight off and didn't seem to grasp the substance of my offer, so I elucidated, 'Unblocking sinks, lifting heavy objects, climbing up ladders to rescue cats – I notice you've had a few extra animals around lately.'

She said those were her friend's cats, she was looking after them for a 'little while'.

'So you're doing OK then,' I said, as she had made no move to invite me in.

Just then a child screamed and someone yelled, 'Bea, where the hell are you, Mungo's scratched Fran!'

Your wife ran into the house leaving me on the doorstep with the door wide open. After hearing various signs of commotion and distress I took it upon myself to step inside.

Fran was in the kitchen crying and holding out her bleeding arm. Your wife was yelling, 'I can't find any disinfectant,' and the blonde was yelling, 'Where are your bandages, we have to take her to the hospital, you can get blood poisoning from cat scratches.' A fat black cat was cowering under a chair and a mottled grey cat was curled up in a fruit bowl on the table. Your dog was running around the kitchen barking. I said I'd get a first aid kit from next door, but I don't think any of them heard me.

Long story short, I administered the appropriate first aid (being St John Ambulance trained), disinfected and dressed the wound (no more than a scratch) and gave my opinion i.e. that there was no point in visiting the hospital. The blonde started googling her mobile for health advice.

Your wife was clearly relieved at my intervention and offered me a drink. 'I think we all need one,' she said, pouring out three glasses of Maker's Mark. I did not decline, thinking this would be a useful opportunity for further close observation.

'Thanks for coming to our rescue, Adrian,' the blonde said with what I can only describe as a meaningful look. Her top was covered in a dried-up white substance. She apologised for looking 'such a fright' (she and Fran had been working on her 'rat sculpture').

'What were you doing to Mungo?' Bea asked Fran. There followed a discussion as to whether or not Fran had pulled the cat's tail and whether or not the cat was a danger and should be immediately taken from the house. Your daughter's nose and cheeks became bright red, she became very agitated and said it wasn't her fault the cat scratched her, she hadn't done anything.

Bea shouted back, 'Of course it's your fault, you've only got what you deserved!' The blonde said she had better take the cats home and Bea said, 'No don't, they can stay until you leave.'

I excused myself, saying I urgently needed the bathroom and I would show myself out.

Adrian

From: khudson@computercorp.com
Sent: 17 August 2018 10.59pm GMT
To: adriansmith@luciouslawnsltd.co.uk
Re: **Report 3**

Very resourceful of you Adrian & many thanks for keeping me informed.

Kurt

Chapter 44

From: Bea Hudson (bhudson9@blueyonder.co.uk)
Sent: 17 August 2018 1.23pm
To: Allie Loff (allie53@outlook.com)
Subject: **Update on experiments**

So big sis, how's it going over there? Are you still upset with me? Hope you are bearing up OK and not pining for Mellow Marty?

Postcard from Mum arrived. She's met lots of interesting people (men that is) since she parted from Janice, including a Polish librarian, an Italian student, who has fallen in love with her, and, most recently, a Bulgarian chef. No mention of bed size. She says she should have done this four years ago instead of all that moping around reading Dad's old letters.

All went well at the lab this morning. We're getting excellent signals in the BLA (inside the amygdala, this plays an important part in the brain's fear response system) again, as well as all the usual sites. Also, we have definite signs of activity in a structure called the bed nucleus of the stria terminalis (BNST) – it's involved in threat monitoring, (also FYI it's twice as large in men as it is in women, and may be responsible for gender identity disorder).

Ben phoned from his sick bed to ask if Hayley had ruined anything yet. I said no, not yet.

Bea x

From: Bea Hudson (bhudson9@blueyonder.co.uk)

Sent: 17 August 2018 5.31pm
To: Allie Loff (allie53@outlook.com)
Subject: **Update 2 on experiments**

A small glitch this afternoon. One of the control group volunteers had an extended sneezing fit fifteen minutes from the end of her scan while watching the spider-less scary film clips that Ben put together. She told us to stop everything, she needed a glass of water. I told her I was very sorry but the scan would be invalid, we'd have to do another one from the beginning. She said, 'I'm sorry dear,' jumped out of the scanner tube and ran out of the room.

As the scanner was booked again at 5pm and we have only two full days left next week to finish our experiment and there was no one else who I could think of to ask to step in at zero notice, I made an executive decision to volunteer myself as her replacement. I thought I ought to, being roughly the same age as the woman who'd absconded. Besides, I felt a moral obligation to share in the distress of our volunteers.

Things went well enough until about halfway through, at the clip of a woman in a dark alley about to strangled by a psychotic stalker. By the end of the experiment, I could think of nothing except going home to down a strong G&T.

I'll be relieved when the last scanning session is over.

Hope to hear from you v soon, Allie.

Lots of love, Bea

Chapter 45

From: adriansmith@luciouslawnsltd.co.uk
Sent: 20 August 2018 7.51pm
To: khudson@computercorp.com
Subject: **Report 4**

9.15am: Your wife left the house carrying a small black leather case and walked briskly down the road in the direction of the railway station.

10.30am: The blonde drove off with Fran in your BMW.

3.15pm: I returned from a lawn replacement job to much giggling and high spirits from your back garden – the blonde and Fran, it became apparent. I couldn't see what they were up to from the terrace or anywhere else in my place. They weren't in the paddling pool as I had initially assumed. At one point I heard Fran say, 'Aren't you going to put on some whiskers?' BTW no sign of any ill effects from the cat attack.

5.30pm: Both went inside then came back out at 6.15pm with cushions and proceeded to do yoga exercises on the lawn (back arches, the downward dog and the lion pose – Jackie does these too). More giggling while the blonde demonstrated (in very short shorts and a cut-off top) and Fran attempted to follow. Then the blonde got Fran to hang onto her back while she went into more downward dogs.

7.10pm: Your wife returned home.

Adrian

From: adriansmith@luciouslawnsltd.co.uk
Sent: 20 August 2018 9.15pm
To: khudson@computercorp.com
Subject: **Report 5**

I hope you don't think I am overreacting, Kurt, but thought you should know about a suspicious incident I observed between your wife and the blonde which took place just now.

I was helping Jacks clean up in the kitchen after our evening meal (fostering goodwill as have had the silent treatment since I made the mistake of saying her new dress made her look frumpy) when I happened to see a movement in your kitchen. The lights were on as it was getting dark and the blinds had not been drawn. I am fairly certain of what I saw even though our two houses are not particularly close. The blonde and your wife came together and locked into an embrace which lasted quite a while. They were standing by the sink. The light was good so I could see your wife's face clearly. Her eyes were shut for much of the time. I did not see the other's face as her head was turned away but I noted her hand move in a regular movement across your wife's back – a gesture of affection (or possibly something else).

I was about to run and get my binoculars (which I had some hours earlier placed in the room next to the terrace for observation of any garden activities) when the women separated and were no longer visible.

Of course, there may not be anything at all in this observation. It is possible that the two women were simply comforting each other as women do. (Bea looked rather more stressed out than usual.) I was concerned however that there may be another explanation of a more disturbing nature, so I took it on myself to slip out into the garden and stand at the fence opposite the smaller kitchen window. It is a warm night here and this window had been left open. (Told Jackie I was going to check the fence as it seemed to be broken.)

During the seven to eight minutes that I listened I heard the two women talking but I could not make out any words. However, I did hear a moaning sound, repeated several times. Unfortunately, I could not tell whose moan it was. After this, I hurried back to Jackie who was calling me to come and watch *Shetland* on the telly.

BTW the fence is now actually broken as I took the liberty of preparing entry for future covert missions. As we had a new fence put up at some expense last year, I'm sure you will agree to cover the cost of any repairs?

Yours, Adrian

From: khudson@computercorp.com
Sent: 20 August 2018 9.35pm GMT
To: adriansmith@luciouslawnsltd.co.uk
Subject: **Reports 4 & 5**

Talk to you about this soon. I'm getting the next flight home.

Kurt

Chapter 46

From: Allie Loff (allie53@outlook.com)
Sent: 20 August 2018 10.27pm GMT
To: Bea Hudson (bhudson9@blueyonder.co.uk)
Subject: **New life**

sorry I've not replied to yr emails, B

not checked my mail for a week

have been with MM, sneaking out when Ray asleep or at farmers meetings

he's asked me to go on tour with him

i've said yes

we leave in an hour

A

From: Bea Hudson (bhudson9@blueyonder.co.uk)
Sent: 20 August 2018 10.43pm
To: Allie Loff (allie53@outlook.com)
Re: **New life**

Allie!! I'm shocked to hear of this sudden decision. I hope you'll be happy with your thirty-year-old guitarist and you enjoy his gigs – and I suppose you'll get to see a decent chunk of Queensland along the way. Though as a middle-aged, no-spring-chicken rock chick, you'll have to get used to fighting off the teenage groupies

Actually, dare I say, I can understand Ray's point of view. He brings you to the country he loves and has missed like crazy for years, hoping you'll be able to make a go of things with him, and instead you're chronically homesick, panic-stricken by anything that moves, especially if it has more than two legs, and generally make a pig's ear of helping to run the farm – all of which would be quite forgivable as you're a townie at heart, and of course emigrating to the other side of the world is bound to be a pretty unsettling experience. But then, to top it all, just because you've been feeling a bit neglected of late and your hubby's not as slim as he once was, you go and throw yourself at the first stranger who gives you the eye and decide to elope with him.

Sorry if I sound cynical and unempathetic. However, 'the grass is always greener' is a useful phrase that often comes to mind when I'm tempted by something alluring but utterly impractical. I would strongly suggest that you get on the first bus back and tell Ray you were suffering from a midlife moment/brain fart/ chronic homesick-induced overreaction.

Got back this evening from uni exhausted after another day dealing with late/menstruating/hyperventilating volunteers, to find a peculiar rash all over my neck. Experiment-induced stress, possibly. Also found Maddie busy finishing her sculpture of a sharp-toothed, pop-eyed rat gnawing through a thick cable (?!!?) She'd forgotten to get dinner so I prepared some soggy broccoli and burnt fish cakes.

To top off the day perfectly, Fran refused to turn off the TV and go to bed. I lost control, shouted, 'Selfish little bitch!' and burst into tears.

Maddie calmed me down. She gave me a relaxing herbal tea and put on her meditation CD – I fell asleep before the end. Now full of remorse.

Let me know how it goes with Van Morrison number two.

One more day of the experiment to go, hope I can last out.

Bea

Chapter 47

What to do about Madeleine?

21/8/18, Tuesday

3.45pm, arrival

Thunderstorm and long taxi queue greet me. Roars from the furious beast up in gunmetal sky. I know how he feels. I'm ready to unleash all on my duplicitous wife. She will not find me merciful. I will not be moved by tears or pleas for forgiveness. She will be sorry for betraying me – and Madeleine will be even sorrier.

A prickly heat deep under the skin is making me scratch as if I've caught fleas, or a nasty case of the clap. Throat now bone dry despite third piece of gum. Soon I will be in that house and I will know the truth. I will see with my own eyes what the hidden cameras have recorded, for better or for worse.

Approach house. All blinds drawn at the front. Wait for minute on doorstep, listening. Faint sound of female voices from within. Insert key and shut door silently. The voices are definitely coming from upstairs. Park my wheelie bag, softly ascend stairs. Giggling, getting louder as I approach the master bedroom.

Hey, keep still! I can't do this with you wriggling about so much.

I grip the door handle, preparing to encounter two naked women in the full torrent of lust.

But they aren't. Goldilocks is standing at the dressing table holding a small pot in one hand and a long brush in the other, with which she dabs gold powder around my daughter's eyes. Then she drops the brush onto the carpet with a gasp.

Fran stays sitting on the stool, facing the mirror. Her face is a fright – lips daubed with crimson, cheeks on fire, lashes longer than Mary Quant ever wore. She's wearing a flimsy gold 'dress' with an overstuffed bra and looks like a showgirl in a Paris nightclub, to be kind.

What the fuck are you doing with my daughter? My voice is loud, if not steady. I note Fran bodily cringe away from me and Madeleine's wide eyes and slackening jaw, as if she's been addressed by Boris Johnson in his cycling gear. Meanwhile, the rash grips my balls like chilli sauce on gnocchi. I am not a maniac, I tell myself. I must calm down, get things in perspective. Things are not so bad. Goldilocks was not doing unmentionable things to my wife.

Madeleine bares her teeth, hands on hips, nostrils flaring like a bull about to charge. Don't you talk to me like that! We were dressing up, that's all. She wanted to look like an Egyptian princess.

With a strong flavour of Soho strumpet, by the look of it!

Fran stares up at me as if I am a two-headed alien. It's all right, Daddy, Maddie was being nice to me. Don't be cross with her.

The plaintive voice and doe eyes do not quench my anger. I take Fran's arm and pull her towards me. Go and wipe that shit off your face this minute, please! And take that ridiculous thing off and put some decent clothes on!

Fran scampers out of the room. Goldilocks glowers at me.

You shouldn't talk to her like that.

She starts grabbing at the melange of boxes, pots, tubes and trays overflowing with colourful substances on the dressing table. On the bed is a heap of bizarre, over-bright clothing, among which I spot the TK Maxx dress Bea wore to a friend's farewell party and immediately abandoned, saying it made her look like a middle-aged woman trying to relive her youth.

Please, don't tell me how to talk to my own daughter. And perhaps you would mind explaining to me what the hell you're doing with Fran, when my wife is meant to be at home looking after her?

Bea asked me to come over and look after Fran, she says after a sizeable pause. She had to go into work.

Work?

The psychopath thingy lab, at the university.

I know where she works, Madeleine. I was expressing surprise at the fact that she's at work at all.

There's an experiment going on today, she needed to go in.

I put on my best barrister's voice.

It's not just today you've been here, is it, Madeleine?

She glares at me, claws at the ready, and rushes out of the bedroom.

I follow her into the 'spare room', now awash with the garish, hippy-style clothes favoured by Mad, tossed across the bed, draped over the backs of chairs, looped onto door handles. Everywhere is a litter of massage oil bottles, candles and sketch books. Incriminating with a capital 'I' to the most dull-witted observer. As Nosey Neighbour pointed out, Goldilocks has secretly set up shop in my house with my wife and daughter.

Madeleine leans over the bed, gathering objects and shoving them into a large canvas bag. Without her display of bravado, she looks a little scared.

It's not what it looks like, Kurt. I'm just staying here to help out with Fran while Bea's busy at uni.

How long have you been staying here? Please, don't lie to me.

Since Tuesday.

Since last Tuesday?

The Tuesday before last, actually.

The Tuesday before last? I repeat with incredulity. So, you've been here for two weeks?

Bea was going to tell you before but she was worried about how you'd react–

Because I might think it a little odd that my wife has handed over the care of our child to her friend, who's never had children herself and doesn't have a clue about how to look after anyone else's? (And obviously has no moral code whatsoever, I refrain from adding.)

Tell me Madeleine, what's going on between you and my wife? Do you give her a little of what she likes every night to keep her mind off me?

I have gone too far. I sound like a paranoid maniac. A disturbingly light-headed sensation is making the ground ripple, as if we are in the centre of an earthquake. Goldilocks edges away from me with an anxious glint in her eyes, simultaneously scanning her scattered possessions as if calculating which ones to grab before running for her life.

Please, I say, take your things and leave. And I would be grateful if you didn't come into my home any more.

You don't need to worry about that, she mutters, turning her back on me as she resumes tossing articles into bags. I'm not planning to come back in a hurry.

And while you're at it... (I retreat to the landing.) Please stay well away from my daughter.

I stomp downstairs. In the kitchen, I find a note in Bea's writing:

Mad, pls walk dog and don't let Fran have any more ice cream!

Pour myself a generous glass of Woodford Reserve Kentucky Bourbon Whiskey and take it to the terrace. Survey the wilderness of our garden (untended flowers and proliferating weeds, trampoline, paddling pool and a clutter of large, pale, rat-like objects by the fishpond). On the other side of my newly broken fence (three planks laid horizontal), wisteria clings to next door's terrace.

The thought of speaking to Adrian again makes me groan. My hand shakes as I put down an empty glass. Realise belatedly that it's raining. Come back inside drenched, in time to meet Goldilocks coming downstairs loaded like a donkey.

She comes up to me. Her eyes are the same level as mine, she's so damn tall.

Just for the record, Mr Hudson, Bea and I aren't up to anything. She loves you and she wouldn't risk losing your love. If you can't see that, you're a fucking idiot.

With that, she's gone.

Could she be telling the truth? I'm tempted to believe her. I need to believe her.

Then I remember last night's embrace, the fun had with the garden hosepipe, the hair grip I found under the sofa while installing the spycams and the skimpy underwear Goldilocks gave to my wife. That woman is a temptress. She has the cravings of a dozen cats on heat and the moral fibre of a slug. I wouldn't trust her as much as I'd trust all the pontifications ever made about Brexit.

6.15pm, search for the truth

Refill glass and pursue the hidden cameras. The tissue-box cam is nowhere to be seen in the kitchen and the prospect of standing on a chair to grope inside the smoke detector from the ceiling does not appeal. The crafty alarm clock, however, is still ticking away on my bedside table. Hands trembling, I open the compartment and remove the memory card. I am about to slot it into my iPad when I am interrupted by the sound of the front door closing. A voice comes up from the hall.

Kurt, is that you?!

I slip the card into my jeans pocket. I descend the stairs slowly.

Bea drops her laptop bag on the hall floor and advances open-mouthed towards me.

What are you doing here?

Darling, how lovely to see you, I say. I was wondering when you were going to make it home. Have you been having a nice time?

I stop three stairs above Bea, who stands three stairs from the bottom of the staircase, gripping the banister. Her face is moist and pink and she's breathing heavily. Her next words come out strained and tremulous.

Where's Fran?

I wait a while to wring out the maximum possible anxiety.

She's in her room taking off the make-up that was plastered all over her face, and the gaudy costume I found her in. Your friend seemed to think it would be fun to dress our daughter up as a hooker.

Where's Maddie?

I threw her out of the house and told her she's not welcome here again. I don't want her hanging around my daughter anymore – or my wife.

Bea's mouth opens even wider. I carry on. My anger is straining at the leash.

I think you have some explaining to do, don't you? You let me believe you were here looking after Fran these past two weeks. I come home and find you out at work and your girlfriend moved in, doing her best to corrupt our daughter!

Maddie is my best friend. I trusted her to look after Fran.

You trusted that woman to be responsible for our daughter? Words fail me. She couldn't look after a guinea pig, let alone a child!

She has two cats!

That woman is a bloodsucker. She'll take what she wants from you and bugger off. I just can't believe you had the nerve to arrange all this behind my back. I go away from our weekend together thinking we'd turned a corner, that you really wanted things to work out. I trusted you.

Bea starts to look guilty.

Darling, I'm sorry. Today was the last day of our critical experiments, I had to be at the lab. I wanted to tell you, I was going to tell you. But it never was the right time. Everything happened at once. Ben fell off his motorbike and Fran bit Molly's finger and was expelled from playgroup and Katie threatened to resign... I couldn't cope with it all. So I asked Mad for help.

A twinge of sympathy threatens to intrude on my outrage.

You're not making any sense, Bea. Why didn't you tell me any of this? Why didn't you tell me you were going to ask Madeleine to stay? Why did you have to go behind my back?

Bea bites her lip.

I was scared of what you'd say. I knew you'd want me to stay at home. But I had to go into uni and keep things going!

So you totally ignored my views and moved in Little Miss Mother's Helper? That was very convenient, I must say. She was on hand for all those other little necessities. Why, I'm surprised you didn't put her in our bed with you – there's plenty of room, with me out of the way.

Her face goes the colour of our rhododendron bush and her voice rises an octave.

You're crazy! How could you think of such a thing? There's nothing going on between us, I've already told you!

She takes a step down the stairs, away from me, then stumbles. She sways precariously. One leg buckles under her. An arm flails out towards the handrail but misses.

Oh shit!

Bea topples backwards melodramatically and might have hurt herself, had not my lightning reflexes allowed me to reach out just in time to catch her. I pull her close. Whatever she's done or not done, I love her more than anything else in the whole world.

Fuck, that was close.

Her face is white now.

I want to believe you, I say.

I swear, Kurt, there's nothing going on. She's my friend, that's all.

So there's absolutely nothing untoward going on between you and Madeleine? Cross your heart and hope to die?

Cross my heart and hope to die.

In that case, why did you tell Madeleine that you didn't want me to find out about it?

Find out about what?

That's what I'd like to know. Your friend said I was bound to find out sooner or later, and you said you didn't want me to know. I heard it word for word, Bea, from my iPhone in the hotel, just a week or so ago. You obviously didn't realise your phone had called mine and was relaying your conversation.

Oh, Kurt! We were talking about your Garmin! How could you think–

My Garmin? What about my Garmin?

I – well – actually…

Bea? What have you done?

Big Ears jumped up for a piece of toast and it fell into his bowl and got all wet, so I sent it off to be repaired, it won't be long now…

A long wail from Fran's room.

Mummy! Where are you?

You'd better go, I say.

Bea reaches the top of the stairs, and turns to face me.

Just a minute, Kurt. Did you come back today on purpose to try and catch me out?

Darling, how could you suggest such a thing? I was missing you like crazy. Then a little bird told me that all was not exactly as I would have hoped, back at the ranch–

What are you talking about?

It's a figure of speech, my dear, it means–

Have you been spying on me?

A spasm erupts in my heart.

I wouldn't put it like that. I've taken a few minor precautions, that's all.

You have, haven't you? You asked that slimy Adrian next door to creep around the bushes at night. Mad saw him standing by the fence the other night, she nearly coshed him with a wine bottle.

She doesn't know about the spycams. I offer up a silent prayer of gratitude.

Adrian kindly volunteered to do what he could to keep an eye on the house while I was away, I explain. He seems to have got a little carried away, by the sounds of it.

How dare you! No wonder the slimeball was so keen to stop over the other evening when Fran got scratched by Maddie's cat.

Excuse me? Fran got scratched by Maddie's cat?

She brought the cats over because her neighbour had to go to a funeral, so there was no one to look after them. They were perfectly all right–

Except that they attacked my daughter! How could you let that crazy woman and her two nutso cats into this house?

They were quite well behaved, once Big Ears had stopped chasing them. The problem was, Fran was pulling the black one's tail...

By this time my face feels distinctly warm and is, quite likely, also the colour of our rhododendron bush. I retire to the kitchen and pour myself another, nearly full tumbler of Bourbon, which I take with me as I survey the house for untoward signs.

Madeleine's artistic implements are bundled into cardboard boxes and plastic beakers on the table in the dining room along with a jumble of wires, cut-up pieces of card, bits of broken wood, bubble wrap and polystyrene. On the hob, a spongy mass erupts from a baking tray, which couldn't have been created by my wife. When was the last time Bea baked a cake? Fran would have appreciated the culinary treats and the unusual play scenarios, no doubt. Artistic mornings and dressing-up afternoons... and what have we here?

I scan the DVDs and Blu-rays in the living room stacked on the cabinet's highest, Fran-proof shelf. *Sex and the City* series one to three, *Mad Men* series one to six – tasteless, but hardly evidence of debauchery. Ditto for *The Exorcist, Terminator 3* and *Mrs Doubtfire*. I scan the room. Nothing remotely suspicious.

Go upstairs to find Fran on her bed, with Selima, being rocked on Bea's lap. Fran sucks her thumb. Her hair is mussed. Traces of tears on her cheeks, now scrubbed of make-up. The remains of black eyeliner on the lower rim of an eye. When she sees me, she screws up her face.

Don't be like that, sweetie, I say. Daddy was upset earlier, but he's not anymore.

Daddy isn't upset with you, darling, interjects Bea. Just with Mummy.

Everything's OK, sweetie pie.

I attempt to kiss Fran's brow but her head dips away. She looks at me as if I've stolen Selima.

Where is Auntie Maddie gone?

Daddy told her to leave, Bea says, moving Fran off her lap. He doesn't like her being here.

Why?

You'll have to ask him yourself, darling.

Fran looks at me, her face scrunched up as if about to cry.

Why are you so nasty to Auntie Maddie?

I exit the room as gracefully as possible. Now I am Mr Nasty.

The search is not yet over, I remind myself. As expected, a careful inspection of the master bedroom reveals little of interest – a book on yoga postures on one bedside table and a bottle of Triple Sec on the other, on top of a badly-spelled, badly-splodged sheet of paper entitled 'Janine Appleyard, Assignment 4 – Dr Hudson, Cognitive Neuroscience 2'.

No bondage, hardcore or homoerotica. Of course, they wouldn't have been stupid enough to leave their girlie magazines and crotchless panties in full view of anyone wandering in – they'd be securely put away. But where? I find myself hesitating in front of Bea's chest of drawers before rummaging through a chaotic assortment of undergarments. Footless tights tangling with garter belts, fingerless gloves grappling with strapless bras and skimpy panties... Nothing out of the ordinary, though. No whips, fishnets or leather knicks.

I try the drawer on the right, usually locked. To my surprise, it opens.

Then a voice cold enough to freeze hell, if not my Istanbul hotel room.

What are you doing, snooping around in my things? What do you think you'll find, a picture of Maddie posing naked?

Shit. Double, triple shit.

Just checking, I say. I'm sorry if this appears to be extreme behaviour, darling. But if you believed I was having a fling with Adrian next door, you'd be concerned too.

I didn't think Adrian was your type.

For a moment, I want to slap her. I want her to know the endless pain of doubting, of imagining the worst. But I say nothing, just slink downstairs to the drinks enclave and pour myself another generous measure of Woodford Reserve.

What have I done? Why can't I simply let myself be loved, rather than risk ruining everything with my paranoia and insecurities? First, I was jealous of our daughter and all of the hugs, kisses, giggles, attention and concern Bea bestowed upon her – and then I was jealous of all the men Bea had ever set eyes on in turn, from Sweaty Mike to the Cranially Challenged Adrian, Nosey Neighbour par excellence. Then, in a climax worthy of a Catholic priest and the cutest choirboy, I decide that my wife is betraying me with her best friend. At this rate, the kind, lovely, intelligent woman that I adore will soon realise she's made a terrible mistake and should not be within twenty miles of a blundering oaf such as myself.

After a while, my hands aren't so steady anymore, nor is my vision. I have a brief urge to go into the garden and throw up. No, that might look bad. Adrian will be loitering by the gap in the fence, ears waggling. And now Fran is coming into the kitchen, hair damp, dressing-gowned and slippered. I hide my glass of whiskey behind the stack of cereal boxes for recycling. She blinks up at me as if I'm a bear that might swipe off her head at any moment.

Hello, sweetie. Don't look so frightened. I love you, remember that. I'll always love you. I'm just having some problems right now.

Do you love Mummy too?

Yes, I love Mummy.

Why are you fighting with Mummy, then?

I'm a dork that's why. A prize dork.

Normally, such a comment would result in a gale of laughter. This time there's not the faintest flicker of amusement.

Fran looks at the floor.

I don't want to be an orphan.

No, we won't let you be an orphan. You're safe with us, Frannie. Very safe. We won't leave you – or each other.

You promise, Daddy?

I promise.

The words slip out. It's too late to retract them, or add a proviso. I have made a solemn promise to my daughter.

I hug Fran and get her a mug of warm milk with a spoonful of honey. Then I retrieve my tumbler of whiskey and iPad, go into the bathroom and lock the door.

7.25pm

Insert memory card in iPad, open video app and transfer video files. Can't get the sound to work. After several minor glitches, sit on the toilet with a hammering heart and begin my private viewing.

Dozens of time-and-date-stamped images of our bedroom pass across the screen. The resolution is not too bad and the camera adjusts well to the varying light levels. Though the DVR is set to record only for a short burst after detecting motion, there's not a lot going on of interest. Just Bea scantily wisping from bed to door after the alarm goes off at 6.45am, performing vigorous leg raises, cycling, etc on the mattress, opening and closing drawers multiple times before selecting each item of clothing, and the like. At night, there's a period of energised tapping into her laptop from her position in bed, propped up against numerous pillows (usually 9pm to 10pm), and occasional flipping through sheets of paper with a red pen and anguished expression before lights out (10pm to 11.30pm).

Fast forward through the weekday routine, the weekend routine. Goodness, I never realised Bea was such a creature of habit. Even the nightly 3am to 4am visit to the ensuite is recorded, complete with toilet flush (fortunately the camera can't see beyond the doorway).

Keep watching despite growing unease. I shouldn't be watching my wife's private moments like this. At the same time, it feels reassuring, this portrait of Bea's fundamental continuity. And I'm watching this stuff for a good reason – aren't I?

July ends. August rolls on. There are minor variations on the theme. Sometimes Fran comes into the room at 2am or 3am with Selima or Mr Gruffy and leaves after receiving hugs. Sometimes Bea gets out of bed around 4am and returns with a plate of toast and peanut butter.

No salacious encounters whatsoever.

I am losing the ability to stay upright, even though I'm still sitting on the toilet seat. My hand lashes out to grab the toilet-roll holder. The alcohol is conspiring with my brain to turn my body into a puddle on the floor. But I keep watching.

Uh oh, what's this? One morning after finishing her stomach-flattening exercises, Bea takes off her panties, leaving her T-shirt on and lies on the bed. Something strange, resembling a banana, is in her right hand. Only it's bright pink and vibrating. Oh my godfathers! Is she going to do what I think she is?

The camera shows little besides a slight wobble of her right hand as it grips the disconcertingly large, pink object. Just the thought of what she is going to do with it freaks me out. What new depths have I sunk to? What sort of man watches his wife pursuing her own private pleasure?

I jab at the fast forward button but nothing happens. Watch in horrified fascination as the pink banana hovers over her bent knees. Hit fast forward again. This time, the frame freezes. The lurid image is plastered over my iPad screen and won't go away, despite pressing every combination of buttons I can think of.

Merde!

A polite tap on the door.

It's Bea. Kurt, are you still in there?

I toss the iPad into the toilet bowl. There's a satisfyingly loud crack. I push down on the toilet-roll holder and attempt to stand but instead lurch into the cistern and dislodge an empty tumbler. The bathroom starts looping the loop and performing aileron rolls. A distorted image of a monstrous bright pink dildo floats before my eyes, then flickers and disappears. I'm going to crash and burn…

Fade to black.

No idea of the time, abandoned in the wilderness of not knowing

Wake to steel knuckles rapping on the inside of my skull. Tongue bloated and furred up. Back of head throbs as if it's been kicked by a mule on steroids.

I am flat on the floor, stiff and cold as a corpse. Not long before that surely, if this keeps up.

Try to move. Thwarted by stab of pain in right knee. Left leg is numb. Right leg is jammed into toilet pedestal.

Roll onto my side into a puddle of alcohol. Blood stain on shirt sleeve. Remove shard of glass from just below the elbow. Ouch. Another shard is stuck in my wrist.

The rapping in my skull becomes a rapping on the bathroom door.

Kurt! Open the door!!!

Croak incoherent reply. Try again.

I can't hear, what did you say?

I'll be out soon! I fell asleep.

What the hell are you doing in there?!

I won't be long, darling. I've just had a minor mishap – everything's under control.

Kurt! What's going on? Open the door will you!

I crawl around the room collecting fragments of glass from the floor. Toss fragments into bin. Fish iPad out of toilet (screen now ominously black), wrap it in copious lengths of toilet roll and place it on the chair on top of the pile of Bea's *Neuron* journals. Then, with supreme effort, I lever myself up off the toilet seat, grabbing hold of washbasin to pull myself upright.

I gasp. A chill goes through me as I confront the image before me. Eyes unfocussed, blinking. Blood dripping from hand. Saliva dripping from mouth. I would not look out of place in a zombie apocalypse movie. What sort of example am I to Fran? What sort of husband am I to Bea? I have let them both down. I have let myself down.

My thoughts ramble in unprecedented directions until the next rap on the door.

Kurt! Are you coming out?

Just taking a pee, I'll be out in a sec!

Hurriedly, I clean my face, remove my stained shirt and staunch the flow of blood from my hand. Then I have an overwhelming urge to pee.

The gush of liquid produces a sensation verging on euphoria until my right knee buckles. I cling to the washbasin for support. The flow of urine continues unabated for another minute.

Opening the door, I nearly topple Bea, stationed on the other side. She pounces on me with a yelp. The ferocity in her eyes pins me to the wall.

What the bloody hell do you think you're doing! You scared me half to death! I've been yelling for nearly ten minutes, I didn't know if you were dead or alive! I was about to get Adrian to break down the door. (She takes in my appearance.) Where's your shirt? What have you done to yourself? Your hand's bleeding – and your head. (She touches my hairline. Her fingertips come away red.) Did you pass out in there?

I was on the toilet and I suddenly felt a bit woozy. Next thing, I was on the floor–

How much did you have to drink, Kurt?

Weariness has ousted her concern. Her voice is icy.

I have fallen over after drinking twice (that Beatrice knows about). I have even vomited into a stranger's hat after several drinks too many at an executive networking event. But this is the first time (excluding the bar in Istanbul) that I've actually passed out.

A few whiskeys, I reply. I wasn't counting.

Bea sighs despairingly.

You've hit your head, Kurt. You need to go to the hospital, you might have concussion.

Sound of feet on stairs.

Mummy! Can I come downstairs now?

More scampering feet.

Daddy!

Fran grabs my waist and buries her head in my stomach. Feel the wetness of her tears and the sobs breaking inside her chest. I don't know where to look, or what to say.

Bea moves her head slowly from side to side. I was so scared, Kurt. I thought you'd had a heart attack or a stroke, or an epileptic fit…

She propels me into the car, saying she's driving me to the hospital to get checked out. Fran comes with us. We are all silent for the entire journey.

8.45pm

We wait in the A&E holding pen for a doctor. Both my wife and my daughter ignore me. Bea holds Fran's hand and from time to time points out to her items of interest around us on the benches full of mumbling, incoherent old men and sullen, slouching youths. I have plenty of time to contemplate the full awfulness of the situation, while pretending to read the copious leaflets with advice on piles, overactive bladders and so forth.

I know perfectly well that nothing can excuse me for scaring my wife and daughter like that. I am an oversensitive, selfish, reactionary brute, well on the way to becoming mentally unstable. On top of all this, I must finally admit, I have a drink problem. A serious drink problem. If I don't do something now, I'm in danger of losing my life as I know it.

Finally, a spotty-chinned doctor takes me into a room and asks me a list of questions, starting with:

- How much alcohol did you drink before you fell?
- Have you ever lost consciousness before as a result of drinking?
  culminating in:
- Have you ever sought treatment for an alcohol-related problem?

By the time he asks the last question, I am deeply ashamed and fervently wish I had stayed at home.

There are treatment programs available for people who find it difficult to control their drinking, the doctor informs me with a raised eyebrow. Many people abuse alcohol because it is the only way they know how to cope with life. They use it to avoid their pain. But there are always other ways.

I mumble something.

After my scan, the doctor finds me in the corridor. He smiles at Bea and Fran then turns to me, his face stern.

Everything looks normal, Mr Hudson, you can go home. And I would advise you to avoid consuming excessive amounts of alcohol from now on. Next time, you might not be so lucky.

With as much dignity as I can muster, I thank him and stand up, avoiding the eyes of the geriatric sitting in the next chair who's listening with interest. I feel like a schoolboy who's been reprimanded by his teacher in front of the whole class. Or maybe humiliating patients is a new cost-saving NHS tactic intended to reduce the incidence of substance abuse.

On the way out, Bea calls for me to wait, Fran needs the toilet.

See you at the car, I shout.

Outside, it's dark. The rain has stopped and the car park is eerily empty. After five minutes of waiting in the car, I think about driving off to somewhere far away and leaving wife and daughter to get a taxi home. That way, I won't have to face them. Also, the car park charge will zoom up to £11 in another minute. I could just cruise round the block, maybe stop in a service station and buy some fuel…

You are avoiding confronting your family, a doctorly voice informs me. Avoidance of pain is not a responsible course of action.

I'm sorry, I say on the way home. I've let you both down.

Are you a drunk, Daddy|?

Who told you that?

Mummy did.

It's true, Kurt. Face it.

10.15pm

Home, at last. Bea rushes into the bathroom before I can remove any leftover evidence of my activities.

What's this doing in the bathroom?

She advances, holding up the mummified iPad.

I was looking at my mail while I was on the toilet, I stutter. It slipped in.

I relieve her of the thing before anything untoward has a chance to appear on the screen. The device appears to be kaput.

10.45pm

The three of us plough through a Thai-Malaysian-Chinese takeaway in silence. While Bea puts Fran to bed, I clear up. Then the two of us are alone in the kitchen.

I hover awkwardly near the fridge. I have an urge to run out of the room and watch the TV – *Mission Impossible*, a rerun of *Only Fools and Horses* – anything so long as it isn't real life. My real life, that is.

I'm concerned about you, Kurt. I think you need to stop drinking.

That sounds like a good idea, I reply.

You're not yourself, anymore. These last few years, you've been different. It's like you've turned into a guy in a movie. A weird guy in a weird movie.

I don't reply. Yes, that sounds like me. A weird guy in a weird movie.

Don't you have anything to say?

I've found it difficult, I guess. The father thing – the husband thing. The whole thing.

I feel myself regressing to a mental age of seven, or less. I try to gather Bea into my arms but she resists.

Are you happy, Kurt? With me? With Fran?

I'm happy, so happy you wouldn't believe – most of the time. Other times I can get – you know.

Tell me.

I question things. I wonder what you're doing with a guy like me. I get crazy with jealousy for no reason. I worry how Fran will turn out, if we're doing enough for her – if I'm doing enough for her. I'm afraid she'll end up like me, a grown up with temper tantrums and a permanent fear that everything's about to go down the plughole. I don't want to inflict that on her, Bea. I want our family to be perfect.

It all splurges out. I can't remember what else I said. (Please, not too much.)

I love you, Bea says. But I don't know...

Her voice falls away. She sounds tired and sad, like a fading rose about to drop its petals.

Kurt, all I know is... I can't bear to see you like this. So lost. It makes me feel lost, too.

Please, sweetheart. I'm not going to turn into a drunken bum. I'm going to do whatever it takes to make you happy, to make Fran happy. I promise.

She nods and smiles weakly. Then says she's going to bed.

When I open the bedroom door, the light is switched off. The duvet is wrapped tightly around Bea, covering nearly everything. I kiss her goodnight on the nose. She doesn't open her eyes.

I briefly contemplate a large glass of whiskey. Instead, I switch on my iPhone and continue with my journal, freshly restored onto my smallest device thanks to the wonders of iCloud.

12.33am

Must stop this damn thing soon. My trusty electronic device might fall into the wrong hands. Fran or Bea might peek inside. I might leave 'What To Do About Madeleine?' lying on a bar stool/bus seat/chair/hospital corridor where a stranger could read this (they would need to discover my start-up doodle first, haha) and transplant my words into an anonymous blog to be read by thousands. It might even become fodder for trashy entertainment and serialised in *The Mail on Sunday*. When I'm dead after a life of unhealthy excess or attacked by a random mugger, Bea might casually peep inside my phone seeking consolation in reminders of the man she loved, to be greeted with the rantings of deluded, obsessional maniac.

Raison d'etre for keeping on with this document – zero.

Evidence for phantom affair – zero.

Evidence for me being unhinged – plenty.

While I couldn't sleep, I read from the start of WTDAM with increasing horror. In places, I sound like a Grade One Nutcase. (Paranoid personality disorder with distinct narcissistic/antisocial/manic tendencies? Manic depressive with obsessive/paranoid tendencies? Hypochondriac with a personality problem?)

3.38am

Have finished checking all the abnormal psychology references on Wikipedia. The more I read about pathologies of the mind, the more I think I have a bit of everything. Is there a category for this, I wonder?

22/8/11, Wednesday

Morning

Bea has arranged for Ben to hobble into the university today to start collating the results of her experiment. She has also informed the university that she needs to take a few weeks off, starting next week, to analyse the results, write them up, submit to journals and put in another funding application. She says Ben can 'in theory' get on with analysing the data without her being there in person. This way, she'll be able to spend more time with Fran. And Katie will come in to help out from tomorrow until school starts in September.

That sounds great, I say.

So, you don't need to worry anymore about me seeing too much of Maddie.

I don't mind you seeing Maddie, darling. You can still meet her for coffee and go to yoga classes together. Only I'd rather you didn't let her see too much of Fran. I think Maddie has an unhealthy influence on her.

And on me.

I admit it, I don't trust her.

Do you trust me?

I'm trying to, Bea.

Can I trust *you*?

Of course you can trust me. I've never looked at anyone else, darling. You know I only have eyes for you.

What about the drink? Can I trust that you're not going to turn into a sad old drunk?

Ouch. An arrow plunging into my heart would not have cut as deep.

I'm going to try as hard as I've ever tried to do anything in my life. I promise.

And you're going to stop imagining that Maddie and I are up to no good?

Yes, sweetheart. I promise.

And you'll tell Adrian to fuck off and leave me and Fran alone?

We come to an understanding.

Afternoon

Informed Adrian that his services are no longer required and present him with the rest of my whiskey collection as recompense for work done to date. Watched his face light up, with commensurate darkening of my own spirits.

Removed smoke-alarm cam from living room ceiling in fifteen minutes while Bea was on the computer and placed it in the dustbin, hidden inside three Waitrose bags. Could not find the tissue-box cam, despite a thorough search of house. Asked Bea if she recalled seeing the plastic tissue container anywhere. She said she hadn't seen it for ages, probably Katie threw it away thinking it was rubbish.

Packed for flight back to Istanbul (7.45am tomorrow).

Evening

Called a babysitter from the emergency list and paid triple the usual rate for her to sit in front of the TV for three hours. Then put Fran to bed and took Beatrice to her favourite ever-so-pricey but ever-so-romantic French restaurant, Le Bon Gout.

Back home, we made up properly. Told Bea she is the mistress of my universe, the only woman for me. She told me that she loved me with all her heart and soul. And while I was away, she had staved off her nightly pangs for me with a new vibrator that she found on the web – but it wasn't anything like as good as the real thing.

Your thing, she added quickly.

I said I was glad to hear it, very glad indeed.

Kurt's vows

1. I will stop drinking excess quantities of alcohol.
2. I will find other, more healthy ways to cope with the vagaries of life.
3. I will do my utmost to be a good husband and father.
4. I will trust my wife.
5. I will not spend any more time dwelling on what Bea might be doing while I'm away.

Part three

Chapter 48

From: Bea Hudson (bhudson9@blueyonder.co.uk)
Sent: 1 Sept 2018 7.09 pm
To: Ray Loff (ray.loff@gmail.com)
Subject: **Allie**

Hi Ray,

I've only just got your voicemail, sorry for delayed reply. It is very strange that Allie hasn't come back yet, as is the message she left on the fridge. I must confess, I have an inkling where she might have gone. She told me in her email about a musician she met recently who asked her to join him on his band's tour of Queensland. I discouraged her from going and got no reply. I haven't heard from her since.

I know this isn't good news. However, on the bright side I doubt she's in any danger so there is probably no need to involve the police. I'm sure that sooner or later Allie will realise what an incredibly stupid thing she's done and come home. In the meantime, please don't you do anything stupid.

Take care,

Bea

From: Ray Loff (ray.loff@gmail.com)
Sent: 1 Sept 2018 7.24pm GMT
To: Bea Hudson (bhudson9@blueyonder.co.uk)
Re: **Allie**

Who the fuck is this guy? How the hell can I find them? I have to get her back.

From: Bea Hudson (bhudson9@blueyonder.co.uk)
Sent: 1 Sept 2018 7.50pm
To: Ray Loff (ray.loff@gmail.com)
Re: **Allie**

Ray,

I understand how upset you are, but this puts me in an awkward situation. My sister trusted me when she confided to me about recent events in her life. It would be wrong to give out sensitive information without talking to her first. But I can't do that as her mobile number is no longer connected – and as I said, she isn't replying to my emails. However, I have sympathy for your situation and want to help as much as I can.

Re the identity and location of this man – all I can say is:
   – he sings and plays guitar in a band
   – he is nearly seven feet tall and has above-average looks
   – he goes by the name 'Mellow Marty'.

Re how close she is to him – well, whatever they may or may not have done together, she only met him a few weeks before she left.

From her recent emails, I think Allie was lured by the idea of an alternative life. You know, a midlife crisis thing. I'm not sure if you know but she was having doubts about the move to Australia – she hated having to constantly brush away flies and watch out for pythons, funnel webs, flies, etc. She didn't like living on a farm in the middle of nowhere but she couldn't tell you. She thought you wouldn't understand and she didn't want to disappoint you.

Don't worry, I promise to get in touch immediately should she contact me.

Bea

From: Ray Loff (ray.loff@gmail.com)
Sent: 1 Sept 2018 7.52pm GMT
To: Bea Hudson (bhudson9@blueyonder.co.uk)
Re: **Allie**

What aren't you telling me? Are you sure she didn't know this guy before? Did she ever say she'd stopped loving me?

From: Bea Hudson (bhudson9@blueyonder.co.uk)
Sent: 1 Sep 2018 9.02pm
To: Ray Loff (ray.loff@gmail.com)
Re: **Allie**

Ray,

I know this must be a huge shock. But I honestly think it's just a fling. She's only mentioned this guy two or three times in her emails, that's the truth. I'm not holding anything back.

There were a few incidental things. She wanted you to pay her more attention, I think. She needed to go out and socialise more – she felt a bit isolated, what with your farm being so far from the nearest 'town', and that having only the one pub full of lager louts and poker machines. But she's certainly never said she was thinking about leaving you or that she didn't love you anymore. (Though she did have a few issues about your weight, to be honest. I don't know how to put this tactfully, I'm afraid. She liked you better when you were thinner.)

My advice? Stop trying to find her. Let her come back to you when she's ready - the animals still need you, even if Allie doesn't. (Sorry if that sounds brutal.) Get back working on the farm as soon as you can. At least feed the chickens, emus etc, and take the dog for a walk!

I do understand how much you miss her, though.

So do I.

Bea

Chapter 49

Bea's notes to stave off
imminent mental collapse

2 September, Sunday

Summary of overall situation

1. Big sister has run off with music bum and no telling when she might be back and when she might reply to my emails. Her husband is losing it and their home/livelihood is in disarray.

2. My team is getting what would be the most exciting research findings of my career, if only we could make sense of them.

3. The research council fellowship runs out at the end of December, so my emerging hypothesis of the basis of the neural phobic fear network may shortly become an elusive memory, unless I can somehow cobble together a convincing case for further funding ASAP to keep the team together.

4. Any funding application I make is unlikely to be accepted unless I get our findings published in a decent journal, and maybe not even then as the science may not be translatable in a short enough period. No one in the UK is interested in backing anything unless it's likely to bear fruit within the next three years, the Prof says, and getting funding is harder than ever with all this Brexit uncertainty.

5. Last week the Prof advised Ben to apply to join the Affective Disorders Group at Manchester as 'the research there is going somewhere.' (Why don't I just give up now?) Ben said, 'No way,' he told me. I am grateful but not much reassured. Anyway, how can I ask Ben and Hayley to stay aboard a sinking ship?

6. Katie is turning into a not-very-benign dictator. Lately she's begun to order Fran around ('Don't leave your tissue on the floor, miss,' 'Don't put your elbows on the table,' and so on) in the disagreeable tone of a Victorian governess. This morning she glared at me when I came into the kitchen at 11.30am in my dressing gown, though I've told her several times that I like to work in bed in the mornings.

7. Maddie says Kurt is 'a jealous lunatic' and wants nothing to do with him ever again. She refuses to come into the house now, in case Kurt materialises. I haven't seen her since That Day except at yoga class last Friday.

8. Kurt has to stay on another month to sort out issues with Turkish staff, most of whom he says are either arguing about how much time off they ought to be allowed for prayers, coffee etc, or offering him backhanders to keep their jobs. He is fed up with it and doesn't want to be without me anymore, but the head of ComputerCorp thinks K is only one who can do the job. Worry about how this away from home working will affect Kurt's state of mind. Twice last week he called in the middle of night, saying he needed to hear my voice. Or was he just checking that I wasn't with Maddie?

9. Have bigger black bags under eyes than usual, feel like old crone in need of magic wand – or failing that, a week's intensive treatment at Champneys (and The Priory soon).

10. As soon as I took him off the lead in the park the other day, Big Ears ran onto the grass and left a big dollop of poo next to a group of women having a picnic. They all stared as I scooped it into a plassie bag and dragged the dog by the scruff of his neck into the bushes. Belatedly recognised one as a mother from Bright Faces playgroup.
11. Mum is missing Janice and has spent far too much money on scarves.

Research

Ben has just helped me finish the data analysis for our August experiments, which is excellent progress. Unfort, I have no idea what to make of the results.

Once again, we've found strong phobic-brain hotspots within the hippocampus and the amygdala. Thank goodness, the data is a lot more consistent than it was last time — Ben's nasty film clips must have done the trick. We found a similar pattern of hotspots across 88% of the phobics.

The strange thing is, we're still getting definite signals from a tiny region within the olfactory bulb. They are consistently present for the spider phobics, but not the control group. Ben's software has ruled out spurious smells, which leaves — well, I'm not sure. For the life of me, I can't work out how an innocuous collection of cells that are meant to be used for filing away smells could be part of the phobic fear network. This part of the brain isn't mentioned in the reported results of anyone else in the field. Did others get the same result as us, but discount it? I will have to think a lot more about this, preferably before the Affective Disorders Group or the Californians get there. Can't submit my paper without some kind of hypothesis to explain this stuff.

One bright spot

Fran seems happy now that I am at home all day, except for three brief visits to uni to have lunch with the team, complete another batch of forms and review this year's teaching schedule with the Prof. Thankfully no first-year psych students, though two hours a week more lectures than last year thanks to the cognitive neuroscience second year undergrad course and two modules for the cognitive brain imaging masters. Fran has been v well behaved in the two or three weeks since I've been home (a record?) – just the usual moaning at bedtime, refusing to eat cabbage/spinach/peas/salad or anything else that is any shade from green to purple. And she hasn't asked once in the last five days if Auntie Maddie is coming back

3 September, Monday

Fran started school today. I walked over to collect her (it is a 'green school' and cars are frowned on, the head informed us in his email, unless they are electric, v small or have a disabled driver). To my surprise and relief, she skipped towards me and told me about her new friends. Her teacher is 'de-lish' though 'wobbly in the bottom'. Well, you can't have it all.

4 September, Tuesday

Dreams of climbing ladders leaning on crumbling walls. Woke in panic as I crashed to the ground.

Spent day ploughing on with this damn paper – in a muddle with it, no coherent argument. Can see all the holes in my thinking. Have I assumed too much? Or have we missed something important along the way?

This morning I overheard Katie saying into her mobile, when she was supposed to be cleaning the fridge, 'Mrs H has very nice work, is very laid back, laying on bed in dressing gown until lunch.' I would have fired her on the spot, only there's no time to find a replacement childminder.

Another email from Ray — he's intending to sleep with as many women as he can find this weekend to show his 'slut of a wife' that she isn't the only one 'who can have fun.'

Not one word yet from big sis. Must stop thinking about her. Have I upset her by being too direct — or by being unsympathetic? Or is she just having such a great time she's forgotten to check her emails? Or don't they have wi-fi/ internet cafés yet in Queensland? And why the hell can't she tell her husband what's going on and why she left?

'Don't know how long I'll be, please don't worry about me' — that must be the most useless note ever. Is she having such a good time shagging this musician that she's forgotten all of her previous life?

Other stuff

Mad's asked me to go to salsa class with her this Saturday. Said yes, though it starts at 8pm and Katie isn't keen to babysit on Saturday nights anymore. But need to have some fun (just a little) or will scream.

5 September, Wednesday

Bribe to Katie worked — tho now hairdryer-less.

8 September, Saturday

Salsa class in the back room of unpromising Streatham pub (forlorn outside, boisterous inside) not far from Mad's place. Emailed Kurt just before start saying Mad and I were off to Legs, Tums 'n' Bums class at the fitness centre, in case he assumed I was only going to pick up men (or women?) Wasn't much chance of either. Felt like a totally unsexy old woman. All the females wore shorts or short skirts with strappy sandals, I was in boots, jeans and an old T-shirt. Everyone paired up instantly, leaving me with a man with bad breath who wouldn't let me go until he'd half twisted off my shoulder in the 'spaghetti arms' routine. It got better later, when I danced with a fit guy with dreads and a tall thin woman with smoky eyeshadow and thick black mascara (Maddie says she's from Croatia and she used to dance in musicals).

Enjoyed the class, could keep up with the steps though not done salsa for ages. But kept wondering if Kurt might be trying to call — he always seems to call just after I switch off my phone. Had planned to make a quick exit then drive home so as not to keep Katie waiting past 10pm, only Maddie insisted I join her and the others for a drink. First social chat for weeks (months?) with anyone except for uni colleagues (not much fun now as Moira is always complaining about her asthma attacks/worthless students and Sweaty Mike reddens and stutters whenever I come near). Nice to be me again, rather than Mrs Hudson or Dr Hudson.

Arrived home forty-five minutes late. Katie ultra sniffy. Told her I was delayed due to a long loo queue. Guilty thoughts at being an irresponsible mother, deceiving wife and lousy employer. Wish I'd stayed on for another two drinks at least, then come home and fired Katie.

9 September, Sunday

Just me and Fran today. Over breakfast explained to Fran that Daddy will be not be home at the end of this week after all, he has to stay in Turkey for 'a little bit more'. She ran off to play with her box of shells.

For rest of the morning she said nothing unless I spoke to her first. Asked her what is the matter, is she missing Daddy? She shook her head and wouldn't tell me.

In the afternoon I took her to Chessington Zoo, thinking that it might cheer her up.

Fran did not voluntarily speak to me in the car on the way there, except to ask if I had any sweets (no), could she have my Samsung so she can play a game on it (no) and refused to play I Spy or sing any of the songs her class is learning with Miss De-lish. Finally, I tried to talk to her about global warming and extinct species but got no response.

When we got into the zoo, told her to hold onto my hand as 'there's lots of people here and we don't want to lose each other, do we?' Made good progress through zoo, helped by Fran's lack of interest in any creatures except giraffes and parrots. With a spurt of frustration, I stopped by the lion enclosure and asked if was she tired (no), upset about Daddy not coming home (no), or upset about anything else (no).

Me: Well in that case, can you try to brighten up a bit! You're jolly lucky I brought you here, I could have stayed at home and had a bath, watched the last series of Mad Men, weeded the garden and finished writing up my research.

F: Can I go to the toilet now?

We found the ladies and I let Fran go into the first empty cubicle. A few seconds later, I went into another. But when I came out, my daughter wasn't anywhere to be seen, and her cubicle was empty.

I rushed outside, circled the toilet block and ran around all the paths in the vicinity, calling 'Fran!' with ever-increasing dementedness. I thought of the other time she'd run away from me in Italy, after Kurt told her off for recklessly running into a woman on crutches and sending her into a bush.

Finally, I spotted Fran on the path ahead, looking wistfully at two boys – or rather the ice cream smeared around their mouths and trickling down their cornets. She looked at me innocently as I strode towards her.

F: Can I have one too, Mummy?

I started to shout at my daughter, who stared into the ground.

Me: Why did you go off like that, Fran?

F: –

Me: Fran, answer me!

F: I don't know.

Me: Tell me!

F: I went for ice cream.

Me: But you knew I was still in the toilet, didn't you?

Fran scratched her elbow. I realised that the two boys were watching me. Adults were tugging at little hands and hurrying past.

Me: We're going home. I've had it with you!

Silence, all the way home. As I drove, my mask of crossness and wrong-done-to-ness firmly in place, my throat tightened and my eyeballs stung with all the tears I couldn't cry.

For the duration of our morose supper of leftover pizza and dressing-less salad, Fran avoided my eyes.

Later, after putting her to bed, I went up to her room again.

'I'm sorry I shouted at you,' I said as she lay there, eyes shut, silky hair piled up on the pillow. I waited a little while but she didn't stir.

Then I shut my bedroom door, switched off my mobile, wrapped up the phone handset with Kurt's thickest jumper and put it into the drawer, then got into bed and cried. For being so useless as a mother, and for being so unable to comfort my daughter that she tries to run away from me. For being alone with a child who needs her father, not me – or Maddie, perhaps.

Chapter 50

Colin Settle
18 Tudor Drive
Woking, Surrey GU21 3NZ
England
(email cmsettle@blueyonder.co.uk, mobile +44 7939 551012)
Gary Settle
14010 RANCHO SOLANA TRL
San Diego, CA 92130
9 September 2018

Dear Gary,

Thanks very much for your letter. I can't tell you how pleased I was to get it, brief though it was. Yes, I'm aware my letters have been on the long side. Afraid I'm not good at keeping things brief.

Re the thorny matter of your heartless seduction of my former wife, your disloyalty to your then-girlfriend, not to mention your disloyalty to me – I accept that you felt justified in doing what you did because Clare had wrongfully told you that I'd refused to have sex with her on our anniversary. (Actually, I'd mislaid my last packet of Viagra, which I'd been saving for extra impetus.)

I can also accept that you haven't yet forgiven me for badmouthing you to your next-in-line girlfriend about what a cad you were for luring my former wife to bed on two occasions before dropping her faster than you could say 'genital warts' – culminating, unsurprisingly, in said girlfriend's hasty retreat.

For the record, I will concede that I may have brought some of my marital misfortunes on myself by neglecting Clare's well-being and being overly absorbed in the inner workings of my hi-fi, the smoothness of my serve and other undeserving minutiae. Perhaps I did judge you rather harshly, bro.

Despite all of our recent differences, I continue (perhaps foolishly) to hope that we can resume our previous cordial relationship, unhindered by the carcasses of the women strewn across our paths.

Before I sign off, I will update you on a couple of things (for the last time, I promise).

My Meetings with Madeleine – I fear you may be right about my perpetual cycles of infatuation/disillusionment with women.

My Cunning Scheme to Rob the Rich to Avenge the Ripped-Off – my misadventure in the reallocation of corporate greed has concluded. On Friday I managed to complete the final transaction (£17,500) only to be promptly propositioned by my deeply disliked junior colleague. (See below for concluding episodes.)

My Meetings with Madeleine

Will get to the nub of the matter. This weekend, over a romantic dinner in the restaurant of our elegant though fading hotel overlooking Weymouth Bay, Madeleine let slip that she sometimes dreams of a rich guy taking her to live in a magnificent villa on a beautiful island, where she would be able to sculpt to her heart's content without having to worry about where she will get the money to pay the bills, replace torn jeans, take Mungo to the vet, get her dental implants done, and the like.

'Where would this island be,' I asked.

'Majorca maybe, or Malta. Or Madeira. I'm not fussy.'

'And what would this rich guy do?'

'Oh, he'd have a job somewhere and come home on weekends, or he'd have a boat charter business on the island… He could help take care of our little girl, too.'

'Our little girl?'

A tentative smile. 'Have I told you, Colin, how much I'd like to have one? Sometimes I have this dream about a little girl. I'm in her bedroom, brushing her hair. I see her face smiling at me in the dressing table mirror, and through the window there's a big garden full of pear trees.'

The candlelight flickers on Maddie's features. She's beautiful, soft-skinned, luscious. She's the one I wake up thinking about with a smile on my face, the one I dream of making Mrs Settle. Then she turns into a scheming seducer, a hard-hearted harlot.

'So all you need now is some obliging rich bloke with a high sperm count and your dream can come true. Or do you see me in that role?'

'Col, don't be silly. What I said before – I wasn't serious. I was being, you know, humorous. Sharing my wacky daydreams with you.'

'You sounded serious to me.'

She pulls nervously at her discarded napkin as if plucking a chicken. 'I didn't mean it like it sounded.'

'You didn't?'

'Of course, other things come into it too – love, attraction... Wanting the same things, a future together. If all that's there, what's wrong with having a bit of money to make things easier?'

Something tells me that this is the time. 'I've never told you, Maddie. It's a bit hush-hush, you see. But I may be about to retire soon. To a sunny island in the Mediterranean, or the Caribbean... I've been working on a scheme to transfer money between certain accounts at my company – quite large amounts of money, actually.'

Her nostrils quiver. Her irises blaze. I can feel her pulse quickening. 'Will it make you rich?'

'No, that's unlikely. The money isn't going to me, it's going to the client accounts. Selected client accounts.'

A long pause. She looks puzzled. Disappointed, perhaps. Other conversations trickle into the gap left in ours.

At last, she says, 'Is this something you shouldn't be doing?'

'You could say that.' While Maddie sips dubiously on her vodka tonic, I explain the principles of my scheme.

She looks into my eyes. 'And what do you get out of this? The satisfaction of knowing you've made amends to some of the people you've ripped off?'

'Exactly. The bosses are going to make me redundant anyway, so I may as well go out with a bang. If they don't catch me in the act and report me to the police, with any luck I'll be in line for quite a reasonable payout when I leave the firm. It might even be enough to start a boat charter business, or maybe a beach chair rental business. Somewhere warm, I hope. By the time they actually realise what I've done, I'll be long gone, and too far away for them to bother with.'

Her eyes are gleaming again. 'Well, I wish you luck, Col… It sounds risky, though. What if they catch you?'

'I've thought of a backup plan. I just hope it works.' I don't mention the fact that, as of forty-eight hours ago, I have technically been caught in the act and my backup plan is about to swing into operation.

Maddie smiles. 'I think your scheme's crazy, but I like it. I never realised you could do something as wild as this.'

She's quiet for a long time, and so am I. Then she leans towards me. 'Don't you ever think about having kids, Col?'

'Not on a daily basis. I've wondered what it would be like, sometimes. A kid or two, maybe a Volvo, a dog… Then I think of the negatives. Would they turn into juvenile delinquents? Would they remember Father's Day?'

'I thought you said you wanted them with your ex.'

'That was then, Maddie. Now – I don't know.'

She looks puzzled.

'Maybe with the right woman. I guess it could happen one day. But I have to say, I'm not too keen on being thought of as a handy stud with a fat wallet.' Did I say that? Surely not.

A cold draught hits our table. The flame wavers. She twists away from me, craning her neck towards Weymouth Bay and the wonders of the Jurassic Coast.

'Sorry, Mad. That was vicious.'

'That's the nastiest thing you've ever said to me, by far.'

She looks upset. I think she is blinking back tears. But I'm not in the mood to be taken advantage of. I'm not going to let myself be duped by a woman, ever again.

'I was exaggerating for comic effect,' I say. 'I don't really think you see me as a handy stud with a fat wallet. But I have to be honest, I don't know for sure. I don't know anything much for sure, with you. Like how you feel about me.'

'You make me happy, Col. I like being with you – I like you very much. What else can I say?'

That you love me? That you adore me and you don't want me to go to a distant island without you, and you can't bear to think of living the rest of your life without me?

Of course, she doesn't say that.

'Let's go to the room,' I say after signing the bill. 'I'm tired, I don't feel like talking.'

We go up to our deluxe seventh floor room with a view over Weymouth Bay and half of the Jurassic Coast, where we go to sleep without even a goodnight kiss.

This morning, on the way back, I said little, pretending to have a headache. I won't be seeing Maddie again. Like water poured into a cracked bucket, my dreams of happiness have trickled away.

My Cunning Scheme

At 7.52pm last Friday evening I completed the final payment to the last of the Lucky Thirteen. I won't burden you with petty details. In a nutshell, with the help of modern technology I transferred seventeen thousand smackers into the account of Mrs Violet Scratched-by-parrot Got-infection Bladder-failing Eyesight-nearly-gone Black, who until that moment had received no whiff of compensation in the three years since she claimed on her health insurance (policy terminated due to 'interrupted payments' together with 'insufficient care taken to avoid injury'; the parrot, though generally affectionate, had a history of becoming aggressive whenever its claws were trimmed).

There I was, shutting down the computer, stuffing a wad of papers into my wheelie bag, having just purged the details of my scheme from the system and mentally patting myself on the back for getting through this last daring deed despite palpitations and a sweat-drenched shirt, when Mr Smarmy Pants himself materialises beside me with a sick-making grin.

'Hold on, Mr Settle, not so fast. You've got some explaining to do.'

I erase my frown and try to assume a nonchalant air as I turn to take in his smug expression, pale pink Massimo Dutti shirt and matching silk tie.

'Hello, Mark. I didn't see you there. What brings you back to the office on such a glorious evening? Shouldn't you be downing a pint in The Butcher's Hook by now?'

'I know your game, Colin, there's no point playing the innocent. I came back to get my squash shoes and you were so engrossed in your little operation you didn't even notice I've been standing three feet behind you for the last ten minutes. I saw everything, chum. In fact, I've even taken a few shots with my phone.'

He holds up his phone screen while I fight a sudden wave of nausea. I take a few seconds to decide that swinging my wheelie bag in his face, though satisfying, would not help the situation. His smug grin intensifies, as does my need to visit the lav quick smart.

'I've had this feeling for weeks that you were up to no good. And now I understand. You've been doing this regularly, haven't you? I must say, I'm surprised. Exaggerating expenses, cheating on overtime – we've all done that. But stooping to this level? I'm flabbergasted. I thought you senior managers got a decent bite of the cherry. What are you going do with that seventeen grand, Col? Get another hi-fi?'

'It's not going into my account, dickhead. It's going to the customers.'

'Oh yeah. Of course it's going to the customers – and then it's going straight into your fat little paws. Do you think I'm thick or something?'

'Mark, I'm telling the truth. I swear on my mother's grave. That money is going to Mrs Black because she's been fucked over royally by us – by me, I put my hand up. I signed to say she should get nothing, even though her life's been ruined, because that's company policy and I knew I would get nowhere fast if I didn't stick to it. So please, just go back home and forget you've seen any of this. None of that money is going anywhere near me.'

'Nice speech, Col, but I don't believe it for a second.' He taps his nose. 'That's your cover story, as clear as daylight robbery. You've got it nicely sewn up with poor old Mrs Black, haven't you? And with all the others – I bet there's others, aren't there? And I bet you've creamed off your share. How much are we talking about in total, by the way? Twenty thousand? Fifty?'

'Seven hundred thousand.' I don't know why I told the little weasel. Bragging?

'I'm impressed.'

'What are you going to do? Snitch on me to Mr Clifford?'

His chest swells like a strutting cockerel who's found a mate. He scratches his well-thatched scalp. 'I'm not an unreasonable chap, Colin. I don't want to see you flung out of here – or languishing in prison, either. White collar crime is the new armed robbery, so I've heard. Insider crime, even worse. The old geezers will want to make an example out of you... Perhaps we can come to an arrangement.'

'What do you have in mind?'

'Well, what would be appropriate? Ten grand of your little transaction my way, and no blabbing?'

'I'm afraid I'm going to have to turn down your offer, Mark. I'm not going to be blackmailed.'

His chest is now flat as a cold chapati. His mouth falls into a leer as foul as any Arsenal fan's after a thrashing by Spurs.

'If that's how you want to play it, Mr Settle. I'll have to do my duty, won't I?'

'I'm not stopping you, Mr Hollis. But bear in mind that snitching on a colleague isn't always the best policy. Especially when you've just tried to blackmail him.'

'My word against yours, I think you'll find. See you Monday.'

For the past three hours, Gary, I've rattled around my flat, wondering if tomorrow will be my Day of Judgement, and if the best way out of my predicament might not be to scarper immediately to St Lucia for a few years. By the time I come back, Messrs Clifford and Spelt will have found other things to worry about. I'll be another name on the list of rogue former employees, cursed in the boardroom and mentioned in cautionary tales related by incredulous junior execs, my photo fodder for impromptu sessions of office darts.

Much as I'm tempted by this plan, it isn't how I want to be remembered. I don't want to be thought of as a cowardly scoundrel who did a runner after getting his own back on the company he hated. I want my reasons to be clear to those at the top. Besides, doing a runner means I'll lose my redundancy payout and have no means of earning a living, as I'll be blacklisted from the world of insurance. And I certainly don't want to be a mug on a wanted poster, looking over my shoulder at every turn, worrying when I'll be charged with fraud and detained at Her Majesty's Pleasure. I must stay and face the music.

If my attempted blackmailer is going to turn me in to our bosses, I need to get there first to present my case. I'll prepare a short statement before going to bed and be outside Mr Clifford's office at the sparrows to hand it to him.

What do you think, Gary?

Hopefully by the time you get this, I will be celebrating my success at the tennis club bar with a bottle of champers. If not, I may well be mouldering in a prison cell, or else cast adrift from society and looking forward to spending the rest of my days frantically seeking get-rich-quick schemes, Poundstretcher shops and two-for-one deals at M&S.

Will leave you to ponder the precariousness of life.

Much love,

Colin

Chapter 51

Colin Settle
Head of Claims Settlement
Clifford & Spelt Insurance
colinsettle@cliffordandspeltinsurance.com
10 September 2018

Dear Mr Clifford,

I have to inform you that for the past three months I have diverted sums of money totalling £702,000 to the accounts of thirteen customers, past and current, without prior authorisation. (Full details are in the accompanying document.)

This was dishonest of me, I freely admit. But were we not dishonest to these customers in the first place, if not also downright cynical and contemptuous?

I do not exclude myself from this judgement – a fact which has caused me increasing unease of late.

My actions were intended to rectify a small part of the damage caused by your policy of 'not letting the customer get away with it', better known to us at the coal face as 'shafting the pricks'. You might view this as a Robin Hood-style gesture, robbing the rich to help the poor. When I embarked on this venture, I saw myself as a rather pathetic, soon-to-be-unemployed senior manager entering late middle age, who had achieved little or nothing of real value in his career thus far. So, I decided to challenge a lifetime of safe, sensible decisions and for once do something I could be proud of in my later years.

I am willing to hand in my notice – and say nothing of my reasons to anyone – on the condition that I receive the full benefits of the firm's early retirement scheme (including, of course, the substantial early-retirement lump sum), together with an assurance that you will not report me to the police or any other authorities for the action I have taken.

If, for any reason, this condition should not be granted, I assure you that I will not delay in explaining the reasons behind my venture to anyone in the media who might be interested (Jon Snow on *Channel 4 News*, for example). I doubt that this will make pleasant viewing for either you or Mr Spelt.

I trust that you will give this matter consideration.

Yours faithfully,

Colin Settle

PS

On making each payment, I contacted each of the 'Lucky Thirteen' recipients to inform them that their unexpected windfall is 'delayed compensation for the ungenerous way in which your claim was handled by us' and that they should not contact anyone about this payment except for yours truly. Several have thanked me already and sent details of how they intend to spend the money.

PPS

As you will no doubt shortly find out, Mr Mark Hollis has learned of my actions re the Lucky Thirteen. I'm sure he will be interested in your response to this situation.

Chapter 52

Gideon S. Clifford
Clifford & Spelt Insurance
29th Floor, One Canada Square
Canary Wharf
London
E14 5DY
10 September 2018

Dear Mr Settle,

I am flabbergasted by the brazen cheek with which you are attempting to hold to ransom the good name of the firm that has supported you handsomely over a substantial fraction of the past two decades. The cock and bull story you gave this morning concerning your 'reasons' for committing such a grave transgression against this highly regarded organisation is not worthy of a journalist on *The Mail on Sunday*, let alone a trusted senior employee.

However, I have resisted my first impulse, namely to contact the police and to insist that the maximum possible penalty for this transgression is brought against you, thereby making an example out of you that would not be forgotten by anyone tempted to follow in your footsteps. After considerable reflection, Mr Spelt and I have concluded that it will not be in anyone's interest for either the police or the legal profession to be involved in what is essentially a private matter.

In the spirit of reconciliation, Mr Settle, I am prepared to accept all of your conditions, including the early retirement lump sum, as long as you will agree to:

a) remove yourself from the building immediately on receiving this letter; and

b) to speak no word of this matter to anyone, for an indefinite period.

Yours, etc

Gideon S. Clifford

Chapter 53

Miss Madeleine Geen

13 September, Session 10, 4pm

Session delayed due to my annual break and Miss Geen being unable to attend therapy since her ninth session on 16 August.

MG: Hello, Nigel. Did you have a good break?

Miss Geen's teeth are even whiter than the last time against her tan. Her long legs are bare under her fringed cotton skirt. Her hair is swept back by a velvet band and a startling pink lipstick graces her lips.

I reassure her that I am very well and that I enjoyed my fortnight's tour of the Italian Lakes with Mrs Rowley.

NR: And I hope you too enjoyed the break from our sessions, Ms Geen? You look very… very… very refreshed, yes.

MG: (An enigmatic smile.) I know this was supposed to be our last session – but could we carry on for another ten weeks? I thought I was over it – all those bizarre thoughts I was having about taking away my friend's daughter. But they've come back.

NR: Would you like to tell me about them?

MG: They're a bit… strange.

I remind her that nothing I hear in this room is strange. Anyway, the stranger the better, as far as I'm concerned.

Silence, save for the chafing of the patient's fingers against the fabric of her skirt.

I ask if she has written down any of her troubling thoughts, as I had previously suggested.

MG: I can't write them down, Nigel, I'm sorry. They're too weird. They make me feel as if I'm going crazy.

NR: What do you think has set off these thoughts?

MG: I don't see Fran anymore.

NR: Why not?

MG: I'm not allowed to. Bea's husband thinks I'm a bad influence on Fran – and he thinks I'm carrying on some kind of lesbian thing with Bea. He told me never again to set foot in his house. I haven't been near the place.

NR: That might be sensible, in the circumstances.

MG: He's still in Turkey but I don't think for much longer. He could pop up at any moment to try to catch us out.

NR: To catch you doing something improper with your friend?

MG: I'm not doing anything improper with her, I've already told you. But Kurt seems to think we're having Friday afternoon dildo sessions and goodness knows what else.

NR: And you would never think of doing anything like that, even if it opened the door to a life in the same house as Fran?

MG: What are you trying to say? Bea's my friend. I'm not this selfish, amoral person you seem to think I am, that everyone seems to think I am…

Her eyes moisten alarmingly.

NR: Everyone?

MG: Kurt, for one – and now Colin. He thinks I'm only after his money – and his sperm.

NR: And that wouldn't be the case?

Miss G gives me a glare like none I have ever received, except possibly that inflicted on me by the departing Mrs Higginbottom after I informed her that my patient list needed urgent pruning and unfortunately her endless ruminations on her damp walls, flat feet and husband's snoring were of no further interest to me.

MG: I like him very much. No, that's not true. (Sighs and purses her lips.) I love him. And now it's too late.

NR: Too late?

MG: He's gone. I left two messages yesterday and he didn't get back to me. Then I found one this morning: 'Thanks for all the good times, Maddie. I hope you find what you're looking for.'

She snatches several tissues from the new extra-large box and wipes the tears from her face.

MG: I didn't care whether or not he was rich. I thought it was good that he had enough cash to look after himself. (Loud sniff.) He didn't seem to have that much, anyway. He wasn't a big spender – we didn't go to flash restaurants or stay in five-star hotels. Not until he took me to Dorset. But he's obviously not strapped for cash. He buys twenty pound bottles of wine and he took me shopping for new trainers when I got a hole in my old ones, and he paid for a plumber when my kitchen tap went.

NR: So, his money was a nice-to-have, not a must-have.

A glare. Two rosy patches appear on her cheeks.

MG: He thinks I see him as a stud with a fat wallet. But I don't. I like – liked his company, and we were good friends. I helped him with his garden, he helped me with mine. I painted murals on his walls and made a giant rat gnawing through a cable for his porch. I didn't ask for things to go any further.

NR: But they did.

MG: On our first afternoon in Weymouth, we went for a walk along the beach – barefoot, hand in hand. I was enjoying the sea and everything, then suddenly he kissed me and said he loved me. I was taken aback, I didn't know what to say. Then a big wave came in and splashed us and I yelped. I think he was hurt that I didn't respond to what he'd said. I didn't tell him that I loved him, too.

NR: Why couldn't you tell him that you loved him?

MG: I didn't know I did. And there's something else. When we had sex, we never used anything. He thought I was taking the pill, but I wasn't—

NR: You were hoping you might fall pregnant?

MG: Maybe, a tiny bit. Hoping a tiny bit, I mean.

NR: What if you *had* become pregnant?

MG: But I'm not pregnant. I'm definitely not pregnant. Will you stop asking me all these questions?

NR: I'm not here to pass judgement, Madeleine. But it occurs to me that your fading hopes of falling pregnant may have induced your fantasies about Fran to return, as it were. Perhaps your attachment to this little girl, and your fantasies about caring for her, symbolise an intense desire for your own child.

MG: Hmm.

NR: The way out of your predicament is clear enough, I would suggest.

MG: What are you trying to say? I should go out and shag every guy I meet so I can get pregnant?

NR: I'm merely suggesting that you accept the reality of your needs and do what you can to fulfil them in the here and now, rather than fantasising about impossible scenarios. The means you choose are up to you, of course, and depend on the practicalities of your situation. There are many possible avenues, if I may be so bold as to suggest. It may be that you need to find another Colin, or multiple Colins—

MG: Multiple Colins! What are you talking about? There's only one Colin. I'm not interested in anyone else, Mr Rowley, put that in your bloody pipe and smoke it! I've had enough of this, you can stuff your so-called therapy!

She snatches her voluminous bag and strides out, leaving a trail of organic nettle teabags across the carpet. I wait for my constitution to recover.

As of this morning, it hasn't. I suspect recovery is some way off.

Chapter 54

N. Rowley
The Practice
13 Old Fellows Court
London SW4 3FZ
14 September 2018

Dear Ms Geen,

I would like to express my deep regret at your sudden
departure from therapy. I also wish to apologise
for any inadvertently offensive or ill-judged
remarks. As you have no doubt realised, Ms Geen, the
therapeutic landscape can be a minefield – especially
for occasionally heavy-handed practitioners such as
myself.

I sincerely hope that you will be able to forgive my
shortcomings and will consider returning for another
ten sessions as you suggested to me yesterday. In
future, I shall try my utmost to refrain from making
insensitive, offensive or otherwise inappropriate
responses.

I very much hope that this proposal is acceptable.
You are, if I may venture to suggest, a highly
intelligent yet deeply troubled woman who would
benefit greatly from continued opportunity to

unburden her innermost thoughts to an impartial yet (I assure you!) sympathetic ear.

Yours sincerely,

Nigel Rowley

Chapter 55

Katie's journal

14 September

Sorry journal long time no write have many things to say but many more things to do, not just taking care of Little Miss but taking care of the Hudson Household, specially Mrs H.

I am getting worried for Mrs H's brain.

Today I find her in washing machine cubbud crying. She says washing powder runs out. I say, It is OK Mrs H, don't worry about it, I will go to shop. She says, No it is not important Katie, and runs upstairs to office to write her Paper (this never runs out). I don't know if I should call doctor or husband or Mad friend. Then see it is 3.10pm and I must go get Little Miss from school or no one will. Mrs H is in world of Paper, Mr H is away in Business World and I am left to cope with Hum Drum of Everyday Life, as Mrs H calls it.

I am grateful however for the many changes since I put foot down. No more am I just ex O Pair or Child Minder. I am Please Katie, Thank you very much Katie. More pay is very nice too, also only three days a week in Hudson Household since my course starts (good thing as Konrad is asking for our flat looking nice too and nice dinner when he comes home).

With my help, the Hudson Household is no longer like inside of chicken cage. Little Fiend is gone, Fran is back. She is nice to me always, says Please Katie not nasty names and does not do opposite of what I say.

We have now:

Morning Routine - Take Fran to school and domestic tasks (not ironing)

Lunch Break - One hour excluding shopping/other duties

Afternoon Routine - Get dry cleaning, shopping, walk dog, collect Fran from school, chop vegetables etc for evening meal

Also we have:

Katie's Rules (I pin to board in kitchen next to Handy Men and Ironing Ladies)

1. Respect shown to Katie at all times
2. No respect - No Katie
3. No bad words from Miss H or Mrs H in Katie's presense
4. No phone calls taken from Mr H unless Mrs H is out
5. No collecting dog poo when I take Big Ears to park

I tell Mrs H I leave space for extra rules, she says I don't think that's nesessary Katie, and makes huffy puffy like she does when Fran will not eat brocolly.

Fran misses her daddy, Mrs H says, she tells me to be more understanding and give benefit to doubts. There has been no more stone throwing or biting fingers, this I am thankful for.

15 September

Mr H phones when I am stirring snow peas. Mrs H is dancing salsa with Miss H.

Who is that? What is that music? Where is my wife?

He has voice like rhinossoros who has lost horn.

Katie, is that you? Please get me my wife, will you?

One minute Mr Hudson, I get her.

Mrs H makes frown at me, turns off salsa cd and wipes neck with dish drying cloth (always she uses, not towel). Today she wears shorts and clingy top. She is getting ready for Advanced Salsa Class on Saturday night, she must get steps right she says (Miss H is going to Sleepover Party with new friends from school, thank god I am not babysitter this time).

Miss H runs out of kitchen to TV room (lucky guess). I make busy with stir fry.

It's my salsa cd, Mrs H says to phone. I'm dancing to keep fit.

The conversation with Mr H goes on. Every so often Mrs H says, Thats all right darling or I'll get on to it darling. Then she says, Hang on in there my love I'll be waiting for you with open arms. She gives big laugh. Open arms, I said!

Then Mrs H asks if can I ask Miss H if she can come speak to Mr H. Miss H says Hello Daddy and talks for long time no stop then smiles like she has hit coconut at the fair.

Chapter 56

From: Madeleine Geen (madeleine.geen@gmail.com)
Sent: 15 September 2018 3.09pm
To: Nigel Rowley (nprowley@blueyonder.co.uk)
Subject: **Your proposal**

Hi Nigel

I got this email address from your receptionist, she said you check it every day. Hope you don't mind me using it.

Yes, I have considered your suggestion.

The answer is no, thank you very much, I am no longer prepared to put up with your unhelpful and often rude remarks.

If you want to hang on to the rest of your patients, I suggest you try to sound less like a pompous, egotistical, cold-hearted old prune.

Madeleine Geen

Chapter 57

N. Rowley
The Practice
13 Old Fellows Court
London SW4 3FZ
16 September 2018

Dear Ms Geen,

I would like to apologise once again for my poor conduct in the therapy room.

Although I was deeply troubled by your reply, I do appreciate your forthright feedback regarding my suitability as a psychotherapist, and have given the matter much thought. Perhaps you have hit the nail on the head, as it were: I am not cut out to be in this profession. This is something I have suspected for some time, but not acknowledged to my innermost self.

It has been painful to admit, but I notice that I often find myself losing interest in some of my patients (not yourself, I assure you) whose catalogues of woes at times threaten to overwhelm both my admittedly limited capacity for empathy, and my increasingly limited attention span. Perhaps at the age of seventy-three, the time has come for me to bid farewell to my life as a therapist.

My wife will not be pleased, I fear. She prefers me to be not seen and not heard during daylight hours so she can freely invite her friends to afternoon tea and tend to domestic concerns. However, Mrs Rowley's reservations do not of course provide a valid reason not to pursue this course of action.

Modern therapeutic norms being as they are, it may well be unwise for me to suggest this, Madeleine. (I hope I may safely call you Madeleine?) But I would like to offer you a metaphorical ear via letters (or electronic media, if you must), in the event that you might wish to continue to unburden your troubling thoughts.

I believe that it is essential to have a channel through which to express the unsayable, those so-called 'unacceptable' emotions that all of us experience at some point in our lives. The written form has much to recommend it - there ought in theory to be fewer distractions and greater powers of concentration at one's disposal. I admit that I find your case of particular interest. Furthermore, this might give me the chance to atone for past mistakes.

I will leave you to consider my offer.

Yours sincerely,

Nigel Rowley

Chapter 58

From: Madeleine Geen (madeleine.geen@gmail.com)
Sent: 17 September 2018 9.19pm
To: Nigel Rowley (nprowley@blueyonder.co.uk)
Subject: **Your second proposal**

Dear Nigel,

I did not mean to push you into early retirement. You haven't been that bad a therapist, you've just rubbed me up the wrong way a lot. I wasn't in a great mood when I replied to your letter – I'd just had some sculptures rejected by a gallery that showed my work last year. I don't think you should give up your career unless that's what your heart is telling you. It's a big decision to make. Perhaps you need to talk it over with your wife?

Thanks for your offer to be my email confidante, Nigel. I assume there's no charge involved?

Actually, there are a few things I wish I could tell someone.

My life is starting to slide downhill. Last week I sold another painting (of three rats on a night out) for £250. But when the woman came to collect it, she told me she needs the money for her TV licence.

The other thing – the guy I was seeing (Colin, he worked in insurance, remember?) still doesn't want anything to do with me. I've called him twice since he left a message on my phone but he hasn't called back. Then I called his company and they told me he'd left. They wouldn't tell me what's happened to him. I thought he must have been caught redistributing his company's money (I don't think I told you about that), so I went over to his place to see what was going on. I got as far as the front gate and went home. (I didn't want to look desperate.) His car was in the drive and his TV was on, so at least I know he's not in prison.

Col was special, I see that now. He was my one chance for a real relationship, and I've blown it. I miss him so much. But I'll have to get by without him, won't I?

I've been thinking about being Fran's 'surrogate mother' again. I haven't told anyone, especially Bea, I wouldn't dare. I imagine Fran living here in my flat with me. I help her get ready for school and make her lunches and stuff. Not just Fran. Sometimes when I see a little girl coming out of the local infants, I want to grab her and take her home with me.

I could go on, but I don't want to bore you with all my weird thoughts. And I know I should be grateful for what I have.

It's Fran's birthday soon and it looks like I'll get to spend some time with her then. I haven't seen her for ages, can't wait. Bea says Kurt wouldn't mind given it's Fran's birthday. I'm going to make a special present for her, so she knows how much she means to me.

All the best,

Madeleine

Chapter 59

Katie's journal

17 September

Very bad day.

I go up to Mrs H's office at one and ask, Do you want lunch today?

Mrs H says not to interrupt her when she is working on Paper. She is still in dressing gown and slippers, hair not seen brush for long time. I take away cup with green mud in bottom from desk and leave her to get on with work on Paper (not one Paper about a hundred Papers, all over floor).

Mrs H comes down at three and asks why I am not at school to collect Miss H. I say Oh dear I have forgotten, I was busy putting away shopping for dinner and cleaning floor where little girl spilled ketchup this morning. Dont worry, I'll go she says, face like black cloud.

When they are back Mrs H says she is sorry she is grumpy today, please can I take Fran and dog out for very long walk so she can get Paper finished in peace.

This she says every day this week with spitty huffy puffy. Today with voice like she is going to cry or scream so I run to get Big Ear's lead.

Miss H jumps up down up down like yoyo beside me as we walk down street.

Can we go to park please Katie?

You know he is not allowed in park, I say. Because he shits in park.

Little Fiend laughs like it is funniest joke she hears in all her life.

Please Katie, can we go to park?

This is every thirty seconds. After five minutes I turn off doggy path and go on road to park. Miss H says she wants to take lead. I am too tired to say No.

In the park, Little Fiend stops at playground then lets dog off lead. Big Ears does Big Shit in front of gate where women in nice dresses come out with their little ones. They look like the women in the Mad Men show Mrs H watches. The little boy points at Big Ears.

Mummy, see the doggy do smelly poo!

His Mummy with strappy sandals and big hat says, Oh how disgusting and gives me Death Stare.

Fran, I say, go and get dog!

He is inside playground now, watering post of swings, and all the Mummies are looking at him. Little Fiend does not move, just watches dog with big smile. Prickly heat comes over my neck and I go myself to get brainless dog.

He gives me innocent look. I bring him back, put him on lead then get out Waitrose plastic bag with emergency sweets and throw sweets to ground.

It is not his fault, Miss H says and rubs her face in his fur.

Please, I say, will you go clean up mess. Take this bag here and put over your hand like glove.

She looks at me like I am crazy.

Please, Fran, do as I say!

Do it yourself!

All the Mummies look at each other. I give dog to Little Fiend, take Waitrose bag, go and pick up all shit myself and put in the dog litter bin (have to ask man with grey hound where it is). When I come back, all Mummies gone and LF is patting Big Ear's head and talking into his big ear.

Dont worry about Smelly Katie. Katie is Ninny Nanny Smelly Fanny.

Is too much. I wish I have shit in my hand so I can rub in Little Fiend's face. Oh yes, I would like!

We go now please, I say, we dont want any more shitty surprises.

Shitty surprises, shitty surprises! sings LF. I take dog lead until we are out of park.

On the way home, I think of plans to pay them all back. I am not putting up with this shit any longer! (This is what Mr H used to say when he comes in from office.)

18 September

After lunch Mrs H says she is still stuck on High Poffisiss for Paper and is going to get drunk or jump off Beachy Head. Get drunk is better, I say. I am joking Katie, Mrs H says.

After I collect Fran from school, Mrs H says she has given up with Paper and is going to drink herself into stew.

At six Mad friend knocks on door. She has golden hair in pony tail and dress to show thin waist and thin legs (OK I am jealous I have rat hair and pudgy legs and no man looks twice at me, except Konrad). Fran leaps up from TV room and gives her big squeeze and says Come to look at my new game, and Mad friend goes after her like dog chasing bone.

Mrs H says, Do you want to join me in drink?

Just one thank you, I say, then I must go back to my sex maniac boyfriend (laugh so she will think is joke).

Noise of jumping feet from Miss H's bedroom.

Fran likes your friend to come here, I say. It is sad Mr H does not like.

Yes, she says, he has bee in his bonnet about Maddie.

I hope it will leave soon, I say. Bee in bonnet is not good.

Since I come back from Poland I hear about Kurt's Commandment, You will not bring Mad Woman into house with my daughter. Also I hear Bea's Commandment, You will stop drinking and behaving like arse. This I learn in little bits when she is in the mood for telling tales on Mr H after watching Mad Men with big glass of very nice orange drink with ice cubes in glass. I taste when she is sitting with feet up and Big Ears licking toes.

Mad friend comes down and pours out glass of Chably and Miss H goes up to room for homework.

Mad says, Here's to the end of your Paper, Bea.

Bea says, The end of my career, more like it.

The wine is going down the bottle very quickly. I say I must go but Mrs H pours me another. I say I must go soon. She says, No Katie, stay.

I go to bedroom to check on Miss H. When I come back, Mrs H is crying again and Mad friend is hugging her. I wonder what Mr H will say if he can see.

19 September

Little Fiend in bed with tummy ache all day and Mrs H is having meeting with Stupid Uni Committy so Katie must Hold Fort. Which means Katie must go up down up down up down to look after Every Little Thing that Poorly Little One wants.

Katie, can you get Mr Gruffy? (big yellow bear with one eye)

Katie, I'm too hot!

Katie, can I watch TV?

I'm getting headache listening to you all day, I say. Why dont you go sleep?

At about four she is calling for me again. I want to go slap her. To calm myself I pour glass of very nice orange drink from fridge. I hear crying and more crying, even when I put TV on loud and close door.

At five I go upstairs.

You shut up and go to sleep now! I am not your slave.

More crying. Snot falling off nose.

Where's my Mummy? I want my Mummy!

She is gone away, she is fed up with you. Everyone is fed up with you!

At six Mrs H comes back. I am on third glass of nice orange taste drink and have nice warm feeling inside.

Mrs H opens door drops work bag on floor, eyes leaping out of face.

What are you doing in here Katie??? My daughter is crying upstairs, cant you hear???

She points up to ceiling like I am deaf idiot.

That's my triple sec you are drinking isn't it??? How dare you!!!

She goes to look at LF. Comes down stairs with red face pointing finger and stomping foot like Mr H.

I want you out of this house this minute! I was crazy to let you anywhere near my daughter!

You are welcome to look after her yourself! She is Little Fiend, I never know such horrible little girl for all my life!

I've never known such a horrible O Pair! Please go Katie, I dont want to see you ever again. I will pay you this week's wages on the internet.

Ok, I say. I will go if you give me good reference, right now in my hand. Or I will tell Mr H what you do with Mad friend, her coming to house and you both getting drunk and dancing and your daughter in next room.

She looks at me like head will explode. But goes to write reference.

Thank you so much Mrs H, I say with big smile when she opens front door.

So long to Hudson Household, I say to self. So long Mr and Mrs H. So long Little Fiend and Shitty Big Ears. I think it will not be so long that all of you will be begging for me to come back.

Chapter 60

From: Allie Loff (allie53@outlook.com)
Sent: 20 September 2018 6.20am GMT
To: Bea Hudson (bhudson9@blueyonder.co.uk)
Subject: **New life, part 2**

Hi B

all is OK, sorry not in touch, no emails here. have left MM, heading to Byron Bay with some greenie hippy new age folks I met at a festival.

pls don't worry anymore. have told Ray everything.

Al xxx

From: Bea Hudson (bhudson9@blueyonder.co.uk)
Sent: 20 September 2018 9.05am
To: Allie Loff (allie53@outlook.com)
Re: **New life, part 2**

Glad you are having fun.

Feel free to send more info.

Your fed-up-with-waiting-to-hear-from-you sister.

Chapter 61

From: Katya (katkowalski@hotmail.com)
Sent: 20 September 2018 11.01am
To: Mr H (khudson@computercorps.com)
Subject: **Important News About Your Wife**

Hello Mr H,

I am sorry to bother you but yesterday I have to resign my position as I see Mrs H drink all the rest of bottle of Curachow with Mad friend, then they dance salsa very close, I do not know where to put my eyes. Fran comes to watch and I must send her back to TV.

I think you will like to know this, Mr H.

All the best from Katie

From: postmaster@mail.hotmail.com (postmaster@mail.hotmail.com)
Sent: 20 September 2018 11.05am
To: Katya (katkowalski@hotmail.com)
Subject: **Delivery Status Notification (Failure)**

This is an automatically generated Delivery Status Notification.

Delivery to the following recipients failed.

khudson@computercorps.com

Chapter 62

Bea's notes to stave off
imminent mental collapse

20 September

10.15pm

What else can go wrong? Come on, Big One Up There, whoever you are, wherever you are, I dare you. Bring it on!

No, I didn't mean it. I am grateful for small mercies, which I will try to list. There are a few, I'm sure.

1. Allie has finally got in touch. And thank goodness she's seen sense and left Van Morrison number two.
2. Fran has got over the stomach upset and is happy that Katie is no longer with us.
3. I too am happy that Katie is no longer with us.
4. I am still a Senior Lecturer in Cognition and Cognitive Neuroscience in the School of Psychological Sciences in the Faculty of Medical and Human Sciences at the best university in southern England.
5. I still have a cramped office with a broken radiator opposite the fruit fly factory in Biosciences, which in summer is full of tiny winged creatures dazed on alcohol.
6. I am not yet barred from conducting research.

7. My team has not yet completely disintegrated, despite the Prof's helpful suggestion that Ben exits into a 'more exciting research area', which would be 'a good thing for a chap of his calibre' and Hayley having just applied for three months leave due to ill health.

8. My paper may be about to disappear down an S-bend with little chance of publication in any respectable journal (feeble brain, inadequate inspiration, lack of credible hypothesis, undue anxiety over what to put in the bloody abstract and general pussyfooting around) but at least it has not yet been rejected multiple times and badmouthed by peer reviewers.

9. Although this year I have been allocated three extra tutees and two extra courses, not to mention compulsory membership of the Gender Equality in Medical and Human Sciences Committee, there will (hopefully) be a few hours left in each week to conduct research.

10. No first year psychology students to teach this year.

11. Lectures do not start until next week.

12. 10am on Monday morning is not nearly as bad as 9am on Monday morning.

13. Kurt has not phoned at 2am for five nights in a row. He has apologised again for accusing me of getting up to no good with Maddie, and swears he has not touched any alcohol since returning to Turkey except 'a bottle of beer' and 'a small glass of wine' with his meal last Saturday night.

14. Mum now back in Haslemere, though with a sprained wrist after falling on some leaves on way back from picking up a carton of milk from the corner shop. She now speaks a smattering of Polish and German, and a lot more Russian — she's going to apply for degree in Russian so she can read original Tolstoy etc. But she is

glad to be home again, especially since her friend Peter from the Film Appreciation meet-up group asked her out.

Anything else?

Oh yes, Kurt's satnav has finally turned up, after numerous delays for spare parts and a factory sit-in, just when I'd given up ever seeing it again. It looks as good as new – no one would ever guess it was once whirling around our washing machine at 60 °C.

And the last thing – Fran and I enjoyed the large, turd-shaped chocolate cake we found in the laundry room on the evening of Katie's departure, in a box labelled 'FOR SHITTY BIG EARS'. Unfortunately, Big Ears couldn't join in, as he's not allowed chocolate.

21 September

Up early to walk to school with Fran. All hunky-dory.

Me: You don't miss Katie at all?

Fran: Of course not, Mummy. Katie is full of shitty surprises.

Me: Where did you hear that?

Fran: From Katie, Mummy.

I hear the Big Poo in Playground story once again and secretly feel a little sorry for our ex ex-au pair.

Fran is looking forward to her first sleepover tomorrow, after her latest best friend's birthday party. I think she'll enjoy it, though she seems a little young for sleepovers. What will they get up to, I wonder? Putting on lipstick, swapping banned computer games and telling exaggerated stories about the shortcomings of their mothers/au pairs? I hope I won't get a bad reputation among this lot of mothers too.

22 September

5pm

Have sorted clean pyjamas for Fran and bought Amy's birthday present, a map of Papua New Guinea (where they plan to go exploring soon, Fran informed me this morning). I said that perhaps they should do a map reading course first – and maybe the odd trip to the supermarket to practise buying provisions.

Spent afternoon pulling my hair out over my paper, all that hasn't already fallen out that is. I know I'm not seeing something important, but what? Why the heck do the brains of spider phobics show activity in the middle of the brain's smell processing centre? Must have gone over same ground a hundred times but nothing sensible has come to me. Ben has triple-checked the data but the hotspot stubbornly remains in the same place. Will just have to submit my paper with this bizarre finding intact, and pray.

5.30pm

Just dropped off Fran at enormous house with ten chimneys and an Aston Martin in the drive – the sort of place where you expect a butler to open the door. Glad we're not in that social echelon yet. I'm quite happy with our falling-apart house (though could do without the cobwebs and dog hairs).

5.45pm

Drowning my sorrows in a large vodka tonic. Well, two large glasses, but who's counting? Have selected my salsa outfit for this evening: a well-above-the-knee flared skirt not worn in twenty years and a skimpy new blouse. My nails are adorned with 'Earth Goddess' iridescent green nail varnish bought this morning — looks rather lurid in this light, but never mind.

I feel sexy again!

I don't have to be home early tonight, hooray!

I am temporarily husbandless and childless. I have thirty-six hours to go before my first 10am Monday lecture and I'm sodding well going to have fun!

6.45pm

On platform at Clapham Junction waiting for the train to Streatham. (A little too much alcohol to drive.) Feel like a bird just loosed from its cage. How long has it been since I've gone anywhere on my own, not counting conferences, seminars, playgroups, Fran's school, the supermarket and an occasional yoga class?

That's how it has to be, according to Kurt. Yes, I'm lucky to have a seventy-hours-a-week job. Even if there's virtually no time left for anything after one's done the childrearing, housekeeping and husband-pleasing.

But it doesn't always have to be like this. I can start doing things on my own, now Fran's going to school full-time. I could learn kick boxing or t'ai chi. So what if we have no cleaner or childminder? Kurt can do his share of tasks from now on...

The train lurches towards Streatham. Grim rows of narrow terraces whizz past my grimy window. The sun lurks behind a thick haze, the train clanks and sways. It smells of fermenting bananas. I'm sticky all over, though I had a shower before setting off.

7.20pm

Order at the salsa pub bar while waiting for Maddie to turn up. Take my glass of wine to a window table. Try to hide my pleasure at several overtly appreciative male glances. My top is on the low side, definitely. Or is it the extra-shimmery eye shadow?

Drink my drink too quickly. Look around at the dolled-up girls and their blokes with fuzzy beards and striped shirts. How young they look. How long do they have left till they're bent-over wrinklies, moping over their absent children?

Feel time swooshing past. In a mere 10^7 seconds, give or take, Fran will have left school and be entering the big wide world, and I will be a post-middle-aged woman clutching at any half-hearted acknowledgement of my remaining attractiveness.

No, I refuse to wallow. I must make the most of every moment. I must Live for Now.

My heart beats faster. What will happen tonight? Will I meet a long-haired, silver-tongued thirty-something singer-guitarist and elope with him to who-knows-where? If one should come up to me this very second and ask me to go with him, what would I say?

I couldn't — I wouldn't.

I love Kurt.

For better or for worse, I've made a promise to him. I'm not going to throw everything we have away by indulging in some spur-of-the moment stupidity.

But part of me envies my sister for what she's done.

23 September

Sunday morning

I wake up in bed beside Mr Gruffy (comfortingly large and warm). Why he is here? Did I steal him from Fran's room?

What happened last night? What the hell happened last night?

Some of it's coming back now...

Don't know where to start. I can't remember much of the details, fortunately.

I clearly remember stumbling into bed a few hours ago, and before that Maddie helping me into the house in the pre-dawn murk. Oh yes, and I nearly fell onto the pavement getting out of the car, just as Jackie next door was putting a bag into the recycle bin. And I threw up on the way home in M's car – Thank God, I got to the window in time. I insisted I didn't need to go to hospital to get my stomach pumped. I really wasn't feeling that bad despite four or five or six glasses of wine, a gin cocktail or two and a vague memory of someone offering me pills. Oh yes, and the two vodka tonics I had before leaving the house.

After second cup of tea

Feel like death. Want to forget everything.

Maddie refuses to go home — she says she will stay here with me for rest of day to make sure I'm OK. Just called Fran — she is fine, she enjoyed her sleepover and will get a lift back this afternoon from Amy's mother.

Checked my mobile and found a 3.21am message I sent to Kurt that I can't remember composing. Did I ask Maddie to do it?

'Having nite out with girls, will be late home, talk later Xxx.' Also, there's fifteen missed calls from Kurt. I haven't called him back. Will wait till I've worked out what to say.

I have been a ... I can't think of a word strong enough. Dazzlingly foolish and irresponsible. A cretin of biblical proportions. An Utterly Bad Wife and an Indescribably Awful Mother.

I don't know if I have the guts to write down the bits of last night that I do remember. But I'm going to try, if only to convince myself what an all-round twat I've been. Then I'll bury this journal at bottom of garden for safely-distant future Britons to enjoy. If they can read its contents, that is. My handwriting has regressed even further lately.

It all started at salsa class. Or perhaps just before, while Maddie and I chatted over our second glass of wine.

Me: This will probably be the last hot night of the year. Summer's over, and soon the year will be over, and...

Maddie: Cheer up, you're not dead yet. There's plenty of time left before you kick the bucket.

Me: I suppose. Have you heard from Colin?

Maddie: No, of course not.

She opened her bag and pulled out her peppermint breath freshener. Neither of us spoke. I felt bad for mentioning him.

Maddie: I'm sure the Croatian woman in our class is either a lesbian or bi. I saw her kissing that girl with the red hair last week, after you'd gone.

That made me pay the Croatian woman extra attention. Clearly, she'd dressed to get it. Her stretch black top left much of her back bare, and ditto for her front. A gold chain clung to her ankle. When it was my turn to dance with her (there were two men short and she knew all of the man's steps), she looked into my eyes and I felt my cheeks warm.

Afterwards I stayed on at the pub with Maddie and some others from the dance class. With a shiver of déjà vu to the bar-hopping nights of my youth, I ordered a whisky and ginger ale. Tonight, I was free to go wherever I chose. There was no reason to get home early and no one to ask where I was.

The air in the pub grew warmer and stickier. The Croatian woman drank from a bottle of beer and flirted with the younger redhead whose ultra-low-waisted white jeans kept revealing the top half of a tattoo. Maddie was occupied with the two guys she'd danced with in class. I chatted to the other salsa dancers at our table while peering at the redhead's tattoo (frustratingly, was unable to make out the design). Then the redhead and the Croatian woman (Vera, I think) started giggling and arm-stroking. After a Bloody Mary (I think) and an Amaretto Sour, I forgot all about my plan to text Kurt to say I would be out late with some colleagues from work.

The next thing I remember, everyone at the table had gone apart from me, Maddie, the redhead and Vera.

Vera: We're going to a party nearby, do you two want to come? It's a five-minute cab ride — there'll be lots going on.

Maddie: (immediately) That sounds like fun.

Me: (thinking about how I was going to get home, but not wanting the night to end) OK, I'm up for it.

The party was in a smart period house. As we waited on the front step, I felt lightheaded, from exhilaration as well as too much alcohol. How long since I'd been to a party on the spur of the moment with someone who wasn't my husband? Then I felt a frisson of fear. I would know no one except Maddie and these two women, now snogging each other.

A woman with cropped hair, a lilac blazer, black shorts and high heels opened the door, 'Hello ladies, welcome!'

The woman headed up the broad curving staircase followed by Vera and the redhead. Maddie paused in the cavernous hall to examine a painting of a woman with waist-length black hair astride a goat under a half moon, then we followed the three women upstairs into a large room with wall-sized windows giving onto the street. The light, from orange and green lamps on low glass tables, was too dim to see anyone properly. The guests were all ages. There were lots of low-cut dresses, vampy looking boas, spiky heels and above-the-elbow black gloves. I couldn't see any men.

Me: Everyone's gay!

Mad: (with a roll of the eyes) What did you expect?

I'd never been to a party like this. I didn't mind what sort of party it was, though. Time was ticking on. Soon there would be no more chances for new experiences. Soon my daughter would be back from her sleepover and my husband would be living with us again, and I would go back to being Dr Hudson, Fran's Mummy and Kurt's Wife.

The woman in the lilac blazer approached with a bottle and some tulip-shaped glasses on a silver tray. We declined. Maddie didn't want to drink and drive and I was feeling more and more woozy.

I went in search of something to eat that might combat the onset of inebriation, only to come face to face with Vera and the redhead groping each other in front of the fridge. I made do with a withered banana from the fruit bowl and joined Maddie on a crescent-shaped white leather sofa.

The music was jangly and discordant, like the early stages of a horror film soundtrack. I wondered when they would put on something we could dance to. None of the other guests seemed to have any desire to talk, to us or each other. Lilac blazer woman stood nearby, still holding her tray, having her thighs massaged by a mature blonde in leopard-print leggings on a footstool.

Me: Is this an orgy, do you think?

Mad: It might be. Look over there.

We both stared at two forty-plus women casually undressing as if they were in a swimming pool changing room. The big bottomed one draped herself astride the arm of another sofa. Her companion, also ample in girth and naked except for a pair of dark glasses, kneeled beneath so that her mouth was unashamedly close to the other's pubic area, shorn except for a vertical black stripe decorated with sparkly bits.

Feeling a sudden urge to pee (had not gone since the pub), I sprang up. My desire for a new experience had vanished. I did my best to negotiate couples in the early and not-so-early stages of intimacy, nearly stumbling over a thick hairy leg. I kept on, out of the room and down the landing towards the only door that wasn't closed.

It was a spacious room. Shell-shaped washbasins, a shell-shaped bath and (three cheers) an old-style, chain-flush toilet. I went inside and was about to switch on the light and shut the door when I saw Vera's face reflected in a huge mirror on the mantelpiece shelf. She was brushing her hair in the semi-darkness.

Vera: Hello, Bea. What's up?

She carried on brushing her hair. It was loose now, long and almost black with a few silvery glints.

Me: I... er... need the toilet.

Vera: You can use it, I'm finished.

Me: Thanks.

I waited. She didn't move.

Vera: (in a softer, husky voice) Come here, darling. Kiss me.

I looked through the open window to a swollen moon. Vera slipped the brush into her bag and turned to me.

Just once, my other self instructed. Just this once.

I kissed her. Her scent gathered around me. Her hands pressed against the back of my head. At the sudden wet fullness on my mouth, I tried to pull away but she pressed me closer. Her pelvic bone dug into mine and I felt the push of her surprisingly dense breasts.

All this time, my body seemed to be entering another zone where the old rules didn't matter. 'Who are you kidding?' it seemed to say. 'You wanted to try something new. Just shut up and let it happen.'

Or was I drunk?

Vera's fingers moved under my skirt and found their way into my pants. Teetering on the brink of collapse, I was grateful for the wicker chair that Vera steered me towards. I was wondering if I should ask for a glass of water in case I passed out, when I realised with horror that my knickers were being pulled down and my skirt was being pulled up. Soon Vera was crouched on the floor, her nose and mouth nuzzling between my legs.

The sensation of the tip of her tongue on my most sensitive part revived me. I giggled — it was like being tickled with a feather. The tongue carried on, joined by a finger. I was telling myself that I must not to enjoy this too much, when I remembered the door. It was still open. I tried to speak, though it was difficult to pronounce any words coherently.

Then the effort of trying to resist what was happening was overtaken by something more earthy. I was dribbling juice like an overripe plum on first bite. No — not juice. I have a horrible feeling that in my excitement I peed into Vera's mouth, just as the redhead came in and shut the door behind her with a sound suspiciously like a bolt closing. She didn't seem at all surprised to see me slumped on a chair, legs open, receiving Vera's unexpected generosity. Pale-faced, without expression, she settled zombie-like on the edge of the bath.

I closed my eyes and prayed for salvation. Finally, Vera extracted her head, wiped her mouth and glanced at her companion with a smile of... triumph?

Trying to find a more ladylike position and simultaneously reach down to the floor to collect my underwear, I was overcome by dizziness. 'Water!' I gasped.

I think it was Vera who filled the toothbrush mug with tap water and passed it to me. Can't remember much of what happened next. I'd rather not remember, to be honest.

OK, it's coming back now. I should get all this out, I suppose, for therapeutic reasons.

The redhead, now semi-naked, kept getting objects out of a large black leather bag, like one a doctor might once have used for home visits — dildos, an assortment of tubes, a long stick with bristles on the end that looked rather like a mini loo brush... Were they intended for me? With wildly beating heart, despite my headache, bleary vision and poor coordination, I managed to collect my knickers, drag them into place and adjust my skirt in about two seconds flat.

Fortunately not. I watched as the redhead administered one instrument after another upon the body of her accomplice, who writhed on the bath mat and thrashed her legs (with pleasure, I think).

At first it was fascinating, if slightly macabre. I gawped at the glistening genitalia (the redhead had squirted and smeared the contents of several tubes with abandon), shocked by this display of female sexual parts in their full, close-up glory (far more informative than the Sky sex documentary that Kurt and I once accidentally turned on after a night out), as well as the sheer volume that could be accommodated by Vera's vagina.

Beginning to feel like a voyeur, I shut my eyes tight. But this only fed my imagination. The rhythmic gasps, grunts, moans and clanks would have been loud enough to rouse everyone in the house, if they hadn't been similarly occupied.

I'm not sure how long all this went on for. No one banged on the door and demanded access to the toilet, as I'd hoped. I tried to get to my feet but couldn't balance, let alone make it to the door. By Vera's ninth — or was it nineteenth? — orgasmic cry, I longed to flee to a remote part of the Antarctic. Then things took a turn for the worse.

The redhead hadn't forgotten me, after all. Leaving Vera sprawled panting on the floor, she rummaged in her bag and approached me with three round white pills in her open palm.

Redhead: Go on, take them. They'll help you relax.

Me: I have to leave, I don't feel well. My friend is waiting for me.

I'm pretty sure I didn't take the pills. I don't remember taking any. Not all of them, anyway.

The redhead rummaged in her bag and produced a dildo, clearly modelled on a stallion's organ. Vera smiled encouragingly at the redhead, who strapped the object to her hips and took a step towards me. I managed to get off my chair and totter towards the door but my legs didn't belong to me and the floor wouldn't stay still. Then from the other side of the door an elephant began to roar and there was a trampling of hooves that quickly turned into a deafening stampede.

Next thing I remember, I was sitting next to Maddie in the back seat of a taxi, thanking her for saving my life.

After fourth cup of tea

What have I done?

I got paralytic and incapable. I lusted after another woman. I let said woman debauch me. I may or may not have taken illegal drugs. I would have been molested by a redhead attached to a ten-inch dildo if Maddie hadn't rescued me. (She got worried when I didn't return and went to look for me, knocked on the bathroom door but heard only sounds of a sexual nature, and went away to check the other loos before returning and demanding entry.)

What would Kurt say if he knew I'd kissed a woman then let her lick my pussy, while another woman watched?

What if he finds out? What if I mumble something in my sleep? What if he interrogates Maddie and forces her to reveal the truth? How much did I tell her?

I am cold with panic. I will have to burn this exercise book before Kurt comes back — or bury it in a far-off field.

What am I going to do? I can't show my face in that salsa class ever again. And how can I face going to uni tomorrow morning and giving a lecture to the second years? What if one of them happened to be at the party and saw me being dragged outside, semi-conscious, clothing in disarray? I daren't go onto the High Street, either. And how will I ever face Fran? She's due home any minute.

The only good thing I can think of: At least I know I'm definitely not a lesbian. Whatever tendencies I may have had in that direction have been exterminated once and for all.

A bit later

Just talked to Kurt on the phone, unintentionally. Picked it up when it rang, thinking it would be Amy's mum re picking up Fran. He asked if I'd had a good night out with the girls. I told him that it had been an 'interesting evening'. Things didn't go to plan, I ate something that disagreed with me, then I had trouble getting home and I didn't feel very well by the end of the evening... Did my best not to lie. Perhaps I didn't, technically. But I lied in my heart and now I feel bad.

Kurt sounded concerned, said I mustn't overdo it. He said he stayed in the hotel last night because he was shattered after a long week. He worked out in the gym, ate a low-fat meal with a small glass of beer then read a book on philosophy (a first?) and went to bed before ten. He has turned over a new leaf and from now on will strive to be healthy in both body and mind.

Me: That's great!

Kurt: One more thing, darling.

I waited for him to say that he's found me out, my mobile called his by mistake ten times during the early hours of last night and all he could hear were unintelligible noises suggesting wanton ravishment... I will worship my husband as long as we both shall live, I promised The One Who Might Be Above, if only Kurt has not found out what I've done.

Kurt: I'm coming home.

I breathed again.

He will refuse to go back to Turkey, even if they threaten to fire him. He has booked a flight home for the morning of Fran's birthday on the 30th, so he'll be able to share the afternoon and evening with her.

Me: That's wonderful, sweetheart!

I totally meant it. I'm so so looking forward to Kurt coming back. Fran needs him — I need him. Here, with me. I've had enough new experiences, especially those involving dildo-toting redheads. Also, I've had enough of vibrators with multiple speeds and attachments. I want my husband back in my bed, putting his tongue in my ear and nibbling my nipples until I'm... Mmmmm. Can't wait.

Chapter 63

N. Rowley
The Practice
13 Old Fellows Court
London SW4 3FZ
23 September 2018

Dear Madeleine,

I am most heartened to discover that you are open to further communication. I am also glad that you trusted me enough to share your thoughts.

Of course, exchanging letters and emails is not the same as therapy. However, I trust my experiences as a therapist will not prove entirely useless in our correspondence – and in my life to come.

I thank you for your kind words, but I have decided to bid farewell to my therapeutic career and embrace the next stage in my life, whatever this will be (trout fishing on Sundays and bridge every Thursday evening does not yet seem an adequate replacement). Yesterday I informed my receptionist and the professional association to which I belong, and today I will begin the task of informing my seven remaining patients.

Unfortunately, I have not yet had the courage to tell my wife, and do not feel able to discuss my career with her as you suggested. She makes a point of telling me how much she enjoys having the house to herself, and I know very well how much she enjoys spending the proceeds of my practice in Harvey Nichols.

But money is not everything, is it? By the way, I sympathise with your artistic disappointment – the artist's way is certainly not an easy one. If you persevere, you may find what you are seeking. The same might be said of your predicament with your former boyfriend. In the therapy room, I always tried to refrain from giving fatuous advice of the kind that a friend might give over coffee. I shall break that rule now, if I may. It seems to me that you should not give up with Colin. Sometimes, things can happen that we cannot foresee.

Turning to your thoughts of snatching little girls from their mothers – as long as this is not something that you would consider carrying out in real life, I do not think this should be something of great concern. We all have socially transgressive thoughts from time to time; such thoughts are, in my view, a necessary part of the psyche, *as long as they are not acted upon*.

I myself have no children – partly through choice, partly through circumstance. To be frank, I find it difficult to imagine why so many people yearn for them. It is a society-induced state, I think, this desire to procreate, an example of how we are guided to do what is expected by the majority. Happiness is to be found in unexpected places, remember. Your way may not be the path of others.

Madeleine, I do not consider your thoughts to be 'weird', as you put it. They do however suggest someone who has suffered from an acute lack of trust in the benign nature of life. This, it seems to me, is a perfectly valid response to life's intermittent cruelties and, I imagine, the setbacks that you have no doubt suffered (though you never were able to discuss them with me), if a somewhat limiting one.

I also have a confession to make.

In recent years I have found myself fantasising while making love to my wife, generally that I am having rather more adventurous sexual experiences. (Nothing scandalous, I assure you.) Lately, these imaginings have become more intrusive. Although I do not blame my wife, I cannot help but see her increasing reluctance to be sexually intimate as a factor; she prefers to receive back, neck and shoulder massages. During these, I frequently find myself thinking about liaisons of a quite different nature.

Thank you in advance for understanding, Madeleine. I trust that you will not be shocked.

Please let me know how things go regarding Fran's birthday.

Yours,

Nigel

Chapter 64

Bea's notes to stave off imminent mental collapse

24 September, Monday

My 10am lecture was not the best one I've ever given. Too many students, too early in the morning. As I reached the lectern, I remembered just how much I hate performing in front of a hundred or so youngsters, half of whom look bored, distracted, puzzled or plain suicidal.

Got through the first half hour by breathing deeply and visualising faces of satisfied students as they leave the lecture theatre. Then looked up at the end of a particularly tortuous sentence composed of long gaps, ums and much frowning and headshaking (thanks to the new material I'd not got around to preparing) to see a carrot-haired girl in the third row, smiling at me.

I'm sure I've never seen her before, but the hair must have been enough to put me in mind of that dreadful bathroom experience. I was riveted to the spot with shock and humiliation. Forgot everything I'd been about to say, ran out of lecture theatre, down the stairs and out into the departmental veggie patch.

I was tempted to carry on out of the gates to the station and onto the first long-distance train, but no umbrella and an ominously dark cloud above. So instead I headed to the Psych Sciences café and had a PG Tips in a chipped mug with Moira, who was just ahead of me in the queue. Managed to hold back my tears, though voice shaky. When we were sitting down I told Moira I can't do it anymore. I can't hack the lectures, or the constant demands for research results, and I can't submit my crazy paper as it is. I'm going to resign.

'No, Bea.' Moira said it three times like a spell, while I sat on the hard plastic chair staring at her. Then she squeezed my hand and suggested I ask for three months immediate unpaid leave — the department can bump my teaching load onto one of our latest intake of Eager Young Lecturers. Or I could apply for stress leave, which would mean I got paid, only that would be a sure-fire path to early retirement and the removal of my 'research active' status. That's what the Prof told Moira anyway, when she said she needed to take stress leave because she was being bullied by a student who didn't like the grade she gave him in his second year paper.

Stress leave sounds tempting, I told her. It can hardly lower my chances of future career success any further. Zilch minus ten is still zilch.

On the bright side, my career is not yet on a par with that of George Price. No one gave him much credit for his theory of altruism and all his other achievements. Of course, I have not yet come up with an amazing theory to blast the world of neuropsychology, and my about-to-be-submitted paper will probably remain unpublished because at its heart is an incredible, unrepeatable fluke. If it does get published, I'll be famous in the world of neuroscience for all the wrong reasons, the butt of jokes in universities across the world for years to come.

Oh well, at least I tried. Who knows, maybe there's still time left to salvage my research career. If only my terminal decline could be delayed for a fraction longer, All Powerful One?

25 September, Tuesday

8.15pm

Haven't been back to uni yet. Can't decide whether to resign or go on stress leave. Think I may have mild post-traumatic stress disorder after the events of the party. Almost everything brings back that dreadful night.

Walked with Fran to school this morning and came home via Marks & Spencer. I was in the checkout queue considering whether to grab a large bar of Lindt when a buxom redhead squeezed past, nudging her rear against mine. All of a sudden I felt faint and nearly collapsed into my trolley.

Later at home watching Big Ears lapping up water in his bowl, I suddenly felt overcome with memories from That Night. My heart was pounding so much and I had to sit down. And every time I see a woman with even vaguely red hair, I have an irresistible urge to run like the clappers.

Onto another worrying thing.

As I was on the doorstep fumbling for my keys, Jackie next door said hello.

Jackie: How are you all?

Me: Fran and I are fine, thanks. Kurt will be home from Turkey soon.

Jackie: (with a peculiar look): Adrian's told me everything, you know.

Me: I don't know what you mean, Jackie.

Jackie: I don't have to spell it out for you, do I? Just be careful, I would. You know what husbands can be like when they get wound up. Especially yours, I should imagine.

Before I could speak, she'd gone inside.

For rest of afternoon, I mulled over her words. What on earth was 'everything'? Whatever her nosey husband might have gleaned from sneaking around spying on me? Just what would that be?

9.45pm

Maddie just phoned to ask how my paper was going but she really wanted to know about That Night.

Mad: By the way, you never told me what happened with those two in the bathroom.

Me: Didn't I?

Mad: You just said you couldn't remember much, you were too sozzled.

Me: Well, I don't remember much.

Mad: Nothing at all?

Me: Vera asked me to kiss her.

Mad: And you did?

Me: I needed to go to the loo. I thought I'd get the kiss out of the way—

Maddie: And then what happened?

Me: You promise not to tell anyone?

Maddie: Cross my heart. Come on Bea, tell me the worst.

I outlined the incident as succinctly as possible.

Maddie: Oh, my giddy aunt! That fucking takes the biscuit!!

Me: Are you OK?

Maddie: Just reeling over. No wonder you were in such a state in the taxi. That's put me right off the idea of going bi.

Me: You were thinking of going bi? What's brought this on?

Maddie: Oh, that party must have triggered something... and Colin giving me the elbow. I was thinking that things might work out better with a woman.

Me: I suppose they could. But then again... Why don't you just go over to Colin's place, if he won't ring you?

Maddie: He doesn't want to see me, Bea. He thinks I'm just out to con him.

I said she had nothing to lose. Then told her I was planning to hand in my resignation on Friday. Maddie said I must swear not to do anything till she comes over and has a proper talk with me. I told her she'd better not turn up again, or the Nosey Neighbours will be onto us. Told her about Jackie's peculiar warning.

Maddie: Don't pay any attention to her, she's a nosey old bitch who doesn't get enough attention. Whatever Adrian said to her is bound to be a pack of lies.

I pondered this while putting Fran to bed. Though it was nearly ten, F said she wasn't tired and insisted on playing with the collection of shells, pebbles and assorted found objects strewn on the floor around her new shell box — a black plastic container that she found in my bedroom.

26 September, Wednesday

8.13am

Woke early in a panic and leapt out of bed.

A redhead was watching me while a huge hairy creature with a tangle of black and white striped legs was roaming over my naked body — arms, legs, neck, belly...

All the time, it kept saying, 'Relax, this won't hurt.' Then, just as Bea Hudson was about to disappear, all its legs dropped off and the spider turned into a bright green snake which slivered away under a rock with a loud BOLF—

Great Hairy Bollocks! I know what I'll put in my abstract. I'll give my perplexing anomaly a name. Henceforth, it shall be known as 'the BOLF' aka Bea's Only Lucky Fluke. (Why not?)

4.10pm

Worked feverishly on the paper's abstract all morning. At last came up with a summary of our findings and a conclusion. Hayley came to my office to proofread the final version (she's been temporarily relieved of migraines after a visit to her Chinese acupuncturist). At 3.30pm I emailed it to the editors of Nature.

Have printed out the abstract and stuck it on my office wall as a souvenir — the version with Hayley's suggested changes tracked.

Chapter 65

How spider phobics may be 'sniffing out' spiders – an fMRI/EEG/DTI study examining the cortical and sub-cortical response of spider-phobic volunteers to fear-eliciting situations using an eclectic collection of brief but extremely nasty film clips

B. F. Hudson, B. E. Smith, H. L. Mistry

We have identified the neural circuit responsible for regulating certain types of phobia-specific fear, which includes the Basolateral Amygdala (BLA) and the Bed Nucleus of the Stria Terminalis (BNST).

In addition, we have identified an additional brain site so far overlooked by researchers in this field, which appears to play a crucial role in spider phobia, specifically. Surprisingly, this site is located within the central region of the Piriform Cortex (Olfactory Bulb) – the primary centre in the brain for processing smells. For convenience, from now on we shall refer to this site as the 'BOLF'.

Our findings indicate that the BOLF is part of an ancient neural circuit providing the olfactory equivalent of visual threat detection.

Though it is well known that spiders possess a keen sense of smell, they are not generally known to be smelly to humans. However, it is ~~just about~~ possible that some spiders produce odours that may be detected by the human olfactory system, and that the detection of a characteristic 'spider smell' would once have routinely triggered a 'spider alarm system' in humans. We suggest that such an alternative non-visual pathway may have evolved which was advantageous to our ancestors, and that a residual smell detection mechanism is still activated in certain individuals, namely spider phobics.

Furthermore, it may be that the complex 'smell memory' encoding carried out in the Piriform Cortex facilitates extremely fast classification of potential predators when arachnophobes are faced with their feared objects – literally, the 'smell of fear'.

Alternatively, the Piriform Cortex may do a lot more than was previously thought.

~~As the grant for this study has come from the Medical Research Council~~ We speculate that a pharmacological agent targeting the BOLF could be employed to 'erase' the fear memory invoked in spider phobics, and so facilitate fear extinction. For reasons ~~of dubious merit~~ outlined in the pages following, we believe that the BOLF would be an ideal target site.

Chapter 66

6pm-ish

Coming out of office, flushed with post-delivery relief, I spied the Prof further down the corridor, ruminating as usual on the incinerator chimneys, and dodged behind a large student standing outside my door (possibly one of my tutees that I'm supposed to meet with once a week). Did not feel in the mood for expounding my hypothesis to a sceptical audience.

Bumped into Mike in the lift, also looking rather sweaty. He has heard rumours about me 'having some issues'. Reassured him I am not yet a geriatric has-been, merely had a fit of incompetence during my first lecture of term. All is well, have just submitted my paper, sorry have to rush or I'll be late picking up Fran.

After dinner

Got email from the Prof summoning me to attend his office at 3pm this Friday. Can't imagine what about. Dismissal? It must be serious to interfere with his Friday afternoon drinks in Room 12 with the faculty VIPs.

Maddie's just called, asking if she can take me and Fran out for lunch at Nando's this Sunday to celebrate Fran's birthday. Said fine, as long as we're back by 3pm (Kurt's ETA).

28 September, Friday
Meeting with Prof

Prof: (Without getting up from desk.) Good afternoon, Bea. I won't beat around the bush – I have a few concerns.

Me: The reason I had to leave the lecture theatre suddenly on Monday – I had a relapse… For years I've had this public speaking phobia.

Prof: (Abruptly, ignoring what I just said.) Have you submitted your grant application yet?

Me: I'll work on it soon. I've been flat out on my paper.

Prof: You probably won't hear from the Medical Research Council for at least three months. So you'd better get on with it, or there won't be any more money to pay for Ben and Hayley past the end of the year.

Me: (Tentatively.) Couldn't the department help out for a while, like it did last year with Jamie's group?

Prof: Jamie was a special case, I'm afraid. (Throat clearing.) You have stiff competition for research funds from elsewhere in this department, you know Bea. Take the PTSD Group, for example. It's attracting plenty of interest from postdocs. One chap has top-notch results under his belt, I understand.

Me: (Glazed look turning to frown.)

Prof: Research isn't for everyone, Bea. Perhaps you should consider concentrating on teaching – you have a small child, don't you? It doesn't pay to spread oneself too thinly.

Left the room with the air of a stepped-on cockroach, without acting on my urge to throttle the Prof (slowly and painfully). I don't think my mouth closed until I was in the loo wiping away my tears.

29 September, Saturday
Nearly 10pm

The weirdest thing has just happened.

I went to Fran's room for the third time and told her to pick up all her shells from the floor. When she didn't respond, I picked up her beach box to do it myself. It wasn't an empty plastic container, as I'd expected. Without its lid, which Fran must have taken off, one can see inside. There's a small hole in the plastic with a lens fastened behind it. Behind the lens is a small box connected with a wire to another small box and another wire (broken) going to a battery.

A month or two ago, this plastic box was next to the toaster, holding tissues. Kurt put it there. I remember saying, 'Why do we want that?' and he replied, 'It makes the kitchen look neater.' Fran must have found it and decided it was perfect for her beach pickings.

Too many questions came at once.

- Is my husband spying on me?
- How long has he been spying on me?
- Are there any other spy cameras in the house?
- Where are they?
- Did he see Maddie giving me a massage?
- Has he seen anything else he shouldn't have?
- What hasn't he seen?
- How dare he do this to me?

The sly bastard!

The slimy, low-down worm!

After midnight

Collected further hairs from the shower floor, finished the latest bottle of triple sec and sent an email to Kurt. Now going to bed.

Chapter 67

From: Madeleine Geen (madeleine.geen@gmail.com)
Sent: 29 September 2018 10.14pm
To: Nigel Rowley (nprowley@blueyonder.co.uk)
Subject: **Your confession**

Hi Nigel,

Thanks for sharing your stuff with me. I'm surprised and quite pleased that you trust me with your secret fantasies!

Have you talked to your wife about them? I think you should consider confiding in her too. She can't really blame you for something you're not really in control of, can she?

I've been making Fran a birthday present. It's a horse, made out of stuff I've found in front gardens and recycle bins. I've sprayed it gold and made a saddle out of some velvet I was going to make curtains from. It's bigger than I expected so I hope she can find somewhere to put it.

Bea doesn't want to meet me for lunch tomorrow (with Fran, as it's her birthday) as we'd planned. She's just found out that her husband's been spying on her and doesn't feel like doing anything except bashing him into a stupor. I'm disappointed, but never mind. I'll just have to pop over with the horse in the morning before Kurt gets back. I want to see Fran's face when she opens it!

All the best,

Madeleine

Chapter 68

From: Nigel Rowley (nprowley@blueyonder.co.uk)
Sent: 29 September 2018 10.48pm
To: Madeleine Geen (madeleine.geen@gmail.com)
Re: **Your confession**

Dear Madeleine,

No, I have not confided in my wife, as I fear she would be shocked and think less of me. We have been happily married for many years, though clearly we do not share as much as some couples do. However, I have never believed it prudent to divulge everything to one's spouse.

I hope Fran appreciates your gift. It sounds delightful.

Yours,

Nigel

Chapter 69

From: Bea Hudson (bhudson9@blueyonder.co.uk)
Sent: 29 September 2018 11.22pm
To: Kurt Hudson (khudson@computercorp.com)
Subject: **Divorce**

I found your spy camera in Fran's bedroom this evening. She has incorporated it into her beach box. Fortunately, it is no longer in an operational state.

I assume there were other spy cameras too?

You don't need to tell me, I don't know if I could bear it.

Kurt, I have had enough. What you have done is utterly intolerable. I cannot stay with someone who treats me like a possession, who tramples over my rights as a human being and thinks it acceptable to covertly watch his wife in her most private moments, day and night.

I want a divorce.

Bea

From: Kurt Hudson (khudson@computercorp.com)
Sent: 30 September 2018 3.03am GMT
To: Bea Hudson (bhudson9@blueyonder.co.uk)
Subject: **Divorce???**

My darling,

As you have not responded to my repeated calls, I will attempt to put into words how deeply sorry I am for the hurt I have caused you. What I did was unforgiveable. But at the time it seemed the only way for me to take control of my incessant suspicions concerning your friend.

I now see how laughable and plain idiotic these concerns were, as were the extreme lengths I went to in order to satisfy myself of their falsity. For my deepest wish was for this vile surveillance to demonstrate your innocence. With hindsight, I should have simply listened to you when you assured me of the truth.

I am a weak, imperfect man. I do not deserve your love. But I love you, Beatrice, with all my strength. Please, my darling, do not abandon me.

When I return, I will tell Madeleine how sorry I am to have tainted her character with my accusations. While I would hesitate to praise her unduly, she certainly did not deserve to become the target of my unfounded suspicions. A garment sent in poor taste, an excess of text messages, an overheard remark misconstrued – any other man would have laughed it off.

Re the spycams – I confess that I planted three in total, all on my first visit home, located in the bedroom, kitchen and living room. The next time I checked on them, one didn't work at all, and despite all my efforts, I couldn't track down the tissue-box cam Fran has just found. What I saw from the remaining camera was minimal (it was that time I locked myself in the bathroom). I swear, as soon as I got to anything remotely private, I fast-forwarded. Afterwards I felt ashamed and furious at myself for stooping to such depths.

Please, my love. Can you find it in your heart to forgive me?

K

From: Kurt Hudson (khudson@computercorp.com)
Sent: 30 September 2018 9.14am GMT
To: Bea Hudson (bhudson9@blueyonder.co.uk)
Subject: **Coming home**

Are you still asleep, my darling?

I love you. Please don't ignore me any longer.

I'll be home mid-afternoon – earlier, if can get on the earlier flight. I'm in a cab on the way to the airport.

Tell Fran I'll see her soon to celebrate her birthday.

I can't wait to see you both. I want us to be a happy family again.

K

From: Bea Hudson (bhudson9@blueyonder.co.uk)
Sent: 30 September 2018 9.49am
To: Kurt Hudson (khudson@computercorp.com)
Subject: **Coming home**

Dear Kurt,

I do not have a heart of stone.

But do you think you can fob me off with a couple of emails? How can a marriage mean anything if there is no trust left, if deceit is the only thing that flourishes?

Not just one 'spycam' – three! Including one in the bedroom!!??

I don't think I can bear to find out any more about your underhand activities. You have reduced me to a spluttering, incoherent mess.

How dare you? You couldn't stop at contaminating my home with your blasted spying devices, you had to engage our neighbours to spy on me as well. Those two next door wouldn't know a donkey's head from its arse, if you hadn't guessed already.

For the record, you might like to know that if I *had* wanted to get up to anything with Madeleine – or anyone else – I certainly wouldn't have been stupid enough to do it at home.

Beatrice

PS

No need to hurry home, no one wants to see you.

Chapter 70

Bea's notes to stave off imminent mental collapse

30 September, Sunday
10am-ish

Feel like have been in a car crash. No more triple sec, ever.

Two emails from Kurt and at least 20 phone messages. He is sorry. Very very sorry.

Should I forgive him?

He's betrayed my trust.

But I've betrayed him too, haven't I?

I've done unspeakable things.

If he knew, he would never forgive me.

I don't deserve him.

It's all v well to take moral high ground, but sometimes you just have to back down and say 'I love you.'

I'll call and tell him before he gets on the plane.

10.15am

Kurt not answering his phone. He must be in the plane already.

Fran just got into bed with me to open my present to her, an enormous white furry rabbit. Got big hug, I am the best mummy ever.

11am-ish

Still have furry tongue and red eyes but I'm feeling a bit better, thank goodness.

No reply from K still.

Maddie's just come over with Fran's present, a horse she made out of recycled household rubbish. It's got cork hooves and cardboard ears and a huge bushy tail made of pieces of copper wire. Fran gave it most of the space on her little dressing table and kissed both Maddie and the horse several times. (Actually, I love the horse too — it must have taken days to make.)

11.30am

Maddie has gone to Waitrose with Fran and Big Ears — I forgot to get any Häagen-Dazs Strawberry Cheesecake ice cream. M's going to stay for lunch as Kurt won't be home for a couple of hours at least.

12.15pm

Mad, Fran and dog not back yet. Called F's mobile and found it ringing in her room. Called M's mobile and got voicemail.

Don't know why they are taking so long. Waitrose is only a ten min walk. Did they decide to stop in the park and eat the ice cream?

1.30pm

Still no Mad, Fran or Big Ears. Called M's mobile again and got voicemail again. Left a message.

Where are they? Trying not to panic or jump to conclusions. The three of them have fallen down a large rabbit hole? They've taken a wrong turn and got lost? But Maddie would have called, wouldn't she? And why is her phone switched to voicemail? Has she kidnapped Fran and dognapped Big Ears?

2.15pm

Kurt has just texted. He'll be home within the hour.

Still no Mad, Fran and Big Ears.

What will Kurt say if I tell him Fran and Big Ears have gone off with Maddie and I have no idea where they are?

Scared of what could have happened to them.

Please God, do something. I know I haven't been your most dedicated follower, but if Fran could come back exactly as she left...

I can't imagine what they could have been doing all this time. Maddie has probably just got engrossed in something and forgotten the time (deciding which brand of ice cream? scavenging bins for future sculptures?) Or she's got stranded somewhere (long queue at Waitrose checkout? a riot in Godalming High Street?)

What if she really has kidnapped Fran?

She's always been close to Fran. A bit too close, perhaps...

Should I call the police? I can't just sit here and wait.

Chapter 71

From: Madeleine Geen (madeleine.geen@gmail.com)
Sent: 30 September 2018 2.30pm
To: Bea Hudson (bhudson9@blueyonder.co.uk)
Subject: **Trip on a train**

Hi Bea

I'm on a train with Fran and Big Ears heading for the New Forest. Sorry not to be in touch before, you were probably worried. I was going to come straight home after we got the ice cream, only we went the wrong way and went past the train station. Something made me go inside. Then I saw there was a train due in ten minutes for Portsmouth via Brockenhurst. I had to get on it. I know you won't understand but please don't worry about Fran, she's safe. I just want a short time with her on her birthday before Kurt gets back. This may be the last chance I'll have to be with her, just the two of us.

Mad xx

PS We ate the ice cream on the train – I didn't get much after Fran and Big Ears had tucked in!

From: Bea Hudson (bhudson9@blueyonder.co.uk)
Sent: 30 September 2.39pm
To: Madeleine Geen (madeleine.geen@gmail.com)
Re: **Trip on a train**

I don't get it, Mad. Why didn't you ask me if you could take Fran out for a while before getting on the train, I wouldn't have minded! I thought something terrible had happened. And Kurt will be here any moment – what the f– do I tell him? Please, bring Fran and BE back this minute.

From: Madeleine Geen (madeleine.geen@gmail.com)
Sent: 30 September 2018 2.42pm
To: Bea Hudson (bhudson9@blueyonder.co.uk)
Re: **trip on a train**

Bea, I'm so sorry I scared you. Wasn't thinking. I must be having a midlife crisis. Or a never going to be a mum crisis. Back later today, by dinner time I hope. Don't worry, we're all ok! Mad xx

From: Madeleine Geen (madeleine.geen@gmail.com)
Sent: 30 September 2018 3.11pm
To: Nigel Rowley (nprowley@blueyonder.co.uk)
Subject: **Latest news**

I have taken Fran and Bea's dog for an impromptu trip to the New Forest. We were supposed to be getting ice cream. One minute I was walking out of the supermarket with Fran, the dog, a tub of ice cream and a bottle of sparkling elderflower tonic on the way to Bea's, the next I was at the ticket office asking for a day return to Brockenhurst. It sounded nice and I was pretty sure it was in the New Forest.

Fran asked why we were going on the train. I said this is your birthday surprise.

What about Mummy?

It's a surprise for Mummy as well as you, we won't be gone for long.

OK, Auntie Maddie.

So here she is, her fringe in her eyes, size 11 trainers waggling above the floor, paint-splattered pink sweatshirt over her jeans. She seems happy to be looking out of the window and pulling the dog's ears from time to time. (Big Ears is sitting on the seat between us, his head lolling onto my lap when the train sways.) The man opposite reading The Sunday Telegraph keeps looking at us like he wants to pull the emergency stop cord and get us put off the train.

I haven't answered my phone yet. It's on silent. It's Bea, she keeps calling but I can't speak to her, not yet. She'll be mad with me and tell me to come back.

Have you got a smartphone, Nigel? Can't imagine you with one somehow. I always see you in a world that time forgot, in a tidy 1950s house with a 1950s wife who makes scrummy desserts.

On the subject of your wife – if your wife isn't much into sex, maybe it's because she's bored with you? She might crave something different, something you haven't been able to give her. Have you ever been to a swingers party? That would be something you could do together. She might like another guy bonking her, you never know. Sorry about that, I'm getting a bit stressed here with this situation.

Fran is my goddaughter, she trusts me and I'm on a train swooping her away from home towards I've no idea what, and Bea wants me to bring Fran and the dog home right away. But I can't give her back yet. She's probably the only child I'll ever have, in a way. I need to pretend she's all mine, just for a short time. With Kurt back from Turkey permanently, I'll never get to see her. Also, I'm not in a rush to get back to Godalming as Kurt will be there and he'll kill me when he finds out I've gone off with Fran! He hates me being with Fran as much as he hates me being with his wife.

I know, I know, I shouldn't have done this. You don't have to tell me.

Madeleine

From: Madeleine Geen (madeleine.geen@gmail.com)
Sent: 30 September 2018 4.37pm
To: Nigel Rowley (nprowley@blueyonder.co.uk)
Re: **Latest news**

It's me again Nigel. I wish you would reply, I could do with some friendly advice. Don't you have a smartphone?

I'm in trouble. We've just sat down for a rest in the middle of a mess of trees and paths with no signs anywhere. I haven't a clue where I am or how to get back to the station. Fran has a blister on her heel and says she can't walk and Big Ears is panting like he needs to drink up the nearest lake. We've drunk all the elderflower tonic and run out of water despite all the bottle top ups from the train toilet's tap.

No idea what to do. No one to ask for directions and the signal on my phone keeps dropping out so Google maps is useless. I can't call Bea even if I wanted to. Just as well, she would totally freak out.

When are we going home? Fran just asked (the Auntie Maddie's have stopped).

As soon as we get out of this effing forest, I said.

Where are the ponies?

I don't know. They were here when I came last time, now they've all buggered off.

I want to go home!

I know, so do I, so does Big Ears!

Actually Nigel, the dog isn't looking so good. His head is on his paws, his eyes are shut and a fat strand of drool is hanging off his chin. I just hope he will last out until we find our way to a tap. The last thing I need is a dead dog.

Madeleine

Chapter 72

What to do about Madeleine?

3/9/18, Istanbul airport

On the plane, at last. Within a few minutes Turkey will be retreating at a rate of 200 km/s and soon I will be home with my family once more.

Tucked under the seat in front of me is a large bag containing my peace offerings — Bea's Coco Chanel perfume and assorted anti-ageing elixirs, and Fran's birthday presents (Turkish delight, a Whirling Dervish costume and a large, dark blue cotton scarf — all I could find at the airport gift shop).

4.15pm, home

I did not expect to have an easy homecoming, following my admission of aggravated suspicion culminating in a grievous rampage of paranoia. But now I am informed that Madeleine has disappeared to somewhere in the New Forest with my daughter and my dog, and my wife has not a clue where they currently are (the New Forest is pretty big), and when they are coming home ('dinner time' could be 10pm to that woman).

When Bea told me this news (cautiously, phone in one hand and empty wine bottle in the other) I was speechless. This cannot be possible, I told myself. This is not the sort of thing that happens to a man returning home for his daughter's fifth birthday, the now not-so-small daughter he has been desperately missing during the many weeks he has been forced to endure a sweaty armpit of a city, by day scouring the arid confines of ComputerCorp's environs for signs of intelligent life, by night reduced to stumbling about in bars, in a feeble attempt to keep his career flowing with the current as opposed to performing ever-diminishing circles around the Spent-CEO Plughole.

I was a turkey for going there in the first place. And for allowing myself to be conned by that conniving blonde bitch.

That woman's not your friend, she's a child stealer, I told Bea, who looked like she had just seen several ghosts.

I really don't know why she's done this, Bea said in a flat voice. She's never done anything like this before.

I sincerely hope not, my dear, I said, or I might be even more alarmed than I am now. If that's possible.

Bea resumed circling the kitchen, occasionally checking her phone or meandering towards the living room windows.

She won't be much longer, I'm sure, Bea said once again. She texted to say where she was going, it's not like she's just run off without a word.

Funny, that's exactly what it seems like to me. One lousy message in all this time. God knows where she is now or what she's getting up to with our daughter.

What the hell do you mean? She would never do anything to hurm Fran.

How do you know? Your judgement of character has been astonishingly poor with regards to your so-called friend.

She would never do anything bad to Fran, I know that. She's a bit messed up in the head, that's all. She's sad that she isn't a mother—

She should be relieved that she can't inflict herself on a helpless child! Except for ours, that is. She's a menace — and a total nutcase. Why can't you see that? OK, I was wrong about you and her having an affair. But I always sensed there was something underhand about that woman—

Bea slammed the door behind her, leaving me alone in the kitchen trying to resist my craving for a double shot of Kentucky Bourbon. My stash of Woodford Reserve has vanished from its hiding place in the cupboard behind a pile of lychee tins and lentil tins. Even my emergency bottles of Gordon's and tequila have gone. Spotted an empty bottle of Triple Sec in the dustbin, above a dozen empty bottles of Chardonnay.

Have I left her alone for too long? Surely, Bea isn't turning into an alcohol-abusing wretch like me? No, I mean like the me I used to be. From now on, I'm going to look life in the face and not take refuge in cowardly crutches. I haven't let a drop of hard liquor pass my lips since that unfortunate episode in the bathroom, and I won't give in now. Bea needs me to be strong. We will resist the demon drink together. We will walk arm in arm and lie side by side — as soon as that woman returns with my little girl. That swine of misspent womanhood, that infernal interloper, brazen child rustler...

God knows what I will do when I get my hands on her. Madeleine will be sorry for what she's done.

5.10pm

Sitting on the terrace with a long glass of iced ginger ale, waiting for the next communication from Goldilocks, musing on what I might say to the woman when I see her. Various combinations and permutations of words, four-letters and up, come in and out of focus.

But I am not a mindless, violent oaf without any shred of self-control. I am a rational, civilised man, and I must behave like one. It's just as well there's no alcohol left in the house.

5.30pm

Called the local police station to report my daughter missing. Got sent around the houses and fed platitudes.

It doesn't sound like a particularly high-risk situation, sir. Call again if she's not back after twelve hours.

Calm down sir, I'm sure your daughter will be back with you soon.

Chapter 73

From: Madeleine Geen (madeleine.geen@gmail.com)
Sent: 30 September 2018 5.45pm
To: Bea Hudson (bhudson9@blueyonder.co.uk)
Re: **Trip on a train**

On way to Brockenhurst station. Sorry to be so long out of contact. Couldn't call, no signal + low battery. We had a few probs with navigation. New Forest is so big!

Will be with you soon. We're all ok except cold + muddy + hungry + Fran limping – blister + I hurt my ankle can't put weight on left foot.

Mad x

Chapter 74

From: Madeleine Geen (madeleine.geen@gmail.com)
Sent: 30 September 2018 5.51pm
To: Nigel Rowley (nprowley@blueyonder.co.uk)
Subject: **Last news**

Made it to station at last after hailed down straggly hiker with backpack who gave us directions + his water bottle + Mars bar + two Nurofen for my ankle (tripped on mole hill).

Now waiting for train to London. Fran not talking, socks off and foot up on bench checking toe. Dog looks better after water, though he peed most of it out on the platform in full view of train heading the other way

I'll plan my next trip more carefully :)

Seriously, I'm not going to do anything like this again. I've learned a lesson. I doubt Fran will want to go anywhere with me, anyhow – and I'm sure to be banned from coming within ten miles of her after today.

Thanks for your letters, Nigel. It's been good to know that you were there.

This will be my last email to you, I've decided. It's time to get a grip on my life (+ hopefully Colin).

All the best, then. I hope it all goes well with your wife. Relationships aren't easy, are they?

Madeleine

Chapter 75

From: Bea Hudson (bhudson9@blueyonder.co.uk)
Sent: 30 September 2018 5.51pm
To: Madeleine Geen (madeleine.geen@gmail.com)
Re: **Trip on a train**

All is not OK here. We are both gobsmacked, flabberstruck, etc. Can't think what has got into you. Why didn't you tell us where you were going?? Kurt has called the police!! Get over here as soon as you can or I hate to think what might happen.

Chapter 76

Text messages between Madeleine and Colin

18.14

Hi Col, just wanted to say hello, seems like ages since we talked. Called you at work the other week but was told you had left already. Hope you're surviving the fallout from your cunning scheme ok. When will you move to the island in the sun? Maddie

18.27

Yes Maddie, I've left my job, at long last. I recently got a big cheque in the post from my former employer, so now I'll have ample opportunity to live it up in some tropical hideaway overlooking the beach. I've heard it's splendid in the British Virgin Islands all year round, the cocktails are excellent and the music isn't bad either. I'm very pleased to hear from you, by the way. If I judged you rather harshly, I'm sorry. I've been burnt before I suppose. Come over and have a drink sometime, anyway. I will be around for a few weeks yet. Colin

18.29

Col, that's super, it wd be lovely to see you. Are you free this evening? I know it's a bit soon but I am in big trouble + would much appreciate your help. Can you poss pick me up from Godalming station about eight + take me to Bea's place? I don't want to go there on my own undefended, I mean on my own. Well not totally, got Fran + Bea's dog with me. Long story, I'll explain later. If you cd do this, I wd be over the moon! M x

18.34

How could I say no to a request like that? I don't get asked every day to rescue damsels in distress. But you've got some explaining to do, missy. Why is Fran with you? And her dog? And why do you want me to come to your friend's place with you?

18.36

Thanks Col, u r sweetest man alive. Promise will explain soon. M xx

18.39

No, I want to know now.

19.13

Sorry for the delay, Fran had to use the train loo then the doors wouldn't open as auto button stuck, so had to call for help, then Big Ears swiped half of a woman's ham sarnie. I had to stop her kicking BE then pay for the lost half. (Nearly ate other half myself, so hungry.) No buffet on the train as it's Sunday. Gave Fran banana + packet of pretzels I nicked from table of guy asleep at other end of train. Due at God. station 7.50pm. Re your questions, I took Fran + dog for visit to New Forest. Things didn't go well. We got lost + injured. Worried what Bea + Kurt will say when we get back. Especially Kurt. Would be good to have your moral support. My car is parked outside their house so I can stop for drink at your place on my way home afterwards (should I make it out of Bea's in one piece that is). xxx

19.15

You took Fran away without permission?

19.35

Explain l8r xxxxxx

Chapter 77

Bea's notes to stave off imminent mental collapse

30 September, Sunday

7.30pm

Not a great day so far. Nothing to eat since lunch. Spent afternoon trying to keep myself calm and Kurt from getting a stroke, heart attack etc.

It won't do any good ranting at me, I keep telling him.

I pray that Mad will be back in half an hour as she texted. Kurt is losing his cool since his fruitless call to the police station. He has been sitting out on the terrace in the gloom. Nothing but grunts or silence when I speak, after his accusation that I'm turning into an alcoholic. Thank goodness he hasn't found the bottles of gin, whiskey and tequila that I hid in the bottom of our wardrobe.

7.45pm

Went out to the terrace again.

Me: Maddie will be back with Fran soon.

Kurt: We hope. I warn you, Beatrice, she's going to pay for this.

I go back downstairs and watch the BBC news for the fifth time. Flooding and droughts, murders and muggings... Compared to all that, our own distressing incident seems fairly minor.

Not all that minor. What will Kurt do when he sees Maddie?

I'm inclined to agree with Kurt, for the first time in a while. She's taken things too far this time.

Chapter 78

Text messages between Madeleine and Colin

20.03

Col, WTFAY? Can't wait much longer, we're going to walk from station though hard with my bad ankle and Fran's blister. Bea's address: Charming Cottage, Summerhouse Road, God. House near on a corner with tiles fallen off the walls and high straggly hedge. Pls come ASAP!!! DON'T CALL ME as my phone battery is nearly gone

20.09

Maddie, I have an uneasy feeling about this. You run off with your friend's child then you turn to me for help. What do you think I am, the closest convenient mug? Much as I appreciate you asking me to be your Knight in Shining Armour, I think this is a step too far. Do you think I am so besotted with you that my brains have turned to jelly? Colin

20.22

Please Col, that's not how it is! Can't tell you all now, am in the shed. Lawnmower against door so Kurt can't get in. He's banging on door, says he will kill me. About to piss myself. Bea shouting at him STAY CALM + HANG ON MAD + dog is barking his head off. Need loo, dark in here, lots of cobwebs & crawling things. Pls pls pls come Col, I will be forever grateful

20.24

Don't be afraid Maddie, I will be with you shortly. Have you called the police? Tell Kurt you will press charges if he lays a finger on you. Col

20.25

Col you're the loveliest guy I've ever known. Bea has called cops but no sign of them, she is going to get help from next door. xxxx

20.26

What is the postcode there? Address you gave not in my GPS

20.27

Don't know postcode. Go to end of God. high street to main road (the other end from Waitrose) and you will see Red Lion pub or Red Dragon. Go up the hill on the other side. Summerhouse Road is on the left

20.37

Pls hurry, Kurt bashing on shed door, he's going to break it down any moment. Christ, he has statue in his hand, a male fertility figure with a big c

20.38

Are you ok Mad? Hang on in there. Can't find Red Lion.

20.39

Kurt's gone mental. I told him I'm sorry I didn't mean to cause harm I just wanted to see Fran once more. He said u crazy bitch I will teach u not to mess with %%^ohshit

20.40

What's going on??

20.41

Thought I was goner for sure. Just peed on lawnmower. Madness here. Bea is throwing apples at Kurt's back

20.45

Adrian next door trying to get statue off Kurt. Great right hook, he's got Kurt in the eye, Kurt shouting at Adrian, he is most useless spy ever + Kurt wants whiskey back. I will try to escape, wish me luck. If I don't get through this, I'm so so glad we met

20.48

Mad where are you? Are you out of the shed yet? I'm banging at the front door. Can you let me in?

20.49

Mad???? Are you OK? Going to climb over side gate, though it looks nasty. I'm not great with heights.

20.52

I am over the gate except for a chunk of my right thigh. Feeling faint, leg bloody, going to sit down for a while in the ferns by kitchen. Are you OK? Please answer.

Chapter 79

From: Allie Loff (allie53@outlook.com)
Sent: 1 October 2018 5.58am GMT
To: Bea Hudson (bhudson9@blueyonder.co.uk)
Subject: **Hello again**

Dear Bea

Sorry to have been incommunicado lately. Just didn't know where I was at, head all over place, body all over place too, hopping from one sofa/bus station to the next.

Decided I did not want to be a rock chick after all, you'll be relieved to know. MM has a nasal high-pitched voice when he sings and isn't as good on the guitar as I'd thought. Also, he smokes weed most nights, which affects his performance in other areas. My excitement waned quickly, as did my cash. He couldn't buy me any drinks because he's paying back a loan. With hindsight I can see he looked on me as a convenient sugar mummy.

Had my phone stolen while asleep on the bus to Brisbane and no money to buy another. No computers where I am now (an 'alternative community' not far from the Queensland coast called Crystal Waters, on the top of a small mountain. Met a kooky girl on bus who recommended it as budget accommodation.)

Everyone here is very friendly, though most believe that aliens from Sirius are about to land (tall with piercing green eyes) and that the end of the world is coming later this year. Everyone is preparing for The End, as they call it, putting up huts in the mountains with messages for the Sirians and flasks of homebrew, gloves and books on self-sufficiency. They say we must all move to a higher place.

Not sure how long I will want to stay here. But for now I appreciate the wholesome cooking and great views.

Re life/career etc – The day after I arrived, I had a flash of inspiration. I'm going to devote the rest of my life to either the healing arts (not sure which ones) or saving the Earth. There are so many important things to be done, it's difficult to know where to start.

Ray and I talked last week. We agreed to get a divorce.

I said I don't think we have any common ground left, and I don't want to be just a farmer's wife anymore. He said he can't forgive me for having it off with a musician half his age (and half his belly, let's face it – I don't have to anymore, thank heavens).

For the first time in ages, I feel that my life is going in the right direction. OK, it's a mess at the moment. But I have to start over, and here is as good a place as any.

How are things in deepest Surrey? Has Kurt got back from Turkey? Hope the time apart did you both good? Did you finish the experiments?

Sorry I did not send Fran a present but I hope my card arrived on time. Wish her many happy returns from me if not.

Love and hugs, Allie

From: Bea Hudson (bhudson9@blueyonder.co.uk)
Sent: 1 October 2018 10.01am
To: Allie Loff (allie53@outlook.com)
Re: **Hello again**

Yes, I'd been wondering where you'd got to after Byron Bay – assumed you'd been captured by a gaggle of weed-infested musicians. Relieved you are OK. Sounds like you've landed on your feet. Be careful of those tree-huggers, though.

Your card arrived today, thanks. No birthday party but it was an eventful day – lots to tell you but no idea where to start.

Love, Bea

From: Allie Loff (allie53@outlook.com)
Sent: 1 October 2018 10.15am GMT
To: Bea Hudson (bhudson9@blueyonder.co.uk)
Re: **Hello again**

The beginning? Whatever you do, don't leave me in suspense.

Not much happening here, most of the gang have gone for their weekly End of the Earth Ceremony. There's lots of chanting and dancing round candles, you get the pic. I prefer to rest in this comfy chair with a distant view of the sea, smelling pines and baking bread. Better get up soon though, it's my turn to cook dinner.

xx

From: Bea Hudson (bhudson9@blueyonder.co.uk)
Sent: 1 October 2018 11.58am
To: Allie Loff (allie53@outlook.com)
Subject: **Showdown at Kurt and Bea's**

All right, will try to do justice to last night's events.

Our homemade action adventure movie started just after 8pm, when Maddie returned from an impromptu unauthorised day trip with Fran and Big Ears to the New Forest.

You should bear in mind that Kurt got back from Turkey yesterday afternoon and was ready to strangle Mad for:

a) making him think (too many texts, too many French films and an inappropriate birthday gift) that she was having an affair with me

b) being a bad influence on Fran (bad TV, bad language and lax morals in general)

c) helping me to look after Fran, without his permission, and

d) taking Fran away on her birthday, without his permission (or mine).

I do not exaggerate – I've never seen him in such a state. He hadn't been drinking but that only seemed to make him worse.

Kurt answered the door. I ran downstairs after him to the three grimy figures on our doorstep. Fran looked as if she'd been camping for a week in the wilderness – face streaked with sweat and dirt, a long scratch across her cheek, hair full of dandelion fluff, her top torn. She ran to me, hid her face in my skirt and started sobbing. Mad looked even worse than Fran – mud splattered all over her jeans. Big Ears looked as if he'd been rolling around in the mud all day – his fur was caked in black gunge. The only bits that weren't were two brown eyes and his slobbery pink tongue. All three reeked of the countryside – to put it politely.

I told Maddie to come inside, get cleaned up, have a cup of tea. She was hobbling towards the kitchen tap when Kurt went into meltdown.

Where the f*** have you taken our daughter? What have you been doing with her all this time? Etc.

Before M could utter a word, he told her she was the most irresponsible woman he had ever met and a bitch, witch, lunatic and she-devil to boot. In response, Maddie spat at Kurt, stamped on his foot, fled into the garden and barricaded herself in the shed.

Next action highlight:

Kurt is thumping on the shed door brandishing our phallus-shaped African fertility statue from the living room mantelpiece (made of stone and quite hefty) and yelling 'Come out of there, trollop!' and the like. I try in vain to calm Kurt down. As usual, my efforts only make him madder.

Mad is making faces at me through the shed window while drawing unintelligible signs on the glass and Fran is watching avidly from the patio, ignoring my orders for her to go up to her room. Big Ears is barking himself hoarse, as are the two dogs next door and by the sound of it, every dog within a mile of us.

I try to distract Kurt from trying to murder Maddie by throwing apples at him, but they are on the small side and my aim is a bit off. Summon Fran. Her aim is much better. Despite being pummelled by apples Kurt keeps on banging on the shed door. Suddenly I realise M is drawing a big letter P for Police. By then, I have flipped several times between stunned and frightened to death. Also, I'm exhausted by apple tossing and tearing my hair out while Fran was missing, and Kurt's reaction to Fran being missing.

After ringing 999 (ask for police and ambulance just in case), I'm tempted to go to bed with a large glass of whatever alcohol I can get my hands on and leave everyone to it. Then the doorbell rings. Reluctantly I let in Adrian from next door, who can't wait to discover what all the commotion is about.

Next thing, he and Kurt are having a boxing match on the lawn, hurling taunts at each other. Fran and I watch from a safe distance. Adrian's punches are more effective than Kurt's. He lands one on Kurt just above the eye. Cue Maddie's hobble from the shed. She grabs the statue that Kurt dropped on the lawn and brings it down on the back of his head. Kurt staggers, curses and reaches out both arms as if to strangle M. She screams and ducks away. Adrian throws himself towards Kurt's legs as if making a rugby tackle but before he can make contact Big Ears bites K's rump (I think he wanted to join in more than anything). There's a furious roar and Kurt takes off like a rocket and lands in our rosebush, moaning and groping his backside.

I have a brief outburst of hysterical laughter.

Maddie stares at me, open-mouthed. Kurt sprawls on his side on the ground, effing and blinding. (There's a big rip in his jeans bottom.) Then he closes his eyes and goes quiet.

Big Ears starts licking his hand. Adrian leaps onto his prone body and starts to slap his face. None of this has the slightest effect. I put my hand on his chest to feel his heart (still beating) then put my hand over his mouth. Thank Christ, he's still breathing.

Maddie kneels down beside Kurt, holds his hand and closes her eyes, muttering, 'Oh my God Oh my God!' I squeeze Kurt's other hand. I'm feeling faint and am about to have a panic attack when Mad's ex-boyfriend Colin stumbles into the garden clutching his thigh (bleeding through his jeans).

Colin: What the hell's going on?

Maddie: (runs to Colin and clings to him) Col!

Adrian: Has anyone got any smelling salts?

Our medicine cabinet contains pretty much everything except smelling salts, so I run upstairs and grab my bottle of eucalyptus oil, which instantly clears the worst blocked nose. It would wake the dead, surely. I charge back towards the garden, dread filling me. Please God, let Kurt be all right. If he wakes up, I'll forgive him for anything. For everything.

On the lawn, Maddie, Fran, Colin, Adrian and Big Ears are gathered around Kurt's inert body. Maddie is holding Kurt's hand, Fran is kissing his brow, Big Ears is licking his cheek and Adrian is tickling the sole of his bare left foot.

Maddie: (between incoherent wails) I killed him!

Me: (shoving a eucalyptus oil-soaked tissue up Kurt's nostril) Shut up Maddie!

Adrian: Someone call an ambulance!

Fran: Keep calm everyone, we mustn't panic.

Everyone looks at Fran. Then Colin limps towards the house and returns with a jug of water, which he raises above Kurt's head. Water streams across Kurt's brow and into his eyes, ears and mouth.

Adrian: Stop, he's coming to!

Kurt splutters and moves his head from side to side. Colin puts down the jug. There's another ring at the front door. I run into the house and let in two policemen and two paramedics.

Me: Thank God, I thought you'd never get here!

I lead them into the garden. The paramedics descend on Kurt, who's now half sat up and sipping from the remaining water in the jug, offered by Colin. The police ask us what is going on.

Kurt: (pointing to the discarded phallus) She hit me on the head with that statue!

Maddie: He was going to kill me!

After several more or less discordant accounts have been given by everyone, the police want to arrest Kurt (for causing a disturbance and attempted assault with a dangerous weapon, I think it was) and Maddie (for kidnapping and excessive use of force in self-defence). But thanks to my strenuous insistence that this was a private matter and no one wanted to press charges, they make do with cautioning both parties.

Policeman 1: (to Kurt, now wincing and tugging at his bottom – jeans at his ankles and his Calvin Klein underpants on display – and Maddie, now bent anxiously over Colin, who's flat on the recliner, trouser leg rolled up, pressing on his bloody thigh with a wodge of kitchen roll) I suggest you two apologise to each other, and try to behave like grown-ups in future.

Me: (while I examine Kurt's bottom, mercifully bearing no sign of teeth punctures but several embedded thorns) Hear, hear! I've had enough. I'm fed up to the back teeth with both of you!

Silence, save for yapping dogs and swishing curtains.

Adrian: That'll need disinfectant – and possibly an anti-rabies injection.

Kurt: (horrified moan)

Policeman 2: You should get that head seen to, Mr Hudson.

Policeman 1: And that arse... We'll leave you guys to make up, then.

Mad: OK, I'll start. Kurt, I'm sorry I ran off with Fran. I lost it, I didn't think of anyone except myself. And I'm sorry I gave you such a big whack with that statue. Only I was scared of what you might do–

Kurt: (rubbing back of head) That was some wallop you gave me, Mad. I'm impressed.

Mad: (turning to me) Bea, I understand if you don't want me to see Fran anymore – and if you don't want to be friends with me anymore. (turning to Colin) Col, I just want to say... (wipes her eyes, leaving dirt-streaked cheeks) I swear I don't want to be with you because of your money. It's nice that you've got some, of course it is, but it's not like I... Oh, shit, what am I saying? I love you. I love you!

Colin: (drops the wodge of kitchen roll he's pressing on his wound and stares at Mad)

Mad: (looking down at her shoes with revulsion) Christ, I've just trodden on a snail.

Adrian: Don't worry, there's plenty more where that came from. They're all over our garden too, they love all the rain we've had lately.

Mad: (to all of us including Fran, now sitting on the lawn beside Colin's recliner, and Big Ears, lying with his head in Fran's lap) So, guys, I understand if none of you want to see me again after this. I'll leave you all alone and go and live somewhere far away. New Zealand, maybe. Or I could just jump off Beachy Head.

Me: (hugging Mad) Don't be so daft, Maddie, you'll always be my friend! You're not going anywhere. And you're definitely not going to jump off any cliffs.

Fran: (dislodging dog and hugging Mad) Don't go, Auntie Maddie! You're my favourite Auntie!

Kurt: (pulling up jeans) I'm sorry I scared you, Madeleine. You must have thought I'd turned into a raving lunatic–

Fran: We all did, Daddy.

Kurt: (to Mad, ignoring Fran) You can come and see Fran again, I won't mind. But please don't take her anywhere again without asking first.

Mad: (turning to Colin) What about you?

Colin: What about me?

Mad: Do you want me to go away, Colin?

Colin: Yes, I want you to go away.

Mad: (lowers voice) You don't want to see me anymore?

Colin: (getting up carefully from the recliner) No, I want you to go away. To the Caribbean. With me.

Mad: You're joking.

Colin: I mean it! Come and live with me. We'll splash in the surf together, laze in hammocks and bob about on boats. I don't care if you spend all my money. I'll help you be an artist and you can help me have fun, while I still can. What's money for, anyway?

Kurt: (drying his eyes with his fingers) That sounds like an offer you can't refuse, Mad.

Adrian: I think you should say yes, lady.

Mad and Colin: (kiss)

Fran: (claps hands with a squeal of delight)

Me: Hey, you two. There's a child watching!

Adrian: (patting Kurt's back) Sorry for that stuff earlier, mate. I was my club's boxing champ in my prime.

Kurt: I can believe it, Adrian. I can still feel that right hook. My face is pretty sore. Almost as sore as my arse.

Leaving Maddie to kiss Colin and bandage his thigh and Adrian to pluck the remaining thorns from Kurt's bottom, I take Fran up to bed, reassuring her that Daddy was going to be all right (though he'd have a sore head and botty for a while). Fran pointed out that Daddy was very silly. I agreed.

What happened next? Oh yes, after Colin left hand in hand with Maddie, Kurt said he was sorry he'd given me so much grief (today plus all the other days). He was also sorry he'd been so hard on Maddie, it didn't take a Miss Marple to see that Mad was mad about Colin. He'd been an idiot to imagine she'd had designs on me – and a half day's visit to the New Forest hardly constitutes a kidnapping, does it? He promised not to be a brainless bozo anymore. Also, he's not going back to Turkey or anywhere else overseas for work ever again. He's told his boss that he's had enough of having to fire people, and if his boss doesn't like it, he's welcome to fire him.

Then to my astonishment, Kurt offered to stay at home and look after Fran so I can become a proper full-time sixty plus hours per week Principal Investigator. He said he could get a part-time directorship or two if necessary, or just become a house husband. Plus my mother could help us out by returning the six cases of Bordeaux she took away on the pretext that they would keep longer in her cellar. We could get a good price for them, now the price of wine is shooting up due to Brexit, and still drink the odd bottle.

Too dazed to reply. Wondered if stress can cause hallucinations.

Kurt and I spent most of the night making up. We promised to be better parents to Fran and better partners to each other. We agreed not to argue over Little Things and only to fight about Really Big Things. We forgave each other for all the bad and hurtful things that each had said and done to the other so far during our marriage. I nearly told him about the party incident (you don't know about that yet Allie, it was while you'd gone missing) but decided it was best forgotten.

This morning, I pinched myself.

Me: Did you really say yesterday you would give up your job and stay at home so I can go to work full time?

Kurt: Absolutely I did.

Me: Let's get it in writing.

Part four

Chapter 80

From: Gary Settle (gfsettle@gmail.com)
Sent: 17 October 2018 6.15pm GMT
To: Colin Settle (cmsettle@blueyonder.co.uk)
Subject: **Planned trip**

Hiya Col,

Your latest letter arrived a while back. Sorry so late in replying. I've never been one for letter writing, you know that. To be honest, when the letter came I was still pissed with you after our heated phone exchange so I tossed it in the waste. I came to my senses though and dug it out a few days later, and have been reading it whenever time permits.

I'm impressed by your exploits at the insurance company. Ripping off your bosses to pay the ripped off – love it! You're a changed man, that's no exaggeration.

How is it all going, anyway? Did you go on the *Channel 4 News*? Have they put you in jail yet? Sincerely hope not.

I've also been entertained by your exploits with the new woman in your life. She sounds like a crazy one! But opposites attract, and if she's got a decent cleavage... I hope you aren't going to give this Maddie up now over some nonsensical idea of her taking advantage. In my experience most women either want you to father their children or spend all your money on them... and some want both, of course. That's just the way it is, pal. If you truly love her, take her on a shopping spree and get her pregnant.

My news – I am making a short trip over your way early December – some country pubs, trips to the theatre, seeing old friends and so on. Have been missing the old familiar places. Quiet over here lately, workwise and woman-wise. Thought maybe we could catch up over a few beers?

Would be great to see you, bro. Long time no see, etc.

Cheers, Gary

From: Colin Settle (cmsettle@blueyonder.co.uk)
Sent: 19 Oct 2018 11.10pm
To: Gary Settle (gfsettle@gmail.com)
Re: **Planned trip**

Dear Gary

I am surprised to hear of your planned visit to the UK in December. Unfortunately, I am about to emigrate to the Caribbean.

The date is set for 15 November. By then, I should have sold this place (have just exchanged contracts) and be scouring Virgin Gorda for a refuge in my own languid corner of paradise. (Remember how beautiful it was when we went sailing in the Virgin Islands with Uncle Jimmy all those years ago?) Although I can't invite you to stay with me in Woking, dear bro, you are more than welcome to visit once I have found my new abode, should you be inclined to dip your toe in the warm waters of the Caribbean.

What do you think, Gary? I can almost hear your gasps of bewilderment. Your boring, never-go-to-a-new-place-when-you-can-go-to-one-you've-been-to-before brother has finally stepped into the land of risk and uncertainty?

I assure you, this really is me. I have not yet been committed to a secure mental health unit or incarcerated in Pentonville at Her Majesty's Pleasure (though I may have come uncomfortably close to the latter). Thankfully, despite the odds, my Cunning Scheme has yielded fruit – financial, psychological and existential fruit. I am no longer Colin Settle the guilt-ridden, about-to-be-axed, settle-for-anything-as-long-as-it's-pointless-and-demeaning cog in the insurance racket, but Colin about-to-settle-in-the-tropical-haven-of-his-dreams.

Finally, I should mention that I have invited the lovely Madeleine to accompany me to paradise. For better or worse, she has accepted. As you know, this was the culmination of a series of improbable events for which I shall be forever grateful. How long she will stay with me, heaven knows. But I hope it will be long enough to inspire the creation of many more giant rats, or whatever her creative juices kindle – perhaps the wildlife out there will provide inspiration – and long enough for me to grow up a little more.

On that note, Gary, I will wish you all the best. I look forward to sitting down with you before too long, having a few beers and putting aside our differences.

Colin

Chapter 81

Diary of a house husband

17 October

9.30am

Just delivered Fran to school, a little late after sandwiches went wonky and I couldn't find her lunch box. But never mind, we had a pleasant drive around the neighbourhood (I've been away so long, I forgot about the one-way street. Teacher, I presume (flat shoes, short hair, blowing a whistle) pointed accusingly at me as I pulled away. Maybe I stopped on those yellow zigzag lines. Or was it a Walk-to-School Wednesday? It's hard keeping up with all these new developments.

Life is definitely on the up, though. Freed at last from corporate slavery, I'm looking forward to many long lie-ins as a gentleman of leisure/philosopher/house husband supported by my loving, hardworking wife while I contemplate the future direction of my life. No more spineless kowtowing to weasels in their echelons of power, shuddering in air-conditioned offices, or wanting to vomit after turbulent flights and aircraft food. Just days spent communing with inner self, and time left over for carrying out all those mission-critical, hands-on tasks of family life.

Contributing to my daughter's well-being – dropping off/ collecting from school; industriously preparing packed lunches; helping with homework; being a shoulder to cry on; attending parents' evenings; escorting to playdates and ballet class...

Contributing to my wife's well-being – sensitive queries re her day at uni; occasional massages offered after stressful meetings; kisses, champagne and flowers delivered at appropriate times...

Domestic bliss, here we come.

Chapter 82

N. Rowley
The Practice
13 Old Fellows Court
London SW4 3FZ
7 November 2018

Dear Madeleine

Thank you for your news and apologies for my long delay in replying. I do hope that you managed to extricate yourself from the scrape you found yourself in with your friend's husband – and I trust that you have managed to embrace Colin? Also, I must thank you wholeheartedly for your advice (though I was slightly taken aback at the time).

Last week I took Mrs Rowley to a meeting of our local swingers' group, which we both enjoyed to the extent that we are considering making these occasions a regular part of our burgeoning sex life. In addition, I am pleased to say that my fantasies have receded of late. This is no doubt due to such outings, as well as my new policy of openly discussing my sexual inclinations with Mrs Rowley. (She has responded most surprisingly.)

Although I cannot yet say I find retired life trouble free, I am making studious efforts to master golf and have been on a preliminary trout fishing expedition. Mrs Rowley finds adjustment to my more frequent presence at home difficult. She has suggested I see some patients again. I will consider this option, subject to my progress in becoming a more tolerant, rounded and compassionate individual. We all have our weaknesses – I more than most.

I wish you the very best for your future life, Madeleine.

Yours,

Nigel

Chapter 83

From: Madeleine Geen (madeleine.geen@gmail.com)
Sent: 3 December 2018 3.11pm GMT
To: Bea Hudson (bhudson9@blueyonder.co.uk)
Subject: **Hello from the Caribbean**

Hello Bea

Having a great time here. Virgin Gorda is heaven.

I don't miss life back home except for you and Fran of course, and Mungo and Giblet, who are still in quarantine. (Colin is happy about that.)

Busy on a new sculpture and getting a studio set up. Col is busy setting up his tourist boat business. We're not too busy, though, for cocktails at sunset from our deck overlooking the bay. Am I making you jealous?

So far we've had only one big fight, about why I lied re losing my virginity to a boy in my English class I had a crush on when I was fourteen (he said I told him it was sixteen) and a few smaller ones (e.g. he says I'm the untidiest person he's ever known and a hoarder). Plus last week we had a tiff about the names we would call our children, if we ever had any.

Col wants to have a baby with me! I said it may be too late, but let's go for it!

Will keep you updated with any developments.

Lots of love to you and Kurt. I hope hubby is behaving himself, and so are you.

Come over and see us soon. There's a guest room with a queen bed for you two, and a sofa-bed for my favourite naughty little girl.

Maddie xx

From: Bea Hudson (bhudson9@blueyonder.co.uk)
Sent: 3 December 2018 6.22pm
To: Madeleine Geen (madeleine.geen@gmail.com)
Re: **Hello from the Caribbean**

I'm green all over, Maddie.

Having a baby is a totally excellent idea. I'm thrilled for you! Fingers crossed it'll happen. Can I be his/her godmother?

I'd love to visit but I won't be over for a while, too much going on here. More news when I get a mo.

PS

If we bring Fran, you must promise not to take her off on any more expeditions.

From: Madeleine Geen (madeleine.geen@gmail.com)
Sent: 3 December 2018 6.29pm GMT
To: Bea Hudson (bhudson9@blueyonder.co.uk)
Re: **Hello from the Caribbean**

Hand on heart, no more Fran-nappings.

Chapter 84

Portrait of a successful scientist

21 December

Paper accepted by Nature subject to satisfactory conclusion of an extra experiment.

CAN'T BELIEVE IT!

27 December

Grant proposal accepted by Medical Research Council!!!

16 January 2019

Paper published in Nature. Whoopeeeee!!!!!!!!!!!!!!!!!!!!!!!!!!!!!!!!!!!!

The news went round the Psychological Sciences Building in one minute, literally. It even managed to eclipse the MPs' vote on the Brexit deal.

Sweaty Mike hugged me and said he'd always known I'd be famous. Moira brought me two glasses of flat Prosecco at the staff bar to celebrate. The Prof smiled at me for the first time in years, and invited me to Friday afternoon drinks Room 12. Fran has told everyone in her class that her Mummy is a Successful Scientist. Kurt cooked me a celebration dinner — yam tagine followed by chocolate fondant with raspberry sauce, not forgetting a bottle of Dom Pérignon. He's also shown everyone in our street the first page of my published paper with my name highlighted in pink (plus the postman, the staff of Waitrose and every café in Godalming, and random strangers he encountered on the High Street). Big Ears gave me an appreciative head butt and let off a big smelly.

6 February

Left Psycho Lab early as it's Wednesday and Prof on prowl for me to give another interview. Came home to an empty house. Fran @ school percussion group, Kurt @ Homebase.

Update on Bea's Only Lucky Fluke

Since the Nature paper came out, the BOLF's existence has been corroborated by several groups (including both our main rivals, I'm even more pleased to report). I'm now researching performance anxiety to see if the BOLF is significant here, too. I have a hunch that the BOLF will be shown to play a crucial role in a range of anxiety disorders, not just spider phobias.

We've been putting people in various anxiety-creating situations, such as asking them to sing the national anthem to an audience of inebriated PhD students listening in the next room via the FaceTime app (Ben's idea).

So far, results have been promising. We've found a strong signal in the usual parts of the brain, especially the BOLF, peaking 180 milliseconds after the presentation of a laughing face image while the subject is singing 'God Save the Queen'. Soon neuropharmacologists will be hot on the trail of a new drug that will consign to history the fear of making an utter fool of oneself in public (especially when delivering one's 10am Monday lecture to a bunch of hungover first years).

We're going to look at social phobics next. The drug spin-off potential is far greater, the Prof says.

As encouraging as these developments are, I find it hard to get excited about them. Too many questions come to me in the early hours.

What am I doing all this for? Do our anxieties really need to be banished? Why did I once think that brain research was the Holy Grail?

Oh dear — I hope I'm not turning into a burnt-out scientist with a macabre death wish.

22 February

It's been all go this week.

Went to a neuroscience conference in Manchester on Monday to give my talk, 'How I Made the Biggest Discovery in Neuropsychology in the Past Ten Years' (actually 8.5). Went to Edinburgh on Wednesday to present my latest paper, on the BOLF's role in performance anxiety. Went to Nonsuch High School for Girls on Thursday to give my talk, 'How to be a Successful Scientist and a Successful Woman'.

Due to give this talk to three WI groups in the next fortnight. (Decided to take the Prof's advice after my first talk and leave out any references to my fruit fly-infested office, emaciated team and pitiful funding, along with the systematic thwarting of my professional goals by the patriarchal environment and heavy teaching and administrative workloads). Communicating my success (and naturally, that of the department/school/faculty/university) is an important job. Besides, I must of course give something back to the department/school/faculty/university/womankind.

Sometimes all this feels totally unbelievable. I had my paper accepted by Nature and suddenly I've gone from a past-it, mummy-track Senior Lecturer, grade Generally Invisible (except when a committee place/unfilled teaching slot beckons) to Someone of Significance. I can scarcely even remember presenting the paper — at a meeting of the Federation of the European Societies of Neuropsychology — I was in a such a daze.

While it's satisfying and a refreshing change to feel valued by colleagues, fellow scientists and the uni hierarchy, there's a downside to my new life. Now I'm a PI and an 'official' full-time member of staff, my weekly hours have reached a new record. I calculated that I did ninety-five hours last week, excluding thinking time on the way to uni, in the bath and while falling asleep. I have practically no time to write in my journal, let alone watch the latest hot show on Netflix or have sex. And I've hardly seen Fran this week. I worry that my daughter won't recognise me soon. Not even my latest generous grant and a team swollen to three eager postdocs, two migraine-free students and Hayley, and minimal hours teaching gormless students/taking tutorials/marking exam papers (and no more serving on committees promoting gender equality in science, hooray!) can make up for becoming a Has Been Mother.

26 February

10.30pm

Sometimes I have the uneasy feeling that Kurt is better at it than me – looking after Fran, Big Ears and the house, I mean. Apart from occasional mishaps, he is doing surprisingly well in his latest role. (Though last week he had a reprimand from the school for delivering Fran by car more than three days a week on average this term and arriving more than thirty minutes late on six occasions without a valid excuse.)

I told him we need to set a good example to Fran. Also, there is no point in slagging off the head teacher, especially when he's within earshot.

I suppose Kurt's temper will not magically vanish overnight, even with the help of meditation, yoga classes and his Headspace app.

On the plus side, apart from a relapse on Boxing Day, Kurt has kept his promise re his drinking. Now he sticks to Carling Light and two glasses of wine on special occasions.

The AA was very helpful after the relapse. (It happened after we disagreed about when the turkey should come out of the oven, what we would watch that afternoon on TV and what we would do about Fran repeatedly kissing Nathan, the cherubic little boy in her class.) We both got drunk on cooking sherry (and the bottle of port that my mother mistakenly brought over for Christmas lunch) and threatened to leave each other at the first opportunity.

The three-quarters of an AA meeting that K attended (full house, as was second week in Jan) was so excruciating, so he told me afterwards, he announced as he left the room that he would need no further help from 'a bunch of preaching, wallowing-in-your-own-misery, alcohol-obsessed meddlers'.

I pray there will be no more relapses — and no more fights that leave me wanting to jump into the arms of Tom Hiddleston.

To support Kurt, since 1 Jan I too have substantially cut down on alcohol. For the last two months I have officially given up glasses of wine with meals (except when dining out with friends, or not with Kurt) as well as all other alcohol, including but not limited to Triple Sec, Cointreau, vodka and ginger ales, gin and tonic, gin cocktails, Prosecco, Chardonnay and cooking sherry.

It is proving more difficult than I thought.

I want to help my husband, of course. As I write, though, I feel a craving for a mint julep coming on. Or a mojito would be nice...

Mustn't slide down the slippery slope, no matter what excuses (marriage, family, work and getting old, off the top of my head). I don't want to get a drink problem — or have I got one already? Nipping out for a secret bottle of wine is tempting, at times. Should have kept details of our local AA, just in case. The thought of turning up there is scary though, especially after Kurt's encounter. Maybe I'll ask Kurt to come too.

I wonder how long he'll be able to keep up this house husband thing? And more to the point, how long will I be able to be put up with it?

Yes, K's cooked some superlative dinners with his latest gadgets — when he's in the mood, and isn't strolling along country lanes/chatting in cafés with fellow members of Godalming Dog Trotters — mostly divorced women, acc. to

Adrian. (Kurt says he needs the 'group support' because Big Ears insists on two walks a day, always poos in the wrong places and pretends he doesn't hear when anyone calls him.)

Also, Kurt does keep the house in good order and nearly always remembers to ask about my day. He even empathises if it's been particularly awful, and sometimes gives me a back (etc) massage! Fran certainly seems to like Daddy being around more. He has more patience with her and is better at explaining things than I am. And now he's got the hang of the kitchen, he makes her nicer packed lunches than the ones I used to make.

I'm starting to wonder, though — are the school mums a bit of a distraction?

28 February

He seems to be getting on rather too well with some of them. Especially the blonde who (Kurt thinks) has had a boob job (she is a 'good 36J'). She told him he was welcome to come along on Tuesday afternoons to the Raunchy Reads Book Club. (He's already going to the Parents' Forum every other Thursday).

Kurt says the book club has only one other man, a 'pint-sized wimp'. Not much competition then, I said. He told me I needn't worry, I'm the only woman for him. To prove it, he's going to get a tattoo of the letter 'B' on his right bicep done at The House of Beauty. I said you don't have to go that far, darling. But am secretly thrilled.

Must go and get the latest on Allie's hunky young Texan, or whoever she's cooking supper with at the mo. Doesn't look like she's going to leave the alternative community soon, esp. since it has a good turnover of men and the world hasn't ended yet. Though it may well end soon in the UK as we teeter over the brink of B*****... It's a good thing I got my grant when I did.

4 March

Worrying developments at home and work.

Fed up with Fran forgetting who I am. These days, whenever I'm home in time for dinner, she greets me with a look of suspicion and bewilderment. Last night when I came into her room to read her a bedtime story, she complained that I didn't know where she was up to (there were multiple bookmarks). Afterwards, she said Kurt reads much better than I do and his cat/stork/elephant voices sound more real.

Didn't know what to say.

Also fed up with people who aren't scientists assuming that I must be a loony with too many neurons and not enough hormones. Jackie next door now greets me with, 'Hello there, how's the research going?' and a pitying smile before hurrying off in case she catches something. Even fellow scientists (male usually) seem to think there's something rather sinister about women scientists who are ambitious, committed and full-time.

7 March

More worrying developments.

Kurt announced over brunch this morning that he's shed his alpha male corporate warrior skin and is luring out his feminine side, which he must think justifies his recent obsessive shopping on Amazon for kitchen gadgets that we don't have space for.

Something new arrives every week. In the past two months we've acquired a Moulinex Stabmixer, a state-of-the-art food processor, a breadmaking machine and a coffee machine that turns itself on and off at appropriate times, cleans itself and tells us when something's wrong.

Then there's all the planning meetings and reconnaissance trips to designer kitchen shops and the homes of 'colleagues' for Kurt's Project To Revamp The House, as well as his regular head/shoulder/foot massages from Christina and Shelley at The House of Beauty (essential for relaxation after a hard day's browsing the latest ideas in interior design, broken up by a spot of gentle reading in Le Pain Très Chère, or whatever our local bakery is now called). He's even started writing a book, How to Become a Successful House Husband (there's a big market, he reckons).

This is all getting a bit much.

12 March

An even more worrying development.

I was about to go to bed when I happened to pass Kurt's new laptop (he was in bathroom). It wasn't hibernating as it usually is, but showing a long list of emails. Naturally, I paused to have a peek.

The third email down caught my eye, to a Barbara Swain: 'Hi Barb, will be half an hour late for book club tomorrow afternoon as I have dental appointment. Looking forward to your cupcakes. Please would you pass on to the others?'

'Your cupcakes'!?! Could that be some sort of hidden code?

What am I thinking? Of course my husband isn't intending to spend Wednesday afternoon groping Barbara Swain's breasts.

Oh my God! Kurt's tattoo!! How could I have been so stupid? I've only just realised. Barbara's initial is 'B' too!

OK, it might only be coincidence. I hope it's only coincidence. But all the same...

I think the time has come for us to go fifty-fifty on the domestic arrangements. Will email Cognitive Science dept. admin tomorrow and ask to go back to a four-day week ASAP. Or a three-day week perhaps. I'll encourage Kurt to follow up on ads for non-executive directors (not many women on IT company boards!) and ask Katie to come back at whatever greatly increased rate she'll agree to.

Chapter 85

From: Bea Hudson (bhudson9@blueyonder.co.uk)
Sent: 14 March 2019 8.21am
To: Kurt Hudson (husband599@homehubbies.co.uk)
Subject: **Bins**

Just a reminder to put the recyling out this morning (before 8.30am!)

See you tonight, darling. Enjoy your day x

From: Kurt Hudson (husband599@homehubbies.co.uk)
Sent: 14 March 2019 9.15am
To: Bea Hudson (bhudson9@blueyonder.co.uk)
Re: **Bins**

Beatrice,

WTF is this empty cardboard box on top of the recycling bin? There's a label on it from a company called Spyware International.

K

From: Bea Hudson (bhudson9@blueyonder.co.uk)
Sent: 14 March 2019 9.31am
To: Kurt Hudson (husband599@homehubbies.co.uk)
Subject: **I spy with my little eye**

Darling, I thought you wouldn't mind. I found the company on the web. They say it's the latest technology, just the thing for checking on all manner of things from naughty children to errant partners – and what's more, foolproof to install. I managed to set up the spycam in just ten minutes in a secret location inside the house!

Now I'll be able to check on how late you're sleeping in – and that you're not doing anything else you shouldn't (involving anyone called Barbara, in particular) while I'm hard at work.

Bea x

From: Kurt Hudson (husband599@homehubbies.co.uk)
Sent: 14 March 2019 9.33am
To: Bea Hudson (bhudson9@blueyonder.co.uk)
Re: **I spy with my little eye**

Are you serious?

From: Bea Hudson (bhudson9@blueyonder.co.uk)
Sent: 14 March 2019 9.34am
To: Kurt Hudson (husband599@homehubbies.co.uk)
Re: **I spy with my little eye**

No, my love. I printed the label myself. Sorry, couldn't resist. B

From: Kurt Hudson (husband599@homehubbies.co.uk)
Sent: 14 March 2019 9.35am
To: Bea Hudson (bhudson9@blueyonder.co.uk)
Subject: **TRICKSY TROLLOP!**

From: Kurt Hudson (husband599@homehubbies.co.uk)
Sent: 14 March 2019 3.38pm
To: Bea Hudson (bhudson9@blueyonder.co.uk)
Subject: **Tattoo**

My darling Bea,

You will shortly witness proof of my boundless devotion to you, and you alone. This afternoon I quelled my anxieties re the prospect of blood poisoning and prolonged pricking with a sharp instrument, and had an extra portion added to my tattoo. The new one now encircles the entire circumference of my biceps. It looks like this:

BEATRICE

Kurt

THE END

Acknowledgements

My thanks to all who've helped me transform my novel from its first incarnation as Everyday Deceptions into what it is now – my editors Philippa Brewster and Jane Read, Mary Flanagan and her students at City Lit's advanced critical workshop, my friends and fellow writers online and off who gave feedback on early drafts and the hardworking team at Bombshell Books.

A special thank you to the early readers and bloggers who reviewed Not Having It All, or helped to spread the word via social media etc.

Author's Note

I hope you enjoyed reading this book. If so, you know what to do :)

For info on my other books and my latest author news, please visit my website at jennieensor.com.